SHADOWRUN

Spells AND CHROME

A SHADOWRUN ANTHOLOGY • EDITED BY JOHN HELFERS

An Imprint of InMediaRes Productions, LLC.

SPELLS & CHROME: A Shadowrun Anthology
Cover art by Björn Hurri
Cover design and interior layout by Matt Heerdt

Published by Catalyst Game Labs,
an imprint of InMediaRes Productions, LLC
PMB 202 • 303 91st Ave NE • G701 • Lake Stevens, WA 98258

ISBN: 978-1-934857-23-6

First Edition: September 2010

info@shadowrun4.com
(Shadowrun questions)
http://www.shadowrun4.com
(official Shadowrun website)
http://www.catalystgamelabs.com
(Catalyst website)
http://www.battlecorps.com/catalog
(online Catalyst/Shadowrun orders)
http://del.icio.us/shadowrun
(cool links)

Catalyst Game Labs is dedicated to producing high-quality games and fiction that mesh sophisticated game mechanics with dynamic universes—all presented in a form that allows beginning players and long-time veterans to easily jump into our games and fiction readers to enjoy our stories even if they don't know the games.

Catalyst Game Labs is an imprint of InMediaRes Productions, LLC, which specialized in electronic publishing of professional fiction. This allows Catalyst to meld printed gaming material and fiction with all the benefits of electronic interfaces and online communities, creating a whole-package experience for any type of player or reader. Find Catalyst Game Labs online at www.catalystgamelabs.com.

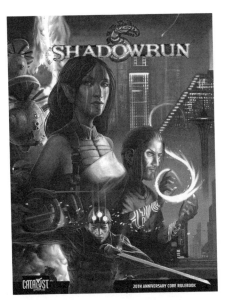

Find out more about *Shadowrun* at shadowrun4.com

CONTENTS

INTRODUCTION

BY JOHN HELFERS

Welcome to what is hopefully the first of many new anthologies of original Shadowrun *short fiction. Before I talk about what a delight it was to edit this collection (it was) or tantalize those of you still reading this introduction with glowing hints of the wonderful stories you'll find inside (they are), I have a brief confession to make, and here seems to be the right place and time to do it, so here goes:*

Until recently, I have had a love/hate relationship with the role-playing game of Shadowrun.

Having been a gamer since dinosaurs walked the earth (can anyone say D&D Expert Rules Boxed Set*?), I've wandered in and out of dozens of RPGs, enjoying some, shaking my head at others. I was first introduced to* Shadowrun, Second Edition *back in college, when the Internet had barely progressed past the gleam in hundreds of computer engineers' eyes, and the technology bonanza we possess today was also unknown (I wrote my term papers on a Macintosh Classic, with ye olde 9-inch monochrome display).*

Since I was also a rapacious fantasy and science fiction reader, I thought a game that combined these elements would be totally cool. And certain things were, like the setting; a depressing, post-punk future Seattle, where magic and science mixed, mashed, and moshed together. Can't miss, right?

But the mechanics of the game, oh, the mechanics. Having never been really mathematically-gifted in the first place, the Shadowrun, Second Edition *rules made me seriously consider switching my major from English to Statistics, or at least sneak a higher-math class into my curriculum to try and get a handle on what was going on in a typical game session. As I recall, the low point was reached when it took our group an entire evening to play one* round *of combat. (As I said, this was Second Edition).*

I drifted away from Shadowrun *after than, but a part of me always pined for what might have been, and any time anyone brought up the game, my reply would always be a combination of longing and annoyance: "yeah, loved the setting,* hated *the rules."*

Of course, all popular games evolve (or else they become less popular, and go into the great circular file), and Shadowrun *was no different. I was pleased to see that the Third Edition addressed a lot of my issues with the rules, and Fourth Edition marked a quantum step forward for the RPG*

itself. Bigger. Darker. Meaner. With more cool characters, cool tech, and even more cool magic. All of which makes it more fun to play, naturally.

But enough of my shameless plugging for the Shadowrun *RPG. This introduction is supposed to be about original* Shadowrun *fiction. Fortunately, my experience with that aspect of SR has been extremely positive. It occurred when my good friend Jean Rabe called me a few years ago and said she had been offered a chance to write a* Shadowrun *novel, but her other commitments were making it problematic to accept doing the book. She then asked if I would like to co-write the book with her. After a microsecond, I said yes, resulting in* Aftershock, *the fifth book in the final six-book series from Roc Books.*

Writing with Jean was tremendous fun, and what was more fun was diving head-first into the Sixth World and being able to do what I wanted to do without having to worry about whether I had a large enough dice pool to accomplish it. The book itself was a true collaboration, with everything from the plot to the characters to each chapter written and reviewed by both of us, and so seamless that when I pick up the published version now, I can't tell where her writing stops and mine starts, or vice versa.

More than likely it was that book that brought me to the attention of Catalyst Game Labs (well, that, and I also edit fiction for them for the BattleTech *website BattleCorps.com) to edit this anthology, which has been my second wonderful experience working with* Shadowrun. *I'd like to thank all of the contributing authors, for handing in superlative stories under an incredibly tight deadline, and also incorporating the cool, new elements of the Fourth Edition game world as well. Featuring new tech like Augmented Reality, which seamlessly melds reality and the Matrix into a new paradigm; to new characters like the Technomancer, who can enter the Matrix* without *a commlink; to new locales for shadowrunning, such as the nasty, lethal, Third-World metropolis of Lagos, in darkest Africa; every story was a delight to read, and every author here a delight to work with.*

I hope you'll agree as you plunge into the following sixteen stories that cover the entire gamut of what the Sixth World has to offer. From a tale that has our not-quite-heroic character playing both sides against– himself, to a story that goes into the heart of darkness that is Lagos, and the choices made just trying to survive in the soul-crushing city, to an exotic excursion beneath the Pacific Ocean off Hawaii to confront a dark entity in the blue depths. We've even included a blast from the past, a classic Shadowrun *story by one of the masters of the SR world, Michael A. Stackpole. Bottom line, there's enough guns, spells, and cyberware to satisfy the biggest fan.*

*I hope you enjoy these all-new stories that explore the gloom of the dark, seamy world that is–and always will be–*Shadowrun.

MAP OF NORTH AMERICA - 2072

✪ National Capital ★ Noteworthy Sprawl — International Boundaries

• City –○– Split City ▪ Noteworthy Area — State Boundaries (U.S.A. circa 1990)

TRADE SECRETS

BY JASON M. HARDY

Renowned as a womanizer on par with Don Juan and Casanova, Jason M. Hardy is alleged to have coded his seduction secrets in his works of fiction. If read properly, books like The Scorpion Jar, Drops of Corruption *and* The Last Charge *could help you avoid ever being lonely again. A similar code has been found in his short stories published on Battlecorps.com and other places, but sadly, those works were found to conceal nothing more than casserole recipes.*

Information was being transmitted by a hundred PANs, and all of it was fake.

At least, that's what Vitriol figured. Broadcasting your real identity—or whatever passed for the actual identity of the people here who didn't have anything that could be called a real name—was like showing up to a masquerade in a t-shirt and jeans. It displayed a tacky lack of imagination.

Visually, the room was a mishmash. Not only did everyone have their own distinct AR augmentation, but many of them were showing off by altering the club's AR overlay. The Clean Heart sported Roman bath décor that was almost entirely virtual—any poor sap without augmented vision would see nothing more than a big, concrete-walled room with a plywood bar over in one corner and benches that looked like they were made from broken chalkboards. With augmented vision, though, the full glory of an ancient bath came to view. Steam rose from a pile of heated rocks across from the bar, benches made of light-colored granite were scattered here and there, and a bartender in a fluffy white robe slid back and forth and served drinks in glasses that sweated condensation.

But here and there, the theme altered. Around Agares, the steam drifting through the room turned to smoke rising above the hellfire that circled his feet. After every step that MidKnight took, black poppies grew, bloomed, and died in the footprints he left behind. And the corner of the room where Blood Sister sat didn't look like a Roman bath at all, but rather like the shadowy corner of a medieval cathedral.

Vitriol thought most of it was pointless. It's not as if their alteration of the AR overlay did them any good. They weren't breaking into any forbidden nodes, they weren't accessing secret information, they were just playing around with a graphics program to show they could. Vitriol didn't bother with any of that nonsense. Sure, he'd disguised his PAN, but all he did was erase it, so anyone who looked for identifier tags on him would see a void, like trying to look into a black hole. He was there, his tags weren't. Effective, subtle, and not work intensive. Vitriol, unlike a lot of hackers, never felt like putting much time or effort into showing off. Blood Sister was pretty much his opposite, always walking around with her own private show like a goddamned performance artist. She was annoying as hell—but she was also one of the best, which was why she got away with it.

Vitriol wandered around the room like a man without a plan. Other people were playing the room like a piano, going from person to person in a particular order dictated by music only they could hear. It looked like a lot of work, the way they did things. All these coded conversations, subtle insinuations, sly gestures. All so much bullshit. Get in, do what you need to do, get out. That's how you deal with systems, and that's how Vitriol planned to handle this gathering. The way he figured it, the less time he spent playing everyone else's game, the less likely he was to be played.

He knew that he was about the only one in the room who looked impatient. Most of the people at these sphinx parties spent a lot of effort to look cool and unhurried, like they didn't need to be there, which was even more bullshit because if they didn't need to be there, then why were they there? For fun? Sphinx parties weren't fun. Everyone was too busy trying to find out what everyone else knew to actually enjoy themselves.

That was the trick of sphinx parties. No one knew how the invitations came out, but you didn't get one—or so the story went—unless you had some juicy piece of info that most people didn't know, but lots of people could use. So everyone here was hungry, everyone wanted what everyone else had, but they weren't about to show it. They kept their faces cool and impassive, and kept the real meat of the evening, the information everyone wanted, electronically coded and out of sight.

Vitriol didn't want to play their game. He wanted to do what he came to do, say what he came to say, and get the hell out. He'd be direct, blunt, straightforward. At a place like this, that was enough to make him a legend. Or at least notorious.

He started walking toward Blood Sister, pressing through the group of people that was always around her without actually being near her. They'd look at the architecture of her AR overlay, they'd admire the textures and the shadows and the way she managed to incorporate the light sources around her into the lighting of her overlay, but they'd keep their distance from the woman herself. With her black cowl and face that was blank, chalky white except for a pair of dark eyes that continually wept blood, Blood Sister had a way of discouraging contact.

He tried pushing one of Blood Sister's fangirls out of his way, but when he reached out to shove the little ivy-covered woman out of his way, his hand went right through her. She was all AR. He had been ready to give her a good shove, so when he didn't contact anything he lost his balance and stumbled, moving away from Blood Sister.

Even worse, he stepped near a dwarf who was sitting at the bar, tossing shot after shot of bourbon down his throat and then tossing shot glass after shot glass over his shoulder, keeping the cleaning staff busy (most of the décor was virtual, but no respectable club, no matter how high tech, ever settled for serving virtual booze). Vitriol tried to dodge out of the dwarf's line of sight, but he was too slow. The dwarf saw him and nodded, looking far too enthusiastic.

"Gemmel," Vitriol said flatly.

"V!" the dwarf said, in a voice far too high and nasal to suit his rough, black-bearded face. The shiny, silver woman sitting next to Gemmel saw her chance to escape and slipped away. "Been too long, too long, way too long. Where the hell have you been, *omae*, what have you been up to? I haven't heard anything about you, which must be good, because when you're doing it right people aren't talking about it, you know what I'm saying? So you're doing it right, right?"

"I'm trying to," Vitriol said, then gritted his teeth and made himself ask Gemmel a rejoinder. "You?"

"Oh, things are great, great, great, you know? I just finished a job, it was a good job, a nice little smash and grab, you know? I mean, I like the undercover sneaking around shit as much as the next guy, but sometimes it's really refreshing to just go in and do what you want to do and not give a shit who sees you do it, am I right?"

Vitriol could just give Gemmel a slight nod and the dwarf would keep talking, keeping him here when he didn't want to be. He stuck his hands in his pockets and hoped his body language looked impatient. But if Gemmel noticed, he didn't care.

The dwarf talked and talked while Vitriol scanned the room, and he saw that the crowd around Blood Sister had thinned. He had a chance, but he might lose it if he took time to politely disengage from Gemmel. But why bother being polite to someone he didn't care about?

He walked away while the dwarf was in mid-sentence.

He strode up to Blood Sister, wondering how long it would take her to see him. She'd recognize him, of course—his hair was now stubbly instead of the bald-scalp look he'd had since he last saw her, but he didn't think that made him look much different. He didn't stand out in this group, however, so it might take some time for her to find him among the freaks.

As it turned out, it didn't take long. He was about five meters away from her when her dark eyes narrowed, squeezing out extra-large drops of blood that ran slowly down her white cheeks.

"Hi," Vitriol said.

The cathedral arch above Blood Sister shook, trembling like an earthquake had just hit the place. Vitriol looked up and instinctively raised his hands over his head, even though he wasn't in any danger.

The archway fell apart quickly, stone crumbling and falling onto and through Vitriol. The first chunks hit the club floor and stayed there, then more chunks came down, then more and more, far more than had been in Blood Sister's display, until Vitriol was completely surrounded by chunks of AR stone.

Bunch of bullshit, he thought, and swept all the rocks away without so much as a gesture. He cleaned the overlay around him until it was once again just himself in his dingy t-shirt and tattered canvas pants.

"Not happy to see me?" he said lightly. Blood Sister did not reply, but the reconstructed archway over her head was already starting to tremble.

"All right, all right, fine. I'll go," Vitriol said. It hadn't been much of a conversation, but it had been enough. "I only dropped by to say hello, anyway."

He turned around and walked toward the exit, hoping he could make it out clean. But there was a demon in his way.

From a distance, Agares did not look all that frightening or even demonic, except for the sharp-toothed crocodile he rode (the crocodile was nothing more than overlay, but Agares still moved like he was riding the nonexistent beast. Vitriol had to admit it was a pretty good trick). Agares had no wings, no forked tail, none of the traditional accoutrements of demonhood except for the reddish sheen of his skin and the nubby horns on his forehead. Once you got closer, though, and saw the eyes blazing out from under the old demon's protruding brow, you gained a full appreciation for the art of Agares' overlay. The face was a wonder of malevolence, with high, sharp cheekbones, a cruel, smirking mouth, and a gaze that cut into you with an almost audible whistle of air.

Vitriol thought the whole package was a little pathetic. In his experience, anyone who worked so hard to look intimidating was overcompensating for something.

"Agares, you old fart," Vitriol said cheerfully. "Did you bring some sulphurous fumes of hell with you, or were you just eating broccoli?"

The crocodile slowly turned to look at Vitriol, but the demon did not move a muscle—except to speak.

"You should stay away from my sister," The hiss of his voice blended almost completely with the steam rising from the AR rocks.

"Oh, you're not related. She's only your sister in the sense that all nuns go to hell. So you're colleagues, nothing more."

"You should stay away from her," Agares repeated.

"And if I don't?"

Fire burned deep behind Agares' eyes, and his lips curled in a tight smile. He stood slowly, then took a step to his left. He was no longer riding his crocodile.

The demon said only one word. "Execute."

The crocodile moved forward.

✪

"Look, I know it doesn't have teeth, but when it bites you it hurts! It fucking hurts, okay?"

Vitriol knew he was speaking louder than he should, so he shut up. He sat against the wall next to the roof door and huddled against the cold wind.

He could tell Harpy was still curious, but also that she didn't want to give him the satisfaction of asking him anything more about it. But they had been on the roof for an hour already, there was no telling how much longer they'd have to be up there, and something had to pass the time.

"So how does it hurt?" Harpy finally asked.

Vitriol knew exactly what she was talking about, but it might be a long night and he needed to take his fun where he could get it.

"How does what hurt?"

"How does a goddamn crocodile hurt, you asshole? You know, the thing you were just talking about?"

"Ah, right, the crocodile," Vitriol said, lightly slapping his knee. "Well, here's the thing. It's a program, right? Software. So it can interact with anything wired into the Matrix. You take your average Hiroki, someone without anything hardwired into their brain, maybe without any implants at all, and it's not going to hurt them much. No access points. But someone like me, I got all sorts of points of entry for it. So when it bites, it's trying to short out anything electronic in me. It didn't permanently fry anything, but it gave me a weird sort of sharp tingling in my brain and throat, like someone was trying to dig a dozen slivers out of the middle of my head with a dozen needles."

"That's still not as bad as an actual crocodile bite," Harpy said.

"Yeah. But it ain't good."

They were quiet again, and Vitriol watched the Manhattan city lights calmly blink and flicker in front of him. It was soothing, which was all wrong, so Vitriol looked at Harpy instead. Her round face, her folded arms, and her eternally arched eyebrow were enough to keep him irritated and on edge.

"Don't you want to know how I finally got away?" he said.

"Not really."

"Oh come on! It was a virtual crocodile trying to fry my neurons! That's kind of cool, right?"

"I guess."

"And obviously I got away from it, or I wouldn't be here. So how did I do it?"

"I don't know," Harpy said. "Some sort of hacker crap. You got out your program and it fought the demon guy's program and yours either won or it distracted this crocodile thing long enough for you to get away. Who gives a shit?"

"It's more complicated than that!" Vitriol said. "It's not like you just launch a program and sit back and wait for it to do its thing! There's all sorts of adjustments you need to make on the fly, moves and counter-moves, it's like swordfighting!"

"It's like playing video games—just a bunch of button-pushing."

"Yeah, but really cool button pushing!"

"Shut up," Harpy said.

"No, hold on, let me explain—"

"Shut *up*." Harpy grabbed her dark sunglasses and threw them on, watching the images that appeared on the insides of the lenses. "They're here," she said. "You're on."

The dark rooftop in front of Vitriol faded as he focused on the image inside his head, a feed from a security camera in the building below. Lochinvar was in the lobby, dressed in his usual black with clips and creases in all the right places. Next to him was the pigeon, a man whose newly implanted scalp hairs did not yet conceal the fact that he was balding.

"No, no, I think it will grow in fine," Lochinvar was saying. "But it's unnecessary, really. Your eyes are—well, forgive me for this, but your eyes are simply extraordinary. I'm not sure anyone could look beyond those eyes and notice anything about your scalp."

The pigeon—his name was Carruthers, if Vitriol remembered correctly—was walking beneath one of the cameras, giving Vitriol a good look at the stubble on top of his head. The skin underneath was turning red.

"Okay, let's move," Vitriol said. He took his focus away from the security footage but made sure he still paid attention to the audio link from below.

Harpy stood, picked up the crowbar she had tucked behind her, and wrenched the rooftop door open with a screech.

Alarms went off throughout the building, but there wasn't any sound. Prometheus Engineering apparently did not feel any need to let any of its neighbors know about break-ins on its property. The people who needed to know about it, though, now knew.

"Oh dear," Vitriol heard Carruthers say through the security feed. "I'm afraid we have to leave."

"Why?" Lochinvar said. "What's happened?"

"It's—I can't really say," Carruthers said. "But we need to leave."

"How disappointing."

Harpy and Vitriol were plunging ahead, going in and out of range of several security cameras and being captured by all of them. Thanks to Harpy's spell, though, the only thing they'd show is two dark, ghostly, faceless images drifting past.

They found the entrance to one of the building's corner staircases and ran into it. The walls here were plain and gray, and while the AR overlay wasn't much prettier, it sure was interesting. Security access points were all over the place, glowing bright red so they couldn't be missed. And security personnel were in the staircase too, a few floors lower, chasing the ghosts their cameras had seen.

"Oh—oh dear," Carruthers said inside Vitriol's head. "The doors are sealed now. I'm afraid we can't leave."

"That's entirely my fault, I'm afraid. Emergencies and crises and such things just aren't my forte. I find I want to talk about what's going on instead of doing anything about it, and that leads to a sort of paralysis that is not helpful in this kind of situation. Which I suppose it's what happening now, as I'm blathering on and not helping the situation."

"It's all right," Carruthers said. "There's somewhere we can go."

"Really? Where?"

"Follow me."

Lochinvar's part was proceeding smoothly, so Vitriol decided to watch his own ass for a bit. Since the staircase was becoming a bit crowded for his tastes, Vitriol pushed a door open and ran into a hallway on the building's fourteenth floor. It was freeing to be able to intrude into a corp building without worrying about setting off an alarm. It's quite possible that he set of three or four additional alarms as he ran across the burgundy-and-green carpeting in the long hallway, but the thing was, none of them after the first one mattered.

Ahead of him, doors opened and guards came out, weapons lowered and ready. There were two of them, and they'd be shooting to kill.

Harpy was ready, though, and she was faster than them. Vitriol didn't see what got them, he didn't feel it, but he saw what happened. One of the guards went down immediately, falling like his spinal cord had been abruptly severed. The other staggered, wobbling and weaving on rubbery legs, his gun firing but not until he had dropped his arm so that all the rounds went into the floor in front of him.

Vitriol was on him quickly, laying the small blackjack he always kept with him alongside the guard's jaw, dropping him like a punch-drunk boxer.

He waved to Harpy, who was lagging a little after casting her spell.

"Come on," he said. "We can stay on this floor for a little bit. There's plenty of room to wander."

Most of the floor looked like it held conference rooms, which made it pretty benign. If this floor had restricted areas, it would already be crawling with guards. Vitriol glanced in several rooms and saw they were all about the same—black, enameled tables surrounded by white, pod-like chairs. The walls of each room had half a dozen screens, and all of them were off. Any one of these rooms would be as good as another, so Vitriol picked one at random and walked in.

He wouldn't have much time—as soon as the guards in the hallway had fallen unconscious, there had likely been an alert sent out to all the other guards, and they'd be converging here.

Then he heard Lochinvar's voice in his ear. Vitriol hadn't changed the volume, so that meant Lochinvar was forcing his way through to get Vitriol's attention.

"I can tell this is a room for executives," Lochinvar was saying. "You don't let the wageslaves sit on this kind of furniture. But what if you're here for a while? Do you just have to sit and wait?"

Carruthers laughed, clearly pleased to be showing off. "Of course not! This room is fully equipped with everything we need to work. You don't think we'd spend any of our time not working, would you?"

"I don't know," Lochinvar said. "These couches appear to be quite comfortable for things other than just sitting around."

Vitriol could almost hear Carruthers blushing.

"They're in," Vitriol said. "Once Lochinvar gets the jack ready, we'll be set."

He hadn't even finished speaking when the node access point appeared before him. It was a black disk, maybe half a meter in diameter, with an ivory inlay that showed a mighty, muscled man chained to a cliff. He had manacles around his ankles and wrists, pulling him into a spread-eagled shape, and he had a terrible gaping wound in his abdomen that, since it was depicted in ivory, seemed clean and sanitary despite the visible intestines.

This was the access point to the Prometheus Engineering executive LAN. It was a network entirely without wireless access—if you didn't plug into it, you couldn't access it, just like the primitive networks of the '60s. Lochinvar, though, had now plugged in a wireless transmitter into the LAN, and now it was up to Vitriol to make good use of it.

The disk in front of him looked so hard, so unbreakable, that Vitriol wished he could take it head on, throw a bunch of agents and maybe a custom mook or two at it and shatter the sucker into a million little artsy-fartsy pieces. But he didn't have time to screw around, and he also had access codes Lochinvar had lifted from Carruthers. Too easy.

He threw the codes at the disk, and it reacted immediately. The wound in Prometheus' abdomen healed, he stood straight and pulled the chains attached to his arms. The edges of the disk pulled in with the chains, then the whole black disk collapsed on itself and was gone. Behind it was a floating circle with a thousand smaller white circles, like little aspirin tablets, hovering in front of him. A thousand files with nothing to identify any of them. And if he was lucky, he had two minutes to find what he needed.

Now it was time for the agents. He let them loose, a swarm of flies buzzing around the little pills, sticking their proboscides into the hard white surfaces, probing for anything that might tell them what

was in the files. They left little bits of fly saliva on the pure white surfaces—an uncharacteristic programming flourish by Vitriol. He kind of
hoped Harpy would glance over and notice.

She didn't. She was too busy watching the hallway outside the
room, waiting for the inevitable approach of the guards. She looked
nervous, which reminded Vitriol that he should probably hurry.

He looked back at the open disk with its thousand pills and saw
that the opening was getting smaller. Something was wrong.

"Lochinvar!" he said. "You didn't let Carruthers log in, did you?"

Lochinvar didn't reply. He didn't hear any noise from Carruthers,
either. Whatever was happening in the room the two of them had
retired to, Vitriol was pretty sure it wasn't good. And now his access
was collapsing.

"Stupid corp bastard should just unplug the transmitter," Vitriol
muttered, then focused on his flies. They were moving fast now, black
blurs skittering over the pills, until all at once they faded away except
for one, and that one had a white pill gripped in its six legs and it was
flying toward Vitriol as the circle around it collapsed. It darted out just
before the entire disk vanished and Vitriol's access was gone.

"Got it, Harpy! Got it!" He turned toward the door. Harpy was
down.

"Oh," Vitriol said. Then he started running.

✪

At least he hadn't been nabbed by contract cops. Places like Knight
Errant and Lone Star were all about wrapping up as many cases as
possible, and forced confessions were a great way to put a "CLOSED"
stamp on a case file. They used torture like plumbers use a snake—
they knew it was usually the fastest way to get the job done.

Come to think of it, Vitriol was pretty sure that Knight Errant
sometimes used actual plumber's snakes in their interrogations. He
shuddered at the thought.

But the people that had him were internal security, Prometheus
Engineering's own people. While they wouldn't mind a confession (it
would come in handy when they were justifying why they had to kill
him), they were more concerned about the truth, a commodity Knight
Errant officers tended to hold in low esteem. These guys needed to
know what was actually going on, which meant that, if they were
smart, torture would be off the table for a while. Torture was good for
a lot of things, but getting an accurate story wasn't one of them.

They'd overrun him soon after he noticed Harpy lying on the floor, and everything had been confusion for a while. They had jammed most of his equipment, and he had to go for a few harrowing moments looking at the world as it really was, without AR overlay. Drab and grey, dull and lifeless. He could have slept with his eyes open—the unaugmented world, as far as he was concerned, provided no interesting visual stimuli.

His equipment was working now, but it wasn't doing much for him. There was only one available node here, and all it did was throw up some AR designed to weaken his resolve. The overhead lights got a little harsher, the table edges looked a little sharper, and there was a slow drip-drip-drip of water coming from an unidentifiable place. He thought about shutting off his AR perception, but he didn't want to give the Prometheus bastards the satisfaction.

There were two big guys standing near the only door to the room, armed and cybered to the teeth. Vitriol briefly experimented with hacking into one of the guy's arms, but he was rejected with extreme prejudice. He was not on his home turf, he didn't have access to outside nodes where he had all sorts of tools and agents stored, plus these guys could probably take his head off with a single backhanded swipe, so he decided to leave their equipment alone for the time being.

Then the door opened and the show started. The guy that walked in was a by-the-book corp security drone, down to the black tie, mirrored shades, and flat head.

"Mr. Vitriol," the man said. "Fake politeness, banal courtesy, tough-guy posturing, blah blah blah. Now that that's out of the way, tell me what I want to know or I'll take it right out of your head."

"Hi," Vitriol said.

The man shook his head. "No, we're done with that bullshit. No banter, no time for you to be a smartass. Tell me what I want to know, etc."

Vitriol leaned back in the wobbly metal chair, casually throwing his right arm over the back. "What do you want to know?"

"Who are you working for?"

Vitriol smiled. "Would you want any of the runners who work for you to give you up so easily? I didn't think so. So I can't tell you—I got professional standards to uphold."

"Fine," the man said, then looked at no one in particular. "Bring it in."

"Who are you talking to?" Vitriol said.

The man focused back on Vitriol. "Not you."

"Okay. And what are they bringing in?"

The man smiled and looked oddly cheerful, even with his mirrored shades still in place. "The nice thing about your operation here, Mr. Vitriol, is that we already know what you were after. We caught you after your agents had pointed it out to you and started to retrieve it, all before Mr. Carruthers alertly terminated your connection." The man smirked. "Convenient, isn't it, that your connection stayed intact long enough for us to find out what you wanted, but not long enough for you to actually get away with it? One might even think we planned it that way."

The interrogator was awfully self-satisfied, but in Vitriol's experience that was a pretty common trait in corp security officers. "Well, you're all very clever then," he said.

"Yes, we are. You were attempting to get your hands on the plans for prototype NT67T/H7, codenamed Project Siren. I assume you weren't just grabbing it randomly, especially since you dedicated so many agents to finding it. So you know what we can do with Project Siren?"

"No," Vitriol said. When you were expected to lie, he figured, why tell the truth?

"We can use it—to be specific, our marketers can use it—to persuade. To insinuate our way into people's heads and make them think what we want them to think."

"Sounds ominous."

"Ah, yes, the deadpan reaction to the major, rather ominous technological advance. You play your role very well, Mr. Vitriol. Sadly, the truth is the project is not yet as powerful as we may desire. We can only nudge minds at the moment, perhaps hasten them to move in directions that they might otherwise have chosen for themselves, without our assistance. It may not be that momentous, but it is a start.

"Okay."

The man tilted his head down and started tracing random patterns on the metal table surface with his finger. "We had to perform a significant amount of brain research in order to develop this product, as you might imagine. Which means that we have a large supply of nanotechnology dedicated toward discovering what is happening in different parts of people's minds."

His head jerked up quickly, and he reached his hand toward Vitriol's head, like he was going to press the tips of his fingers through his forehead and knead whatever he found in there.

"We have the tools to reach in there, Mr. Vitriol. Into your brain. We can find what's in there," He leaned back. "So you can tell us what we want to know, Mr. Vitriol. Or I can send in the agents that can find it for me."

"You can't do that," Vitriol said. "No one can do that."

"But we think we can."

"Who gives a shit? All that means is that you're delusional."

The man gently shrugged. "That may be," he said. "But we're delusional enough to try it."

"Fine," Vitriol said with a casual wave of his hand. "Waste as much time as you want. You don't have anything that can do what you're saying."

"But we have nanotechnology research that interests you enough to break in and attempt to steal it. So you know we have nanites here that can affect your mind, and we're willing to use them. They are nanites that have some kind of effect—if they didn't, we would never have continued Project Siren long enough to catch the interest of whoever hired you. We have nanites that can affect the brain, and we're going to put them into your skull.

"But maybe we don't know what we're doing. Maybe we have these nanites that can do things to your brain, but not the things we think they'll do. And we will put these things into your brain and let them run wild and we will see what they do to your mind. Are you willing to see what the results will be?"

Vitriol wished his eyes hadn't grown wider, but he knew they had and there was nothing he could do about it. "You can't do that. You can't just take someone off the street and inject things into their brain!"

"First of all, Mr. Vitriol, we didn't just pull you off the street. Second, while human testing is sometimes frowned upon by the more squeamish corporations, many of us know that the use of human subjects can provide great advances in learning. So when you are whatever you'll become after this, Mr. Vitriol, you'll know that you helped the cause of science."

"I don't think this is necessary," Vitriol said, wishing there was something, anything interesting in the room to look at.

"You're prepared to talk? About your conversation with Blood Sister, perhaps?"

"About what? What do you—" He kept a nervous eye on the room's door. "Okay. I'll talk. Let's negotiate."

"Not that kind of talking, Mr. Vitriol. The kind where you tell us what you want to know."

"I can't—"

The door to the room opened, and a man in a long white coat walked in holding a small metal box. The man with the sunglasses waved his hand abruptly in front of Vitriol's face.

"It's too late. We'll do it my way."

"But—"

"We're done," the man said, and walked out of the room as the man in the white coat approached.

❌

Vitriol didn't go out for a while after that. For a few days he simply didn't feel like it, and after that he stayed in because he thought it would be best to lie low. He didn't go home, either—his home was a dump, and he didn't want anyone to find him there. He stayed at a hotel, the type of place he could afford with the money he had earned, with a false identity that came as an additional form of compensation.

When he finally went out again, he avoided his usual haunts, even staying away from a sphinx party he heard about. But there are some things in life that, like chronic headaches, cannot be avoided no matter how hard one tries, and one night Vitriol found himself in the same bar as Gemmel. He was not able to avoid the dwarf, and he was surprised to realize that he didn't want to. He should probably know what other people knew about the incident.

Gemmel didn't make him wait. He plopped down net to him on a stool, easily climbing up on it even though it was almost as tall as he was. Vitriol glared at the bartender to let him know he should stay away for a time. The bartender, who did not seem anxious to move from his padded stool at the other end of the bar, looked away from Vitriol and Gemmel.

"Hey, hey, Vitriol, did you hear?" Gemmel said, brown beard bobbing. "Did you hear about the nun?"

"What?"

"The nun, the nun. Blood Sister. Sold out. Went corporate."

So that was their game, Vitriol thought. "What do you mean?"

"What do you think I mean? She got a steady gig, shadow ops for Prometheus. They might even put her on the official payroll someday."

"Wow. Never thought she was the type to go corporate."

"So why do you think she did it?"

"Don't know," Gemmel said, scratching his head. "How does anyone ever get anyone to do anything they don't want to do? They had something on her, I guess."

"Yeah, I guess."

"Maybe that's what was bothering her. She seemed like she was kind of in a bad mood, don't you think."

"Yeah. For about the last five years."

"No, I mean recently. Recently she was in an even worse mood. You saw it, didn't you? That night at the sphinx party? Didn't she seem like she was in a really bad mood that night?"

"Yeah."

"So what did you talk about?"

"Nothing," Vitriol said. "Nothing at all." Then he smiled and walked out.

The Manhattan streets were shiny in the night, almost like they were wet. The air was heavy, and the scent of rotting garbage never really went away on days like this.

Vitriol wasn't paying much attention to the street, though. He was playing around with the twin images, twin memories in his mind. In each of them, he was talking to Blood Sister at the sphinx party. In one of the images, they had briefly exchanged hostile words while the nun's church collapsed on him, which is what really happened. In the other, they had a brief exchange that strongly indicated that Blood Sister was behind the Prometheus Engineering break-in.

It was a ludicrous image. Anyone who really knew Blood Sister would know she wouldn't ever work with Vitriol, and she wasn't the type to organize a run on her own. But the people at Prometheus didn't know that. Vitriol had talked to Blood Sister so he could put a memory in his head, and then he played with the memory so it would give out the information he wanted it to provide. When the Prometheus people had found the custom-designed memory in Vitriol's head, they had believed it. Especially since they had heard about the conversation and wanted to know what it was about.

So they had brought Blood Sister in, and they had apparently gotten what they wanted from her. And Vitriol was quietly let go—the people who hired him apparently saw to that, and although Vitriol couldn't know for sure how that happened, he believed they could order around his former captors because they were their superiors.

It was a shame about Harpy. She was the sacrifice the run needed to look right. Lochinvar hadn't been seen for a while, and possibly only Carruthers knew of his fate.

Prometheus would move forward, thinking they had gotten what they wanted—not only did they have Blood Sister's identity, but they seemingly had proof that their memory retrieval nanites worked. Never mind that Vitriol had forced them to work, pretty much waving his fake memory in front of them as hard as he could, so they didn't have a choice but to find it.

Vitriol's employers had lied to him about who they were, he had lied about what Blood Sister had said, then his employers had lied to the rest of the Prometheus Engineering corporation about the capabilities of their nanotech program. And the world continued spinning 'round. Vitriol knew that there was only one secret to survival in this world—stay at least one lie ahead of everyone else. ⊗

SPELLS & CHROME ■ 25

BLOODY FINGERS

BY JASON SCHMETZER

Jason Schmetzer is a writer and editor in the cornfields of Indiana, far from corporations or dragons. His work is found in many Catalyst Game Labs products, crossing the BattleTech™, MechWarrior™ and Shadowrun™ lines. He is currently managing editor of the BattleCorps/subscription website.

2070... somewhere south of London

They'd gone to ground in the Barrens.

Deke blinked his cybereye's overlay off and inhaled slowly. His eyes—normal vision now, no AR—tracked slowly right-to-left, mostly unfocused. He was watching for movement, for telltales, for things that might not be tagged with an RFID or broadcasting a mesh signal. The sun was nearly down, anyway. If one of the 'nappers was stupid enough to light a stick, he'd see it. Or smell it. The doxy buggers.

"Deke," a bud in his ear whispered. "No signs."

Deke twisted his head. Lincoln was nestled in a gully a hundred meters to his left, rifle presented but protected by a ghillie suit. A blink brought his AR back up, scattering icons across his vision, but Lincoln wasn't broadcasting. The subvocal they were using was burst-transmit—if one of the 'nappers caught the signal, they'd think it was background noise. Unless they were good.

But they're not good, Deke reminded himself. Good kidnappers wouldn't have grabbed the daughter of the local *oyabun*. He thought-clicked a reply to Lincoln and went back to studying the building he thought they were hiding in. It had been a restaurant, once upon a time. Now it was a ganger hideout.

In the Barrens.

Deke blinked the overlay away and sighed. He'd sworn to never come back here. And if he didn't need the nuyen the bunnie had promised so bad, he never would have. *But a samurai has expenses.* And so here he was, a half-klick from the shack his mother had birthed him in, sitting the near-misting rain and trying not to think about his childhood. *And one job away from getting off this bloody rock for good.* There was good money to be made in Europe for a man who was good with his hands.

"Deke," Lincoln whispered.

"Shut up," Deke snarled.

"The lackey is back."

Bollocks. Deke twisted around and watched the yakuza mage low-crawl forward. He was wearing a black skinsuit, no armor, and he carried no weapons. He was the weapon, of course. And ink. Lots and lots of ink. Deke had seen him without his shirt back at the meet. He was covered in tats. *A good little yak. The bloody hell am I doing working for yaks in London?*

"It is time," the mage whispered.

"It's not," Deke whispered back.

"They will soon detect us," he said.

"If you keep talking and moving around, you're right." Deke ground his teeth and turned back to the ganger shack. AR showed him old dots, tags from the restaurant days that were still powered. The detectors, for example, were still up. So if they approached from the drive-thru side there'd probably be a chime announcing the arrival of the next consumer-drone sucker to purchase his ration of trans-fat and obesity. The gangers had probably left that there—it was cheap security for them. A gang that could swipe the bunny's daughter had some sophistication. Not smarts, of course. But so-phistication. *And maybe...* Deke ducked his chin to whisper to the mage behind him.

"Any like you in there?"

"Like me?"

"Spooks? Magickers? Seers-through-walls?"

"Let me see." There was a still moment, where Deke had the un-comfortable feeling someone was walking on his soul, and then the yak mage spoke. "One of them has some small talent, but he isn't trained. There are nine, by the way."

"Where?" The yak shook his head. "Armed?"

"I could not tell."

Deke sucked air through his teeth. "Guards?"

"I could not tell."

"You're not helping, you know."

"Nor am I hindering," the yak said. "The *oyabun* sent me to make sure his interests are looked after, and that his daughter survives this ordeal." Deke heard something in the man's—*well, the ork's*—voice. He looked back, but the sun had set too far for him to see the man's face without calling up his cybereye's thermal settings. "You are being paid. I am to watch, and assist as necessary."

Deke snorted. "I'm so grateful." The mage made no reply.

"Deke," Lincoln whispered. "It's now or never."

"Yeah," Deke whispered. "All right. On my signal."

"Rog-o," Lincoln said.

Deke rolled his head around on his shoulders, stretching the sinews of his neck. His fingers ran across his torso and thighs—subgun, pistols, a half-dozen balanced knives wrapped around one thigh. He blinked the combat overlays up, visual light only. No starlight, no thermal. It was a restaurant—there would be stoves, and lights. He sent a quick diagnostic check through his commlink. All implants ready, firewalls up. His kit—both physical and mesh—was secure.

"All right," he whispered, and then slithered forward.

The hide he'd selected was above the restaurant, and his path forward was downhill and mostly wet—*good English weather*—and the gullies would hide him for most of the descent. The slings kept his subgun tight against the small of his back, no whispers, no rattles. Dad would've been proud. Fast and silent, the old SAS vet had said. Deke was both. He low-crawled into a culvert and risked a look.

A half-klick from where he crouched, his mother had borne him just before things had gone in the pot. His dad had been called up and snapped up into the unpleasantness before he'd even really gotten to know him, and then his Ma had started doing what was necessary to feed them and give them a roof—*roofs, really, since the tricks never let us stay long*—and Deke had gotten the start of his education in the realities of the Sixth World.

The drekking Barrens.

More and more dots popped up on his AR. Deke shut his mesh down to internals, closing off the queries from parking bots and restaurant menus. The remote aiming reticle from his gun flicked off his overlay, but Deke knew how to shoot without his implants aiming for him. He could bring the mesh back up quickly enough, but anything that wasn't wired direct would broadcast, and he needed to be unseen.

The misting rain thickened into a good English drizzle, not heavy enough to block his sight or raise a noise, just enough to start swallowing the small sounds of odd noises and his movement. Deke let the grin show—*good English weather*—and just for a moment forgot where he was and why.

Yaks. In the Barrens.

"I'm going," he subvocalized. The processor smashed those two words to a zip-squeal and burst it out to be picked up by Lincoln's mesh. That was his signal—that meant that anything Lincoln saw through his scope that wasn't an early-middle-aged former SAS commando carrying a little yak princess out the door was a target for the big rifle he was snuggled up with. Deke gathered himself into a crouch, brought his subgun around, and triggered his mesh.

Then he sprinted.

His AR came active again and filled with dots, RFIDs sensing him and firing off announcements and queries. He made the ten meters between himself and the access door he was aiming at in about five seconds, which was about fourteen and a half seconds longer than it took the first of the over-the-counter security bots to see that his mesh wasn't one of the gangers and trigger what passed for an alarm.

That's right, kids, he thought. *Run outside, where my friend Lincoln can see you.*

It was forty seconds before the door opened, and a boy with iridescent facial tattoos ran out, cradling an old Ares repeater. Deke grabbed him from behind, swung him around and into the side of the building, then dropped him. The muzzle of his submachine gun was already pointing down—a single round was all it took, and all of that in the span of two seconds and a half-yelp of noise from the ganger. Deke ignored the tapping of the boy's foot against his as the body's nerves reacted to the loss of its brain. He was listening, his cyberear attuned for echo and canceling the masking rain noise.

A boom echoed through the night, so close it almost covered the mallet-striking-soft-meat sound of the large-caliber bullet hitting its target from around the building. Deke didn't bother looking in that direction. Lincoln's ghillie was more than enough cover to conceal him from the likes of these pukes.

Seven. Deke heard footsteps coming, but they stopped before they appeared out the door. He frowned, looked down. The dead boy had dropped his Ares where someone in the hallway could see it. *Damn it*, he thought. Then he slid away from the doorway.

Bullets punched through the light metal of the door as one of the gangers inside lit through a whole magazine. Deke grimaced as hot bits of metal flecked against his face, but none got in his eyes. He squatted, subgun ready. His cyberear had already adjusted for the noise of the gunfire. Footsteps.

One set of footsteps. The clatter of a magazine hitting the floor. No answering click of a new one being seated.

Deke stood up, slipped his gun around behind him on its sling, and clenched his fist. Precise pressure from his ring finger against a specific part of his palm triggered a mechanism in his fist. A ten-centimeter blade slid from between his ring and middle fingers of his right hand, mono-edge sharp. Deke stepped around the door and took two long steps.

The ganger was maybe eighteen, fit but with the added paunch around the midsection that a young man gets when the near-constant exercise of youth is replaced with the sedentary complacence of one's early twenties. He was fumbling with a magazine for the bullpup-style subgun he was carrying. He saw Deke, and his eyes went as big as saucers. His mouth opened, ork's tusks prominent.

"Shite—" Deke heard, but that was all the man had time for. Deke swung an uppercut at the kid, hard enough that when it landed it lifted the ork ganger off the floor. He didn't fall, though, because his jaw was caught on the edge of the blade protruding from Deke's fist, the blade that quickly sliced through the jawbone holding it in place. The kid collapsed, blood and bits of bone and gray matter leaking out of the gaping hole in his chin.

"Bloody hell," Deke whispered. "Another kid."

Six.

A message window popped up on Deke's AR. ALARM TO CITY— DON'T KNOW WHO. Deke blinked the message closed and pulled one of the matte black automatics from his thigh holster. *A remote alarm? All the way out here? For* gangers? He looked down.

The dead kid's arms were tattooed.

Oh, shit. These weren't gangers. They were yaks.

Rival yaks.

Deke drew in a deep breath and flashed a warning to Lincoln. His instincts screamed at him for standing in one place this long. He crept around the body and down the hall, pistol presented. He'd only used a single round from his subgun, and there were still twenty-nine more in the magazine, but he didn't want to be spraying bullets around in a room where his paycheck—*I mean, the little yak princess*—might be held.

Deke moved toward the front of the building. He'd been in restaurants like this one before—there'd be a little maze of rooms in the back, then the kitchen, then the main dining room out front. He kept the pistol leveled and moved steadily. His boot soles made no noise, not even being wet. Nothing jingled.

"I see you, runner," a voice said. Deke jerked the pistol around toward the source of the sound, but it was a speaker in the ceiling. "That's right. I'm watching you."

"Nice to know," Deke said, resuming his advance. He came to a junction, turned toward the front.

"I wouldn't go that way, runner," the voice said.

Deke went that way.

When he'd been ten his father had gone out to deal with looters or something—his mother was never good with stories—and never came back. All he had of him were memories of the brief times they were together when his father had been on leave. Times when the man had been drinking and spilling his soul to his eight-year-old boy, confessing his sins and passing on a veteran's wisdom in his catharsis.

"Never do what the blokes want, lad," he'd said one night, eight or nine deep in his pints. "They say go left, you go right. Nine times out of ten, they was just misleadin' you anyway. An' if they weren't, well...you'll know where to find them."

An alert pinged on his AR as Deke passed a junction in the corridor, barely a few meters away from the large swinging door that had to lead into the kitchen. He's just entered a mesh zone, an overlap. Most of the area around here was dead zone—no Matrix—but a node had just popped up. Deke frowned.

A buzzing in his ears erupted. *Jamming.* That meant they knew about Lincoln. Deke gritted his teeth and reached around to a small pouch on the small of his back. He pulled out a small canister, twisted the top, and nudged the door open far enough to shove it through. As he expected, a hail of gunfire tore through the door the instant it moved.

The flash-bang exploded. The light was blocked by the door, but the sound carried through like a punch, and even though he'd prepared for it, it still dazed him for a second. And a second was all the bloke needed.

ALERT. Red letters flashed across his vision. "Bloody hell," Deke mumbled. His overlays started twitching. The hacker was messing with his mesh—with his own bloody network—and although he'd not fully penetrated the OS, he was trying. And he might succeed. Deke was a samurai, not a hacker. He had hackers on retainer that updated his mesh. But he wasn't one himself.

"Shit." He shut down all of his unwired network. Targeting crosshairs dropped off his overlays. Reports stopped pinging from the arrows and dots scattered around the restaurant. Deke squeezed the grip of his pistol, cursed the seconds he'd lost dealing with the hack, and charged through the door.

A troll lay on its side just to the side of the door, its thick hide smoking. *Bloody fool must've grabbed the grenade*, Deke thought. He drew back a foot and kicked, but the impact did little more than jostle the giant. He grunted and spun, taking in the rest of the room.

And the three guns pointed right at him, held by the last five gangers.

"I told you I could see you, runner," an elf said. His eyes were glassy with overlays—he'd been the one speaking in the corridor. That made him the hacker.

"And here I am," Deke said.

"You're here for the child," the elf said.

Deke looked around. He didn't see any children. "I am. Her father wants her back."

"Thinks 'e own the place, does he?" a human said from one side. Deke glanced at him. He was almost forty, dirty, with the look of a man who'd done his lazy best to get through life on bravado and cowardice. Deke looked at the gun in his hand, flashed an enhancement through his cybereye, and then ignored him. His pistol's safety was still on.

"He doesn't care, Cyril," the elf said. "He's just a runner, not a yak."

"Then let's shoot 'im an' be done," Cyril said.

"Let's not," the elf said.

"Wise choice," Deke said.

The elf laughed. "You're hardly in a position to negotiate," he said. "Your sniper outside can't help you, and we've got you covered. I can sense your augments, runner. I know you're wired—a relic, really, these days—and although I shut down your mesh, you're still dangerous." He brandished the Ares in his hand. "You might get me, but not all of us."

"True," Deke said. "But..."

"But what?"

Deke smiled. "Now, yak."

Someone walked on his soul. Power wafted through the mana, wrapping itself around the weapons of the gangers like ethereal fists and ripping them from unyielding hands. Deke brandished his pistols as all the gangers' guns slammed themselves against the wall behind him and clattered to the floor. A moment later the yak ork sorcerer walked through the hallway door behind Deke. His eyes and his tattoos were alight with unholy fire. He'd been watching through the small vision slit. Or at least, that had been the plan.

"You should not have taken the child," he said.

"Couldn't come yourself?" the elf spat. "Had to get *gaijin* help?"

"When a need arises, one secures an expert," the mage said. "Where is the child?"

The elf snarled a half-heard curse. Deke swallowed.

"Where. Is. The. Child?"

"Sod off, yak," Cyril said.

The mage looked at him. His lips moved with silent words, and suddenly Cyril was screaming, was writhing, and then was on fire. Deke stepped back, pistol leveled, but the yak was only interested in Cyril. After a moment the body collapsed and stopped screaming, but didn't stop to burn. The scent filled the small space.

The yak turned back to the elf. "The child?"

"We sold her."

"You sold her."

"To Tamanous." The elf looked at Cyril's corpse and then back at the yak. Deke had to give him credit. If he was scared—*and by all the dragons in the Sixth World* Deke *was scared*—he didn't show it. "Got a good price, too, a young thing like that. Had just the right blood type."

"Why would you do that?" the mage asked. "You knew we would come after you. You knew who she was, who her father was." He frowned, which made his tusks more prominent. "Why would you do something so foolish?"

"Because this is England," the elf said. He spoke the best Queen's English. "And you're just an import. And it's time you remembered it."

Deke looked at the mage. The ork raised an eyebrow, but didn't speak. Deke swallowed, and rebooted his mesh. It came back up clean, but there was a waiting message from an unknown sender. He looked at the elf. The elf looked at him. "What's the plan?" Deke asked.

"We renegotiate," the ork said. "Let's go?"

Deke turned toward him. "What about them?"

There was a strange, wet noise behind him. He turned, saw the bodies lying on the floor, faces frozen in distended caricatures of horrible pain. Blood leaked from their eyes.

"What about them?" the ork asked, and walked through the door.

Outside, Lincoln came down to meet them. He had the hood of his now-soaked ghillie suit thrown back and his rifle cradled in his arms. He looked at Deke, elf's ears upturned and a smile on his face. "Payday, mate?"

"Not yet." Deke slipped the safety on his pistol and slid it into his holster. "You said renegotiate," he said to the mage.

"I must contact the *oyabun*," the mage said. "Please do not leave." He sat down where he stood, into a puddle, black skinsuit splashing muddy water. His face went blank.

"What happened?" Lincoln asked. Deke filled him in. Lincoln looked at the mage, his hand unconsciously stroking the receiver of his rifle. "Bloody hell, mate."

"Yeah." Deke looked at the ork on the ground. He didn't seem to be there. He called the message up on his screen. It was text only, but he recognized the elf's hand on it. The way it spoke was the same.

>*I don't blame you, runner. Nuyen is nuyen. But beware the yakuza. We've stained their honor, and they'll want that hidden. You know. Be wary. As the man said, you are an expert. But you're not yakuza.*

Deke read it twice, then deleted it. The ork had not stirred. He was communing, or something. Deke caught Lincoln's eye, then set up a link through the mesh. Text only. He glanced down.

>*Can the yak get on our mesh?*

Lincoln glanced down, then shook his head.

>*He killed everyone in there.*

>YOU TOLD ME THAT.

>*Yeah, but he did it without blinking. He didn't ask which harvester they sold the girl to. He just gakked them.* Deke looked back at the building. There was a bit of smoke rolling out of the open door. Perhaps Cyril had spread.

>*One of the gangers left me a message.*

>WHAT?

>*On my mesh. He tried to hack it—succeeded, I guess—but I shut it down. Told me to be careful. Said we're not yaks. Said to watch out.*

Lincoln glanced down at the zoned-out yak mage. He still hadn't moved. >SO YOU'RE WORRIED.

>*Yeah.*

>KILL HIM?

Deke shook his head. >*Not yet. We need to find this little girl, get paid. We need more information.* He looked down at the ork. >*And a better plan.*

Lincoln shrugged. >I'LL BACK YOUR PLAY. He disconnected.

Deke looked around, trying to ignore the taint in the air of cooking meat. It wasn't the first time he'd smelled it, not even the first time he'd smelled it in the Barrens. He dropped an overlay and looked around, watching for mesh telltales or odd dots or arrows. *Nothing.* The shack was right down the road.

"We're leaving now," his mother had said, a couple months after they'd gotten the word about his dad. "We're not coming back here. We're never coming back here."

Yet here I am.

The mage stirred.

"We're going back toward town. The girl has been sold to the Leaf gang, and their harvesting center is ten kilometers that direction." He climbed to his feet and looked between Deke and Lincoln. "This is acceptable?"

"Our contract was for the gangers," Deke said.

"Your contract was to retrieve the *oyabun*'s daughter."

"From the gangers." Deke jerked a thumb over his shoulder. The rain was keeping fire from spreading outside the building, but the smoke was still there, and the smell. And, Deke knew, later that night there'd be a moment where his hand would spasm and he'd see the face of the ganger he'd punched to death. "That's done."

"I said we would renegotiate." The ork returned Deke's gaze evenly.

"Now."

"Very well. I will increase your payment by forty percent for the added labor."

"Sixty."

"You are haggling?"

"We could walk away now."

"You haven't completed your contract," the yak said. Lincoln stepped a step to the side, away from Deke's side, adding some distance between them. The ork looked at him, then back at Deke. "Even if you did, the *oyabun* would hunt you down."

"Fifty percent over the previous amount," Deke said. His palms were sweating inside his gloves but he kept his voice even. "And you deposit the first amount now, into our numbered accounts. Before we take another step."

The ork smiled. It was not pretty. "Done." He turned and walked back toward the slope they had come down. Their vehicle was waiting there, and as Deke drove at the ork's instructions he had Lincoln check the status of their accounts. They'd barely gone a klick when Lincon sent a message through Deke's mesh.

>MONEY'S THERE. NICE PLAY.

"How do you know it's the Leafs?" Deke asked.

"That was the information I was given," the mage said. He stared out the side window, but his fingers moved every so often in intricate movements and his lips moved as he subvocalized words. Deke watched him out of the corner of his eye.

"Given?"

"By those with the information," he said.

"You know, you could start trusting us," Deke said, after a short period of silence. "We're doing what you want."

The mage turned his head and looked at Deke. "Trust is not necessary, runner. Your skills are needed, and so you are employed. More information would not make it any easier for you to shoot people."

"I need to know about the Leafs."

"There are six people in the facility as of six hours ago. When we get there I'll be able to update that number."

"Update?"

"I can sense it."

"So you can lead me right to the little girl?" Deke smiled. "That'll make it easier. Might even be able to get in and out without killing anyone." He made an indicated turn and slowed. The flashing neon sign of a tree branch was blinking ahead in the distance, and his overlays were starting to pick up more lively dots and arrows—current ones, even. Not leftovers.

"I cannot tell you where people are," the mage said. "Only how many."

"Seems rubbish, to me."

"Everything has limits, runner. Even in the Sixth World."

Deke didn't slow down as he passed the Leaf organ harvesting center that masqueraded as a private care facility. He just rolled past, not even looking. Lincoln would be looking, he knew. He'd cross-load the feed through his mesh later. And the yak was almost glowing as they went past.

"There are twelve people in that building," he said.

Deke drove to the next side street, signaled the turn like a normal driver, and took it. He pulled into the first alley he found and parked the van, then opened his mesh up while Lincoln transmitted what'd he'd seen. Deke watched the replay at double-speed, watching for anything that would indicate he should slow down, but saw only what he expected: a harmless-looking building, unfortified, hiding in plain sight.

"Plan?" Lincoln asked.

"Depends," Deke said.

"On?"

"On whether one of those twelve people is the little girl." He looked to the ork. "You realize we may be too late."

"She is still alive," the mage said. "She must be."

"Then the smart money is some of them being doctors." Deke took a deep breath. "That means fast."

"Fast is more dangerous," Lincoln said. A ping sounded in Deke's head. >WHAT'S PLAN?

"Yes, it is," Deke said. >*Insurance.*

"The girl must not be harmed." The mage was looking in the direction of the building, but his attention was still on the small team. "Can you extract her?"

Deke smiled. "That's what you're paying me for." He glanced at Lincoln, thought for a second, and then shrugged. "Life's dangerous." He shifted his weight, then directed his attention to the ork. "You and me need to talk."

"We are speaking."

"Tell me about your mojo."

"My what?"

"Your magic. You can sense people. And I know you can kill people. I've seen that bloody well up close." Deke swallowed against his suddenly dry throat. "Can you just knock everyone in there unconscious?"

"Perhaps," the mage said. "If I could see them. But the spell for that is very dangerous to small children. I would not chance it with the *oyabun*'s daughter at stake."

Deke opened his door and climbed out. They were parked behind a small suite of offices—all seemed deserted, and all the arrows were reading closed. He clicked through several overlays, but there didn't appear to be any security related to the Leafs directed at them. The rain hadn't changed, but there was more light. This close to London—or this far from the Barrens—there was the beginnings of a dedicated zone. If he'd been so inclined, Deke could have probably accessed the Matrix.

"When I go in, will you know who I am?"

"Only if I can see you," the mage said.

Deke nodded. *This might work.* "If I were carrying the little girl, would you be able to tell? Without seeing us, I mean."

"Only if I can see you. Magic is not like a vid camera." The ork climbed out of the other side of the van. He paused a moment, turning his face upward to the rain. When he looked down, Deke saw calculation in his eyes. "What is your plan?"

"I will go in. I will find the little girl. Once I have her, I'll either carry her out or put her on my back." He beckoned at the mage. "Once you see us, you put everyone else down for a nap." He snapped his fingers. "We walk out."

"Seems simple enough," Lincoln said. >HOW DOES THAT HELP ME!?

>*Patience.*

The ork considered for a moment. Then he climbed back into the seat he'd recently vacated and closed the door. The window rolled down enough to let sound out. "I can do this," he said. He rummaged for a black skullcap and climbed back out. "I must get on the roof. There are skylights."

"Well..." Deke went to the back of the van and rummaged around until he came up with a dingy old peacoat and slipped it on. It was large enough that it hung to below his waist and halfway down the backs of his hands.

"You're going in like that," Lincoln asked.

"That's right."

"Through the front door."

"That's right."

>ARE YOU TRYING TO KILL YOURSELF?

"That would seem unwise," the yak said.

"Against other runners? Absolutely. Those gangers we just left? Get me nicked and sold off without a second thought." Deke shrugged his shoulders to reseat the peacoat over the bulge of his subgun at the small of his back. "Here? Just what the doctor ordered."

"You're insane," Lincoln said.

"They have to have a front," Deke said. "People must wander in off the street, arrows or no. They're a medical office, for dragon's sake. I'll just walk in for a consult." He grinned a nod at he ork and started walking, head down, hands deep in the peacoat's pockets.

>HE'S GOING TO KILL US.

>*Not before we get the kid.*

>RIGHT AFTER.

Deke snorted. >*Probably.* He glanced around the sidewalk as he came around the building he'd parked behind. There was no one else on the streets, and a quick flicker of his overlays confirmed no active sensing. He shut back down as quickly as he could, content to do more than zip-squeal text with Lincoln. It was maybe a hundred-meter walk to the clinic.

>*Get on the Matrix. Get us a rigger, right now. We need a drone here in ten minutes. Pay whatever you have to. But we need wheels.*

>THAT SHORT WILL COST.

>*Death costs more.* Pay it.

>THE PLAN?

>*Find a hide. Somewhere you can bear on the roof and the front of the building.*

>I CAN'T LOOK TWO DIRECTIONS AT ONCE.

>*Watch the front. You don't need to watch the ork until I've got the girl.*
>ROG.

Deke clicked the messager off and concentrated on the task at hand. The front of the Leaf clinic was brightly lit, just like most of the other 'corp clone businesses around here. Deke walked just beneath the sign and into the front door without hesitation.

A white-coated receptionist looked up when Deke entered. He was young, maybe twenty-four, a dwarf. He was sitting on a high stool, short arms manipulating an AR keyboard in front of him. Deke's mesh registered a query from the dwarf but returned nothing, not even a carrier.

"May I help you?" the dwarf asked.

"I need a doctor," Deke said.

"Your SIN?"

"It's my hand," Deke said, holding up his right arm.

"I understand, sir," the dwarf said. The nameplate on his uniform read SANCHEZ. "But I need your SIN to begin processing your application."

"It hurts," Deke said. He stepped to the desk. A meter of countertop separated them, but Deke didn't doubt there was at best an alarm button—at worst a gun—beneath the countertop. He poked his arm across the desk. The dwarf frowned.

"Sir, I'm afraid—" he gurgled the rest, as the monoblade in Deke's hand penetrated his forehead.

"That's better," Deke said. >*It's on*, he sent to Lincoln.

Alarms screamed to life around him. An armored door collapsed near-instantly across the entryway he'd just passed through, and doors snapped shut across the exposed corridors. Deke blinked his overlays up. His mesh came up and his AR went haywire with warnings.

"Bloody hell," Deke murmured, and crouched in front of the dead dwarf's desk.

"Sometimes they're ready for you," Deke's father had once said. "Despite surprise, the buggers find out you're coming or they're ready to be surprised. Then all you can do is cause as much chaos as you can and hope you slip through amongst it."

Deke shrugged out of the peacoat and flung it toward the door. He brought his subgun around and chambered a round. Then he reached into the baggy pockets on the thighs of his dungarees and pulled a small gray charge. He rolled around the corner of the desk, slapped the charge against the nearest blast door near where the latch would be on a normal door, and then smashed a flat metal plate overtop it. Then he rolled back around to duck and cover behind the desk.

He tripped a control in his mesh.

The explosion was a small one, but even small explosions are loud in small rooms. Deke's ears—well, his real one, not his cyber—were ringing, but he staggered to his feet and smashed his shoulder against the door. The plate groaned and then snapped with a crack. Deke shoved his way through and led with the subgun.

Overlays washed across his vision as his mesh interrogated the arrows and dots and other RFID tags in the building. A sketchy map began to take shape in wireframe, but Deke ignored it for now. There were no doors off this corridor, so he had only one way to go. He went.

A man stumbled across the T of the corridor in front of him, moving right to left. It could have been an elf, or even an ork. It wasn't a girl. Deke didn't hesitate. He triggered a three-round-burst from his subgun, two of which removed the person's head at the throat quite nicely. The third buried itself in the surprisingly sturdy door.

The reports of the gun were quite loud, loud enough to penetrate the ringing in Deke's left ear. He reached behind him again and came back with a flash-bang, which he primed and rolled down the corridor. He came to a stop against the opposite wall of the T-junction. Deke crouched and opened his mouth. His overlays flickered to masking, and he closed his left eye. The explosion was even more devastating than the door charge had been.

>TWO DOWN IN FRONT. Lincoln was getting some work after all.
>SWEEPERS.

That left nine, one of which was the bunny's little girl. Deke ground his teeth and moved toward the junction. Sweepers from around back of the building—sweepers being those blokes who'd try to come around the building and get behind him—in less than thirty seconds meant a disgustingly high state of readiness. Either these Leafs were real pros, or they were real nervous having the bunny's daughter getting her organs removed in their building.

Either option would get Deke killed.

Two more forms loomed out of the darkness ahead as he went left at the T. He brought the subgun up and fired twice, six rounds. Three to each form. Both of them collapsed as Deke darted forward behind his bullets. They were women, in hospital greens. Harmless.

Still dead.

"There's two kinds of people in the world, lad," his first sergeant in the SAS had told him once. "The kind that matter and the kind that don't." Deke had frowned then, and the sergeant had clapped him on the arm. "On an op, there's those you're there for and those you aren't, and those you aren't are disposable. They get in your way, you move them. You don't leave problems behind you."

Deke stepped past them. He didn't look down twice.

Seven.

>THE ORK IS DOING SOMETHING.

Deke swore and shouldered a door open. An empty breakroom, full of spilled coffee and dots screaming fire warnings. Deke swung around.

A flicker of light made him jerk back, but not far enough. Something tugged at the subgun for an instant, right before the front half of the barrel dropped off. Another flicker of light, and Deke looked away from the end of his gun lying on the floor and down the hallway. A man in heavy gloves twirled a length of line. Monofilament. As sharp as the blade in Deke's fist.

"Runners," the man spat.

"Corps," Deke spat back.

"You're not getting out of here," the sec man said.

"Darn," Deke said. He dropped the remains of his submachine gun and held his hands out toward the man. The sec guard snarled and swung his line. Deke, his overlays ready, tagged the line in flight and stuck his right hand out, fist clenched. The line jerked in the air and went taut, the end wrapped around the edge of the monoblade protruding from Deke's fist.

"Nice trick," the sec guard said. "Not nice enough." He jerked.

There was another tug as the monofilament sawed through the blade and swung free. The man spun, unbalanced, gathering the line back to himself. It took the low-mass line barely a second to writhe back under his control.

Just in time for the bullet from Deke's pistol—the one he'd drawn with his left hand even as his right registered the tug of the monofilament cutting—took him in the shoulder and spun him around.

Deke switched the gun to his right hand, advanced two steps, and put four more rounds into the downed sec man. The fourth round entered the man's head through his right temple. It didn't—that Deke could see—come out.

"Works," Deke said. *Six.*

>DON'T GET COCKY.

Deke's cyberear picked up the footstep even as he chuckled at Lincoln's comment. He spun around, gun ready, but not fast enough. Bullets crackled down the hallway as the man—the elf, Deke saw—held down the trigger on the submachine gun he held. The first round crashed against the right side of Deke's chest, but it bounced off his dermal plates and ricocheted away. The others—twenty-eight or so, his mesh told him—flew on steadily higher trajectories as the recoil raised the barrel.

Pain flared through Deke's chest at the impact. The armor was subdermal, after all... he had a right-big gouge through the flesh and muscle of his chest. He let himself fall to the corridor floor but kept a tight grip on the pistol in his right hand.

"Did I get him?" the elf asked.

"No," Deke snarled. He fired.

Five.

Deke gathered himself and stood. His chest burned, but he didn't have any trouble breathing. He replaced the magazine in his pistol and moved down the hallway in the direction the man with the sub-machine gun had come from. A large pair of double-doors were at the end of the hall. Deke bulled through them in a rush.

The room was brightly-lit from a bank of lights on the ceiling. The light was harsh, actinic. Four men stood around a table, trays and instruments all around them. A small form was on the table, covered in green surgical blankets. There was blood on the blankets.

"Get out of here!" one of the men said. "You're not sterile!"

Deke swallowed. There was a lot of blood on the blankets. More on the aprons of the men, and on the tools scattered on trays around them.

"Did you hear me?"

Deke shot him.

The others yelped and backed away from the table. There were no other exits from the room except the large doors Deke had come through. He brandished the pistol and the men whimpered and backed against the wall. Sheep. Deke stepped closer to the table and jerked the surgical blankets back.

She was perhaps nine years old, and pale. Or, even healthy she'd have been pale. She was certainly pale now. Her body was lined with incisions and stitches. It looked as though they'd already had their harvest, but they'd taken the time to close her up. Deke looked around. "Where are they?"

"They?"

"Her bits," he said. "The bits you lot took out."

"In the tank, of course," one of the men said, pointing. There was a small stasis unit near the wall, glowing with a full charge. "We had to protect them."

Deke looked down. He blinked, hard. Several times. He heard his father's voice in his head.

"Don't let them fool you, lad," he'd said, one of the last times Deke had seen him. "They'll tell you about rights and liberties and what's right. They'll sell you a whole load of bullshit, if you let them. But it's real simple." He'd taken a swig of his pint and looked Deke straight in the eye. "The world doesn't care. Nature, she don't care about your rights. A tornado doesn't care about your right to life. Viruses don't care. A wolf, he don't care about your right to protection. He's gonna eat you, 'cause he's hungry and you're soft. Don't be soft, lad. Be the wolf."

Deke looked at the little girl. Her hand was bandaged. He reached down and pulled the bandage back. Her pinky finger was missing, as was half of her ring finger. Deke frowned. "You're going to sell her fingers?"

"No," one of the docs said. "That was by instruction."

"Instruction?"

"Mr. Johnson. He told us to take off her fingers." The doc glanced at the others, but they weren't talking. "Said it'd send the message he wanted."

Deke blinked again. He holstered his pistol and gathered the small child up. Several tubes pulled free of her arms. Machines started beeping, and his mesh picked up a persistent warning about moving patients. He cradled the girl to his chest. As if she were his own.

"What are you going to do now?" the doc asked.

"Wait."

"Wait? For what?" Deke said nothing. The doc frowned. "What are you wai—" he collapsed. A wave of dizziness passed through Deke, and the yak princess whimpered. The doctors collapsed. There was a crash from outside in the corridor. Deke set the girl back down and stared at her. *The ork*—Deke looked up but saw nothing through the skylight.

>HE'S COMING IN.

Deke inhaled. *The world doesn't care.* He opened the stasis tank and looked inside. Everything was sealed and tagged. He searched for a moment before he found the items he was looking for. They were quite small, and the miniature field generator barely held them, but they fit into the now-empty pocket at the small of his back. Deke closed the tank and turned around, facing the door. He drew the pistol.

Maybe I'm just being paranoid. I got the little girl back. He squeezed the grip of the pistol and looked around. The doctors were unconscious, not dead. He saw one's chest rise and fall. His finger twitched on the trigger guard.

The ork walked through the double doors and stopped. He looked around, taking in the dead doctor and the others lying unconscious on the floor. He looked at Deke, who nodded at him, then at the little girl.

"*Chikusho*," he whispered. Then he turned his gaze on the doctors. "*Eta!*" he spat.

"You have docs that can put her back together?" Deke asked.

>WHEELS ON THE WAY.

"We have doctors," the yak said. His tattoos were still glowing, and even Deke, who was about as magical as the mud on his boots, could feel the energy crackling in the room. The dead doctor's body burst into flames.

"So we're done?"

"She has been disfigured."

"You have docs. You can fix her," Deke said.

"Not that," the yak said. "Look at her hand."

"It's only a couple of fingers. You can get her cybers, or bud them."

"It is *yubitsume*."

"Yubi-what?"

"*Yubitsume*. It is a yakuza thing."

Deke loaded a message to Lincoln. "But we got her back. We're done."

"Her father will not be pleased."

"That he's getting his daughter back?"

"That she is missing her fingers. That she has been dishonored, and through her, the entire *kai* has been dishonored. I have been dishonored." The ork stepped closer, leaned down. "Why would they do such a thing?"

"Because they were paid to. Just like me."

"Like you?"

Deke gestured. "Wake that one up. He told me. His Johnson had him take her fingers off. I don't know what mess a couple bloody fingers makes, but those were his instructions."

The ork stared. He walked around the table and nudged the unconscious doc with his foot. The man moaned, and shifted a bit, but did not wake up. The ork grunted, kicked the others. They all had the same reaction.

"No one can know of this," the ork murmured.

Deke swallowed. >*Get to the wheels.*

>MORE YAKS. COMING UP BEHIND ME. GOOD GUYS, I THINK.

The ork swung around. "Lincoln is moving. Where is he going?"

>*Ping me every two seconds. Let me know you're still there. Watch the new guys.* Deke shrugged. "Maybe he saw something." He took a step toward the door. A light flashed on his AR, every two seconds.

Deke clenched his jaw.

The ork inhaled deeply. The tattoos on his face and arms flared brightly, and the ork shuddered with exertion. "I have friends outside now," he said.

The light stopped flashing on Deke's AR.

The ork's eyes opened, turned toward Deke.

Deke shot him, two rounds, in the stomach. The ork cried out and collapsed, arms wrapped around himself.

"Dragon's piss!" Deke swore. He moved quickly around the small table, where the ork had fallen. Using the toe of his boot, he rolled the ork over. As soon as the yak was on his back, Deke planted a knee in the center of his chest and leaned down. The pistol, traces of smoke and cordite still wafting from the barrel, notched itself between the ork's eyes.

"Is Lincoln still alive?" Deke demanded.

"Yes," the ork said.

"Transfer the money."

"I cannot," the ork said. He groaned in pain, and then opened his eyes and stared at Deke. "It requires me to commune, and I cannot while in this much pain."

"Then do it tomorrow."

"Why should I, when you have betrayed me?"

Deke laughed. "Tell your bunny that he owes me what was promised. Whether he wants his little princess back or not, he'll want the secret kept. I'll keep his secret. Lincoln and I, we're getting off this rock. But I'm taking some insurance."

"We will hunt you dow—"

Deke reached behind his back and pulled the stasis pack out. He brandished it in front of the ork's face. "I have these." The ork's eyes widened. A finger and a half lay nestled in the sterile package. "You come after me, these come out."

The ork grunted in pain as Deke shifted his weight and stood. "I don't care what you all do around here. I'm getting out." He slipped the fingers back into their pouch above his belt. "But I want to be left alone." He aimed the pistol. "Do we have a deal?"

The ork stared at him, then yelped as Deke pushed down with his foot before nodding at the runner. "We do."

Deke smiled. "Then so long, lad," he said. "And remember. They world may not care, but you do. And I've got these bloody fingers." He smiled, a full, toothy smile, and spun and slid out the doors with nary a whisper of noise. *The yaks outside are on the wrong side of the building.*

And was gone. ✪

BETTER THAN

BY JEAN RABE

Jean Rabe is a long-time Shadowrun *player who favors trolls that use bows and arrows. She is the co-author of* Aftershock, *a* Shadowrun *novel she happily penned with this anthology's editor. In addition, she has written two dozen novels and more than four dozen short stories. In her spare time ... such that it is ... she plays a variety of games, tugs on old socks with her dogs and tries unsuccessfully to put a dent in her growing stack of to-be-read books.*

Moses loved the night. Not because he could see better in it—which he could due to various enhancements in his cybereyes—but because that was when the snakes crawled out onto the sidewalks.

Moses loved to watch the snakes.

Pink, grass-green, blue, day-glo yellow, purple, they slithered into the low spots still filled with rainwater from the late afternoon deluge. They shimmied into splotches of beer and butted up against pretzel pieces puked from the drunkards tossed out of bars along Western Avenue. They slipped into puddles of piss provided by Seattle's vagrants.

Reflections from the neon signs was all they were, so his chummer Taddeus had said.

But Moses thought they looked like real snakes—beautiful, colorful, electric, eclectic, squirming, mesmerizing, fireworks-come-to-ground-just-for-his-very-own-pleasure snakes.

He stood on the corner of Western and Seneca, eyes locked onto a thick cherry and grape striped snake that twisted seductively in the water pooled between his size-eleven feet. He liked this city because it rained almost everyday.

The snakes only came out for the water.

"And the child grew, and she brought him unto Pharaoh's daughter, and he became her son. And she called his name Moses: and she said, Because I drew him out of the water." Moses liked that particular Exodus quote because of the water part. His father was a minister in Renton, a fire-and-brimstone Baptist ... or was that Lutheran ... who'd named all his children after significant folks from the Bible. Ruth was the oldest, followed by Jacob, Abraham, and Isaac. Moses was the youngest, and the only one who'd remained wholly human. Father said it was a sign that Moses was destined for great things. Moses thought it was a curse. He didn't have his sister's naturally-keen hearing or Isaac's tough skin. He didn't have Abraham's fine-looking tusks or Jacob's affinity for magic.

So he had to turn to tech to compensate. And tech was damn expensive.

He touched the tip of his boot to the pool, sending out a ripple that made the cherry-grape snake dance.

The snake had crept down from the overhead neon sign advertising Live Nude Dancing Elves. Moses idly wondered if any place advertised dead ones. He tapped his foot and the snake wriggled faster.

Moses hadn't given the snakes much thought until a handful of months past. That's when the microscopic vision subsystem implanted in his cybereyes malfunctioned. The series of minute optical lenses, designed to magnify objects up to a thousand times their normal size, splintered during a fight with a trog razorguy. Moses, who'd emerged battered but victorious, had been on a run with Taddeus and a few others into the Barrens, and they didn't pull enough nuyen from the job to get his lenses replaced. Didn't matter—he was kind of glad he hadn't, as rather than magnify the snakes they now enhanced their color and sometimes spun pieces of them away like one of those toy kaleidoscopes kids looked into. The cracked lenses made the snakes breathe, too—Moses saw their sides moving in and out, and when he cocked his head just right, as he was doing now, he could see their tongues flicker from between their invisible fangs to taste whatever interesting things were in the water.

In fact, Moses hadn't realized Seattle's sidewalks had snakes until the lenses cracked.

"Move it!" This came from a muscle-bound troll who cursed and stepped off the curb to get around Moses. "Go stand somewhere else, you ugly vatjob!"

Moses flicked his tail at the oaf, but the troll was quick, already on his way down the street. Moses liked his tail—it was one of his favorite modifications. A meter and a half long, covered with tiny lizard-like scales with mirrored surfaces, it had a built-in light at the end that he sometimes read by. It was one of those balance tails, weighted and grafted onto the base of his spine and keyed to a processor that monitored his center of gravity.

He'd gotten his shaped dermal plating at the same place he'd bought the tail—from his trusted ripper doc. Paid almost full price for the plating and had it stylized with ridges at the elbows, bumps across his forehead for the heck of it, and made to look like he had great abs and a broad chest.

Made him look better than human.

It was decorated just above his heart—not with tribal art or hieroglyphs like most favored—but with "EXD 3:6" in reference to the Bible verse: "Moreover he said, I am the God of thy father, the God of Abraham, the God of Isaac, and the God of Jacob. And Moses hid his face; for he was afraid to look upon God." Moses hadn't been able to find a verse that at the same time mentioned Ruth, but then she had a whole book devoted to her.

He had Doc add a wet sheath over the top of the plating some months ago, save for the spot on the chest with EXD 3:6 on it. It was a variant of a dermal, but modified to feel cool and slippery, sexy, glistening ... sort of like snakeskin.

The cherry-grape snake writhed faster as Moses continued to stare.

The sheath was great because thugs had a hard time grabbing onto him. He'd tried to get a chameleon modification with it, but Doc said combining those features was a few years away. So he settled for adding a near-meter-long head of fiber-optic hair, bright orange with a cascading effect of yellow and red at the tips to make it look like fire. Because he styled it often, it was wearing a little thin in places and sections of it needed to be replaced.

That's why Moses had come down here tonight ... to get some nuyen to pay for more hair and some other enhancements. He had his heart set on getting some horn implants. He'd been fitted a year or so ago for bull horns, but decided they were a little too big, and too expensive. Last week he'd put some second-hand goat horns on layaway, at the same place he'd get the hair replacements—from his trusted ripper doc. Bright, white horns with a mother-of-pearl glaze—fixed implants, as the retractable ones were a little out of his price range. Doc promised that the horns wouldn't itch.

Some of Moses' other implants did, and scratching them in public had gotten him banned from more than one establishment. The penile implant was the worst, with its mentally-controlled gel reservoirs and synthetic skin that he had some sort of allergic reaction to. He hoped he could remember to ask Doc for some more ointment for the rash.

"Nuyen," he said. "Came down here to get me some." He repeated "nuyen" until it became a mantra that twisted in time with the cherry-grape snake. "Nuyen for the tech-fix."

"What's he starin' at, ya think?" The speaker was an elf, a live one, but she wasn't nude or dancing. She was wearing a sand-colored plastic dress that crinkled when she crossed her arms in front of her probably-enhanced chest.

"The puddle. Maybe he lost something in it." Her companion was also an elf, face painted garishly and lips three times any natural size. "Didja lose something in it, mister?"

"Lose? Lose yourself. Get lost," Moses said. They stood too close to the water and made it harder to see the snake. He heard the sand-colored dress crinkle as the pair strolled away. The snake could swim freely now.

An ork peddler walked by, selling hot soyjerky. Passersby commented on the spicy smell. Moses couldn't smell it. He couldn't smell anything.

Moses had a direct neural interface connected wirelessly to the various built-in computers nested in the implants that allowed diagnostics checks—and said checks told him several things were either malfunctioning or were overdue for maintenance ... his failed nasal receptors for example. They'd been out of whack for the past eighteen ... or was that eighty ... months. His enhanced taste buds didn't register anything either. He could be eating ... well, pretty much anything ... and not hurk it back up because of the taste. He only ate to keep his strength up and because his super thyroid implant demanded it.

"Should get 'em fixed," he said. "Maybe."

He'd need a lot of nuyen for the repairs. He had Kevlar bone-lacing with RFID sensor tags, a blood circuit control system, and a data-jack engraved with elaborate Japanese kanji-signs that he couldn't read ... it was a used model and so he hadn't been picky.

"Nuyen," he said. "Sashayed down here to get me some."

The encephalon he'd went under the knife for six or so months back hadn't helped. Hardwired into Moses' brain, it was supposed to boost his information-processing. It only seemed to scramble things now. At least the math subprocessor unit whirred along without a problem; he could calculate rent and utilities in a nanosecond, and it doubled as an alarm clock. His internal GPS worked without a proverbial hitch, too. It's how he found his way to this corner without making a single wrong turn. Too bad he hadn't thought to load his sister's address into it. What was her name? Ruth. Yeah, that was it.

"Ruth. Nuyen. Nuyen. Nuyen."

The radar sensor was another matter. It was supposed to emit terahertz and ultrawideband radar in frequency pulses, analyzing Doppler and bounced signals. It never had worked right—another piece of used equipment he probably shouldn't have had installed without first asking Doc for some sort of warranty. At least it functioned as a motion detector, except that it never registered the snakes. He'd remember to ask Doc for a warranty on the pearlized goat horns.

Once more he thought about taking what little nuyen he had stashed away—coupled with what he was going to score tonight—and spending it on repairs to his existing systems. But he really wanted the goat horns, and he was being good by repairing at least one of enhancements—his fiberoptic do. Besides, if he spent all his nuyen on repairs, he'd never be able to afford the cyberfins he'd been thinking about. Saw an advertisement for them a couple of days back ... or was that a couple of weeks ... or months?

His memory played tricks sometimes.

"Nuyen," he said. "Came down here to get me some."

His regular ripper doc could implant the webbing between his fingers and toes so he could manage the butterfly and backstroke in record time. Of course, Moses knew he'd have to take swimming lessons first.

The two elves returned, the sand-colored plastic crinkling a little louder.

"Geese," Moses pronounced them. It was the right neighborhood for hookers. The women were looking for someone to dock with—for nuyen, naturally—their gander probably somewhere close by for safety. Moses wouldn't mind docking with the one with the overlarge lips, but he needed to save his cred for the hair replacement and the fins ... and to fix something. What attachment was he going to repair? Besides, his father had taught him to stay away from those kinds of women. They were sinful. Moses was SIN-less

"And the Lord said unto Moses, Behold, thou shalt sleep with the fathers; and his people will rise up, and go a whoring after the gods of the strangers of the land, whither thy go to be among them, and will forsake me, and break my covenant which I have made with them. Deuteronomy thirty-one-sixteen."

"Talking all Biblical. Still looking in the puddle, he is," big lips said. "Yo, Clint." She sidled up to Moses. "You interested in a little whoring, maybe we—"

"Get lost," Moses said.

"S'matter, don't like elves?"

"Live nude dancing elves," Moses said, looking up at the sign again.

Big lips shuddered and swayed down the street, arm-in-arm with plastic dress.

"Tadd would've spent his nuyen on them geese." Moses missed his old chummer.

The last time they were together Taddeus told Moses he didn't discriminate enough, that he bought pre-owned cyberware on the black market when he should be shopping at legitimate places. "The legal clinics won't deal with the stuff you're putting in your brain," Taddeus had said. "Who knows where that stuff came from? I oughta turn your doc into the authorities." Tadd said other things, too, but Moses hadn't had his data filter turned on, and so could only remember a few sentences.

Ripper docs, shadowclinics, Taddeus wouldn't have anything to do with them, Moses knew. But then Taddeus didn't have near the modifications as Moses. Taddeus wasn't quite better-than-human. Tadd was still mostly human.

Moses had been better-than-human for several years.

"Nuyen. Nuyen. Nuyen."

He liked his ripper doc 'cause he could pick up modifications that weren't exactly legal, and he never had to supply an ID or SIN. And it wasn't like he had these things done in a back-alley filth parlor with half-used, unsterilized medkits at the ready in the case of accidents. It wasn't technically a black clinic or a body bank. His Doc had a real medical degree and operated out of the basement of a tattoo parlor, a real high-end underground clinic. Moses had done his research before going under the knife. Doc hadn't had his license pulled for any of the usual reasons—too many malpractice cases or amputating the wrong limb. He'd simply experimented a few times on a few unwitting and later protesting patients ... and got caught. Moses wasn't unwitting; he underwent each modification with both insect-like compound cybereyes wide open, and he didn't care when Doc suggested a little muscle doping now and then or a little trial genetic infusion.

And Doc was a real ecologist, as green as they came. He believed in recycling—bioware implants, nanoware, cyberware, augmented limbs. Because Moses bought most of his stuff second-hand from Doc, he could afford the integration system for all his simsense and networking devices and the bundle of skillwires with multi-functionality. He wouldn't have been able to buy tricked-out cyberears if they'd come right off the assembly line.

Moses thought he might ask Doc if those ears could be tweaked just a bit, so he could hear the snakes. The cherry-grape one might have some juicy secrets to share. He glanced back down at the puddle. Yep, the snake was still there.

Doc was good at providing discount prescriptions. Moses had to take three ... or was that four ... pills a day to stave off biosystem over-stress, and another couple pills to treat his temporal lobe epilepsy. The latter malady was an acceptable side effect of having so many cyber implants. Doc said the condition was chronic and degenerative and that if it got much worse Moses would need corrective gene therapy or maybe a little brain surgery. If Doc was going to go back in Moses' brain, maybe he could finesse something with the memory center or somesuch. Moses really wanted to remember his sister's address.

Taddeus had called Moses an aug-ad, an augmentation addict, and said he wouldn't go on anymore runs with him until he got his head straightened out. Moses figured Tadd just didn't understand about not being satisfied with being human. Moses was almost there ... satisfied ... but not quite. He just needed a few more adjustments. He had mood swings because wasn't quite happy with things they way they were now. Sure, he was better-than-human, but he could stand to be a little bit better than simply better-than. Tadd was probably just pissed about the mood swings. He'd be back. Him and the others would come crawling to Moses for help on another dip into the shadows.

Crawling, like the cherry-grape snake was crawling. Moses watched it slither to another puddle. He followed it.

"Gotta go this direction anyway," he said. "Up the hill." His internal GPS told him he had two more blocks to go, all uphill. "And the Lord said unto Moses, Get thee up into this mount, and see the land which I have given unto the children of Israel."

Two more blocks up, around the corner, and then down an alley and he'd have plenty of nuyen for the hair and the swim fins and ... what was he going to have fixed? His fang implants? Only one of those had snapped off.

"Two more blocks for the nuyen."

The snake obliged him, slithering along as if a guide, though a few storefronts later it changed color, turning yellow now, and then green. When it split in two and turned sky blue, Moses realized it wasn't the same snake, and it wasn't nearly as pretty. He'd go back and find the cherry-grape one later, after he scored his nuyen.

One more block. "Just one more, and what—"

Just short of the next corner Moses saw the rude troll who'd called him a vatjob. He was leaning over a human woman sporting rabbit ears and a fox tail, vulching her, maybe hitting her up for drugs or nuyen or ... .

"Oh, it's the vatjob." The troll turned to face Moses and stuck out his jaw to look menacing. He had a submachinegun in his right hand, barrel pointed at the pavement. The other passersby on the sidewalk gave him a wide berth. "Mind your own business. Bit-brain bakebrain whackjob nutjob vatjob." The twin blue snakes cavorted around the troll's big sandaled feet.

Moses cleared his throat: "And it came to pass in those days, when Moses was grown, that he went out unto his brethren, and looked on their burdens: and he spied an Egyptian smiting a human ... er Hebrew, one of his brethren. Exodus two-eleven."

"Definitely a nutjob vatjob." A line of drool spilled over the troll's lower lip and extended to the pavement, striking the head of one of the blue snakes and sending Moses' temper flaring. "This is between me and Foxy Foxtail, so move it." The troll raised the gun in threat.

"And he looked this way and that way, and when he saw that there was no man, he slew the Egyptian, and hid him in the sand. Exodus two-twelve."

"What are you talking about you—"

"King James Version." Moses' wired reflexes kicked in and he bent and pulled a combat knife from a sheath in his boot and hurled it using all the strength in his synthetic cyberarm. Should have been wearing body armor, Moses thought as the troll dropped to his knees. The troll shouldn't have relied only on a secure long coat that he hadn't even bothered to button. Moses threw a second knife from the other boot, finishing him.

"And he killed it," he quoted. "And Moses sprinkled the blood upon the altar round about. And he cut the ram ... err, troll ... into pieces; and Moses burnt the head, and the pieces and the fat. Leviticus eight-nineteen and twenty."

The fox-tailed human squealed and sprinted across the street, leaving Moses to stare at the twin blue snakes undulating in the spreading troll blood.

A lone goose in a barely-there skirt screamed and drew Moses' attention away from the snakes.

"Nuyen," Moses said. "Nuyen. Nuyen. Nuyen. Came down here to get me some." He kicked the submachinegun away. Moses didn't care for guns. Sure, he could use them, and he had a smartlink for a heavy pistol he lost on a corp-run. But he preferred knives because they didn't make as much noise. He turned the troll over and retrieved his knives. He shoved them back in the boot sheathes, more worried about speed than the blood, and rifled through the troll's pockets as gawkers came to stand over him. "A credstick. Good. Got me some nuyen I wasn't expecting. Not a whole lot on it, though."

"It's the puddle guy." The goose in the crinkly dress was back.

Couldn't she find someone to dock with? Moses wondered. She was pretty enough. Maybe she ought to lower her price.

He slapped the side of his head with his palm, rattling the GPS just enough to get him back on track. "Around the corner. Down the alley," he said. "Later," he told the elf-geese. Then he was gone, his wired reflexes giving him a boost of speed that took him around the edge of the all-night pharmacy, down half a block and into the alley. He didn't hear any sirens, but he figured sooner or later someone would call about the troll bleeding out on the sidewalk. It had been self-defense, hadn't it? The troll had been carrying a gun, after all.

There weren't any snakes at the mouth of the alley. There was plenty of water for them, as Moses sloshed through one puddle after the next as he made his way around trash receptacles sitting outside the backdoors of bars, sex shops, and diners. But there weren't any neon signs, and it was the signs that gave birth to the best snakes. Moses felt better when there were snakes around. Moses was supposed to have snakes.

"Exodus four-three and four," Moses said. Why was it he could remember the Bible verses so easy but not the color of the whatever-it-was he had on layaway with Doc? "And he said, Cast it on the ground. And he cast it on the ground, and it became a serpent; and Moses fled from before it. And the Lord said unto Moses, Put forth thine hand, and take it by the tail. And he put forth his hand, and caught it, and it became a rod in his hand." He sucked in a deep breath and went farther down the alley. "Thy rod and thy staff, they comfort me."

A cat hissed and shot in front of him, disappearing behind crates stacked at a barber's back door.

"Hurry with this," Moses told himself. He wanted to get the nuyen and get back out on the street. Find that cherry-grape snake again and ogle it a little longer before he visited Doc and had ... what was that he was going to the clinic for? "Hair." He was pleased that he remembered that. "Hair and—" Hair and something else. He'd put his mind to it after this was over. Put his head to it. "Head. Head. Head."

Moses scratched the bumps above his eyes and brightened. "And he put the mitre upon his head; also upon the mitre, even upon his forefront, did he put the golden plate, the holy crown; as the lord commanded Moses. Leviticus eight-nine."

What was his sister's address? Eight Nine something. Ruth, right? Yeah, Ruth. Wither-though-goest-Ruth.

Halfway down the alley, that's where the GPS tugged him.

"Didja bring the nuyen?"

Moses stopped, peering into the shadows, insect-like compound cybereyes separating the grays and blacks and finding the man ... dwarf ... thickset, grubby-looking. They all were dirty-looking, the ones who dealt in these sorts of things.

"Did you bring the beetles?" Moses returned.

The dwarf stepped away from the wall.

And the good ones were rich.

"Nuyen. Nuyen. Nuyen," Moses whispered. His ears whirred and clicked, picking up the dwarf's heartbeat and the slow slap of his shoes in the puddles sadly devoid of snakes. Moses needed snakes. Picking up the dwarf's breathing. Insect-like compound cybereyes with heat-sensors finding the dwarf, finding rats scurrying along in either direction, finding garbage piled up outside the back door of a Chinese restaurant, finding things he didn't want to get too close a look at. Finding nothing else.

For once, Moses was glad he couldn't smell anything.

"Did you bring the beetles?" Moses repeated. He heard the faintest of whirring and clicks. The dwarf was checking him out, too. "I'm alone. No guns."

"I know."

"The beetles." Moses added a hint of desperation to his voice, like he was a junkie in desperate need of a fix. He was, but not for the beetles. He remembered the goat horns he had on layaway. If he didn't pay them off and get them installed soon, he'd lose his deposit. "Did you bring the beetles?"

"Better than life," the dwarf cooed, stepping closer.

"Better than human," Moses said, thinking about the horns and the fins and echolocation bioware and maybe some extended volume for his lungs and elastic joints for his knees.

"Better than anything," the dwarf said. "Yeah, I have beetles. You have nuyen?"

Moses pulled out the troll's credstick. Good thing he'd run into the troll. He'd forgotten his meager credstick back at his place. He hadn't forgotten it the last time he pulled this stunt, or the time before that or before that. Had to have a credstick to make them think you were actually buying something. Had to have the black market contacts to get the names and locations of beetle-sellers. Better-than-life chips were still illegal and you couldn't buy them just anywhere. He didn't want the chips, just the credsticks the beetle-seller would have on him. It was a theft that would never be reported. Moses had done this a dozen times. Or was that two dozen?

"Yeah, I got the nuyen. Let's see the chips first." Moses waved the stick higher. He knew the dwarf had some sort of enhanced vision that would let him pick out the details. "Why don't you—"

The back door of one of the bars opened, spilling sickly-yellow light out into the alley and reflecting off the puddles. Moses caught a glimpse of a snake, but it wasn't a pretty one. Only neon bred the pretty ones. He tried to look away, but it *was* a snake, and Moses was supposed to have snakes, wasn't he? Maybe if he cocked his head he could see it breathe. Maybe if—

The dwarf barreled into him, fist slamming into his stomach, plating absorbing it, but the momentum sending him back. Moses' tail lashed out, whipping around the dwarf's muscular forearm. It was a cyberlimb, all metal, no flesh, fingers ungodly strong and grabbing at the tail, squeezing, breaking some of the mirrored scales.

"Damn you!" Moses cursed. He couldn't afford to have the tail fixed, not with all the other plans for modifications. Not unless the dwarf had lots and lots of nuyen for selling beetles. Moses' bone lacing made him strong, and he used that might now to bull-rush the dwarf, bringing his knee up into the smaller man's chest, pushing him down into the puddle to smother the ugly, yellow snake.

The dwarf had dermal plating, too. So Moses changed his tactics, pounding his fists against the dwarf's wide, ruddy face.

Voices intruded, maybe the man who'd opened the back door and birthed the ugly snake. Someone with him, voices panicked at what was transpiring in their alley. Make it fast, Moses thought. Don't need someone calling Lone Star. Not that he was doing anything illegal. This was self-defense. The dwarf started it. Moses just intended to finish it.

"And Moses said unto the Lord in Exodus four-ten, O my Lord, I am not eloquent, neither heretofore, nor since thou has spoken unto they servant; but I am slow of speech, and slow of tongue. But let me be fast of fist. Let my wired reflexes fly."

Moses pounded harder until he heard bone crunch. The dwarf didn't intend to just stay down and die, though, struggling frantically to reach something at his side, succeeding, and pulling free a heavy pistol that he shoved up against Moses' side. The dwarf fired three times, the first two bouncing off the dermal, but the third punching a hole in the plating and sending a round deep inside.

Moses registered the pain, but shoved it to the back of his mind and continued to pound, listening to voices spilling out in the alley, listening to the dwarf curse, and hearing another round fire and find its way inside. Then he heard the dwarf cough and felt blood spit up against his face and onto his lips. Good thing he couldn't taste. Dwarf blood would probably taste bad.

The dwarf heaved once beneath him, and then fell still. Moses dug through his pockets, finding credstick after credstick after credstick. Twenty five of them—his math subprocessor unit counted things instantly. The proverbial motherload. He shoved them in his own pockets. They wouldn't all fit, so he stuffed the extras in his kangaroo pouch, which had been a handy modification. Then he pushed off the ground, one hand pressed against his wounded side.

The voices came closer, accompanied by feet slapping through puddles filled with ugly yellow snakes. The backdoor to the bar was propped open wide and sickly light poured out.

"Are you hurt?"

"Who are you?"

"What happened?"

There were more questions from the quintet of barmaids and bartenders. Moses ignored them all and whacked his free palm against the side of his head, kicking in the GPS and tugging him back out the alley, onto the sidewalk and around the corner of the all-night pharmacy.

Maybe he should go in the pharmacy, he thought. Buy some painkillers and bandages.

But Doc's wasn't terribly far away, five or six blocks tops. Doc could repair the damage from the dwarf's slugs, put him under for that and do some modifications and hair-grafting at the same time. He certainly had enough nuyen on all these credsticks. Get it all done at the same time. Had the dwarf shot up some of his computer interfaces? Were more systems damaged?

"Nuyen. Nuyen. Nuyen. Got me lots of that." Moses staggered up the street, past the body of the bled-out troll that was still lying on the curb, passersby walking around it. No sign of Foxy Foxtail, whom he probably saved.

Lightning flickered high overhead, followed by a boom of thunder that drowned out the music spilling from bars and sex shops. It would rain soon, thank the Lord, Moses thought. Rain and fill the low spots so the snakes would have more room to swim.

He watched the snakes as he went, pushing himself between the throng out on the sidewalk, struggling to watch the snakes between all the feet. Bright blue, grass-green, violet, day-glo pink, chartreuse, they shimmied all along Western Avenue. Moses followed the cherry-grape one, and with his free hand fingered one of the many credsticks in his pocket.

How had he gotten so many credsticks?

What was he going to spend them on?

Hair, he remembered hair. He came down here to get him some of that. Hair and ... hair and ... pearlized goat milk for his sister Ruth. Intreat me not to leave thee, Ruth. Where thou lodgest, Ruth.

"Where do you lodge?" Moses mused.

He'd deliver the milk tonight, if only he could remember her address. ✪

CALIBAN

BY PHAEDRA WELDON

Phaedra Weldon is the author of the urban fantasy series, Zoë Martinique Investigations published by Berkley. She has written in the Star Trek *universe and writes fiction and source work in the* BattleTech *universe for Catalyst Game Labs. She was recently tapped to write a novel in the successful SyFy series,* Eureka! *Her fourth book in the Zoë series,* Revenant, *is scheduled for a June 2010 release. Her first* Shadowrun *novel,* Dark Resonance, *about a reluctant Technomancer and a familiar Netcat, will be published in 2010.*

I have a problem paying 1,000 nuyen for a cup of fancy, swill-tasting soycaf. So when some gacked-up ork blows it into ceramic fragments before I can even choke it down—it sort of sets the mood for the rest of the day.

I make a better cup at home—but I wasn't at home that morning. I was in Los Angeles—the last place I ever wanted to be. I'm more at home in Seattle—a long way from my present location. I was doing a friend a favor, and getting shot at in the process.

Welcome to 2072.

My name's Derek Montgomery, but most of my chummers call me Dirk. I've sort of built up a reputation as a shadowrunner over the past sixteen years. I never call myself that—I'm a detective for lack of a better word. Shadowrunners take on a variety of jobs that respectable clients don't want to get their hands dirty with.

I've only dipped in that pool when it was necessary—or I was tricked into it. I still cherry pick when I can, and then beg when necessary. I've pretty much kept my choices to surveillance and recovery over the years—though I have been pulled into some pretty complicated situations.

This profession sometimes takes me to different places—not always the more exotic locales like Hong Kong—nobody throws that kind of nuyen my way. And since I'm more of a Seattle name, not much about my reputation has gotten past the borders. Lately the routine had become too much of just that—a routine. I did want to get out of the rain—see some sunshine.

Los Angeles wasn't my first choice, and neither was this coffee shop across from the Mega Tri-Plex (that's the local term for the three Megacorps buildings for Horizon, Ares and Shiawase).

I was here to do a favor for an old friend's "nephew." But let's get it straight—I knew the guy I was meeting wasn't really her nephew—because Naomi Takashi didn't have siblings. Naomi's an old friend of mine from my short-lived Lone Star days who was now the Central Administrator for Wireless Augmented Reality Reconnaissance at the Lone Star facility in Seattle. The fact she had asked me for a favor—that was enough for me to say yes before I knew what it was she wanted.

I had a skeletal sob-story fit for the latest teen trideo—of a brother looking for his sister who disappeared. Yeah, I'd heard it before. Null perspiration.

But hell—it was Naomi—and I owed her my life ten times over.

So I'd e-mailed the guy—a Knight Errant employee named Kazuma (that's KAH-zoo-mah, as Naomi corrected me forty times) Tetsu. Tet-sue. His e-mails were professionally encrypted—scaled so that I'd have to enter a password on my end to read them. It was a bit annoying but I liked the guy's eye for security.

We'd arranged to meet at Cup O' Sin on the corner of Dreking and Expensive at ten o'clock. I'd only been there ten minutes before I saw him entering the shop—that was less then two minutes before the ork and his buddies blasted in with weapons firing.

Just my kind of day.

He was tall and slender and young looking—like most Japanese I'd known. Naomi was my age and I swear she looked as young and beautiful as the day we'd first met. His hair was fashionably cut around his face and ears then pulled back in a long ponytail behind him. It looked as if it'd been dyed a reddish brown as well—but at least it wasn't something like bright pink or yellow. He wore an expensive suit, black with a mandarin collar and black silk beneath. On his lapel was the KE pen the local branch's employees wore as a badge as well as his SIN that allowed them access in and out of Knight Errant doors.

I kept my attention fixed between my contact and the three coming through the front. It was obvious in a pinch they weren't actually aiming at anything or anybody—more so firing off their weapons to create a panic. My guess was to chase customers out of the shop.

But then there was always the path of the stray bullet—which found my client somewhere in his upper body. With a grunt I ducked, pulled out my Colt Manhunter and chambered a round. It wasn't so much that I was worried about this kid's life—but my own. If something happened to him, Naomi would blame—and possibly kill—*me*. At the very least she never speak to me again.

And as a professional, I couldn't exactly afford *not* having her as one of my key contacts for information in the Lone Star database.

As others scrambled out and the three intruders made their way in, I moved quick and low around them and to the right. Kazuma lay on his face behind a felled shelf of token coffee mugs and sugary sweets. I saw blood on the back of his suit and on the polished tile floor beneath.

But he hadn't let the wound take him down as he moved slowly, half-dragging himself toward the back of the shop to the counter, a black leather messenger bag draped around his shoulder. If that's where his gear was stored and one of the shooters saw it, they'd come after him and take it.

Tech wasn't as expensive as it used to be—but still—from the size of the bag I assumed he had one of the new slimline commlinks with an RFID tag on it. Shit-heads like these were always looking for a quick steal and a quick fence.

With a glance around I moved in behind him, keeping the over-turned shelf between us and the intruder's view. Colt in my right hand, I crouch-stepped over him, threaded my left hand and arm beneath his left side under his arm and pulled him forward with me.

My back gave a slight protest—he was heavier than he looked—and I was getting too old for this.

Original intention had been to get him out of the shop—but it looked like that exit was blocked, and he'd also started to fight to get free of me. I figured whoever didn't get out in the first few seconds was going to be either a hostage or collateral.

"*Baka* let me go!" he hissed at me as one of the shooters, a bulked up, chromed hulk, chased a nice-looking girl out of the shop and then dragged her back in again. Uh oh—that didn't look good for her. "What are you—" the kid said in a much louder voice.

I slapped a hand over his mouth and yanked him down to the floor with me to watch the shooters' actions.

The ork noticed his companion dragging the girl back in by her hair and moved in himself. If this was gonna be some twisted bit of thrill sex I was just gonna have to drop the kid and do my part. Can't stand by and watch as some innocent piece of endowment gets gacked.

But ork took his weapon and held it by the firing end and smashed it hard into his companion's head. The side *not* covered in a chrome dome. Blood gushed over the thug's face and he lost hold of the girl. She screamed but was at least smart enough to get the hell out of there.

"What the hell did you do that for?" Chromedome demanded as he reached behind him and drew a katana from his back.

Ork didn't appear to be too afraid of Chromedome's weapon. He was in his face, his own weapon righted and the barrel inches from the guy's bloody nose. "We ain't here for that. You do your part and you get paid. You fuck up again, and I'll cap your ass and chop you for parts."

Chromedome sneered and re-holstered his blade.

A few other customers were trying to get by and Kazuma was moving in my arms. I pulled my hand away from his face and whispered, "Keep quiet."

But that just wasn't going to happen. "I have to get back there," he nodded in the direction he was going. "Behind—" he winced "behind the counter, to the right. Central server and network key."

Oh? I didn't ask how this kid would know that—I just did what he said. I released him and he kept low. I crouched down as well but noticed there was a blood trail left by his clothing. That little detail was going to give us away eventually—but at the moment it couldn't be helped.

"I'm in," said the third intruder, another human that'd set up a small odd shaped box near the register. He'd donned a pair of goggles and AR gloves—dude was interfacing with the shop's PAN through a home-make comlink.

So they were hacking into the shop's network. But why? It was a coffee shop. The only thing they'd find was an inventory list, payroll records, and maybe what next week's soy-drek of the day was going to be.

Kazuma was moving again and I followed him, hoping like hell none of them noticed the motion behind mister hacker. It wasn't that I couldn't defend myself—I was pretty good with my Colt Manhunter. But I had no idea if Kazuma here was armed, could shoot, or how bad he'd been hit. I also didn't know what kind of weapon mister hacker had. The fact these guys were hitting a shop bright and early on a Tuesday morning, full of customers and witnesses, was just a little crazy.

He moved behind the coffee shop's counter and to the right, just past the employee john and kneeled in front of what looked like a blank part of the wall. I kept myself low on my knees, my Colt aimed at the back of mister hacker as Kazuma held up his left hand in midair. It looked to me as if he were playing an invisible piano—but I knew he was logged into the Augmented Reality of the coffee shop's PAN.

I didn't see a commlink on him anywhere, no wires, so I assumed he'd done the mod thing and converted his data-jack to a wireless receiver—internal 'link. And since I didn't see any goggles or shades—I assumed his eyes were cyber-enhanced as well.

Now see? Why would a young, good-looking kid like this do that to his body? Me? There wasn't an artificial piece of hardware anywhere. Not even a data-jack. Never had a need for it. Yeah, I'd used the commlink and goggles rig now and then so I could get a taste of what AR might be like—having advertisements, e-mail and calls always in the peripheral of my vision.

And you know what I thought about it?

Crap. My mind stayed busy enough without all that shit being dumped in there on a continual basis. The Matrix was easier today to access than ever before—I'd never liked VR back then and I sure as hell didn't like it now.

There was a click and the door popped open. I pulled it out just enough to shove him inside, then piled in behind him.

The room was little more than a four-walled coffin, complete with an empty desk, an old data-jack outlet in its surface, and several brown, unmarked boxes. A broom, mop and apron hung on a nail behind the door.

I closed the door as quietly as possible. Kazuma reached out with his left hand again and tapped invisible keys. He was favoring his right arm where the bullet had apparently went through his shoulder.

Abruptly he waved at the air with his left hand and then collapsed hard against the wall. When he moved I saw a bright smear of blood he'd left behind. I holstered the Colt and coaxed him into helping me remove the messenger bag and jacket. Kazuma unbuttoned the front of his shirt and winced as I peeled it back from the wound.

Yep—right shoulder was a bloody mess. Reaching into the right pocket of my coat, I retrieved an old penlight I'd gotten from a client a few months back—self-charging little tool. Wasn't sure how I'd lasted this long without it—especially with my aging eyes.

He winced and closed his eyes as I pulled material out of the wound, but kept quiet. Turning his face away, I got a good look at his profile and noticed his hair had shifted, exposing a long, slender ear.

"You're an elf."

"Is that a problem?" His voice was surprisingly deep.

"No—it's just that Naomi didn't mention that." Now I was sure he wasn't her nephew.

His eyes opened at her name and he turned his head to look at me. "You're Derek Montgomery?"

I gave him my best smirk. "Is that a problem?"

He almost smiled. Almost. But then schooled his features into something a bit more stoic—which of course looked strange on his face. I'm not a judge on guy's looks. Especially when it's common to polish up one's appearance cosmetically these days. But looking at Kazuma— I'd say he was kinda too pretty for a guy. Being an elf and Asian—that was a double whammy. Androgyny was the curse of being both.

There were more shouts on the other side of the door and then a scream.

Kazuma looked at the door and I noticed just a flicker of panic in his expression. "We need to call the PCC—"

Ooh. I waved my right hand at him to stop. "Let's not get too hasty, okay? I'm sure local authorities can handle this." It's not that I had a problem with the PPC cops—my problems were more inter- laced around Lone Star—but I wasn't in the mood to deal with *any* sort of authority at the moment.

He frowned at me. I noticed he had dark green eyes, not dark black-brown like Naomi's. And I also noticed with a slight shock that they *weren't* enhanced; these were human—or rather elven—eyes.

I looked at both of them. Cyber eyes—though you could buy the newer enhancements with life-like cosmetic qualities (mostly used by kids who were doing it behind their parent's backs)—always had a tell-tale sheen about them. Not like an animal's eyes that went red or silver in bright light—but more of a different hue. A signature that I'd always used as a marker. It let me know they were seeing things I had no access to.

This kid's eyes didn't have that. They weren't cyber.

So—how had he seen the shop's AR? Or even been able to tap this room's security? Unless he had on a pair of those smartlink con- tact lenses. That *could* account for the green tint to his eyes.

"I'm going to check on our friends outside." He leaned his head back on the wall and closed his eyes.

"Hey—Kazuma," I tapped his cheek. He looked incredibly young and he was looking incredibly pale. With a wound like that and no medical treatment—elf or human—he was going to go into shock. I wasn't a doctor, and I sure as hell couldn't play one in the trid. "Hey— look at me."

He blinked slowly and his expression looked—familiar. Only where had I seen that look before? Not on *his* face—but someone else I'd known a long time ago. It was the expression of someone being in two places at once.

"They've dismantled the auto-security call-out," Kazuma said, though his expression didn't change. "Looks like they've already hacked into the main control. Damnit—the ECCM's still working, but it looks like they're not trying to jam the main signal."

I was still wondering how he was seeing this—so I reached out and moved his hair away from the sides of his temples. There was no datajack. Nothing. Not even a scar where one had been removed. I would swear he was accessing remotely—but was he *in* the Matrix? I didn't see how—most of the time if a decker was submersed in VR then they weren't accessing their meat sack except to breathe, much less speak.

How the fuck was he doing both? "Do you have security clearance for this server?"

He nodded slowly. "I do now."

What the hell did that mean? Was the kid hacking his way in? Well, he *was* Knight Errant and he'd known about this room—which made me think he was either pretty high level or he'd worked in the sector before—maybe even for the PPC. I figured I'd ask him later—after we kicked these assholes out.

"Kazuma—can you figure out what they're after?"

"I don't—" He frowned, and his full, lower lip trembled. "How could they know this? I didn't know that door existed on this server. Ponzu—track sinister seven, subsection 66.77-pop2. Find out where that thing is going."

Ponzu?

Wasn't that a sauce?

Kazuma blinked rapidly as he looked up at me. He was shaking. "I-I'm cold."

"Shock." I glanced around. There was nothing in here that I could use as a blanket—except my coat. With a sigh I stood and removed it, careful of my weapon and laid it over him. I really needed something to staunch the bleeding—but the wound was a through and through—a hole in and a hole out. The wound was bleeding steadily and if we didn't get out of here soon, this kid was gonna expire.

And then I'd have Naomi to contend with. That was not how I intended on ending this little venture.

As I tried to fasten his coat around him as a bandage my hand pressed against something hard and ungiving. I pulled the coat back and found a hidden back holster around his middle containing a Fichetti Security 600. I slipped it out and checked the magazine as Kazuma's eyelids fluttered. Fully loaded.

I nudged him and held the gun up. "Can you use this thing?"

He squinted at me and nodded. "Yeah—I can use it. My Grandfather taught me."

Grandfather? Was that supposed to mean something? I held it out. I wasn't surprised a Knight Errant techie boy had a weapon—I think I was just slotting him into a stereotype and suspecting he had a katana hidden somewhere. "Think you can use it now?"

He nodded and reached out with his left hand and grabbed it. "Why?"

"Because we have to get out of here, that's why. If I understand what you're saying, those jack-heads out there are looking to steal this server—why I don't know—but that means they'll be trying to bust down this door any minute and I'm not sure—"

"They're not after this server," Kazuma said and he cleared his throat. He also sat forward and took in a deep breath. He tried not to wince from his shoulder and I noticed he wasn't using his right arm at all. "They found a back door I didn't know was there—it was probably written in by the coder for this server's original service before it was re-purposed. But they got an Agent in through that door. I've sent my own program after it." He swallowed. "I'm afraid it's trying to hack into Horizon. *Baka*."

I wasn't going to pretend I fully understood what he was saying—but I was knowledgeable enough to know that using an Agent to hack into an outfit like Horizon was gutsy. "I'm not sure how they can find a link between the two PANs—"

"Horizon owns this city block as well," Kazuma said as he winced. He was honestly fighting to stay with me. This kid had guts, I'll give him that. He nodded to the wall behind him. "This is part of a redundancy system—an off-line backup for Horizon's client list. It was scheduled to be taken off-line next month and remove the node."

There was more shouting from outside the door, and I thought I heard the siren call of a local authority posse. Great. Things were about to get heated. I looked back at Kazuma. "Are you saying there's a way for them to hack into Horizon by using *this* PAN?"

Kazuma nodded. "Yes—I'm—*baka*—" he jerked and his eyes closed again. At the same time there was a barrage of foul language from the other side of that door.

Nuts. I couldn't hear exactly what they were saying—I was blind. If I had my commlink I could hack the shop's security system myself—but I didn't. I eyed the bag on the suit jacket. But if Kazuma did...

I grabbed up his bag and rummaged through it. As I suspected—inside was a Novatech comlink and a pair of gloves and shades. I pulled them out and slid the gloves on, then slid the shades on. They were blank—no image. I took them off and checked the commlink.

It was off.

I looked at Kazuma—if the link was off, how the hell was he accessing the PAN? Was my first guess that he had an internal 'link, right? Which meant he was using his own secured PAN to chase after the hackers?

That was just stupid on several levels—having an internal 'link nowadays—especially since the Technomancer and AI scares was just stupid. If someone listening to all the drek out there about Otaku Nightmares being Technomancers didn't see a physical commlink they'd kill this kid. Straight up. I'd already read about too many "mistakes" like that in this crazy-ass world

The other problem was if the Hackers noticed him and fought back with any sort of attack—like a black hammer or even some sort of databomb—he was gonna suffer some serious dumbshock from running hot sim. I switched the commlink on, set the protocols, and discovered the commlink's ID wasn't his, but someone named Hitori Tetsu.

Ah...Tetsu. The missing sister?

With a shrug I donned the goggles again, connected to the PAN, and was instantly barraged by the daily specials (which correlated with Kazuma's assessment that they hadn't tried to jam the signals) as well as a flooded inbox of email, texts and coupons available from PRADA international.

PRADA huh? So—the Tetsu family was well off. Figures.

Even as I looked around the room I still saw the desk and a small pop-up window identifying the type of datajack and the IP address. The damned thing even informed me what company manufactured the broom and a red blaring message warned that the mop had a known defect in the rotary connection.

Wow...what a rush. And then I looked at Kazuma.

And got nothing. Not even a PAN identifier or ID.

Now—I wasn't completely savvy on the latest wireless craze that'd pretty much rerouted the world in the past seven years—but I had been paying attention enough to eek by. Had even set up my own PAN and had my commlink spoofing alternate IDs from a dataset I'd bought with good nuyen.

But from what I understood, an active PAN should show some sort of ID to it.

Or was his on private or something? Either way—it was time to apply a little of my own hacking skills.

I heard the yelling outside through the door and grabbed up one of the ear-buds from the shades and stuck it in my left ear. Now I could hear as well as see all the craziness being picked up by this 'link.

As I looked around, I found a pop-up that told me there was an access panel to the left of Kazuma. With a grunt I moved over him on my knees and then felt along the wall. Two pushes and the pressure plate disengaged.

The opening revealed a slate gray surface with several lights flashing in what looked like random patterns. There were also two datajacks to the right. Reaching over his legs, I pulled up the bag and looked for cabling.

No cabling. What I did find was a small prescription bottle for some hi-test painkiller. The label tag opened a new AR window before my eyes. Kazuma Tetsu's name showed up as the prescription recipient. His address flashed up as well. 1000 miligrams of Nanoprofen. Wow. That was strong stuff. What was he taking it for?

"Derek," came Kazuma's voice to my left.

My left? Kazuma was to my right. But when I looked at him he was still sitting with his eyes closed. With a pounding heart I looked to my left.

There was something there—visible only in the shades in a third AR window. It was Kazuma—sort of. But he looked more like a trideo anime character than a person. His hair was bright red and he still had the ponytail. He wore a tight fitting black suit with a high collar, and the handle of a katana jutted up behind his right shoulder.

Now that was stereotypical.

His eyes were large and green and bent up on the ends like a cat. "Kazuma?"

He nodded. "Matrix icon," he said. "You're wearing my sister's comlink."

Oh great. I didn't even want to know what this commlink's persona resembled.

I nodded to him. "It was the only one you had in the bag." I kept looking at him, but the AR windows didn't give me any more information. Not even a handle. "You care to tell me how the hell you're doing this? I mean—you got an internal 'link?"

Kazuma's cartooned face smirked. "No, I don't care to tell you. I should have told you to put those on sooner—makes this much easier to work in VR and solicit your help. I found the Agent they sent to the Horizon node—and I destroyed it."

I was impressed. Confused as hell but impressed. "So—this is good?"

"Yes and no," he smiled. "In truth the Agent was seemingly benign, with little to no security to it—but when I destroyed it—some sort of other program triggered and it followed me back here. The hacker noticed the blood trail leading to this room."

Oh.

That was bad.

He held up his right hand and an animated keyboard appeared beneath his fingers and he reached up to an animated AR window. "I've been able to infiltrate their equipment and I've locked the outer doors."

I narrowed my eyes at him. "You did what?"

"They can't get out that way."

"And the authorities can't get in."

He nodded. "I know. I sent a message via KE to the locals—PPC—telling them a KE security agent was inside and working on delivering the criminals. They'll keep the corner surrounded until everything is secured inside."

Oh good grief. "Kazuma—you're losing a lot of blood—"

"Which is why I need you. I can't concentrate on too many things right now—or I'll fade—lose consciousness. So I'm going to have to let go of the door when they hack it. I'll be semi-conscious and that's all I'll need to work. You're gonna have to stall them. Use my hidden gun holster and let them take the Colt."

I was about to protest.

"They'll think they've disarmed you. I'll need you to hide Hitori's commlink—I don't want them to find it. There's a storage compartment to the right of the panel. Put it in there and I'll lock it."

Uh huh. As I watched and listened to him I was starting to get a suspicion I didn't like. "Kazuma—does KE have a monitor on you? I mean—will they sense your vitals and send a wagon?"

"They do have a tag—but it can't read me right now." He smiled. "My commlink is in the pocket of my jacket. You'll need to pull it out."

Ah! So he did have an external commlink. I moved to his jacket and fished inside the pockets, finding it hidden inside the inner breast pocket. It was a Novatech model as well, slim line.

It wasn't on.

I looked back at him. He smiled. "Turn it on."

My suspicions came to an ugly head just then. This kid was accessing the PAN as well as the Matrix—or at least a small part of it with no commlink. I moved back and sat hard on my ass. "Kazuma—are you—?"

His eyebrows arched up.

Something started banging loudly on the door. I jumped, not expecting it.

"They've started hacking the door," he said.

It sounded more like they were banging on it.

He wasn't going to answer me. And if it was true, and Kazuma Tetsu was a Technomancer, could I blame him for being quiet? Given the current climate? He worked for a powerful mega-corps, for crying out loud. If they even had a slight bug up their butt that someone in their security department could do what he could, he'd vanish from the registry of the living so fast even Naomi wouldn't remember him.

The banging continued as I did what Kazuma suggested. Two pushes on the panel by his head and the bag and gear fit just inside. I replaced the panel and watched as Kazuma's physical left hand came up and typed again on an invisible keyboard.

I heard the click. I also heard the whine from the door as well.

Shit.

I placed the commlink in his hand and he held onto it. And I knew if I still had his sister's 'link on I'd see his ID flash up in an AR window. I removed the hidden holster from Kazuma and placed it on my own waist—it barely fit. I was a bit wider than my elven friend. The Fichetti fit easily into the hidden seam of my coat as I slipped it back on.

"I found their IDs," Kazuma said softly as I put his coat back on him as well. "The ork's name is Harold Burton—limited enhancements; cyber-eyes, right arm, and an artificial heart. He's blind in his right eye—has a down payment on a new eye."

I was impressed—this guy was hacking into their actual records—not spoofed ones.

"The human is Sylvester Van. He's had a half-replacement of a cyber-brain. His left eye is equipped with a target laser that is connected wirelessly to the firearm. He carries a katana—but isn't as skilled at using it yet. He has a blog—and his third lesson is tomorrow at noon. He has aspirations of being a samurai."

With that I had to laugh as I braced for the door to open.

"The one hacking is called..." Kazuma frowned. "I can't—" he winced and suddenly put his hand to his ears.

The door opened with an ear-shattering bang.

Sylvester—Chromedome—was the first one in and he pointed his katana directly into Kazuma's chest. I couldn't tell from my angle if it slid in or not. I hoped like hell it hadn't. "Found him! He's in here!" He moved the blade's end to the pin on this lapel. "And he's Knight Errant."

Seeing me, he moved the blade into my face and I held up the Colt in one of my hands. "Don't kill us—this man was wounded. Just let us leave and no will—"

"Shut the hell up!" Sylvester yelled. He jabbed me with the end of the blade, right into my chest. Luckily it only pierced the leather of my coat and not my skin—but he didn't have to know that. I made the appropriate noise and allowed him to grab the Colt from me.

"Get out of here," he said as he pulled on my collar and yanked me to my feet. He might be stupid—but was definitely strong. Pulling me out of the room, he pretty much tossed me to the right and into the arms of the ork, Harold.

I really had to squelch a laugh at that one. And that wasn't hard seeing as how his fist made contact with my face.

His cyber-enhanced fist.

I saw stars before I even hit the ground. I'd also managed to fly over the coffee bar at the same time. The force of the blow was supposed to incapacitate me.

And it almost did.

Almost.

I landed against the far wall—close to where Kazuma was originally shot—and just lay there, waiting for the room to stop spinning. I watched as they yanked Kazuma out of the room as well—and he half-stumbled, half-walked as he was presented to the Hacker behind the counter by Sylvester.

The hacker narrowed his eyes at Kazuma, and I suspected he had smart lenses on, reading the ID tag from the now active commlink. "Well, a Knight Errant boy," he said in a voice full of phlegm.

I took that moment and tried to focus on the cameras. They were moving independently, zeroing in on me, on the front door and on the scene at the bar. Was that Kazuma?

A cry from that side of the room caught my attention and I looked back in time to see Harold using his huge cyber arm to squeeze Kazuma's wounded shoulder.

Damn—if they kept that up he was going to pass out. I wasn't sure what the rules were for Technomancers, but I was pretty confident if he went unconscious, whatever he was doing in the PAN would stop. And then the doors would be open and these drek-heads could go free.

The hacker grabbed Kazuma's chin and turned his face to look at him. "You realize what you just did? How much nuyen you just lost us? All I had to do was retrieve one file, one damned file—and you destroyed my gateway." He leaned in close. "Your ID doesn't say it—but that accomplishment tells me you're pretty rich with the KE cred—which means you have codes. And I want those codes," he removed his hand and then produced one hell of a rifle and pointed it at me where I half-lay, half-sat in a dazed heap on the other side of the room. "Or I shoot the old guy."

Old guy?

Kazuma's eyelids flickered and he slumped forward. The Hacker cursed again and then moved the rifle over Kazuma's shoulder to point at Sylvester's head. "You overdid it!"

Harold's eyes widened. "Boss—hey!"

Harold came from the back, a scowl on his face, his tusks grinding back and forth. "Jarod—the main server is back there. I found an access jack—but I can't even start to hack in. Everytime I try to I get bounced back."

Jarod nodded. "No, but this kid can. And he will—" he looked at Sylvester. "Get that juice—the stuff you got off that kid you geeked last week."

Sylvester looked crestfallen. "Aw, man. That's my stash—besides, if you give it to the dandelion eater, he might die."

"I don't give a shit as long as he's awake enough to give me the codes," he pursed his lips.

"Can't you just hack his 'link?"

"The codes aren't in his 'link, shit-head," Jarod said. "Knight Errant security keeps the codes closely monitored—they're changed out during sporadic intervals and each Errant Agent is given the secure location for those codes. He'll have to give them to me himself."

As I lay there, watching and listening—feigning being wounded but not feigning that much—I was amazed at how much this drek-head knew about Knight Errant protocols. Either his Johnson had given him the information or he'd actually worked for KE as an Agent at some point.

Either way, I needed a distraction. As Kazuma anticipated, they didn't frisk me for any more weapons—taking the most obvious. I still had access to the Fichetti—but I would need some sort of distraction to draw it. Any movement on my part might compromise whatever Kazuma had in mind.

Though at the moment I wasn't sure how any of this was gonna work, since he was out cold. And from the blood pooling on the floor—I didn't give the elf much more time in this world.

"Wake him up," Jarod said. "If nothing else, we need him to release the doors. We'll take him with us and find a good shaman to take the information from his brain."

Uh oh. I honestly didn't know if that was possible—but the image of Naomi furious at me—that was very possible.

As if on cue, the side soy steamer came on, sending a hot, steaming blast against the counter. This caused the machine to wrench and fall forward.

It was funny, but it wasn't. All three of the shit-heads turned and fired on the poor steamer, riddling it full of holes. Kazuma fell to the floor in a dark heap on his right side, his face turned away from me. He was still.

A little too still.

"*Stopstopstopstop...*" Jarod called out. The shooting ceased. The steamer, dead.

And the Fichetti was in my hand, concealed and fully loaded. Thirty rounds of ammo—and the bastards weren't even paying attention.

The blender abruptly came on as well. Full of something the barista had been making before the ork barged in, now slurped and spewed into the air, splattering the three amigos.

"What the hell is going on here?" Jarod called out.

"Otaku!" Sylvester shouted and ran to the front door. He banged on it repeatedly and tried to wrench it open. "There's a ghost in this system—"

I was up on my knees, tugging at the downed shelf I'd used earlier for cover and used it again as I filled Sylvester with a good dozen holes, then without letting go of the trigger I moved the gun to the bar and nailed Harold when Jarod ducked.

With a grunt I released the trigger. Damn. I got to get me one of these!

Silence was golden in the room and I could hear Jarod breathing. I was sure he was trying his damnedest to open the doors through the PAN—I could hear the circuitry vibrating. But he wasn't breaking through Kazuma's security.

And that's when I'd made my mistake—glancing back at the doors as they moved on their own. Jarod was up and moving around the bar, his weapon trained on my head. *Idiot!*

"You're a Technomancer...aren't you? You're the one messing with everything. I can't hack in or out of anything—there's something in there—in the door to Horizon. It was some monster you put in there, wasn't it? You can't—" and he was looking around at something I sure as hell couldn't see. "What is that?"

I tried to bring my gun up, and his attention was on me again.

"Damned freak—" he started to scream and I saw his finger tightening on the trigger. I pulled my pistol up, knowing I'd be too late—

And then a hole abruptly appeared in the center of his forehead. Bone, flesh and gray matter flew out and he lowered his gun, and fell backward.

I looked past him to see Kazuma standing by the bar, his left hand holding my Colt, a half-smile on his pale face. I was still half laying on the ground behind the shelf as he straightened and very calmly walked over the broken glass, ceramic, and blood to me as he pocketed my gun, then held his hand out to me.

I stared at it as if it had nine fingers, but I took it and he sort of helped me to a standing position. My head ached, and I was thinking maybe I should throw back one of those pills he kept in his bag.

The doors suddenly released, opening just a tad and I noticed the cameras moving back to their original positions. I could see men in uniforms moving in from their hidden positions in the streets around us.

Then he had my gun in his left hand again, spun it around and handed it back to me, hilt first.

I took it and offered him his. He shook his head. "Not...yet."

"You weren't as badly hit as I thought," I said as I re-holstered the Colt. "Were you?"

"*Sukoshi*," he nodded. "I am. But I at least had to make sure you survived this little venture." He gave me a half smile. "Or Auntie Naomi would never forgive me."

"Auntie?"

His smile faded. "Uh oh—"

"What is it?"

"If you'd be so kind as to keep my gun, holster and the bag hidden back there," he started to lean at a weird angle. "I'm going to politely...pass out."

I caught him as he fell forward into my arms.

✪

Three days later, I found myself actually inside one of the dormitory complexes for Knight Errant. It was located in the Bunker Hills area, and it took three levels of security, as well as the presence of a bandaged but healthier looking Kazuma Tetsu to escort me to his apartment.

It was a nice place. Spacious and completely automated. There was an ambient light change as I stepped in front of the sensors.

"It's looking for your 'link," Kazuma said as he moved to one of the white, cushioned couches in front of a roaring fire. It was close to nine and my transport back to Seattle left at midnight. Flanking the fireplace were floor-to-ceiling windows overlooking greater Los Angeles. "If you had one, you'd be given a choice of decor preferences."

I shook my head as I stepped down to the living area. Kazuma moved to a bar and pointed to the well-stocked shelf. I nodded and he poured me a scotch, wet. He knew his stuff. And when I tasted it— it was the real thing. Not synthohol. It burned all the way down.

He sat on one of the sofas and I sat on the other. His right arm was still in a sling—fixed to his chest to restrict movement. Apparently he was allergic to several of the latest muscle mending medications and had to let it heal naturally. He had a ceramic, green cup in his hand. Tea, I assumed.

I set the glass on the coffee table between us and retrieved his bag from my jacket. Kazuma immediately dug into it and pulled out the prescription. To my amazement the kid took two of those pills out, popped them into is mouth and took a swig of tea.

"You get headaches a lot?"

He nodded and put his left hand to his forehead. "Since the Crash."

I chewed on my lower lip. I hated delicate situations—especially since there was nothing delicate about me. "Is that when it happened?"

He sighed as he looked at me. "I was online, yes. With Hitori, my sister. We were both caught at the same time. When I came to, I was in a KE facility. My grandfather and Hitori were with me. Knight Errant had treated me, as they treated all their employees who were caught. Many died—they said I was lucky."

I looked at him. "About your sister—"

He put up a hand. "As I said in my message. I'm going to step back for the moment. It's been three weeks. She said when she went to work for Ares that she would be gone a month. As you saw her 'link was still active, and her apartment is still open."

"But don't you find that a bit strange?" I said. "Why didn't she take her 'link with her? Why leave it at her apartment for you to find?"

Kazuma looked at me. "I don't know. I don't even know if the Crash affected her in the same way it affected me. What the other day taught me is that I'm not as prepared for those kinds of surprises as I need to be. I'm not—there's more I have to learn before I can face what I think is ahead of me. I have to do better at defending myself."

"You seem pretty good with a gun."

"That doesn't make me prepared," Kazuma said. "That makes me lucky. I have a lot to learn, and I have some ideas. But what I'm most concerned about right now is that my secret—what I am—remain a secret. Naomi trusts you. Should I?"

"Does Noami know...about what you are?"

Shaking his head, he looked crestfallen. "No. And she can't. It could compromise her job. They're on the alert to look for Techno-mancers—even suspected ones. I can't," he winced and put his left hand to his forehead.

"Headache?"

He nodded. "There is a song...a sound...that I can't escape from. It's in my dreams...and in my thoughts all the time. It's lulling me into the Matrix...and I'm not sure I can fight it off much longer. There's no assurance that little things like the coffee shop—that one day they won't point their fingers at me."

"Which is why you keep an active 'link."

"Yes."

Sighing, I sat back. "You want me to keep looking for Hitori—in case something happens to you."

Kazuma nodded. "I'm going to give you the information. You'll find it encrypted in your inbox sometimes. Always look for Dancer. That's my online handle."

"So-ka. Is that the icon I saw?"

He smiled. "It was a drawing my sister made once. She always wanted to be a cartoonist. Hitori would be the only one to recognize it." Kazuma looked at me. His face was flawless, and his ears hidden artfully beneath his hair. At a glance no one would suspect what he was capable of. "Will you do it? Will you help me and keep my secret?"

"You're an idiot, you know that, right? Taking this all on your-self."

He smiled. "Baka."

"Aho."

His eyebrows arched.

I nodded to him. "You call me the minute you hear anything, and I'll do the same." I stood then and moved to the door. He was beside me. A good half-centimeter taller, wiry, and lean, the old chummer faces the new.

"*Arigato*, Mr. Montgomery."

"Chummers call me Dirk."

He made a face. "Chummer?"

"*Omae*," I said. "*Oyasumi*, Tetsu Kazuma," I used the correct form of his name and bowed.

Kazuma bowed from the waist as well and nodded. "*Oyasumi*, Dirk Montgomery, *omae*."

With a nod, I left the apartment and stood just outside the door before strolling down the drive to where a car waited for me, compliments of Kazuma. Tonight was cooler than the previous night when I heard back from my own contacts.

The hit on the coffee shop was pointless—it'd been nothing more than one of a dozen false hits within a sixty-meter radius that Tuesday—hits on Horizon owned establishments. All of them coordinated with Knight Errant. Code; *Caliban*.

That would explain that punk hacker knowing so much. He'd been a plant, a KE mole. Why? I didn't know.

Yet.

I decided to do a bit of digging into Caliban myself—give Kazuma a break. If something snagged, I'd be back in Los Angeles before the sun was up.

They could count on that. ○

NO SUCH LUCK

BY MATT FORBECK

Matt Forbeck has worked full-time on games and fiction since 1989. He has designed collectible card games, roleplaying games, miniatures games, and board games, and written short fiction, comic books, novels, nonfiction, magazine articles, and computer game scripts and stories for companies including Atari, Are-naNet, DK Publishing, High Voltage Software, Turbine, Ubisoft, Del Rey, Wizards of the Coast, Games Workshop, WizKids, Mattel, IDW, Image Comics, and Playmates Toys. His first original novels, Amortals *and* Vegas Knights, *hit shelves in the summer of 2010. For more information, visit Forbeck.com.*

"Deal me in," the dwarf said as he limped along the sumptuous Sioux carpet that sprawled across the wide, polished parquet of rare Yucatan woods. He snickered as he watched the gazes of the men drift inward toward their commlinks, silently demanding that their high-paid security forces earn their exorbitant wages by showing up to take out the trash.

He gimped his way closer to the table, enjoying the growing look of fear on the faces of each the four suits sitting there as they realized that help would not soon be coming. He grunted along on his good leg, favoring his battered knee, and he reached into the fraying pocket of his torn and tattered jacket, fished out a packet of paper, and pitched it into the middle of the table.

The men recoiled as if he'd tossed them a grenade. Then one of them leaned forward and peered at the bound-up papers through tight, beady eyes set deep into his hatchet-shaped face framed by a haircut that cost more than the dwarf made in a week.

"Real money," the dwarf said. "The stuff we used to use before electronic transfer. Before trusting the corp banks was mandatory."

"Is it real?" a white-haired man at the table said. The dwarf heard the telltale click-wheeze of the man's cybernetic lungs. The man stared at the money as if it might sprout legs and fangs and attack.

The dwarf laughed. "Probably not, but then what is?"

He hopped up onto the only empty chair at the table and stood on it. His eyes still barely came to the level of the men staring at him. He flicked his chin at the man stroking his pianist's fingers along a large tray of thick, colored chips.

"That's a hundred thousand nuyen." The dwarf waved a thick hand at the decaying paper. "Count it if you like."

The man's pencil-thin moustache peeled back in a sneer. "That won't be necessary."

The dwarf smirked at that. He reached out for the chips, but the hatchet-faced man slapped a hand on the felt between the banker and the cash.

"This is a private game," the man said.

The dwarf stuck out his bottom lip at that and gazed out the high windows overlooking the sparkling Chicago skyline—or what was left of it. The space where the Sears Tower had once stood still gaped like a missing tooth.

"So it is," the dwarf said. "And it's being held in a private club." He smiled at that. "And yet here I stand."

The white-haired man coughed, then spoke. "Subhuman species are not permitted in the club."

"The club? Is that what you're calling it these days? Short for the Policlub, eh?" He looked at his own stunted height, then gave the men a knowing wink. "Pardon the pun."

"Humanis is a charitable organization devoted to protecting the rights of a humanity besieged on all sides," the banker said, a hint of amusement in his voice.

"Or so your commercials claim," the dwarf said as he doffed his grimy baseball cap. Nanite-inked tattoos snaked and danced beneath the skin of his bald scalp, forming hypnotic shapes like a living screen-saver trapped inside his skull.

He leaned forward and put two hammer-like fists on the table. His braided beard, streaked through with gray, grazed the green felt.

"Let's not mince words. We're worldly souls. You're bigots. Wealthy ones too. You get nasty people to do terrible things to people like me, and you pay them well for it because it keeps your hands clean."

A small gun appeared in hand of the fourth man at the table, the one who'd been silent until now. He looked young and strong, although the dwarf was sure he'd been surgically sculpted that way. He could smell the bioengineered pheromones wafting off the man, designed to tell everyone within range who the big dog at the table must be.

Despite all that, he held the gun like a little boy.

"I'm not afraid of you," the man with the gun said through rows of perfectly straight teeth.

The dwarf laughed. "Go ahead, boy. Pull that trigger. Give it your best shot."

The man hesitated. A bead of sweat ran from his temple.

The dwarf leaned farther over the table, nearly crawling on to it. He pointed right at the center of his forehead.

"Go ahead and shoot, son." The dwarf's voice dripped with contempt. "I can take it. Or when you went in for all that cosmetic surgery did they remove your balls because you were clearly never going to need them?"

The gun barked in the man's hand, nearly leaping from his fingers. The bullet zipped high over the dwarf's head and crashed into chandelier overhead. Flying shards of crystal rained down and sliced into the dwarf's exposed skin.

The dwarf pushed himself back to stand on his chair. He reached up and picked out the bits of crystal still embedded in his skull.

The white-haired man with the plastic lungs gasped. "Lucky Wurfel," he said. "You're supposed to be dead."

A rivulet of blood trickled down the side of the dwarf's head. He snorted at that. "No such luck."

"Lucky?" The man with the gun had lost his expensive cool. His hands shook so hard that he dropped the weapon on the table. It went off again.

This time, the bullet tore through Lucky's jacket and creased his ribs. He grunted in pain and grabbed at his side. When he pulled his hand away, crimson coated his palm.

"Oh, my God!" the gun-dropper said. "I'm—I'm...."

"Sorry?" Lucky said as he straightened back up.

The man scowled at the dwarf. He glanced at the gun again, and his fingers twitched.

Lucky nodded. "I didn't think so." He pointed at the man with the chips again. "Deal me in."

"So we can play against a dwarf named Lucky? I don't think so."

"You got something against free money?"

"I don't want you taking mine."

The white-haired man interrupted. "The nickname's meant to be ironic, like calling a fat man 'Slim.' This son of a bitch has the worst possible luck."

"Huh." The hatchet-faced man gave Lucky a look like he was sizing him up for a body bag. "Seems that would have killed a 'normal' man by now."

Lucky grunted at the man's racism. "Dying's easy. Living with pricks like you around, that's the real challenge."

The hatchet-faced man shifted in his seat but refused to meet Lucky's eyes. The dwarf stared at him for a moment, then turned back to the banker. "So," he said, "do you want my money or not?"

"Why do you want to play?" the gunman said. "I mean, you're going to lose, right? What's the point?"

"Because I want to tell you a story," the dwarf said. "And interrupting a game of cards is rude. "

The white-haired man nodded at the banker. The man reached out and scooped up the packet of bills. Without counting the money, he pulled 100,000 nuyen worth of chips from the tray in front of him and pushed them across the table toward the dwarf.

Lucky swept the chips into a pile in front of him. Then he looked each of the men—every one of whom hated him and anyone like him, he knew—and grinned.

"All right," he said. "Let's play."

The hatchet-faced man dealt. Lucky spotted him slipping cards from the bottom of the deck as he went, but he didn't bother to say anything. He knew he was going to lose, after all. He expected it. The game meant nothing.

"So," the white-haired man said. "What's your story?"

"Yeah," the too-handsome man with the gun still sitting in front of him said. "You're about to pay us a lot of money to listen, so out with it."

Lucky gathered in his cards and looked at them. They read 2, 3, 4, 5, 7. All of them were clubs, with the exception of the 7, which was a spade. He put the cards down in front of him and tossed a 1,000 nuyen chip into the center of the table.

"I wasn't always the unluckiest dwarf you'll ever meet. Well, I mean most people. I suspect idiots like you don't run into a whole lot of dwarves in your corporate boardrooms.

"I was one of the first dwarves ever born. When I came out of my momma, imagine what a surprise that must have been. At first they must have just thought I was a little small. Maybe just a bit behind the growth curve. By the time I got to school, though, they must have had their suspicions. I know when I finally went off to middle school, for sure, they had more than guesses that I was a, well—"

"Freak." The man with the gun sneered at Lucky.

The dwarf shrugged it off. "Maybe. Hell, probably. They even talked with some doctors about how to surgically lengthen my not-so-long bones.

"After they talked with enough specialists, though, they realized that they didn't have some kind of genetic anomaly on their hands, but a child in the vanguard of a new resurgence of an ancient race."

Lucky held up his hands to stave off the scoffing.

"Save it. You think I'm a freak of nature, and I think you're a murderous bunch of assholes. Maybe we're both right, but that's not the point of the story. So, if you'll let me go on?"

The others looked to the white-haired man, who nodded his assent.

"Back in those days, there weren't a whole lot of things a dwarf could do. I didn't fancy joining the circus, thank you, so I had to forge a new destiny for myself. When I was eighteen, the computers all crashed, and my identity was lost. I took that as a sign and never registered with the rebooted systems. Instead, I slipped into the shadows, and I've never come out since.

"The year I turned twenty-eight, I was a hardcore shadowrunner. That was back in '39, back when it all went bad. I lost a lot of friends in the riots on the Night of Rage."

Lucky stopped for a moment and gazed up at the spot where the Sears Tower had once stood. Although it had been gone for so long, it still felt like someone had cut off one of his limbs. When he got this close to it, it almost seemed like he could still feel it out there, teeming with thousands of lives.

He didn't bother drawing any cards. He just kept the ones he'd been dealt. Still, he called every bet and every raise.

"My parents worked downtown, right near the Sears Tower. They died the day it went down. I was somewhere off in Manhattan, still trying to help clean up, to make a difference after the riots."

The banker threw down the winning hand and raked in the chips. The deal passed to the white-haired man, and the cards came sliding across the felt again. Lucky didn't even bother to look at his cards this time. He kept playing mechanically while he talked.

"As you might imagine, all that made me pretty mad. I was a real revolutionary for a while there. I cut off all contact with humans.

"As far as I was concerned, you guys were the enemy. A dead-end branch on the evolutionary path to the top of the food chain. If I'd have had my way, I'd have pushed all the resurgent races into havens on the West Coast and then nuked the rest of the continent until it was a sheet of glowing, green glass."

Lucky paused for a moment to relish the looks on the faces of the men staring at him. They were used to being the haters, not the hated, and the swap in positions discomforted them.

"Instead, after a lot of soul searching and no little amount of beer, I decided to switch tactics. Instead of doing runs for anyone with enough credits to spare, I swore I would only take on contracts for missions that would help the resurgents and do something to keep disasters like the Sears Tower from ever happening again.

"I specialized in curses."

The breath in the white-haired man's plastic lungs caught. Lucky was sure he was the only one who noticed, as it came at the end of another hand. The gunman won this time, and after raking in his winnings he started to deal as well.

"Magic came back along with the metahumans, as I'm sure pisses every one of you off to this day. You probably think the only kind of magic is eeeevil magic, but you're as wrong about that as you are about everything else.

"Magic is a tool. It doesn't tell you how to use it. You just pick it up and do what comes naturally.

"If you have a chainsaw, for instance, you might start knocking down trees. Paul Bunyan might hate the chainsaw, but every other lumberjack around loves it.

"If you decide to use it for something more, ah, antisocial, though—like knocking off heads instead—then you're the evil one. The murderous urges come from inside you. The chainsaw is innocent."

The gunman shook his head. "But that's not true. Magic doesn't work that way. You just mentioned curses."

"Yes," the banker chipped in. "Aren't you supposed to be cursed?"

Lucky tapped his temple with a thick index finger. "Exactly," he said. "Magic can be bad, just like people can be bad. Curses are bad, but they're not the worst."

The dwarf called the bet and raised it again. He waited for play to continue, but the hatchet-faced man held up his hand for it to stop.

"What is it then?"

"What?"

"The worst sort of magic. Does it have anything to do with something that causes perfectly normal women to give birth to genetic freaks?"

"Do you know to keep an asshole in suspense?"

The man shook his head.

"I'll tell you later. Now see that raise or fold."

The man tossed in his chips, and Lucky began speaking again.

"I got sent on one of my last missions back in '45. I wound up at a secret base up in northern Michigan, near Sioux St. Marie. The scientists there had located a cursed artifact of some sort or another and were trying to weaponize it."

The gunman scoffed. "Are you telling me that some of those damned elves were trying to figure out a way to throw the evil eye at a whole city at once?'

Lucky waited for the man to stop chuckling at himself. Then he started in.

"Ever read *The Lord of the Rings*?" he asked.

The gunman shrugged and shook his head. The hatchet-faced man and the banker followed suit. Only the white-haired man seemed prepared to admit he'd ever even heard of the books.

"I've seen the movies," he said. "The trideo remakes, not the originals."

"Yeah, yeah, yeah," the gunman said. "The ones with the dwarves in them." He glanced at Lucky as the others nodded in recognition at last. "I'll bet those are your favorites."

"In *The Lord of the Rings,* there's this dark lord named Sauron—"

"As in 'the Sons of Sauron.'" The white-haired man glared at Lucky. "Who did you say you worked with again?"

"I didn't," said Lucky. "But I try to avoid those pro-metahuman wackos whenever I can. Their agenda is almost as stupid as the crap you Humanis idiots spout."

The gunman started to say something, but Lucky cut him off. "That's not what I'm trying to get at here. This Sauron—the one in the book—he had a ring of power. *The* ring of power. It corrupted anyone who touched it. Drove them mad."

"Including him?"

"He lost it."

"How'd that happen?"

"Just go back to school, learn how to read, and then open the fucking book. That's not my story here."

Lucky waited for a moment for the gunman to sit back in his chair and shut up.

"All right. Imagine—now, I know that's hard for calcified brains like the ones you guys tote around in your skulls—but imagine, if you will, what would happen if you could take that cursed ring and atomize it."

"Atom-what?" The hatchet-faced man scowled.

"Grind it up into a fine dust and then mix it with an aerosol spray," the white-haired man said.

"I see someone paid attention in chemistry class," Lucky said. "Now, imagine if you did that with the One Ring. If you could grind it up and aerosolize it, think about how many people you could corrupt at once. And they'd never stand a chance of not getting infected by it."

"That's insane," the banker said. "Nothing like that's ever been done before."

"Insane," the dwarf said, "but not impossible. In any case, that's what these scientists had set out to do."

"Are you saying they had the One Ring? I thought those books were supposed to be fiction."

Lucky gestured at himself. "Do I look like fiction?" Instead of waiting for an answer, he just shook his head. "No, there's no such thing as the One Ring, but the scientists up there near the Soo Locks didn't need an artifact like that. Instead, they had something else."

"Which was?"

"Ever hear of the *Edmund Fitzgerald*?"

The men at the table stared at him with blank looks.

"Nobody listens to the classics anymore," Lucky said. "The *Edmund Fitzgerald* was the most massive ship to ever sail the Great Lakes. It went down in a storm in 1975, almost a hundred years back. Twenty-nine men died."

"So what does an ancient wreck have to do with anything?"

"The *Edmund Fitzgerald* didn't go down due to mechanical failure or due to the storm. It went down because it was cursed."

"Bullshit." The hatchet-faced man cleared his throat and spat on the floor. "That's too early. Before the aberrations began."

"Back in the 'good ol' days,' right?" Lucky shook his head. "You Humanis schmucks never get it, do you? Magic isn't something wrong with the world. It's the natural way of things. It waxes and wanes through the centuries like the moon in the sky.

"Just like during a new moon, though, even when you can't see magic, it's still there. It's just waiting for its time to shine again."

"That's just a bunch of Sixth World crap," the banker said. "The same foolishness street shamans and other charlatans have been spouting forever."

Lucky smiled. "Believe what you like." He gestured at himself. "I think the facts are on my side."

"So what sank the *Edmund Fitzgerald*? The One Ring? Or was it made of white gold this time?"

Lucky shook his head. "A sailor on the ship had been having an affair with a Chippewa woman, the daughter of the Bad River band's chief. When she dumped him for another man, he stole something from her home, an ancient spear that had been part of the band's history ever since they'd taken that name.

"'Bad River.' Makes you wonder what must have happened for a whole band to get slapped with that name."

"No," the gunman said. He had his hands flat on the table before him, framing his still-smoking gun. The fingers of his right hand twitched toward it. "I don't wonder. I don't care."

"Course not. It's not all about humanity, is it?" He looked at each of the men in turn. "It's about white, male humanity. If you ever got rid of the metahumans, you'd just turn on each other again. Blacks, Hispanics, Asians, women, gays. Anyone who's different from you in any way.

"Hell, if you got rid of them, you'd start in on the people with brown eyes. Or black hair. Or crooked noses.

"It's not about preserving rights with people like you. It never is. It's about preserving power. Yours."

The men stared wordlessly at Lucky. After a moment, he continued.

"The *Edmund Fitzgerald* went down because the spear the sailor stole was cursed. Of course, the spear sank with the ship, and it sat at the bottom of Lake Superior for decades before someone finally figured it out and then went to find it.

"Ares Industries got its hands on the damned thing, and somebody there decided that it wasn't enough to have a cursed spear around. After all, a spear can only affect one person—or ship, or building, or whatever—at a time. The Ares eggheads set their sights higher than that.

"So they ground it up, mixed it in with some nanites, and aerosolized the whole mess."

Lucky let that sink in for a minute.

"You're fucking nuts." The hatchet-faced man folded his hand. The chips sat untouched in the middle of the table.

"Ever heard of anthrax?"

The men squirmed in their seats.

"People hear the word 'anthrax,' and they break into cold sweats and then reach for their ultra-antibiotics. Remember the attack in Sacramento last year? Killed three hundred orcs before it was done."

Lucky stared at the silent men. "Yeah, I expect you do.

"The funny thing about anthrax is that it's usually harmless. Cattle everywhere carry it. You can pick it up by walking through any pasture. It's more common than cow pies, and only about as annoying as stepping in one of them.

"But you refine it and then aerosolize it, and it's deadly.

"Imagine doing that with a cursed spear."

The men remained quiet. The white-haired man ran his tongue along the inside of his lips as if he had something to say, but he kept it to himself.

Lucky shrugged. "Wasn't my idea. I just got mixed up in it."

"Someone else from inside Ares got wind of the plan and hired me and my team of runners to go in and put an end to it. They'd lost the argument in the boardroom, it seems, but they weren't willing to just let it rest.

"Of course, they didn't exactly tell us everything about what we were after. Just that we had to snatch it and then confirm its destruction."

"Everything went smooth as silk at first. Our decker—that's what we called them back in the days when they still had to jack into a system—he blew through their IC defenses like they were made of toilet paper. Our mage took out most of the security with a nappy-time spell, and I took care of the rest of them with less than a single magazine."

Lucky's hand pulled an imaginary trigger as he spoke.

"Then, when we got our hands on the package, it all went to hell. Matrix feedback fried Bones's brain. Misha's spells fizzled in his fingers at the exact worst time. My guns jammed.

"I grabbed the package and high-tailed it out of there. The others were already dead. Our rigger scooped me up, and we zoomed away, watching the Soo Locks vanish in the rear-view mirror.

"We would have made it, too, if it hadn't been for the rain—and that damned moose.

"The damned thing went right through the windshield and crushed Jeremy dead. I sat there, stuck in the shotgun seat, and watched as we spun out of control and smashed into a stand of pine trees.

"The fucking airbags saved my life."

Lucky closed his eyes and took a moment to collect himself. He pinched the bridge of his nose with his thick, stubby fingers until the screams in his head went away.

When Lucky opened his eyes again, the men were still staring at him, waiting for him to continue.

"The package shattered in the crash. All that dust. It got all over everything. Into everything.

"Everything.

"Me."

Lucky coughed at the memory, and the men around the table all jumped.

"There's a reason most people figured I died on that day. The paramedics that showed up to save my life were killed when the damn car exploded just after they pulled me out it. The kind man who stopped to give me a ride to the nearest hospital, he blew a tire on the way out of the parking lot and died in the resultant crash.

"The hospital itself suffered a gas leak shortly after I was admitted. The blast destroyed an entire wing of the place."

"How?" the white-haired man said. "You—with luck like that, you should be dead a dozen times over."

"Sure enough," said Lucky, "and that was just the start of it. It took me a while to twig to just what was going on. I'd taken a number of head injuries, after all. Eventually, though, I figured it out.

"The scientists had gotten it right. They'd turned that single cursed spear into uncountable millions of tiny little curses, and all the ones that hadn't gotten scattered all over the wreck had worked their way into me.

"I'd become—I am—a living curse. I'm kind of the anti-Midas. Everything I touch turns to shit."

The men stared at the dwarf. The banker actually edged his chair away from the table.

"It's all right," the gunman said. "He hasn't touched any of us."

Lucky reached over and picked up a card, then grinned. "True enough," he said. "But I didn't have to."

As he held the card up—the Queen of Hearts—the symbols on its face began to morph. Soon, he held the 2 of Spades.

"The nanites," the white-haired man whispered.

Lucky tossed the card down on the table and rubbed the moving tattoo on his scalp. The inkiness under his skin leaped toward his touch like iron filings to a magnet.

"They get into anything I touch for more than a few seconds. And then they do the same to anything—or anyone—handling that."

The gunman snatched up his gun again. "This—this game's over. I'm through playing around with you, stunty."

"Go ahead and fight it, kid," the dwarf said. "Give it your best shot. I've been at it for years, and I can't get it right. I'd love to see someone win."

"No," the white-haired man said to the gunman. "Don't—"

The gunman pulled the trigger. The gun exploded in his hand. He fell to the ground, clutching the raw stump of his wrist for a moment before passing out from the shock.

The banker leaped to his feet, knocking over the tray of chips as he went. He took three steps away from the table before he slipped on one of those chips and went sliding into the plate-glass window that Lucky had been staring out through before. The glass gave way as if the sealants all around it had somehow rotted away, and it and the banker tipped out into the wide-open Chicago night.

The hatchet-faced man snarled like a caged animal. "I don't believe you," he said. "This is all just some more of the usual metahuman propaganda you freaks propagate."

"I went into hiding right after I became cursed," Lucky said. "The sorts of things that happen to the people I come into contact with, they're not pretty. I can barely stand to watch.

"For assholes like you however, I'm happy to make an exception."

Lucky stepped onto the green felt in front of him, then beckoned the man toward him, taunting him to try to knock the dwarf from his perch. The hatchet-faced man lost his temper and lunged straight for Lucky.

The dwarf swung a meaty fist out and smashed the hatchet-faced man's nose flat. He felt the bones inside shatter and go straight back into the man's brain. The man fell to the floor with a sickening thud.

"Wouldn't your curse have taken care of him?" the white-haired man said.

"Eventually," said Lucky. "But who wants to wait for something like that when handling it yourself is so satisfying?"

"What about me?" the white-haired man said.

"You're already history. You were dead the moment I came into the room. Just like all the security guards you've been waiting on to show up since then."

The white-haired man clutched as his chest as he broke out into a sick sweat. "My heart."

"Imagine that," Lucky said. "What are the chances?"

"But." The white-haired man gasped. "What about you? Why doesn't the curse kill you too?"

"Because," Lucky said as the man collapsed on the table, "that would be letting me off too easy."

The dwarf got down from the table and strolled toward the door. As he reached it, he looked back over his shoulder at the four dead men. They'd engineered the deaths of hundreds if not thousands of metahumans. They'd have killed Lucky on the spot if they'd had an honest chance—not that he'd given them one.

They'd deserved to die, and he felt good about their deaths.

And more than a little jealous. He'd hoped one of them might have finally been able to release him from his curse. But no such luck.

He spat one last thing back at them as he left the place.

"Lucky bastards." ✪

EXPECTATIONS

BY KEVIN KILLIANY

Kevin Killiany has been the husband of Valerie for three decades and the father of Alethea, Anson, and Daya for various shorter periods of time. He has written for Star Trek *and* Doctor Who *in addition to several game universes, most notably* BattleTech™ *and* Mechwarrior™. *When not writing Kevin has been an exceptional children's teacher, drill rig operator, high-risk intervention counselor, warehouse grunt, ESL instructor, photographer, mental health case manager and paperboy. Currently Kevin is in family preservation services, is an associate pastor of the Soul Saving Station, and is managing to fit short stories in while working on his third novel. Kevin and Valerie live in Wilmington, North Carolina.*

I rolled my left hand against the sidewalk, pushing off with the edge and heel before momentum broke my fingers. Hunching my shoulder, I tucked my chin to my chest and did my best to turn the headlong dive into a semi-controlled tumble. The plascrete pavement rolled up my elbow and across my shoulders as I pulled my Colt Manhunter free.

Ice seared my knee. I saw a flash shot image of slashed slacks and a mist of blood as it swung past my face. Flechette round. Dumb luck or my suit had kept the razor slivers from shredding anything more vital than dermis and capillaries.

I ended my roll flat on my stomach in two fingers of water. Dog kept to his feet, daintily avoiding puddles, as I wrapped both hands around my Manhunter and lined up on—

Nothing.

Or more precisely, a ten-meter-high wall of absolute blackness; flat and unreflecting in the orange glow of the sodium lights.

From the layout of the buildings, the black nothing was covering—or filling—an alley. But it could have been a straight shot to the bowels of the Deep Lacuna for all my eyes could tell me.

Then the scent of the spell reached me and everything became clear.

❌

Sight is the easiest sense to fool. Folks notice smells, twitch their ears when the sound's not right, scratch where it itches, and spit out what tastes suspicious, but when it comes to sight, they pretty much run on autopilot.

Which kinda makes you wonder why Fun City spent so much time and effort making their little piece of security look like it was stuck one hundred and twenty years in the past. Don't get me wrong. I'm as fond of pink stucco as the next guy, and riding in the replica of an antique car with no roof and decorative fins was—in the argot of the illusionary period—neato.

But good as the augmented reality overlays were, they didn't hide the fundamental wrongness of the picture. A picture made worse by the not-quite-right scent of orange blossoms they were using to not-quite-mask the stench of the Harbor wafting in over their western wall.

Technology's not magic; this's good enough for mundanes.

"It's February. Real orange trees are full of fruit."

"What?"

I looked at the woman sitting next to me—more like across from me, the back seat of the ground car was that wide—and realized I'd spoken aloud. That happens sometimes when I'm focused out; I forget what I'm doing.

"Talking to myself," I answered. I patted Dog absently. Dog hated to be touched, but the sight of the gesture—man patting loyal twelve-kilo companion—had a universally calming effect.

The woman, who had introduced herself as Rachel, tilted her head to one side, weighing whether she was satisfied with that. The driver skewered me with a gimlet glance; no trust there. These folks had me on constant scan, they knew I wasn't transmitting. But I reminded myself that this wasn't Pasadena, and the local mundanes were suspicious of folks who weren't so mundane talking to themselves.

"My father worked in the groves," I lied by way of disarming explanation. "It's the wrong time of year for orange blossoms."

"Ah." Rachel's teeth flashed white against her dark skin as she smiled. She had an exotic Afro-Latina look—more striking than pretty—and all of her original equipment. Rare in LA. Athletic build beneath the expensive suit, and strong features that I bet looked damned formidable when she ...

Focus, Bastion.

So focus I did. Ignoring the very real cloud of approving pheromones being produced right next to me, I spread my senses wide.

My eyes, least trusted of my senses, reported we were passing through a suburban merchants' district, circa 1959. Neatly dressed people—most in period costumes marred by chrome—strolled beneath manicured trees, admired vintage shop displays, or noshed beneath bright awnings in sidewalk cafes. Surface readings were smiling faces, clean streets, cops who waved—even the squirrels looked happy. Everything so saccharine I felt my teeth rotting.

Speaking of teeth, I counted the teeth-grating "silent" buzz of no less than twenty-seven drones industriously surveilling our block of boulevard. A lot of beautiful people were sharing the fascinating minutia of their daily lives with the grateful world.

Pasadena has it's P2.0, of course, the constant circulation of personal broadcasting and voyeurism that used up Dog knew how much bandwidth, but nothing on the scale of Fun City. In Pasadena the idea that P2.0 was more addictive than BTL was a wry-smile joke. In Fun City the addiction was pretty much a given; if not a religion. Everyone seemed to be trying to point their best profile in all directions at once.

For a moment one of the automated spy-eyes—doing a passable impression of a curious hummingbird—dipped out of the general swarm to pace the car. A cherry-red replica of a 1957 Cadillac convertible cruising majestically down the boulevard must have triggered its "this might be interesting" circuit. The car flashed the drone a signal I only imagined I heard and the roving eyeball turned away; no doubt scrubbing any images in the process.

My canine nose, as always, gave me more information than my ears. I closed my eyes and lifted my chin as I sampled the breeze. Beneath the Harbor stink and the ersatz orange blossom and the omnipresent electric ozone of the AR skins was the faint frisson of spell work. Basic security wards on the businesses for the most part, with more than one illusion—pretty much a staple in the land where image was all. Nothing—

A stench of fear. Bitter sweat and raw emotion flooded my senses for half a second and then dissolved.

"What?"

Rachel's question tipped me to the fact that I'd shed my relaxed pose. Ol' gimlet eyes was watching me, too, having evidently puzzled out a use for the mirror glued to the windshield.

"Nothing significant," I said, glancing down at Dog's relaxed form for confirmation. "We just passed close to something."

"Magic?"

My ears pricked at the note of alarm beneath her casual tone, but I dismissed it. Low-level paranoia over matters magic was par for a mundane who'd hired an occult investigator. Anybody who paid my opening highball price up front without hesitation had to be scareder than most.

Gimlet's ever-watchful gaze regarded me from the mirror. I hoped the car was on autopilot.

"Someone having a very bad day." I patted Dog again, pretending I didn't notice his reproachful glare. "Nothing involving us."

"Us?"

"Nothing involving me, anyone I care about, or anyone in the car."

I braced for follow-up questions. A lot of folks who don't use magic believe the trideo myths and expect mages to "read" spells in a glance, discerning everything from its purpose to the shoe size of the caster.

But Rachel just nodded and absently copied my gesture, stroking Dog's back.

I shrugged apologetically, but Dog was having none of it.

Gimlet caught the wheel when it began turning, belatedly restoring the illusion he was driving as the Cadillac navigated a narrow opening framed by signs warning us not to enter. I had a fleeting impression of a 1950s garage and then we were through the back wall and climbing a steeply curving tunnel that made no effort to emulate the 1950s.

Regularly spaced along the featureless walls were motorized slug guns slaved to armored sensors that followed every curve of our stately spiral. Not terribly sophisticated, but whoever was sitting in the control center would have no trouble from anyone in the tunnel.

Our spiral ascent ended in a round room—high ceilinged and about thirty meters across—with one of their patented armored gun cams at each compass point. The car stopped in the middle of the room, facing floor-to-ceiling metal doors flanked by two human guards in light armor.

A tall specimen with dead white dreadlocks stood slightly to one side, somberly resplendent in an ostentatious costume of studded leather and flowing cape. From his elegance and arrogance I took the posing mage for an elf; but when his scent reached me I realized he was just a pretentious human. Noting the martial runes inlaid in ivory and silver along the length of the ebony quarterstaff in his grip, I took a chance and guessed horticulture was not his specialty.

As soon as the four of us climbed out—Rachel and Gimlet on one side, Dog and I on the other—the Cadillac backed silently out of sight down the tunnel with ponderous dignity. Presentation; real showmanship is in little touches like that.

The worthy in classic wizard garb regarded us regally as the two guards stepped up to check us out. Professionals, they checked Rachel and Gimlet as carefully as they checked me—scanners, then a pat-down. Making sure I hadn't planted anything on my escort for later retrieval.

One of them surprised me by having the presence of mind to scan Dog. Nothing showed but canine, of course: twelve kilos of terrier-sized hound packaged in russet and white stockings. The goon visibly relaxed and finished the quick rub-over with a scratch behind the ear he probably imaged Dog enjoyed.

"What is he?" he asked. His gravel voice implied a poorly healed throat injury.

"Basenji."

"Thought so."

"Some kind of spook dog?" the other goon asked with a hint of nerves.

"African hunting dog," the dog fancier answered. He took another breath to elaborate, but caught Rachel's cocked eyebrow in time. Sketching an apologetic salute, he stepped back without a word.

I'd been pretending to ignore the costumed mage by the door throughout the guards' inadequate pat-down. With no other legitimate distractions, I went for slightly startled—like I hadn't noticed he'd been giving me his best steely stare for the last forty-three seconds—when I met his gaze. Must have looked authentic, because the moment he thought he had my attention he struck a more dramatic pose, the fist on his hip pulling his cloak open enough for me to see the runed hilt of a mageblade.

The astral scent of his weapon conveyed much; as did the fact he thought such a display was necessary or prudent. I made a point of ducking my head a bit, keeping all responses in the physical as I let him know I was suitably impressed. Then I ignored him again, focused on following Rachel's hips out of the chamber.

They led me down an unadorned hallway and through what was evidently the servant's entrance to a penthouse office only slightly larger than the garage. There were ornate doors at one end and a panoramic view of the sun setting beyond L.A. Harbor —which was itself made beautiful by distance and lack of smell—at the other. In between was a plush expanse appointed with objects so ugly they could only be art and antiques that were probably real. Subtle restraint by Fun City standards.

Not so restrained was Julius vanVijrk. Swathed in silk and reclining on a divan, the sole proprietor of vanVijrk Revitalization made a passable case for becoming the default icon for self-indulgence.

I managed to avoid tripping while kicking myself for not demanding six times my usual fee and made it safely to what was evidently the minion's audience position—just to the right of his natural line of sight and nowhere near the guest chairs.

"Sebastian Automne," Rachel presented me, making the Hispanic mistake of pronouncing the final *e* in my nom du job.

Julius stopped pretending he couldn't see us and turned his hooded eyes to regard me with evident boredom. No doubt my cue to perform some obligatory obeisance expressing joy and gratitude for being in his presence. Since he was the guy covering my rent for the next six months, I dropped my chin an inch—acknowledging his eminence.

"Ork magic," Julius pronounced in lieu of greeting. "Can you handle it?"

"Yes."

I spent the longish pause watching Julius puzzle out I'd finished talking.

"Yes?" he demanded. "That's it?"

"If you don't trust my answers, don't ask me questions."

I felt Rachel shift weight. Dog, sitting next to my foot, turned his head to eye me.

For his part Julius stared at me like I'd grown a second head for a long three count. Then he laughed—a single, phlegmy bark.

"San Bernardino," he slapped the ornate table at his elbow, rattling the wine decanter. "You can handle ork magic."

Now that was useful. Very few people knew about San Bernardino. And if Julius thought 'ork magic' had been the challenge on that case, he'd been given corrupted data.

"We are undertaking a tremendous project—one that will improve the quality of life for thousands of people," Julius explained, his jowls quivering with passion, "And orks are trying to destroy everything."

I cocked an inquiring eyebrow—standard tactics for getting folk to say what's on their mind.

"Because they're orks," Julius snapped at the prompt. "Without honor, incapable of rational thought, no sense of debt to their betters. Trust them and they turn on you."

Julius took a couple of deep breaths, impressing me with the amount of flesh he could lift with only his diaphragm.

"Forgive me," Julius said after calming his nerves with a sip of wine. "Pembroke, a dear associate of mine, lost his granddaughter to orks only yesterday."

"Orks?"

Julius cast me a suspicious glance and I hastily replaced incredulity with inquiry.

"There has been sabotage," he explained. "My people have not determined how it is being done, but they tell me the magic involved is definitely orkish."

I refrained from telling Julius his people were either idiots or had learned to tell him what he wanted to hear. Judging from the contrast between Rachel's respectful demeanor and racing pulse, I suspected the latter was endemic to his organization.

"I wanted outside talent, a specialist, to deal with this threat," Julius was saying. "I made inquiries. Someone well placed in the thaumaturgical department at CalTech recommended you as an innovative investigator with a nose for the exotic."

I did not wince.

That last phrase was a direct lift from Jesalie's master's thesis— an otherwise fine piece of research into the world of occult investigation marred by a few romantic misconceptions. Last I'd heard she was teaching intro-level courses at Pasadena City College. Evidently she'd parlayed that into a weighty position at CalTech since. Good for her.

I made a mental note to thank her for boosting me for a high-nuyen gig. Then full memory kicked in and I amended the mental note to read: 'arrange for a third party to convey my gratitude.'

"Rachel," Julius interrupted my mental noting. Then, apparently taking a deep interest in the Harbor at sunset, he presented his profile.

I looked to Rachel and she indicated the door through which we'd entered with a sweep of her hand. Subtle confirmation of my suspicion we'd been dismissed.

A short trip farther along the staff corridor led to a much smaller chamber without windows occupied by a large oval table with chairs and decorated with Gimlet eyes and the trideo idol mage. Hector and Franz respectively, I learned when Rachel made introductions.

"Ork magic?" I demanded.

"That wasn't me," Franz said in a heroic baritone. "The lackeys he calls security merely confirmed his paranoia."

"And as a card-carrying combat mage you don't bother to tell him there's no such thing?"

Franz shrugged. He probably meant to imply there was no point in arguing with Julius, but the message I got was he found his boss's ignorance useful.

"However misidentified the source, the sabotage is real," Rachel said. "And magic we can't identify—and can't defend against—is involved."

"Show me."

The data dump was devoid of business-specific details such as costs and materiel sources, but the overall picture was clear enough. There was a major project scheduled for the near future, date obscured, that would reclaim most of a shallow bay in the east Harbor, near where the I-5 bridge launched toward Downtown. Looked like sixty to eighty blocks to my untrained eye.

"vVR is bigger than folks think," I said.

Hector grunted, Rachel smiled, and Franz looked disdainfully down his nose. He had a good nose for it.

"That is an upcoming Horizon Corp project," Rachel said. "They don't know we have this projection."

I refrained from comment.

The visual updated and a stretch of real estate about three blocks wide connecting the newly reclaimed land to the northwest corner of the Fun City enclave glowed a cheery gold.

"This is the vanVijrk project."

Julius wasn't pulling terra firma from the briny, he was revitalizing rubblefield—buildings tumbled by the Twins. Areas of L.A. abandoned by their previous owners were a wilderness of SINless squatters and street gangs lacking the chops to control profitable turf—free land for anyone with the nuyen and balls to rebuild. vVR was building a secure, upscale conduit linking the new Horizon enclave to the northwest corner of Fun City, with the cheery gold spreading out to cover a half dozen blocks hard against the outer face of the Fun City wall. An area that already had a more somber color code of its own.

"That's the center of the PCC resettlement."

"Pueblo Corporate Council-built refugee camps are temporary shelters and classified as undeveloped land under reclamation protocols," Rachel briskly quoted—whether from regulations or an investment prospectus I could not tell. "Refugees have no legal standing. Refugees displaced by legitimate redevelopment are permitted to apply for housing at another facility."

I nodded sagely. One did not question the rationalizations of one's paying clients. Which may have had something to do with Franz staying mum on the absurdity of 'ork magic.' I didn't bother changing my opinion of him.

Aloud I said: "I take it folk currently living in the neighborhood Julius is about to revitalize are primarily orks."

"That portion of the refugee camp *is* predominantly, but not exclusively, ork," Rachel acknowledged the coincidence. "Mr. vanVijrk has reason to believe it is a Sons of Sauron stronghold."

"Julius believes his problem is racism?" I asked.

Gimlet—Hector—pursed his lips. I made a mental note to scale back the sarcasm.

"If ork separatists are sabotaging his project," I went on, infusing my voice with professional analysis, "He needs street enforcers, not an occult investigator."

"The sabotage has relied on magic in every case," Rachel said. A dozen sad blue dots appeared along the happy golden corridor of vVR revitalization. "Either direct assault with damaging spells or obscuring spells shielding saboteurs."

Data windows blossomed beside the blue dots. A quick read told me a couple of the "shielding spells" had been sloppy security. But in other cases the spellwork was very sophisticated—performed by someone with skill and long periods of uninterrupted proximity to the target.

"You're still framing the central skeleton of the elevated causeway," I said. "Are the buildings underneath occupied?"

"The refugees and squatters near the camps have not been evacuated, and there are no doubt squatters in the rubblefield," Rachel said. "The buildings will not be leveled until phase two, when their construction materials are recycled to build the walls enclosing the ground-level cargo concourse."

"Good," I said, rising. "Are my quarters in this building?"

"Excuse me?"

"First I need to feed Dog," I explained. "Then I need to rest. Come midnight, Dog and I will stroll the length of this project of yours and see what we can find."

✖

Sight is not my forte. I've been told my visual illusions stink out loud and I never have much luck penetrating visual effects thrown my way. It's a limitation, but I've learned to deal with it. Case in point, flat in a two-AM puddle staring over the sights of my pistol,

I was not surprised my eyes couldn't pierce the dark nothing filling the alley.

Giving up, I canted my ears—*listening* to the alley. A rustle without weight—a dried leaf or scrap of paper in the breeze. A drip. No life—not even rodents. At least nothing moving.

Cold seeped into my chest and belly. I hoped the water I was lying in was only leaching away my body heat and not soaking through my jacket. Ballistic should be waterproof, right?

Still not willing to get to my feet, I lifted my chin a little, focusing my canid olfactories on the alley. Scents of garbage, mostly vegetable; urine from a few hundred rats—all of which were still not moving; something remarkably soapy-clean; and a lingering trace of gunsmoke.

That last one surprised me by being a recipe I recognized. Lone Star custom, the rent-a-cop corp's trademark homebrew for the Ruger Thunderbolt. As far as I knew it didn't increase the effectiveness of their favorite sidearm—but the sinus-stabbing jolt of cordite was their way of making sure everyone knew they were the ones pulling the trigger.

Which made no sense. Fun City had their own gunsels. There was no reason for a Lone Star or a Knight Errant or even a Pueblo Corporate Council constable to be within a dozen klicks of my puddle. Of course, the fact the shooter had missed me at forty meters implied there wasn't. And since when did Thunderbolts fire flechettes?

Guerilla saboteurs using disposable assets and disinformative clues? Unheard of.

Dog, evidently certain nothing was happening, found a dry piece of pavement and sat. I lay prone and soaked in an empty street with my gun lined up on blackness. After six slow breaths during which nothing at all moved, I decided Dog might have been on to something.

The darkness began fading. Either my inaccurate assailant was towing the spell directly away from me as he made his escape or he was long gone and the blackness was dying a natural death.

The normal dark revealed the alley wasn't exactly an alley. Light from the sodium lamps mounted high on the skeleton of the vanVijrk causeway washed over the front half of what looked like some sort of delivery area: A space just deep enough to let long-haul trucks get off the street and broad enough to let them back up to a pair loading docks barely discernable in the far wall. The back of some no-doubt once fancy establishment facing the next street.

A fading thermal glow emanating from a person-sized metal doorframe between the docks implied it had just been flash-welded shut. I had a momentary hope my incompetent shooter had melted himself into the door, but there was no scent of seared flesh. The quartz-glass security window that had given him line of sight on me was too small even for my narrow frame and carving through the metal would take time. It looked like my shooter had made his escape and sealed off pursuit.

If it weren't for that soapy-clean smell from somewhere inside the blind alley, I might have believed I was alone.

Abandoning the illusionary safety of lying prone in a puddle, I got to my feet. The ice in my knee had turned to fire and the damn thing nearly buckled on me. I stood a moment, letting my knee adjust to the weight. Opening my long coat, I flapped the heavy fabric to circulate air. A stupid move when going into potential combat, but I wanted my shirt to dry.

Besides, if anyone in the alley wanted me dead, the first shot would have passed to the left of my right ear.

Trying not to limp, I moved toward the alley and the soapy-scented witness who might have some answers. Dog kept pace. The tick of his trotting toenails against the pavement brought home the fact that the world around us was absolutely silent. This near the refugee camps the street should have been alive with late-night entrepreneurs and their clientele. Either the jungle drums had warned the natives to stay away or something was persuading folk to take their business elsewhere.

By the time I reached mid-street, the part of my brain that understood the vagaries of breezes and the wafting of scents had narrowed her location down to three or four square meters of deeper shadow between an overflowing dust bin and the right-hand loading dock. And there was no doubt it was a *her*. Mixed with the soapy cleanness was the unmistakable musk of a young human female.

Human-*ish*, I amended, with an acrid tang I couldn't place. I'd never smelled anyone quite like her.

Once my nose told me where to focus my ears, I found her breath—slow and shallow as she tried to be silent—and her heart hammering like she was on the last leg of a marathon. I didn't swing the muzzle of my Manhunter toward her—let her think I was still trying to puzzle out an empty alley as I cut off her escape.

Truth was, I was ignoring the alley and casting my senses wide to search out who else might be about. I counted seventeen whos else at the very edge of my senses, none moving in our direction. Dog moved a little away from me, following a path that made sense to him. I didn't bother turning my head to follow.

Three entertainment drones in loose formation whirred overhead, ignoring me as they searched the sprawl for exciting footage to pipe back to their masters in Fun City or Hollywood. Evidently one guy with a gun leveled into an alley did not constitute exciting footage.

Solidly between the very clean girl and her only chance to escape, I lowered my gun. I wasn't quite trusting enough to put it away, but muzzle to the ground was a pretty universal sign of nonaggression. I let her know I knew where she was by pointing my face directly at her hiding place.

The breathing stopped.

"Come on out," I said, putting no power behind the words. Just basic, civil communication. "I don't intend to harm you."

I stood silent through the long pause that followed.

Finally the girl shape rose from behind a busted crate of junk beside an overflowing dust bin. She stood, not moving, until I holstered my Manhunter. Then she stepped hesitantly into the open.

I saw immediately why she had a *human-ish* scent—one of the few cases of sight trumping scent. She was mid-Expression.

Sometimes when an ork and a human got together a kid resulted. If dad was human and mom an ork, she'd have a litter of orks with maybe a human thrown in. If dad was the ork and mom human, the kid looked human until puberty. Then it was a fifty-fifty crap shoot; emphasis on the crap. At an age when most humans were getting sweaty-palmed over the idea of their first date, hormones hit the poor kid with seventy-two hours of metamorphing hell.

By the time the process was fully done, there'd be no sign she'd ever been human. But mid-process ...

Mid-process she should be writhing in ungodly agony as her bones grew and shifted and her muscle mass doubled. I caught another whiff of the acrid beneath the little-girl-changing scent and the penny dropped. She was sweating out some expensive pain killers. Real high-end stuff if it was keeping her upright and scream free.

I could see my little ex-rich girl's Afro-human features had once been aristocratically sharp, but now her high cheekbones were spreading, flattening as her face became broader. Her tusks were barely big enough to protrude, but her cheerfully bright jumpsuit was stretched taut across her bulking form.

A cloud of pubescent hormones and pheromones washed over me. I twitched as the scent registered. The girl caught the motion and stopped, covering her mouth—her new tusks—with one hand. I knew Dog was amused at my reaction, but I didn't give him the satisfaction of looking in his direction.

"It's all right," I said, knowing how stupid that had to sound. "You surprised me is all."

She didn't react. She just stood with her wide eyes staring at me over her concealing hand, blank with fear. And/or expensive pain killers.

Her jumpsuit was expensive—some sort of upscale school uniform with all the identifying logos cut off. Neatly, like whoever had dumped her had cared that her clothes kept her warm. Or maybe they were just thinking about appearances. The hand not covering her mouth held the strap of a kid's shoulder bag blazoned with advertising that declared her loyalty to a half-dozen trendy products. Among other things, she was a fan/member of *Gang Life! L.A.'s most popular teen P2.0 network!* I wondered if she was plugged into the network now, if anyone was seeing what her life had become. I doubted it. Beautiful people were not interested in the way real life could screw you over.

The bag was nearly empty, but had once been stuffed with what smelled like high protein soy bars, and toiletry articles—including that expensively effective body wash. The fact that she had such a carefully packed bag told me whoever'd dumped her hadn't wanted her to suffer. Too bad they hadn't wanted her at all. What kind of person abandoned an innocent kid who'd never been on her own to the sprawl beyond the refugee camps and packed her a lunch?

Family. Nothing but. From the gilded enclave of oh-so-human perfection I was working for.

"My name is Bastion," I said, hoping the silence hadn't stretched too long. "What's yours?"

"Monica," she said, moving her hand just enough to speak. "Monica Pem—"

Her face crumpled. The name she'd been commanded to never say again got lost in a despairing wail.

I had my arms around her before I thought about it. Pembroke. This was the "missing" daughter of Julius vanVijrk's dear friends. Lost to the orks. For a long count I just held her, letting her sob her heart out against my still damp chest while I stared into the now natural dark of the alley and weighed options.

❷

"What the *vut*?"

Monica tried to bury herself in my chest—the guttural challenge instantly transmogrifying her wracking sobs into a terrified tremble that threatened to rattle my teeth.

I shifted my weight, shielding the kid with my body before looking over my shoulder.

The broad street was still empty, but now a knot of three ork males stood dead center in the only way out of the alley. My nose belatedly warned of a distant fourth I couldn't see. Ignoring him, I focused on the more immediate threat.

My canine nose told me two of the three were a sibling set, and all of them about Monica's age—but full-blooded orks, which meant near-adults with twice her height and three times her mass. I caught the whiff of a pricy floral cologne that had been hip in the clubs around Lacey Park about eight months back, but there was nothing effeminate about their visage. They were dressed for the street—waterproof boots, synthleather thick enough to be body armor and improvised clubs.

I smelled machine oil, gunpowder, and brass—at least two slug throwers—and altered my assessment of the tactical situation accordingly. Screwed pretty well covered it.

"Cruising for some local exotic?" Demanded the ork who was not a brother. "Humanis get hard for a *ken* joytoy?"

For nearly three tenths of a second I considered explaining I'd been down here on legitimate business and the girl had found me, but common sense kicked in. A, I wasn't all that sure my business was legit, and two, these jokers didn't give a damn. Anything I said would be *shpita*.

If it came to a firefight I'd never get clear of the girl in my arms fast enough to get off a shot. Worse, ork punks habitually blended maximum firepower with minimum accuracy. From the looks of things, it was a smart money bet any rescue attempt these warrior wannabes launched would kill Monica.

Don't let the urgent distract from the essential.

I filed that bit of philosophical flotsam where it belonged and kept my gaze level—trying for something between "not scared" and "not confrontational"—while I worked on the problem.

Conventional street wisdom has it that if you kept your mien cool and didn't look like you're looking for trouble, four out of five times you can avoid a fight. Standing in a blind alley facing three angry-looking orks with my arms around one of their girls, I didn't think my odds were quite that good, but I gave it my best.

My three dance partners spread out, positioning to keep me the center of attention. The diverging smells of gunpowder told me right and left carried the guns while the fine mineral oil and steel straight ahead told me middle man favored a blade. Ork tradition would dictate a combat axe, but that would have been redundant, given his twisted steel club. From the scent of sandalwood and the cut of his long coat, I was betting katana.

Keeping all three in my gaze was a trick, but I managed without nervous head jerks.

Visually occupied, I set my canine ears and nose to sweeping the street. I still hadn't pegged where the fourth strain of *eau d'ork* originated and I strongly suspected that bit of information was vital. I had a sense the real danger was watching and waiting while these picadors got the measure of the *gaijin*.

In my arms, Monica's seismic shudders had subsided to a tremble. I hoped that indicated she was getting a grip, but under the circumstances exhaustion was the more likely option.

"*Ujnort vut.*" The third ork, the one to my left, revealed himself as a minimalist. Also not much of a curser if he thought "non-ork shit" was a cutting remark.

Dog, ever battle savvy, found a spot a few meters in front of me and sat down. He looked expectantly from one ork to the other, as if hoping for a treat, but none of them acknowledged his presence. Apparently unbothered by the lack of attention, Dog yawned hugely, then rolled his head over his shoulder to cast a sideways look back toward me.

It took me a moment feel safe taking my eyes off the ork turks. I turned my attention to the curly mass of black hair pressed against my chest.

"Monica," I murmured. "Look at them."

She scrunched against me tighter. In her heart I was her kind; her protector. The protection part was a given, but the her kind part was no longer true—her genetic expression was unstoppable. In another— day? two?— she'd be fully ork and this scene would not be happening. She was already ork enough that the three thugs—and by extension their distant leader—read her as one of their own. Which, from her size, meant a child of five or six. Hence the chivalrous hostility.

"It's all right, kid." I was getting sick of that phrase.

Monica pulled her head away from my chest and tilted her face up toward mine.

"They need to see so they can understand."

She hunched back down. Pressing her forehead against my sternum, she rocked back and forth. I could imagine her eyes scrunched shut in denial.

Guttural growls made what the gang imagined clear.

Focus.

A new scent. A fifth ork; female. Near the fourth, wherever that was.

The breeze swirling in eddies worked against me. I might never have gotten a fix if Dog hadn't simply pointed his nose left to sniff the new smell. A shape—two shapes—in the dark beneath a stoop across the street. A doorway I'd walked past ten steps before getting shot at.

Now that I knew where to focus my senses, I picked up the heady tang of magic. There was a weaving back and forth between the spaces surrounding the ork woman in the shadows. She was one used to both worlds.

I tasted long enough to be certain this was not the magic that had blanked the alley, then withdrew.

"Kid," I said, keeping my voice low and comforting.

I pulled my left arm—the one on the side away from our audience—down and got my hand between Monica and my chest. Finding her chin, I lifted gently until she was looking up at me. Her face, shielded from the others by the hunch of my shoulder, caught a few rays of sodium light. It wasn't as wet or as blotchy as you might have expected from the amount of crying she'd been doing—which was good, because I wasn't sure I could keep a grip on the situation if our ork audience thought I'd been hurting her.

"You got choices. There are places besides the sprawl, orks that aren't squatters," I explained, pitching my voice to her alone. "Don't think facing these guys means you have to stay with them or on these streets. I got places you can go, people you can count on."

I cocked an eye at the three ork toughs. They were about where I'd left them, shuffling their feet and growling ork-like noises. I didn't speak or'zet well enough to track everything, but the gist of it was spurring each other on mixed with hints of disgust that no one had smashed my skull yet.

I was peripherally aware of the two shapes beyond them moving forward.

I looked back down at Monica, her chin still between my thumb and finger. She was gazing at me with something like surprise.

"You've got choices," I repeated with better grammar. "And the first one is how we go about getting out of here.

"These young gentlemen," I tilted my head in their direction, inspiring a fresh chorus of growls, "Are trying to rescue you and I do not want to hurt them. We need to show them what's going on before things get out of hand. Okay?"

Monica licked her lips, flinching slightly when her tongue hit a new tusk. She nodded.

I let go of her chin and put the arm back around her shoulders. Lowering my right arm, I turned her slowly until our audience could see her clearly in the streetlights.

There was a moment of silence.

"Huh," minimalist ork quipped cleverly.

The two from the stoop paused mid-street. Standing in the full glare of four sodium lamps, they were still shrouded in shadow—as though they'd brought the gloom of the hidden doorway with them. I knew the reality was I was being persuaded not to look directly at them, but I didn't bother pressing the issue.

"She got dumped," I explained. "She asked me for help."

"How you plan on helping, *ujnort*?" middle ork demanded. "What you think you going to do with her?"

My ears pricked at his awkward phrasing. My guess was street jive was not his default argot. Which appeared to support Julius' Sons of Sauron theory—you'd expect ork separatists to speak or'zet exclusively.

"I was thinking I'd take her home."

"You got a nice apartment?" Second ork, ranged to my right, gestured vaguely with his club. "Maybe some pretty pictures and toys for her to play with?"

"Pasadena," I said, keeping it simple.

"What's that? A Humanis dumping ground for freaks?"

Second ork was clearly the humorist of the group.

"It's a blended community," I said to Monica. "No ghettos. And between the college and the university there's a lot of opportunities."

I didn't come right out and say she could do a lot better in Pasadena than in the L.A. refugee camps, but no one in the alley misunderstood what I meant.

"She belongs with us."

The woman's voice was low, but it seemed to resonate off the plascrete beneath my feet. The alley walls didn't so much echo as repeat her words.

I was not surprised to discover the middle of the boulevard was no longer shrouded in darkness.

The speaker was ancient by ork standards and wrapped in several layers of symboled robes. Her hair was gold. I mean the metal, not blonde. Most folks would have thought it was a wig, but the filaments grew from her scalp. Fine as optical fiber, they were braided into intricate patterns—an echo of the web that connected her to the astral and to the city.

Her eyes were white with cataracts but she had no trouble keeping them locked on me as she strode forward. The black staff in her hand rang softly against the plascrete; metal, no doubt crafted from whatever she considered the bones of the world around her.

Middle ork shifted, making way for the street shaman without looking at her.

"This is our child, a daughter of this city." The resonance wasn't illusionary. I felt the vibration through my soles. "She belongs with us."

I felt Monica tense beneath my arm.

Another step, halfway between us and Monica's would-be rescuers, the shaman stopped as though she'd hit a wall. Her eyebrows—silver wire, I noticed—climbed toward her hairline. She looked down at Dog, sitting with his tongue lolling from his grinning mouth, and then back up at me. It took no great leap of logic to deduce what had happened; Dog had raised the astral curtain enough to let her know what she was up against.

The shaman gathered herself, and for a moment I thought she was going to try to overcome. I braced myself as well as I could while maintaining my reason, and tried to anticipate what attack would make sense to an urban.

Instead, she relaxed visibly. "Respect."

"Respect," I agreed and dropped the confusion spell. If she was giving respect, the three tough guys weren't going to give trouble.

For their parts, the bully boys blinked and muttered, looking disoriented as their minds suddenly cleared. The erstwhile comic gave me a bug-eyed stare, apparently the only one to realize why they'd been too bewildered to attack.

Monica stood straight as her own uncertainty evaporated. She didn't pull free of my arm, but she was no longer leaning against me for support.

My own cranium took a deep, cleansing breath. Don't try this at home, kids.

"This child is as connected to this city," the shaman said, speaking clear and straight, with none of the drama and declaration of her earlier pronouncements. "She belongs here."

"That's her choice to make."

"She has made it."

I wasn't surprised when Monica stepped forward, breaking her contact with me.

"Wait a sec, kid."

She turned back to face me. She looked excited, anticipatory, maybe a little nervous. Pretty much confirming what I already knew. You can't get complex expressions like that under compulsion.

I took her too-young hand in mine, pressing one of my old-fashioned business cards into her palm.

"If you need us, send 'Bastion Chien' to Pasadena."

Monica smiled, her eyes clear despite the pain meds.

"You're a good man," she said.

She turned away again. The shaman half-turned her head, indicating the street behind her. Monica walked past the old woman, close enough to touch but not touching, and joined the older ork male still standing in the middle of the boulevard.

The shaman's white eyes were on me. I thought of six clever things to say in as many heartbeats and kicked myself for each of them. Instead I kept my eyes locked on to her gaze and bowed, leaning forward about thirty degrees at the waist.

She acknowledged the respect with a deep nod to me and then a bow of her own to Dog. Without a word, she turned and made her way across the street to the shadow beneath the stoop. Monica and the ork fell in step behind the shaman as she passed.

The three toughs were still milling and bemused, looking after the shaman and back to me a few times. Two of them knew something they didn't understand had happened—the third wasn't talking. I cocked an eyebrow; he flinched. No doubt when he felt they were safely out of range, he'd tell his chummers how close they'd come to death by magic. Eventually the three decided they couldn't see me and headed off into the night on whatever mission I'd interrupted.

Leaving Dog to watch the street, I strolled over to the dustbin Monica had hidden behind.

Five minutes later I was on the street, headed back toward Fun City. The sidewalk, empty throughout the little passion play, was again busy with the foot traffic of late night. People scurrying with heads down, hoping not to be noticed; others strutting their stuff, ready to do business.

I bought a skewer of scorched and seasoned meat from a vendor with a trash can grill. Catching a troll hooker's eye, I flashed her a grin and a wink, earning a raucous laugh in return.

Julius was not going to like my report one bit—but I was no longer interested in what he thought.

○

"Horizon?" Julius looked pale.

"You were right in that there are orks involved," I said. "But they are being used as cats' paws."

I described the darkness spell, again, in detail.

"A spell of that size and density requires both native ability and a thorough grounding in thaumaturgy—at least a university education. Something well beyond the resources of the refugee camp.

"There are ork street shamans," I dismissed the ilk with a wave. "They *might* be responsible for the concealing spells—that's a simple matter of dissuading people to look in a given direction. But the direct assaults were carried out by a mage or mages who can command corp-sized salaries."

"Horizon?" Julius repeated.

"If we posit there's another corporation that wants to stop you from linking the new Horizon enclave to Fun City, Horizon is the corp that fits the bill."

"I was providing them with a service ..."

"Unasked."

Julius couldn't quite muster a glare.

"You were anticipating a need you were not supposed to know about. It is not beyond reason to suspect Horizon might not want an outside agency calling attention to a project still in the planning stages," I styled my summation on a popular trideo barrister, narrowly resisting the urge to parody. "It also takes very little imagination to assume Horizon would want to maintain exclusive control of all access between this future enclave and Fun City—already their enclave in all but name.

"Given these assumptions are valid, I think they were showing uncharacteristic restraint. Assassinating you would have solved the matter more quickly, cheaply, and thoroughly."

I counted three before Julius closed his mouth.

"Rachel," he said and presented his profile.

She would have turned us right, leaving the sanctum, back toward the garage exit. Instead I turned left, heading for the room where she had briefed me on the job fourteen hours ago.

Rachel hesitated, then followed.

I could not help but notice yesterday's approving pheromones were missing. It also seemed that Dog, whom she'd pretty much ignored previously, now occupied much of her attention.

I was not surprised when Franz and Hector appeared some distance ahead, vectored for rendezvous.

I preceded the trio into the meeting room and made a point of sweeping around to the far side of the oval table without hesitation. Let them think they had the safety of covering the exit. I remained standing and Dog jumped onto a chair next to me so he could see over the table.

For their parts, Hector stood watching me, Rachel divided her attention between me and Dog, and Franz had eyes only for Dog.

"Two out of three conspirators talk to street shamans."

"What?" Franz glanced at me to ask.

"You three are lucky Julius ignores lackeys," I answered. "Bad acting can be a fatal flaw."

"What makes you think—"

Rachel stopped, her eyes big on the Tiffani needler in my hand.

I kept my eyes on Rachel, peripherally aware of Hector's reach for whatever he carried. The big man stopped mid-motion when the tiny weapon left my hand to clatter on the table.

"Your sister, on the other hand, could make a fortune in the trideos."

"Sister?" Franz asked in a puzzled tone that almost redeemed my respect for his acting abilities.

"You're mistake was trying to spook me into a reaction in the garage," I told him. "A seldom smart way to assess an opponent. Once Dog had a whiff of your mageblade, I was able to smell your work everywhere."

"That makes no sense."

"Okay," Rachel cut of my cuttingly clever retort. "What is it you think you've got?"

"Three smart people who work for a self-absorbed, dangerously ambitious idiot and trying to banish Dog will get you killed, Franz."

The mage lowered his hands.

"Make that two point five smart people," I said. "Julius had concocted a scheme anyone with half a brain could see would piss off Horizon—if only because it revealed someone was selling their plans to idiots.

"My bet is he knew but did not care that he was going to level the hometown of half his faceless minions."

"What?"

"Hector, a refugee camp and its environs do not do that well without a steady infusion of outside resources. It's an economic model as old as haves and have-nots," I spread my hands, including my audience. "Loyal sons and daughters with jobs in the promised land sending home all they can."

"If your speculations were true," Rachel said. "If. All we'd have to do to stop him is tell Horizon."

"At which point vanVijrk Revitalizations would disappear in puff of greasy smoke and all of you—and likely your families—would become either dead or broke or both. You had to convince Julius he was waking a monster without waking the real monster. However Julius, Humanis to the bone, looked at your carefully crafted evidence and saw his own monster—and made wiping out the refugee community an even higher priority. You couldn't tell him he was jumping at the wrong shadow without showing your hand, so you had to find an outsider to connect the dots."

"And out of all L.A. we picked you?"

"If those college kids pretending to be street punks hadn't been from Pasadena, I might have considered that a long shot," I agreed. "As it is, I think someone took Jesalie Pilar's hundred-level culture of street magic course at City College. I've met enough freshmen over the years to know she makes a minimal attempt to conceal my public professional persona while dwelling exhaustively on my affinity for scents. Inadequately informed, you convinced Julius I was a big deal and staged a little drama to convince me Julius was up against the big boys and the orks were innocent victims.

"My guess is your sister's expression was an added bonus—you probably had some suitably innocent waif originally cast for the role of guide through whatever expository journey you'd concocted," I shrugged. "I spoiled things by going off script and your shaman friend had to improvise."

Rachel shook her head.

"I have no sister," she said, and I lost my mental bet with myself that she'd deny the whole thing.

"Olfactories."

"An olfactory scanner can't identify individuals," Hector seemed glad the conversation had hit on an area of his expertise. "There's no way to establish family relationships by smell."

"For a chemsniffer it's impossible," I agreed. "For a dog's nose it's inevitable."

Hector made an inquiring noise.

"He's a mystic adept, talented in all the usual detection, inquiry, and discernment skills. Nothing obviously remarkable about him," Franz explained, bearing down just a bit on the *obviously*. "His key investigative tool seems to be an animal attunement of an intensity that strains credulity."

Hector looked unenlightened.

"He's got an open channel, for want of a better word, to the dog," Franz explained. "He experiences through the dog's senses. He sees and hears and smells everything the animal does."

"Not so much see," I corrected. "There's a reason you've never heard the phrase Basenji-eyed." I stopped short of explaining my limitations in the optical sphere.

"Franz here cast that darkness spell through a quartz security window in a steel door he'd welded shut to ensure Dog here didn't get a whiff of him. Effective, but like the potent sanitizer Monica used to get rid of the gunshot residue after shooting at me, it called too much attention to itself.

"Speaking of smell, the touch I really liked was loading needler ammo with cordite gunpowder. I suspect that was your handiwork, Hector. You don't need a dog's nose to smell that stench, and everyone knows it's used only by one of the big corps' favorite head-busters and that *they* only use it in cannons too big for little Monica to handle.

"Franz didn't realize that was wasted effort," I spared that worthy a smile. "I already had his astral scent from his mageblade."

"That's the second time you've spouted that nonsense," Franz snapped.

"But that nonsense isn't what's really got you pissed," I countered.

Franz made an angry gesture at Dog. "You have neither the skills or the power to craft this vessel or bind a spirit into it."

"Not even close," I agreed. "That is no vessel, that is my dog; a real dog really named Dog, now possessed by a free spirit with no name he's willing to tell me but answers to Dog."

The three took a long hard stare at Dog. He grinned back a canine grin, all sharp teeth and mocking eyes. He clearly had no intention of showing them what he'd shown the shaman in the alley.

"You've said you feed Dog, and that you need to rest after doing so. And from that confrontation with—" he stopped himself mid-word. "In the alley, we know Dog loans you his energy for spellcasting; so there's a quid pro quo in play.

"I can see the shape of it, but I don't understand the mechanics," he frowned. "This is not ... usual."

I considered explaining, but didn't see the point. Jesalie hadn't figured it out in a month of living with me; there was no way I was giving away the trick of my trade to some one-off customers who'd never see me again.

Franz had been right when he pegged me as unremarkable. I like to think I'm unique, but if you were to graph the talents and abilities of all the psychic investigators in LA, I'd be about dead center on the bell curve. What made me was my partner.

Dog, by which I mean the free spirit possessing Dog the Basenji, gives me direct access to astral data—way beyond my ability to assense. But he gives it to me in doggish: very little sight, lots of smells. Where top-dollar wizards see an astral fingerprint, I get an astral scent. You can research it—believe me, I have—and find enough evidence to make a case for the way Dog conveys information being dictated by the limitations of the creature he's inhabiting.

Personally, I think he does it because it amuses the hell out of him.

Like Franz said, everything is quid pro quo. So what does Dog get from me? Hard to say. He explained it once, I think, but I'm not sure I followed. Call it context. Interpretation. Maybe it's because he's a dog; maybe it's because he's a spirit, but everything we people do seems random. Dog finds humans fascinating; he just needs me to understand the natural world.

"So," Rachel said into the stretching silence. "What do you plan on doing with this information?"

"I'm kinda torn between telling Julius and getting killed or telling Horizon and getting killed," I shrugged. "One of the things that makes me unremarkable is the fact that I honor a confidence when there's no compelling reason not to."

Hector and Franz glared with varying intensities, but Rachel's smile was wry.

For a moment I considered asking about the Pembrokes. Maybe they were her grandparents. Or maybe there was a network of families helping kids make it out of the ghetto into the promised land. But it was none of my business. Nothing here was.

I circled the table, Dog preceding at a thoroughly terrier-esque trot. The three made way.

"If Monica wants to go into the business, tell her to call," I said in the doorway. "I can connect her with some resources. She's got my card."

"Business?" her sister asked.

"Investigator," I said in dripping ain't-it-obvious. "She can play a role, keep her wits while loaded on painkillers in the middle of a confusion spell, and—to come that close with a needler at forty meters and *not* hit me? She's a hell of a shot."

Rachel smiled unexpectedly.

"She says you moved so fast she almost hit you."

"Story of my life." ✪

WHERE THE SHADOWS ARE DARKEST

BY STEVEN MOHAN, JR.

Steven Mohan, Jr. lives in Pueblo, Colorado with his wife, three children, and surprisingly no cats. His short fiction has appeared in Interzone, Polyphony, On Spec *and* Paradox *as well as several DAW original anthologies. He has written nearly half a million words of* BattleTech *fiction and has been tapped to write the first novel of Catalyst Game Lab's line of* MechWarrior *novels. His short fiction has won honorable mention in* The Year's Best Science Fiction *and* The Year's Best Fantasy and Horror *and he is a former nominee for the Pushcart Prize.*

Abiola Fashola was on his way to meet with the Yoruba street gang that ran his neighborhood when he saw the old man. A cold shiver of dread rippled through the troll's massive body.

The funny part was he didn't know why. Abiola had never seen the old man before.

He didn't *look* dangerous. The old man was human, but then most Yorubas were human. He wore olive drab work pants and a bright yellow shirt. He was big around the belly, suggesting he got quite enough to eat, though how he managed to do that in the Shomolu quarter of Lagos was a mystery. His skin was dark, his hair the color of iron. His chin was clothed by a wispy, gray beard.

So he didn't look dangerous and he wasn't doing anything unusual. The old man stood in the busy street haggling with a fishmonger whose cart was loaded with the rich variety of fish that could be caught in Lagos Lagoon: three-eyed fish and no-eyed fish, fish with parasites and fish with stumps where fins should be, fish that *looked* fine, but were loaded with heavy metals or bacteria or magical maladies.

The Yoruban quarter was pushed right up against the poisonous lagoon, which the people of Lagos used as dump, toilet, bath, and larder all in one.

The cart's contents turned Abiola's stomach. He had eaten better when he'd been a merc—too bad he couldn't stomach the killing.

He was tempted to dismiss his feeling as nerves, but he knew better. The shiver meant his dreaming mind had seen some danger his waking mind had missed.

The first time it happened to him his merc unit had been working some Igbo raiders that were coming out of the jungle to harass the oil workers that fed the Lagos pipeline. It seemed like cake duty, drawing a fat corp paycheck from Global Sandstorm (washed through the Edo Kingdom, of course) to hunt down some irregulars.

Only the irregulars didn't turn out to be so irregular. Later Abiola learned they were mercs drawing their own fat corp paycheck from United Oil (washed through the Igbo Kingdom, of course.)

Anyway, it had been a pretty summer day and they were working their way through some small family farm that had met some unfortunate and violent end.

They were on the north side of the farm, moving through fields that weren't growing anything but knee-high grass. The jungle rose up before them like an emerald wall, so close that Abiola could hear the cries of monkeys, the chatter of birds, the buzz and click of insects.

They moved across the farm using standard infantry tactics. First squad would sprint forward, while second stood back ready to provide covering fire. First would stop, establishing cover, and then the two squads would trade, second exposed, first concealed.

First had taken cover behind a truck turned over on its side, men laying prone behind the truck's engine block or its bed, AK-97s pointed at the jungle.

Second readied itself to rush forward toward the burnt-out hulk of a tractor forty meters from their position.

Abiola shivered.

It wasn't that he was a coward. He didn't fear combat. He was used to being bigger and more powerful than the men he fought. And he was a devout Christian, so he didn't believe this life would be his last. He did not want to die, but neither was he paralyzed by the thought that death might be waiting for him around every corner. Abiola Fashola was *not* a coward.

But suddenly he couldn't move.

So when second squad moved out, they went without him.

Giving Abiola a ringside seat when an Igbo ambush cut down every last man before they could reach the tractor's limited cover.

He would never know for sure what had caused him to freeze. Maybe his dreaming mind had looked out into the jungle and recognized the signs of danger: a glint of sunlight on steel, a fern stalk snapped and broken, the sudden peculiar silence of birds.

Whatever it was, from that moment on Abiola believed in it. So he took his fear of the old man seriously.

Abiola turned and hurried down the street, telling himself that things in Lagos were not always what they seemed. The old man could be scouting for the flesh-trade or he could be a corporate hit-man, a merc recruiter, a drug runner.

Abiola did not wish to find out.

He ducked down a side street, took another turn, and ended up on Ikorodu Road.

In the late afternoon, Ikorodu was a snarl of traffic, an impossibly long line of cars and trucks so old they still ran on gas. Mixed in with the cars were darting motorcycle taxis called *okadas*, construction yellow *danfo* busses so crowded that people hung out their open doors, and the occasional caravan of trucks on their way to Victoria Island in the company of tanks and APCs.

None of them going anywhere.

A brown cloud of smog hung over the go-slow. Horns honked and men cursed. Boys no older than six worked their way between the stalled cars, hawking gum, newspapers, steamed bean cakes, sweating bottles of Gulder beer, anything that might sell to the trapped commuters.

In the chaos, no one noticed a hulking troll moving down the sidewalk.

Abiola Fashola was big even for a troll, two meters sixty-one and pushing three hundred twenty kilos, only the last ten of which were from too much Star beer. His skin was dark chocolate and a pair of ornate horns the color of bronze began at his forehead and curled around like a ram's. He wore camouflage pants from his merc days over heavy work boots. A black t-shirt revealed muscular arms that could pop a human skull like a balloon. A meter-long machete hung from his belt by a lanyard.

He also wore a simple gold cross hidden beneath his long, black beard. Abiola had great love for the baby Jesus, but he tried not to let it show.

In Lagos, universal love and brotherhood was the kind of thing that could get you killed.

As he walked down the street his vision swarmed with augmented reality objects, ghostly icons floating over reality, powered by the mesh network that blanketed the road.

Most of it was garbage, spam pop-ups offering to increase the size of certain parts of his anatomy. (Like he needed any part of himself to be *bigger*.)

He powered down his comlink and looked around. No sign of the mysterious old man. Maybe it'd all been in his imagination, after all.

Abiola weaved through the crazy, crowded streets of Lagos, following Ikorodu Road another couple blocks before ducking east again.

After losing the mysterious old man, Abiola almost felt good. Until he heard a cruel voice behind him say: "If it isn't Mr. Troll," and he remembered the errand that had brought him here in the first place.

✪

They ended up in a little bar, Abiola nursing a Star beer the street gang bought him. Abiola loved Star, but this one tasted a little off. Bottled beer went for five naira, but he couldn't help thinking this one had cost more.

Abiola raised the bottle in a gesture of respect and said, "Thank you for the beer, Babafemi Kosoko."

Yeah. This one had cost quite a bit more.

The bar was small, a ramshackle collection of salvaged wood over a dirt floor. It was filled with the six or seven area boys Babafemi had brought with him, all of them armed with automatic weapons and wicked looking knives.

Babafemi and Abiola sat alone at a battered table. Babafemi was young and handsome. He wore jeans, real western blue jeans, and a pale green t-shirt that proclaimed: *I don't have an attitude problem, you're just an asshole.* The boy couldn't be older than twenty.

His given name meant, "Beloved by his father."

Babafemi flashed a lopsided grin, bright against his dark face. "We've been watching you, Abiola Fashola. Trolls are rare among the Yoruba people. Especially ones who used to be mercs."

"That part of my life is over," said Abiola carefully.

"Yes, but you still have the skills, no? You don't have to be a merc, but you still have the *skills.*"

Abiola took a pull of his beer.

Babafemi was not human, not really. Oh, he was biologically human, Abiola was sure of that, but the part of human beings that made them feel for others of their kind, that held them back from terrible violence, that caused them to reach out a helping hand when none was required, *that* part of Babafemi was utterly missing.

Abiola hated killing, he was sick to *death* of killing, but he would have killed Babafemi for a quarter-naira and he would have taken the job without a second's consideration. He would've taken no joy in it, but he would have done it anyway for the same reason one puts down a rabid dog: because the world would be a better place without Babafemi in it.

Except instead of killing Babafemi, Abiola was going to end up working for him.

"The 38 Dragons have forgotten their place," said Babafemi. "They've been giving us trouble."

"Isn't their place down south where Shomolu bumps up against Surulere's northeast corner?" asked Abiola. "Maybe they're giving you trouble because they've got their backs to a killing field. If you talked with them, maybe you could work something out."

A thin, cold smile knifed across Babafemi's young face. "Oh, we're going to work something out. It won't involve talking, though." The boy leaned forward. "And the Ammits would like your help."

An ammit was a giant crocodile. The awakened species terrorized the swamps and creeks of Lagos. It was a powerful and dangerous creature, but Abiola understood that calling yourself an ammit didn't *make* you an ammit.

These boys, these terrible boys played at being soldiers, played at being *monsters*. They called themselves tigers or crocodiles or dragons or lions, but in the end all they did was kill each other.

And whoever else happened to be in the way.

"I don't know," said Abiola softly.

"Eighty-five naira," said Babafemi, "and plenty more where that's from. Every time you join us for one of our little parties."

Abiola stared off into the distance. Eighty-five naira and a bottle of beer. How had he come to sell his soul for so little?

Babafemi leaned back in his chair, and slapped one of the young men crowding the bar on the arm. "Or you could always become a fisherman."

Everyone laughed at Babafemi's grand joke.

And that's really what it was about. Choices. He could go work for one of the corps, who were less decent even than the mercs they hired. Or he could eek out a meager living, just another poor *maghas* paying tribute to Babafemi or some other petty thug while the poverty of Shomolu drained the life out of him.

Or he could go back to carrying a rifle for anyone with the naira, go back to killing for money.

No, there weren't any other choices.

So he would be a soldier in the gang wars. And why not? He'd just be killing another Babafemi on the other side. Hadn't he told himself he was willing to do that, just a few minutes before?

Abiola cleared his throat. "You're just going to kill the Dragons, right? We're not going to ... hurt any innocents."

Babafemi's face screwed up into an expression of faux shock. "Innocents?" he said. "My boys and I would *never* hurt innocents." A broad smiled stretched across his handsome face. "But let me tell you something, Abiola. Isn't no one in this world who is *really* innocent."

Then Babafemi laughed out loud to show he didn't really mean it.

Even though Abiola knew he did.

✪

The western sky was on fire with the sun's death, molten orange shot through with gold, fading to dark blue and then purple. Beneath that magnificent sky the cool air of dusk carried the rotten stink of garbage and the rattle of automatic gunfire. Teenagers grunted or cried out as bullets took their lives and their bodies fell upon the mounds of refuse they sheltered behind, just one more piece of garbage for Lagos to bear.

How did I come to this place? Abiola wondered.

A bullet spanged off the 50-gallon drums of sludge Abiola crouched behind, sparking orange as it ricocheted away.

Sure, this is a lot better than being a merc, he thought sardonically.

He fired his AK high into the darkening sky, hopefully giving the Dragons something to think about without actually killing any of them.

The Dragons were making their stand at the back end of their territory, up against the short border with Surulere.

Babafemi said it was because the Dragons were afraid to come out and face the Ammits, but Abiola wondered. People whispered that dark things sometimes came out of the spooky Surulere and took the weak, the old, or the very young. Maybe the Dragons were back here to protect their neighborhood.

The border was a place of garbage. No metahuman would step foot in Surulere, not even to throw away refuse. So the people stacked their garbage here, dotting the border with stinking mounds of rotting filth.

Which gave Abiola an idea.

He glanced left, saw Babafemi crouched behind a pile of garbage, firing away with his Ares Viper Slivergun. Abiola drew a deep breath and shot out from behind his cover, crouch-running toward the gang leader. He dove behind Babafemi's pile of garbage.

"Hey, nice trick," said the boy. "You know you can get killed doing that?"

"I know how to end this," said Abiola breathlessly.

Babafemi's face brightened. "Yeah?"

"They won't fall back into Surulere."

Babafemi snorted. "Who would? That place's walking death."

"All you have to do is set a trap on either flank. Then we push them hard in the center they'll flee—right into our hands."

Babafemi scowled. "Too complicated. Good thing *you're* not in charge."

Abiola opened his mouth, but Babafemi cut him off. "Wait." And then he disappeared.

Abiola turned and fired a burst at the opposing side to keep the Dragons on their side of the twenty, thirty-meter no man's land.

Babafemi returned carrying a little girl in his arms. She was maybe eight, her eyes wide with terror. She shrieked as Babafemi wrestled her to the ground. She flailed at him with her little fists. Babafemi hit her hard in the face and she went limp.

"Hey, Dragons," he shouted. "Got one of your little sisters here. Surrender or I'll kill her."

"You can't do that," whispered Abiola fiercely. "These guys are thugs. They're not going to give over because of her."

Babafemi shrugged. "Then we'll just have to keep plugging people until they *do* give over."

Abiola looked down at the dazed little girl and then back up at Babafemi. He almost killed the gangster right then. But that would only make him at war with the Ammits, which was a sure death sentence.

And it would do nothing to help the civilians caught in the crossfire.

"Don't kill her," said Abiola. "I have another idea."

"What's that?" asked Babafemi.

But Abiola was already charging into the no-man's land, firing his AK straight and level. A Dragon popped up and Abiola laid him out with a well-aimed burst.

Fire sliced through Abiola's left arm, but he kept going.

He arced around a pile of garbage and caught the surprised gunner just as he was turning. Abiola roared and smashed his fist into the boy's face.

The Dragon dropped like an unstrung puppet.

Another gangster stepped toward him, his rifle leveled at Abiola's chest.

Abiola reached forward with his left hand, pushing the rifle's barrel up so that it fired over his shoulder. Then he dropped the Dragon with a blow from his right fist.

He sprinted toward *another* garbage mound, this time dodging *Ammit* fire and caught two more Dragons.

"Down on the ground," Abiola growled.

One of the men went for a knife and Abiola shot him dead.

The other got promptly and eagerly onto the ground.

Suddenly the sound of gunfire started to die off. Finding an enraged troll behind their lines was enough to scare the Dragons off.

Wearily, Abiola settled to the ground his back to the garbage mound. He was shaking with the after-effects of adrenaline and his left arm throbbed with pain.

For a moment he closed his eyes.

When he looked up again he saw Babafemi looking down at him, smiling from ear to ear.

✪

The full moon shone down on Babafemi Kosoko's paltry victory, its silvery light joining the firelight of the burning garbage mounds. The Ammits had set them afire to celebrate their defeat of the Dragons, filling the border with a choking smoke that tasted gritty in Abiola's mouth.

Seventeen boys and men had died and for what? So the Ammits could gain three more recruits (captured Dragons) and round up eight civilians—all women and children.

And so Babafemi could proclaim his superiority to all.

Babafemi raised his voice above the drunken hoots of his men. "I thank my good friend, my *brave* friend, Abiola Fashola, who greatly aided our victory."

A ragged cheer went up.

Abiola bowed his head, but could not bring himself to speak.

"Tonight our brother showed the true heart of an Ammit."

Abiola swallowed. This was what he'd been afraid of. He did not want to join Babafemi's gang. Doing limited jobs for them was quite different than being *one of them.* "I thank you," began Abiola, "but—"

He was cut off by one of Babafemi's lieutenants. "What should we do with these?" he asked, pointing at the frightened pack of women and children with the barrel of his assault rifle.

"Kill 'em," said Babafemi.

"*No*," Abiola barked.

A cloak of silence suddenly descended over the makeshift camp, only broken by the crackle and hiss of the dirty fires.

"No?" Babafemi whispered.

Abiola licked his lips. "I mean no disrespect, Babafemi Kosoko. Only . . I thought the reason for this mission was to show the people of Shomolu that the Ammits could protect them better than the Dragons."

"Which they'll see if the Dragons' people end up dead," insisted Babafemi.

And suddenly Abiola saw it. Most of the people of this neighborhood had run away during the fighting. If Babafemi killed those few who remained there would be no one to object if those who paid protection to the Ammits took over this land. In his own crude way, Babafemi was building political support and he wasn't going to let the lives of a few women and children stand in his way.

Isn't no one in this world who is truly innocent.

"*Wait*." Abiola was sweating, reaching for something, *anything*. "Without me you wouldn't have beaten the Dragons."

If the group of Ammits had been silent before, now their silence was *arctic*.

"Is that so?" asked Babafemi in a low, dangerous voice.

"Let them go," said Abiola. "For your new brother. *Please*."

Babafemi looked long and hard at Abiola, his dark eyes glittering in the firelight. "All right," he finally said. "For my new brother."

He turned to the cowering women and children. "You all may take your lives and go. *Into Surulere*."

Abiola stepped forward. "But no one ever goes into—"

Babafemi turned and looked coldly at him, and suddenly Abiola understood he had pushed this little dictator exactly as far as he could. If he said one more sentence, one more *word* it would be him who ended up dead, his great body sprawled atop a makeshift funeral pyre.

Abiola's mouth clamped down around the sentence he'd been about to speak.

Satisfied, Babafemi turned back to the women and children. "*Go*," he shouted.

No one moved.

"*Go*." This time he fired his Slivergun at the ground near them.

Shrieking with terror the women and children fled across the road that divided Shomolu from Surulere, running towards their doom.

Abiola remained, watching them go until they were nothing more than dark shadows in the silvery moonlight.

I am a fool, he thought. *Basic pack psychology. I challenged the leader so he had to deny me to reestablish his dominance.*

"Come on, *brother*," Babafemi sneered, "time to go."

The Ammits started to walk away from the garbage dump, but Abiola watching the horrorshow wreathed in shadow where two women and six children had just disappeared.

Then, without knowing he was doing it, he began walking, *toward* Surulere. Before the Ammits realized what was happening, he was already gone.

❌

Surulere was silence.

It was a bombed-out district empty of life, empty of *hope*. Rubble choked the streets. Most of the buildings had been burnt to the ground. Those that hadn't were pile of charred brick, blackened timbers reaching into the night sky like claws. Even after all this time, Surulere still smelled like charcoal.

But what really got to Abiola was the complete absence of sound. There were no human sounds of course, no laughter, no music, no shouts, but also missing were the sounds of insects and animals, absent was the *whir* of the giant beetle called Jauhekafer, gone were delicate flutter of batwings. Even the wind was still, as if the air itself was reluctant to visit the dead streets of Surulere.

The shuffle of Abiola's feet as he picked his way through the debris was the only sound that disturbed the funerary silence.

Surulere was a place of unmatched horror, even in Lagos.

During the first VITAS pandemic the district's entire population had been wiped out. A million people had gone to their deaths sick and panicked, crying out for help that would never come.

After the plague had run its course, nothing stirred in the district to break the silence.

Some said Surulere was still haunted by the ghosts of all those dead, others that the district had been colonized by the ghouls called *sasabonsam*.

Or something darker still.

A shiver wriggled down Abiola's spine.

Sure, he thought, *like I need to be warned I'm in danger now.*

He saw no sign of the women and children who had been chased into the darkness. It was as if the street itself had swallowed them whole.

And then, at last, he *heard* something.

A scream. A *human* scream.

Abiola ran toward the sound. He turned the corner and saw the women and children huddled together. A trio of *sasabonsam* circled them.

The ghouls were tall, their small bodies riding on slim legs that made them look almost like they were walking on stilts. They turned as Abiola came around the corner, and he saw smooth skulls and gaping mouths filled with sharp triangular teeth. Eyes filmed with white.

The ghouls were drooling.

Abiola *roared,* pouring all his pain and frustration out in a low, powerful sound that came from deep in his chest and rolled out into the world like distant thunder.

Then he dropped his AK-97 and sprayed the closest monster with bullets. The thing dropped, jerking spasmodically.

But its brothers were on him in an instant.

They skittered towards him on those long, slim legs, reached for him hungrily with their claws. Abiola pulled into his trigger and—

Nothing.

He was out of ammo. He threw the AK down and tore his machete off its lanyard, wielding the big blade like a knife in his great hand.

He would go down fighting, but he knew he *would* go down. He could kill these two, but not before they scratched him, infecting him with HMHVV, turning *him* into a ghoul.

Abiola would kill himself before he let that happen. He swallowed hard and took a step forward.

And then he heard something to his right. He and the ghouls both looked.

The old man.

He stood next to the women and children, about ten meters to Abiola's right, a placid smile on his round, dark face. Abiola's heart sank. His first guess had been right after all. The old man *had* been involved in the flesh trade, selling his fellow man to the sasabonsam.

This was what he thought as the old man raised his arms. Suddenly lightning flashed from the old man's palms, jagged arcs of bright, actinic light burning the ghouls down until there was nothing left but their smoking legs, somehow still standing.

"Come," said the old man, "it is past time we leave this place."

✪

The two men stood on the border between Shomolu and Lagos's dark heart as the women and children gathered together what little was left of their lives. Around them the garbage fires still smoldered.

"You are a master of Surulere," Abiola whispered.

The old man chuckled. "Hardly. Dark things live in that district, perhaps darker even than the sasabonsam."

"But you entered Surulere and came out again."

"To save you, my young friend. To save you. You might say I've had my eyes on you."

"Like Babafemi Kosoko," Abiola said bitterly.

The old man's eyes crinkled with amusement. "Not exactly. Though, I, too, admire your skills."

"Why have you been following me?" Abiola asked, the words a threatening rumble from deep within him.

"Abiola means, 'born in honor,'" said the old man softly. "Maybe I wanted to see if that name suited you."

Abiola turned that over in his mind for a minute. Then he said, "Who are you?"

"My name is Obi Akinlaja. I am a shaman, a master of Yoruba magic, of juju. I follow the old ways."

He turned and pointed at the dark stillness that was Surulere. "That may be Africa's future. Death. Evil. Darkness." He shook his head. "But not if good men and women will stand against it. I am putting together a team to run the shadows. I can't promise you it will be safe. But I can promise you it will be *right*."

Abiola glanced at the two women and six children picking at the broken remnants of their lives. They were homeless and heartbroken and terrified. But they were also *alive*.

He had done that, him and this funny old man.

Abiola's throat suddenly tightened with emotion. After plunging into despair and desperation he'd come out with a prize he'd never expected.

Hope.

He reached forward and enclosed the shaman's tiny hand in his. ✪

IN MEMORY OF

BY BRADLEY P. BEAULIEU

Bradley P. Beaulieu is a SpecFic writer who figured he'd better get serious about writing before he found himself on the wrong side of a lifelong career in software. His story, "In the Eyes of the Empress's Cat," was voted a Notable Story of 2006 by the Million Writers Award. Other stories have appeared in Realms of Fantasy, Writers of the Future, Orson Scott Card's Intergalactic Medicine Show, *and several DAW anthologies. He lives in Racine, Wisconsin, with his wife, daughter, and two cats, where he enjoys cooking spicy dishes and hiding out on the weekends with his family. For more, please visit www.quillings.com.*

I'd been in the noisy kafé with my handler for nearly an hour when a yellow alert flashed along the right side of my vision. A quick acknowledge of the alert produced an AR popup showing that someone in the kafé had been caught observing my conversation one too many times. I couldn't see him, so I tapped into the camera feed from my Toy Poodle, Skittles, who was sitting in her carrying bag on the chair next to mine. The superimposed feed showed a tall, unassuming Aboriginal in a threadbare suit, sitting alone at a table near the corner. I rewound Skittles' feed—the histogram geography of the business district and the curving grace of Sydney Harbour Bridge panning in time with the slow rotation of the kafé—and found that he'd come in nearly an hour ago, a few minutes after I'd arrived.

Despite the tetched-grandmother persona I wore for the benefit of Sydney's sprawl, I was careful when it came to business, and took things like this seriously. My handler, a young elf with delusions of self-importance, caught my mood and stopped subvocalizing immediately. I tapped on the table three times in a place only he could see. Though our business wasn't quite complete, he immediately nodded and stood, saying he'd see me next Thursday, which meant he'd contact me again in a few weeks.

As he left, I masked my discomfort by breathing in the scent of my steaming mug of kaf while studying a chiphead sitting at a nearby table. Then, using the Resonance that had been with me since the crash, I reached out and probed the walls around the Aboriginal's PAN. My eyebrows rose, though I quickly brought my mug up to my lips and slurped to cover the mistake. His walls were *good*—not state-of-the-art, but close, and not at all what I expected from a guy who looked like he'd just dragged himself in from the outback. I might have been able to crack it, but as closely as he was watching me, as ready as seemed to be for such a thing, he would have sensed it.

Skittles captured his vitals using the instruments clustered in her skull, and I sent them to an identification service I paid more than just a little to use. It usually returned a positive match that was ninety-eight percent accurate within a second, but this time it took nearly five, and when it *did* return, it gave me something I'd never seen before: a non-match, which meant that the government and most, if not all, of the corps would have no idea who this guy was. It did, however, give probable indications that he hailed from the Northern Territory, perhaps the Tiwis—with some Western European ancestry thrown in for good measure.

I had two choices: call in the security firm I kept on retainer or invite this bloke over. Had he been a random gawker, I would have just ignored him and left, but it was clear he'd been hoping to find me here in this my favorite kafé, and I'd be damned if I'd give it up without a fight.

Moments after I sent him a polite request to join me, he picked himself up, wove through the crowd, and sat across from me. His skin was the color of moist earth, and his hair was wild, going in all directions. His clothes—twenty years behind the times—smacked of someone consciously trying to look like a dreg, but strangely enough his smile, pleasant but knowing, made it seem like he knew I would see through it, and that he didn't care if I did.

No, it wasn't that he didn't *care*. He had *wanted* me to understand that not all was as it seemed. He would have been disappointed if I *hadn't* noticed. And that was when I realized then that this was a much more dangerous situation than I'd given it credit for.

He had an open channel into his PAN for subvocal communication, so I patched in.

Have a name? I asked while a waitress with glowing red piercings sprinkled all over her face poured me a refill.

Macquarie will do. You're Mav?

I nodded, smiling politely at the name he'd given—Macquarie was the most common alias for Aussie clients who wished to remain nameless, the equivalent of Mr. Johnson in the UCAS. *What can I do for you, Mr. Macquarie?*

He sat forward in his chair, looking at Skittles with a pleasant smile on his face. Before I could stop him, he had reached out to scratch Skittles' ear through the holes in her carrier. Skittles bared her teeth and snapped, and Macquarie snatched his hand back, frowning and shaking his finger. He pulled a napkin from the table's dispenser and used it to staunch the wound.

She doesn't like strangers much, I said.

He glanced at Skittles, frowning at the red blotch on the otherwise white napkin. *I have it on good authority you're the one I need to talk to.*

Whose authority?

He leaned back into his black plasteen chair, gripping his finger, silent.

I can find out, I said.

Perhaps, but by then our dealings will be done.

What makes you think they're not done already?

He paused, glancing at the crowd over my shoulder. *All I need is a simple data drop.*

Not my cup of kaf...

I pay well.

Money I've got. Not strictly true, but it wasn't something he needed to know.

Then perhaps the target will interest you.

I waited—my expression appropriately blank—as dozens of nearby conversations washed over us.

Cylestra, he finally said.

And why would Cylestra interest me?

Cylestra has the largest database of Tamanous agents south of the equator.

I prided myself on maintaining my composure, especially during negotiations, but I found my eyes thinning at what he was suggesting. And I saw within *his* eyes a look of hunger. He knew he had my interest. Clearly he also knew that my second husband had been taken by a Tamanous ghoul nearly thirty years ago. Liam had gone to Adelaide for a sales conference. He hadn't shown up on the second day. The search for him began in earnest on the fourth, and on the fifth they'd found him floating in the Myponga Reservoir south of Adelaide, missing one lung, both kidneys, and his liver. He'd had a bad heart or they might have taken that, too. I'd married twice since then—divorces, both of them—but Liam's death still haunted me.

I realized my jaw was clenched so tight my molars ached. That Macquarie knew this about me was disturbing. Combine that with the fact that he had the capacity to obtain an encrypted tunnel into one of the better guarded biotech corps made the situation frightening, and I'd always told myself that if my alarms were going off, they were going off for a reason, and I'd better listen.

Skittles had started barking—she'd always been a good pooch that way. I shushed her and said, "That's all right, girl. We were just leaving." Without another word, I broke my connection with Macquarie, picked up Skittles' carrier, and left the kafé, taking the transparent pedestrian tube that curved down and around the building toward street level.

Shortly after we joined the flow of busy morning traffic, Skittles resumed her barking, and I saw in my AR overlay that she thought the situation dangerous enough that she had activated the tranq gun hidden inside her throat. I brought up Skittles' video feed and found Macquarie forcing his way through the crowd toward us. I sent a command to Skittles that forced her to calm down—dealing with the fallout of a tranq was sometimes more trouble than it was worth—but I *did* prime a signal to SkySec that if not defeated within one minute would result in a security team being dispatched.

Macquarie ran in front of me and blocked my path.

I nearly let Skittles shoot him. But there was something in his eyes, a desperation that hadn't been there before. His heart rate was up; so was his breathing. He was pinging my subvocal channel over and over, pleading for a new tunnel.

He was truly worried. It had been a bluff inside, an act, something to get him in with someone bigger than he was used to dealing with.

I should have kept walking—I should have—but in the end I was curious about him, about his story. What had driven him into the sprawl to find me? What wrongs did he hope to right? And who stood to get hurt once the scales had been balanced?

Why Cylestra? I asked after reopening the channel.

He shook his head. *I'm not paying you for that.*

You're not paying me anything, as I recall.

The database means nothing, then?

I bit back my reply. *You could get anyone to use an open tunnel. Why me?*

There can be no traces of the drop. I can't leave this to an amateur.

Since the moment I'd heard the word *Tamanous* in the kafé, my mind had been feeding me memories of Liam I'd long since thought forgotten—the brain had a funny way of squirreling those things away and bringing them back when they were the most unwelcome. In my thirst for revenge, I'd contacted over a dozen shadowrunners, paying

them what little I made to search for his killers. They'd found nothing. All of it had been wasted money. Then came the crash of '64
and along with it my newfound gifts as a technomancer. What I had
viewed as a blessing quickly became a curse as I failed to master even
the simplest of techniques to manipulate the Resonance I could feel
all around me, every minute of every day. It seemed like the harder
I tried and the more I focused upon my goal, the further away it became. After several frustrating years, the anger became too much to
bear, and I gave it all up.

In the months that followed, without even trying, my abilities
began to soar. I'd taken it as a sign that searching for Liam's killers
was, in the grand scheme of things, fruitless. Strange that now, when
I thought I'd finally managed to leave all of it behind, an opportunity
to exact some revenge was presenting itself. *Karma at work*, I told
myself.

A troll shouldered his way through the tunnel, nudging both me
and Macquarie aside. Skittles barked at his retreating form.

Will you do it? he asked.

Give me the key and the package.

The tunnel's good for another three days, he said while transferring
the data through a secure socket.

Come to the kafé in two days, and I'll let you know how it went.

He nodded, a curious look on his face, and then he turned and
walked away, moving through the crowd as if he'd been living in the
sprawl all his life.

Before I lost sight of him, I tagged him and sent a request to Sky-
Sec, who in addition to straightforward security dabbled in surveillance—they leased time from the city's traffic cameras for just this
purpose. With any luck, I'd know where Macquarie was holing up by
the end of the day.

✪

I returned home and released Skittles from her carrier. She circled
around the room several times before jumping up to the beaten
brown chair she'd long ago claimed as her own. She barked several
times—no doubt still excited from all the goings on—before finally
settling into the familiar curves of her hopelessly matted pillow.

No sooner had I sat down on a recliner and ordered the windows to shutter themselves than I received a message from SkySec:
they'd lost Macquarie. I sent back a request to provide details—I

needed to know how he could do such a thing—but my hopes were small that a useful answer would ever be returned. The pretty penny I paid every month was worth it, but SkySec was not known for value added service.

After swiveling the chair away from the windows, I reclined and gave my aching knees a rest. It was time to find out what I could about this deal.

I was curious about the Trojan, but given how Macquarie had lost SkySec, the possibility of finding out more about him was simply too tempting, so I decided to have a little look-see before getting down to business. I knew a probable place of origin, and I knew he had a beef with Cylestra, so that's where I began.

It was at times like this, when I was physically tired but mentally curious, that the Resonance called to me most strongly. Sometime I found myself having to fight the urge, but now, luckily, I could simply let it take me. And it did. The reality around me shifted, and though there was a brief moment of reorientation, it quickly felt like I belonged there, perhaps more so than the physical world. There, I was *part* of the world, and it was a part of me. I was not bound by the frailty of my form, nor the aches and pains that had collected like driftwood along the shore. Here, I was free to go where I would, unfettered.

I bent myself to my task, sifting through tera after tera of news releases, images, blogs, vlogs, memory uploads. I took each of them and played them against the others, building the pieces of the puzzle first and then, one-by-one, piecing them together until the picture began to form.

Finally, twelve hours after entering, I found it.

Eight years ago, an Aboriginal girl named Sindala Hendesa had, with the consent of her parents, joined a drug trial to restore her failing kidneys. It was a process that was advertised as costing half as much as growing a new one, and since it was a final-phase trial, it was subsidized and would cost them even less. Cylestra was administering the program through a loosely veiled partnership with the Northern Territory government.

Bathurst, and especially Sindala's village, was not wealthy. The doctors were subpar, as was the nearest hospital, which was where Sindala would have been taken had the Cylestra medical team not offered their services, so it was natural that Sindala's parents would jump at any small increase in their daughter's chances. The treatments continued for several months, and Sindala showed signs of improvement.

But then there was a reversal. Sindala's organs—not just her kidneys—began growing at an alarming rate. By the time they decided to drop her from the program, her lungs had enlarged by thirty percent; her heart was twice as large as it should have been, and her kidneys had tripled in size. Within another few months, many of the subjects began experiencing similar issues, forcing Cylestra to abandon the trial altogether. Shortly after, Cylestra simply picked up and left, side-stepping the repeated requests for follow-up visits.

Sindala's father, of course, was my Mr. Macquarie—real name, Koorong Hendesa—and her mother was Allora. As Sindala's health deteriorated, Koorong and Allora fought in the courts for Cylestra to pay for new organs. Their lawyer, one of the few that would agree to take on a small-stakes claim against a Double-A corp, tried to argue that the side effects were much more damaging than had been accounted for in the initial discussions with the Hendesas. The judge, in the end, ruled for the plaintiffs, but it was a sham—the Hendesas were awarded the exact sum of money they had paid to Cylestra, an amount that would fail to even dent the mounting bills and future treatments that Sindala would need.

After the trial, with Koorong and Allora's savings drained, the village chipped in, but they could afford little more than an ancient dialysis machine.

Sindala died two months later.

An alarm from the lobby of my apartment complex broke my train of thought. I tapped into the intercam and found Koorong speaking feverishly into it.

"Please, Mav, let me in, we need to talk." He pressed on the button for my apartment feverishly. "Mav—"

"I don't appreciate clients following me home, Koorong."

He paused at the use of his real name. "Can I come up?"

I let him in, and a minute later he had reached my apartment on the 132nd floor. He gave Skittles a look of consternation that I couldn't quite interpret. Perhaps the bite earlier...

"We have to leave," he said, "Now."

Skittles measured an extremely high heartbeat from him, and I could tell just from the sound of his breathing that he was anxious.

"What's happened?"

He glanced back at the door, then Skittles, and finally back to me. "I'll explain it all later. But please—"

His eyes widened as he looked over my chair to the windows beyond. Shadows were playing among the shutters—something large obstructing the sunlight. The entire apartment was soundproofed, but there was the telltale whine of jets could be heard.

I triggered the windows to drop their shields. The kevmesh armor shot downward from its recessed compartment above the windows, fast, but not fast enough.

Guns opened fire, stitching bullets across the apartment. The windows shattered, spraying glass over the confined space. The whine of the jet engines became suddenly and overwhelmingly loud. Bullets stitched a trail across the wall, in a heartbeat eating up the distance from the yellow acacia in the corner to Skittles' chair.

I had already begun rolling to the floor, but before I could even touch the carpet I felt something burn along my upper thigh and then my backside. Then something hotter than I had ever felt in my life bored deep into my lower torso. As the shields finally slammed into place, I looked down to find blood welling from a hole in my gut, not the bright red one saw against their skin after a small cut, but blood of the dark and deep and deadly variety. I knew just from looking at it that I would soon slip into shock, but that knowledge seemed to slow time down, seemed to sharpen my senses, not deaden them.

Koorong was on the floor, looking at me with wide eyes and a worried face as bullets tore viciously into the shielding. Skittles was barking and running around in a circle. She nipped at Koorong's arm until I found the presence of mind to call her away.

The guns ceased firing, bringing a relative silence, but the change in volume felt deadly because it made me think that the only reason they had stopped was that something more powerful was on its way. Koorong must have sensed this as well, because instead of tending to my wound he moved behind me and picked me up under the armpits and dragged me toward the front door.

We made it halfway before an explosion tore through the shielding. The armor did not completely give way, but it was close. Fire rolled across the apartment, the force of the blast threw us backward.

Koorong was up again in a moment, dragging me, though not nearly as quickly as he had moments ago. Still, we made it out into the corridor as the second blast came in. Skittles followed us, flames and smoke licking at her heels. The door slammed shut with an almighty boom and bowed outward, but it held. *It'd better hold*, I thought in a moment of insensate humor, *or I'd be asking for my money back*.

The heat of the wound in my side had ebbed, replaced by a cold, tingling sensation in my fingers and cheeks and nose. When we made it to the lift, Koorong pressed the button marked 150 instead of the one that would take us to the lobby.

"Where are we going?" I asked.

Ignoring my question, he pulled up his pant leg. Underneath was a simsilk leg sheath with a myriad of small pockets. From one of these he took a yellow wad of sticks and mud, which he squeezed tightly in one hand. The thing cracked and popped like miniature fireworks. He pulled my shirt up and placed the balled up wad onto the wound, and like a spider unfolding its legs, the thing expanded until it covered the wound completely.

Skittles, surprisingly, only watched.

The wound began to burn white, blazing hot. I stifled a scream as he repeated the process on the other side, where the bullet had exited—or was that where it had entered?

I passed out momentarily.

When I woke, he was dragging me up the stairs that led to the roof's access door. Normally it would be secured, but for some reason it opened for him.

Skittles launched herself past him.

"Come back, girl." My voice was weak, and Skittles paid me no mind.

Outside, it was dusk. The sun seemed to have broken into a galaxy of lights that lay golden against the landscape of the sprawl.

"Where are we going?" I asked again, unable to form a more coherent thought.

Koorong pulled me to the edge of the building, mumbling words under his breath as the immensity of the sprawl came into full display beneath us. I grew dizzy.

The whine of the jets intensified. They knew we'd escaped to the top and were coming after us. Skittles was barking so fiercely I thought she might damage her voice box. Koorong pulled me up to the lip of the building as the jet's roar increased sharply.

I glanced over my shoulder and saw, cresting the edge of the building, a four-engine tilt-wing with a cluster of serious looking weapons fixed to the belly. Within the partially mirrored surface of the cockpit's windshield were two pilots, one sitting higher than the other.

Then they were lost from view, for Koorong had taken a step forward, pulling me with him. We fell, slowly it seemed to me. I looked up and saw Skittles, looking down, barking madly, the transparent blue concrete at the edge of the building ablating from a hail of bullets striking it.

"Skittles!"

No sooner had I said her name than she was whisked off the building and into the air. She followed us down as the wind began to roar. In my terror I thought the sound was due to the speed of our descent, but it soon became clear that the airstream was rushing upward so quickly that it was slowing us down. Then it was *carrying* us.

We began slipping sideways, at a slightly downward angle, through the byways of the sprawl, passing building after building as the people inside them stopped and stared. We went two klicks in less than a minute, Skittles floating close behind us, silent for once.

We came down near a small park. The pain in my abdomen returned as we fell to the ground. Koorong lay next to me, panting heavily in between hard coughs. Despite the wind, he was sweating profusely. Skittles hobbled over—she'd picked up a severe limp, though whether it was from a stray bullet or the landing I didn't know—and began licking his forehead until he defended himself.

And then I passed out for good.

○

I awoke in a Spartan room with strips of lights running along the ceiling. I was lying on a gurney. Every part of me ached—the bullet wounds especially, but they were less painful than I would have guessed. I tried to access the net, but failed. Already my skin was beginning to crawl at the realization that I could not feel the Resonance. I tried to reassure myself, reasoning that we were in an insulated bunker of some kind, but this did nothing to calm my growing sense of anxiety.

I turned my head and saw a cage in the corner of the room. Skittles was inside, but for some reason I couldn't sense her through my normal connections.

"Skittles?" I said, hoping she would wake.

She didn't move, and my heart sank.

"Skittles, dear?"

Then she did move, though it was slowly, as if she'd been sorely wounded. As she stared through the wires of the cage, a great sense of relief washed over me.

"There, there, girl—"

I stopped as the sound of an opening door echoed dimly into the room. The click of footsteps came softly at first, growing louder. I turned my head, that simple motion painful. Against the far wall was a hallway that took a shallow angle up and into the darkness. Koorong stepped into the light with an unreadable expression on his face. I wished Skittles' sensors were working. I felt naked without them.

"How long has it been?" I asked.

"Nearly a day, but the sedatives I gave you should have kept you under for at least another twelve hours."

"Where are we?"

He paused. "We're safe."

"That's not what I asked."

He pursed his lips, and the chocolate skin over his eyebrows furrowed. "For now that's the best I can offer."

"Then tell me this, or I'm getting up and hobbling out of here. How did Cylestra know I was investigating them? I hadn't so much as touched the tunnel *or* the packet you sent me. I was only searching for information about them, about you, passively."

He glanced toward Skittles. I followed suit, my eyes thinning, an uncomfortable feeling forming in my gut. "What did you do to my dog?"

"She'll be fine."

"Tell me!"

"It's a virus, low level, innocuous. It gathers information and transmits it to my wife, in the Matrix."

I thought back to the kafé, when Skittles had bit him. He had done that on purpose, and I'd completely missed it. "Why?" I asked. "Why monitor *me*?"

"It's well known what you can do."

I shook my head. "I gather data, for the right people, for the right price. How's that going to get your daughter back?"

His face screwed up in anger. "I'm not trying to get her back, I'm trying to make them pay!"

"What's that got to do with me?"

"Allora needs to know how you do the things you do."

"There are dozens of technomancers around Sydney."

"You're more than a simple technomancer, and you know it."

"You think she can learn what I know in a few hours?"

"No." Koorong began pacing across the cold concrete floor. "We've been studying you for months. We learned much by simply watching, and even more during the hours Skittles was feeding her data. She only needs the last few pieces of the puzzle."

"What can she possibly hope to do with it? I *read* data."

"It is by knowing how data is read that data can be planted." His face grew angrier as he talked. "Allora will take Cylestra down, bit by bit, brick by brick, until there's nothing left."

"And the Tamanous list?" I asked, thinking of Liam. "Does it even exist?"

"It might." He seemed to deflate as he spoke. "I don't know."

I tried to sit up, but the bullet wound flared like a red-hot iron. It was only pain, though. I sat up, grunting through gritted teeth as stars danced before my eyes. I nearly fell back, but managed to prop myself up, breathing heavily, sweat tickling my brow and armpits.

"Please, lie down. It's not safe to move yet."

"I'm leaving, and I'm taking Skittles with me." Despite those words, I didn't move. I couldn't. I knew I would simply fall if I made it to the concrete floor; I certainly wouldn't make it to Skittles' cage. *Maybe in a few minutes*, I told myself.

"Even if you could leave—which you can't, not like this—I need you. This isn't over."

"I'm not helping you anymore."

His expression hardened. "My wife is in danger because of you, and you're going to help get her out of it."

"*I* placed her in danger? Who fed that poor excuse for a Trojan to my dog? Who thought transmitting from my apartment directly to Cylestra's intranet was a good idea?"

"You had me *followed*. Two of Cylestra's sister corps have people inside SkySec. They must have run a search after sensing the incoming trace."

"How does that place Allora in danger?"

"Because I went to see her! I'm fortunate I masked myself halfway there, but they'll find her soon. We have to go to her. You have to show Allora what you do, so she understands completely."

I took shallow breaths to stave off the dizziness as rage boiled within me. I was angry not because Koorong had fooled me—I'd been fooled before and I'd be fooled again—it was because I'd fallen for such simple bait. I had jumped at the chance to avenge Liam's death too quickly. You never get what you pay for when the price is too cheap.

As I gripped the edge of the gurney, my knuckles aching, I found myself thinking less about Liam and more about Allora. She was a woman who had lost her child. Liam and I had never had children, but I was sure that if I had, and I'd lost her to a corp, I'd bloody well be trying to do something about it. And it wasn't just about Sindara.

It was bigger than that. Cylestra was multinational. How many others had found a similar fate to Sindala? Dozens? Hundreds?

Koorong had an expectant look on his face. He knew—or had a good idea—that I would agree to help, even after his duplicity. Was I really that transparent?

I supposed I was. "Where is Allora?" I asked.

"Not far."

✪

I watched as Koorong melded into the surface of the graffiti-covered wall behind him. He was still there, just camouflaged, but the effect was so successful that standing only a meter away I could hardly detect his outline. He claimed it would work for both of us, and as long as he was able to concentrate, it would be enough to get us inside Blaxland Heights, a massive tenement project on Sydney's southwest side, without being seen by cameras. Indeed, when I looked down I couldn't see my own hands, even when while wiggling them.

Ready? he asked subvocally.

I checked the Blax's meager security system again. Allora had created several back doors, and Koorong had given me the keys. The path we'd be taking was populated, but by nothing that would cause any alarm.

Ready, I said.

We padded across the street toward a courtyard that sat below the fifty-story complex. I could still feel the bullet wounds, but barely. The yellow wads had taken a while to kick into full gear, but they had healed my injuries to the point that the skin had closed over with bright pink scar tissue.

Skittles—also covered by Koorong's spell—followed close behind us. I'd disabled her barking except for the direst of emergencies. I had nearly left her in Koorong's underground safe house, but had found that I couldn't. She'd been my most steadfast friend for the last twelve years, and it felt too strange going without her. I would actually think about her *more* if she wasn't with me, which would only lead to mistakes.

We wove through a steady stream of traffic until finally passing through the entrance. What met us was a gallery that was probably meant to be impressive, but its grandeur was dimmed by the half-filled stores that lined each side and the smells of disinfectant that could not quite mask the scent of decay. As we walked, avoiding the traffic of Blax's mishmash crowds, the sights and sounds of in-your-face AR marketing clashed with what was once a stark and under-stated interior.

We headed in nearly two klicks—taking turn after turn and esca-lator after escalator up through the alternating clusters of strip malls and domicile-hives—until finally reaching a massive atrium whose dirt-caked windows ten stories above served only to make things gloomier. We had gone halfway through the atrium, skirting a group of chipheads sitting in a circle on the synthsteel floor, when an alarm from Blax's northern end flared within my AR display. I had tweaked Blax's system to trigger a low-level alarm for anything or anyone that seemed out of the ordinary, and further filtered it to trip a higher-level alarm for corporate-type squads, and finally a third if Cylestra or any of her sister corps were sensed. This alarm was the highest priority.

They're here. No sooner had I subvocalized the words than my feed to Blax's security system was cut off.

My heartbeat quickened. Of the seven hired samurai we had spaced around the complex, I triggered four to go after the pair of trolls and half-dozen men that had entered Blax's northern end. The others I kept in reserve in case Cylestra had sent in more than one team.

We continued to the edge of the atrium and took the lift to the thirty-seventh floor, our camouflage finally fading away on the ride up. When we exited, Skittles began barking fiercely. Before I could shush her, the rattle of gunfire broke out somewhere far below. We turned a corner and rushed down a dimly lit hall to an apartment as screams and a small explosion shook the air.

Skittles, sticking her head out between two of the nicked bars of the atrium railing, picked up three of our samurai beating a quick retreat into the open space below.

Things had gotten worse much faster than I'd anticipated. I sum-moned the remaining samurai to assist, hoping they could catch Cylestra's men off guard—though with the amount of preparation the enemy had already shown, I knew that hope to be slim.

We ducked inside the apartment, and Koorong immediately tapped a sequence on a holopad inside the door. The space was very cramped, but it otherwise looked like it belonged somewhere far, far away from the sprawl. The walls were a rich, earthy gold, and the room had been decorated with Aboriginal masks and pottery and ornate, dried flower wreaths. And it smelled ... like nature. It was jarringly at-tractive after the stark, gray labyrinth of Blaxland Heights.

We rushed down a hallway to a bedroom, and there, lying on a gurney not unlike the one I had found myself on only hours before, was Allora. I knew that she was two years younger than Koorong, but she looked at least a decade older. Her cheeks were sunken, and her skin was a sickly shade of brown. Her eyes rested deep in their sockets, and though the pictures I had found of her on the net had shown a healthy young woman, *this* Allora was grossly thin.

Hurry, Koorong said as he pulled a heavy, rolling tripod from the closet. Mounted upon the tripod was a heavy machine gun. He locked the wheels and lowered the gun until it was horizontal, and then he nodded toward Allora meaningfully, almost angrily.

I searched for her PAN, but found nothing. I scanned her form and found a wired connection leading to an old, reliable Renraku hub.

She's hardwired?

Koorong looked at me, confused for a moment, but then a look of horror and understanding came over him.

I'll have to go through Blax's WAN.

His eyes widened, and his gaze darted between me and Allora several times. *You said it yourself, they have control over it now.*

I sat down in a synth-leather chair with permanent depressions in the cushions. *Can't be helped.*

Another explosion sounded, much closer than I would have thought.

"Go!" Koorong said out loud as he trained the barrel of the machine gun on the door.

I leaned back and connected to the WAN.

I was immediately assaulted by a prehensile arm emanating from a massive, floating piece of IC. The thing was like a god of the seas from eons ago, black with hundreds of tendrils wavering in an unseen wind, all of them ready to strike. It lashed out again and again, but I had learned more than a few tricks in my time and wouldn't be caught so easily.

I sent out several paladin sprites in the next few milliseconds, and while the IC was deciding which of those to attack, I tethered several of its arms to the one of the paladins, forcing it into a regressive loop that would take precious seconds to unravel.

At the same time, I activated the encrypted tunnel to Allora. Immediately, and for the first time, I could feel her. She was indeed hidden deep within the maze of Cylestra's net, and she was fighting to remain hidden, for it was clear that Cylestra was now digging recklessly in order to find her.

I probed, hoping to create a stronger connection with Allora, but every time I did Cylestra's IC whipped its arms toward me. Only by feinting and launching more paladins was I able to keep them from striking home.

But then something changed. An alarm had been raised, and all proximal firewalls flared red, limiting traffic to secure channels only. I'd anticipated that, but the IC had activated an enhanced sniffer subroutine. The IC—even with the sniffer—wasn't good enough to catch me if I was careful, but it was more than adequate to make sure I remained separated from Allora.

I was growing desperate. The squad Cylestra had sent would reach the door any moment, and if I reached out to Allora in any significant way, the sniffer would find us both. I tried again and again, using all the complex forms I had learned over the years, but none of it was working.

At the back of my mind, I sensed an alarm from Skittles. The squad had broken through the door. I released the inhibitors that prevented her from launching tranq darts without my approval, hoping it would help Koorong, if only to a small degree. When I did so, I felt the telltale remains of Koorong's virus.

And that's when it struck me. The solution was crystal clear. The only thing I wasn't sure of was whether I had the time to do it.

Using Koorong's virus—a truly masterful piece of ware—as a model, I altered the sprites I'd used earlier. It was rushed, and I knew there were holes, but I only needed several good seconds. After adding some tracerouting, I released the paladins, moving as close to Cylestra as I dared. I could tell they'd found Allora, but had not yet been able to purge her from their systems. I commanded the paladins to ping loudly, forcing the IC to split its attention.

The dark and deadly arms turned and attacked. I nearly got caught in the initial onslaught, but was able to slip away as they fell upon the duplicates. Immediately I spread my awareness among the sprawl, pulling together the previous data I had earmarked regarding Sindara. I had not gone further at the time, thinking the other patients irrelevant, but I found more and more participants, building a case of circumstantial data that, when viewed as a whole, would paint a very uncomfortable picture of Cylestra's medical practices.

As I continued, I felt the data stream from me, through the paladins, and all the way to Allora. She was feeling everything I was.

I hoped it was enough. It would have to be, because the IC—even though it had nearly succumbed to Koorong's virus—had finally traced the signals back to me. It began boring through my defenses. The pain was worse than the bullet wound, for I felt it everywhere. It was nearly impossible to think, but I couldn't leave. Not yet.

I sent the information to all of the district attorneys that were responsible for the patients in Cylestra's kidney trials, and several more copies to the most independent news outlets I knew.

And then I dropped out.

I woke to the sound of rapid, heavy gunfire.

In front of me, a chromed up troll lay unconscious in the hallway, two darts sticking out of his neck, another from his right cheek.

Next to me, the rotating barrel of the machine gun stopped as the bullets ran out. Koorong glanced over at me, realizing I was back. "Is it done?" he asked while feeding another belt of bullets into the gun.

"I—"

My words were cut off as a stream of bullets tore into the room. Koorong's shoulder blossomed red, and he howled in pain. The gypsum board above me crumbled as I dove to the floor. The bullets stopped a moment later, and in the following silence I heard a series of sharp puffs as Skittles' dart gun fired.

The short burst of gunfire that followed ended with a horrible, high-pitched yelp. Moments later, there came the sound of a body falling heavily to the floor.

Koorong was silent. Unconscious. I searched for Skittles' signal, but the only response I received was a simple readout showing that nearly all of her systems had been destroyed but that the one of last resort—the thermite grenade tucked into her chest cavity—was active and waiting for the signal to detonate.

Two more sets of footsteps approached the entrance. They stepped into the forward room a moment later, their boots scraping noisily over the detritus of battle. There was a moment of silence: the men taking caution after so many had unexpectedly died.

The grenade's active status blinked in my readout, but I didn't think I could do it—didn't know if I could kill her, even to save myself—but the moment I saw the shadow of the first of them stepping into the short hallway leading to the bedroom, a fear so expansive welled up in my chest that I gladly grabbed for the chance Skittles was offering me.

I crab-walked into the corner, curled up into a ball, and gave Skittles the affirmative.

The grenade detonated a split-second later.

Even with my eyes shut tight, everything went white. The explosion was deafening. The shockwave pounded every part of me at once. Debris blew into the room and rained down for long moments, and I swear I felt the section of the building we were in sway back and forth.

As the sound of pattering debris filled the room, I slowly got to my feet and brushed away the powdery white bits of wall that had fallen over me. I coughed as I waded through the cloud, looking for Koorong.

I found him lying in the closet, dead, three bullets—red on white—stitched across his chest. I turned away immediately, unable to look upon him like that.

I turned to the gurney. Allora was still there, but when I touched her neck to find a pulse, I found nothing. I stared at her for long moments, feeling like a sister—in cause, if not in blood. Sadness welled up inside me and begged to be let out, but it was not something I could allow to happen. Not now. Not here.

I left the apartment quickly and wandered in a semi-random path toward the nearest exit from The Blax. I found no resistance. I hitched a ride on an old-style water ferry and took it to the north side of Sydney. Then I paid for a coffin hotel with anonymous cred. Several hours of sheer terror followed where I was sure I would be found and shot dead where I lay, but eventually it became clear that I wouldn't be followed. Not today, at least.

And finally, hiding in that small, darkened space, I allowed myself to cry.

❂

I didn't dare get a new SIN in Australia, and I didn't dare keep myself anywhere near Cylestra's sphere of influence, so I headed for Tokyo. I set up shop and began taking very simple jobs—data scrubbing and the like—and then one day I was sitting in a seedy bar drinking a truly horrible cup of kaf when a Japanese man in a black suit walked in and headed directly for my table. The look on his face as he wove through the tables was one of serious intent.

Seven months had passed since the devastation in Blaxland, but I knew immediately he was somehow connected to it. I hadn't had the heart to get another dog after Skittles. I *had*, however, picked up a gun. I reached into my purse, but before I could wrap my shaking fingers around the grip, the man slipped one hand inside his suit coat and pulled out a chip the size of a thumbnail. He set it carefully onto my table, then turned and left.

I grabbed the chip and held it tight in my fist. Only after the attention of the others patrons had returned to other things did I slip the chip into a reader inside my purse.

It contained, I found, a SIN. Fiona Douglass. Born within six months of me in Scotland. Her parents had moved to Brisbane when she was twelve, and after graduating early with a degree in datalytics, she'd moved around Australia—not surprisingly to many of the places I had been, both before and after Liam. I could tell already that it was a consummate job; Fiona Douglass had no doubt died recently, but I had few doubts that it would be difficult to tell that without speaking directly to people who'd known her.

I was now Fiona Douglass.

Before I knew it, tears were welling in my eyes. I sniffed and wiped them away, sipping the bitter kaf to camouflage the outward signs of my utmost joy.

Allora had made it. She hadn't died in that apartment in Blaxland, she'd jacked in. Permanently. A ghost in the machine.

I tapped into the net and began sifting—in an extremely passive manner—the history of Cylestra over the past few months. It was something I had avoided since leaving Australia, but with the arrival of this news it felt sufficiently safe to have a look. What I found was a series of events—communication leaks, misplaced orders, a downtick in sales—that made it clear that Cylestra was on a slow and steady decline toward a death of its own. Corps the size of Cylestra could not truly die; if it performed poorly for too long, it would be swallowed, in whole or in part, by another corp, but when that happened, Allora would be there. She would be absorbed as part of the merger, and she would hound the new corp until the biotech wing was deemed too inefficient to justify its continued existence. She would eventually, inevitably, exact her revenge.

After sitting back in my uncomfortable seat and savoring these realizations, I got up and left the bar.

It was time to get a real cup of kaf.

And then it was time to find a dog. ☉

FADE AWAY

BY STEVE KENSON

Steve Kenson's first published work for Shadowrun *was an essay in the second edition of* The Grimoire. *This led to writing the adventure "The Masquerade" in* Harlequin's Back *and working on over two dozen books, including* Awakenings, Magic in the Shadows *and* Portfolio of a Dragon. *Steve has written seven* Shadowrun *novels, including* Crossroads *and the first Kellan Colt trilogy, beginning with* Born to Run. *He maintains a website at www.stevekenson.com and a LiveJournal at xomec.livejournal.com.*

You move down the corridor confidently, not striding, because striding implies a sense of arrogance, not humble duty and responsibility. Still, it's a confidence born of power, of the certain knowledge you can handle anything that might come at you. You know—deep down—that you are up to the challenge, that you were born to be, made to be.

Although you are humble, this place is still beneath you. You step over loose piles of garbage in the hall with the barest sniff of disdain. The place reeks, the stench of human filth and misery is strong in your nostrils, almost threatening to choke you, but you push it aside. You flex your fingers inside their close-fitting, black leather gloves; feel the fine leather creak slightly, the steely strength in your tendons and muscles.

The background noise in the corridor is a mix of broadcast programs and sprawl music barely muffled by cheap, particleboard doors and sheetrock walls worn paper-thin. The noises coming from behind the door ahead and to your left are grunting, animalistic, matching the filth and desperation of this setting. They're tantalizing and disgusting at the same time. Is it distaste for them or for what needs to be done that wells up in your throat? Tasting the flat, metallic bile, you grab hold of it, turning disgust into anger into power.

[LOWER: EMO_TRACK]

Your booted foot blurs as it lashes at the door. You barely feel it as the jamb disintegrates from the strike, splinters of formerly glued wood-substitute flying. The flimsy chain on the inside tears off, still stubbornly holding onto the fragment of the frame it's firmly screwed into, as if to proclaim it is the weakness of the structure and not it that had led to this. Things seems

to drop into slow motion, and a part of you watches the splinters and fragments fly, detached, fascinated.

The door flies open, banging against the inside wall, but rebounding only slightly. You're inside before it can do so, the world around you moving so slowly you can pick out every detail. You savor it: the shocked, startled looks spreading across the faces of the man and the woman locked together on the ratty sofa against the wall, the man simultaneously pushing back with his arms to rise while reaching for the crumpled mass of clothing strewn on the floor. Vivid tattoos crawl along his muscled chest and arms: blue-green dragon scales, golden carp, there, between his shoulder blades, a blooming lotus.

Then you have him by the throat, lifting him off the woman, pinning him against the wall next to the couch. Cheap paint and sheetrock chip and crumple where his head hits. He has enough air to grunt once in pain before your fingers close his windpipe and he starts to choke. As if your hand was around her throat as well, a scream arrives stillborn from the woman's mouth as little more than a hiccup or faint yelp. She starts to move, but there's a gun in your other hand, and you level it back in her direction without even looking. The sounds of her movement stop and there's only a faint whimpering.

The man you've pinned glares at you with dark eyes, slight epicanthic folds betraying a mixed heritage that strikes a momentary chord of familiarity, but elicits no mercy or slackening of your grip. You watch with a certain fascinated detachment as a full range of emotions play across his face in just a few seconds: surprise and shock give way to rage at your intrusion, a furious desire to strike out at you, then puzzlement at the inability to escape your grip. Hands claw at the leather sleeve of your coat, feeling more like caresses through the thick material. Confusion starts to give way to panic, a desperate need for escape, for air. The man's face starts to redden. There's a slight ache along the length of your arm, but you savor it, the burning in your muscles as your grip remains, unrelenting, tightening. You do not look away, still aware of the faint whimpering from the couch behind you—gun leveled there—but no other signs of movement. The man's feet bang against the wall , just centimeters off the floor. Someone bangs back from the neighboring apartment and you stifle a laugh: are they hoping to quiet the noise or do they think they're playing a game? They might think it is more foreplay, and not the main event.

The tapping dance of his feet slows, then stops, the clawing at your arm grows feeble, then his arms fall, limp and helpless. His eyes remain locked on yours, but then start to glaze and roll back in his head as the struggles give way to nothing more than deadweight pinned against the *wall. You wait with a terrible patience, drawing out the silence that dares anyone to interrupt it. The only noise is the background babble of music and soundtracks from outside and a few last half-hearted thumps from the other side of the wall.*

When you release your grip, it's almost a surprise, like a spring un-coiling. The body drops limply to the floor, like a wet sack sliding down the wall. You lower your other arm for the first time, bringing the sleek, flat-profile pistol down to your side, and turn away from the dead man– knowing his fate with a cold certainty–back towards the woman on the couch.

It's as if you notice her for the first time. She's young, and still fairly pretty for a whore, her neo-Egyptian style makeup giving bold, dark em-phasis to her wide eyes and half-blood features, dark hair spilling loose and wild around her face. Again, a slight feeling of recognition stirs deep inside you, along with something else. She has managed to grab the soiled sheet covering the couch and pull it up to cover herself, although the half-hearted effort is largely forgotten in the spectacle that unfolded before her; one small breast peeks out around the edge of the fabric. The nipple is small, dark and still erect...

[PAUSE_PLAYBACK]

"Did you fuck her?"

"What?" Kage murmured, turning away from the dark rain-streaked window toward the figure lounging on the bed behind him.

"I said, 'did you fuck her?'" Tomashi replied with a sigh, punctuat-ing his words like he was speaking to a child or an idiot. It was a tone Kage found irritatingly familiar.

"I...no..." he said quietly, eliciting an exaggerated huff of frustra-tion from the other man, who slapped his hands down on the mat-tress for emphasis.

"It would have been better if you had fucked her," he muttered to nobody in particular. "That would have been hot. You could have taken her right there after you did him..."

"I didn't," Kage repeated, somewhat uselessly, "I..."

"Shut up," Tomashi countered without any real heat. "Don't spoil it. I still want to run the rest." But as he settled back against the pil-lows of the bed, Kage's commlink buzzed softly. He answered, eyes remaining on Tomashi who glanced over in idle curiosity.

"Hai," he replied to the clipped voice on the other end of the line. *"Hai."* Tomashi lifted himself up on his elbows, which emphasized his

slight but growing paunch, the look on his face making it clear he knew who was calling. Kage disconnected the line.

"Your honorable father—" he began.

"My honorable father can go fuck himself," Tomashi interrupted.

"He's here," Kage forced in, before his charge could go off on a lengthier rant.

"So?"

"He wouldn't care for..."

"You're right. He. Wouldn't. Care." Tomashi said. He produced a flat-profile pistol from under the pillows on the bed and made a show of checking the magazine and the slide, sighting along its length at nothing in particular in a corner of the room.

"Where did you get that?" Kage asked, already knowing the answer. The weapon was a familiar one. There was a cold knot in his stomach.

"Where do you think?"

"That's not a toy."

"Sure it is, just like you." He swung the pistol around to point in Kage's direction, causing the other man to fight down the urge to reach for his own weapon, holstered under his coat.

"Do *not* point that thing at me!" he said through clenched teeth, taking a fractional step towards the lounging Tomashi.

"Or what...? You'll kill me?"

Stepping in, grabbing the hand holding the gun faster than the eye could follow, pinning the wrist in a vice-like grip...

"No..." he said quietly. "No, but it's careless, and dangerous, not everyone has my... restraint."

Tomashi just laughed, slowly releasing the hammer of the gun and deliberately raising the barrel towards the ceiling before lowering it to the bed.

"Something to be said for going out in a blaze of glory," he mused, more to himself, looking longingly at the gun. "Better to burn out than to fade away."

If so, you're well on your way, Kage thought. Even if he was able to protect Tomashi from all outside threats, including the strong temptation to beat him within a nanometer of his life, he couldn't do anything to protect him from himself. A fascination with simsense programs had blossomed into a full-blown obsession, perhaps even addiction.

Tomashi had long since given up popular sims like *Shadow Super-Mage Talon* and *Ninja Slayer IX.* Even the so-called "California Hot" and "Kong Chips," with their barely legal signal levels and boosted emotional gains, were not enough to satisfy him. Tomashi was into what many called "real sim." It wasn't the pre-packaged, carefully edited programs sold in stores, recordings of staged events and the experiences of simstars, but raw "wet record" sims of real action, real events, of the kind of life he didn't have.

He tried a different tack: "Your father is concerned about you... and so am I."

"My father is concerned about his reputation and his legacy," Tomashi countered bitterly, "and you're paid to be concerned about me."

"No, I'm not," he countered, just as coldly, "and you know it."

"Sure you are. You're paid with your life, and your honor, and all those things you can do." He gestured vaguely towards his own head with the pistol he held in his hand, as if all those things were stored up there, which, in a way, they were. "I have a pretty good idea just how much all of your mods cost." He waved his free hand—and not the gun—in Kage's direction.

"I'm sure you do," he shot back, "especially..." but then a knock sounded at the door and Kage went to it, shooting the slightly younger man a penetrating look. It was a familiar routine and his duty gave him something to hold on to in situations like this. Out of the corner of his eye, he watched his spare pistol disappear beneath Tomashi's pillow. He'd have to deal with that later.

Even though they were as safe in the *oyabun*'s home as they could be anywhere, Kage approached the unknown behind the door like a possible threat. It was his job. He opened the door a fraction, his concealed hand hovering near his weapon.

"Yojimbo," the man on the other side said, and he bowed slightly in response.

"Kanaga-*san*," he replied neutrally, sliding the door open further for the *kobun* to enter the room, if he wished.

"The Chairman wishes to see you."

Kage wondered if he detected a hint of gloating in the *kobun*'s voice. He knew full well Kanaga was a traditionalist who did not approve of half-breed "samurai" guarding the *oyabun*'s son. He frequently criticized Chairman Shigeda's policies, in fact; Kage never understood why the *oyabun* tolerated him, but Kanaga was efficient, and the Chairman liked men willing to challenge him, to a point. Such tolerance was a part of the "New Way" Shiegada-*sama* and his organization espoused.

He bowed in acknowledgement of the message, as if delivered by the voice of the *oyabun* himself, and Kanaga turned and walked away from the door. Kage gave a quick glance back before he followed, but Tomashi was already settling back onto the pillows and restarting the sim-feed. He sighed, closing the door behind him as he left.

The room down the hall was the *oyabun*'s personal study, and sometime office, although he conducted little official business there. It was appointed in a lean, minimalist style enhanced by virtual installations. Displays, input devices, and other necessities could appear as needed via the oyabun's personal commlink and the other discretely hidden Matrix nodes in the room. Kage knew full well that he entered through an invisible web of scanning beams, tiny cams, and mics—every action observed and recorded. *Another typical night for me,* he mused somewhat bitterly. He was only grateful Tomashi hadn't thought to activate his sim-rig to record this as well.

The *oyabun* did not speak at first, leaving Kage standing just inside the panel doors as Kanaga withdrew and they whispered closed. Although they looked like traditional rice paper, they were actually a far tougher polycarbonate composite. The Shigeda-*gumi* was a progressive one, after all, and the Chairman (he preferred that title whenever possible) sought to blend old and new practices suited to the Sixth World. The virtual rendering decorating the wall opposite the windows was symbolic of this: based on the first famous commuter-captured photo of the Great Dragon Ryumyo in Japan, displayed across the Internet in the days just after the Awakening at the end of 2011. The iridescent dragon and the sleek bullet train were a contrast between the ancient and modern, the mythical and technological. The paired swords displayed on the polished wood credenza were replicas using modern carbon steel with monofilament diamond edges. The calligraphic wall scroll, on the other hand, was authentic, from the 1800s, as Kage recalled.

Chairman Shigeda stood in front of the window to the side of the room's low desk, arms clasped behind his back, looking out into the rain spattered darkness through the carbon-composite windows in a manner Kage found achingly familiar.

"My son," he began in a low, firm voice, "is not worthy of your efforts, Yojimbo."

"Shigeda-*sama*..." the *oyabun*'s hand went up, cutting off any further protest and indicating he was not looking for vain denials of what they both already knew.

"Still," he continued, as if not interrupted. "Tomashi is safe in your care. I know this. You were made to be his perfect companion and protector... as his mother wished."

His perfect plaything, Kage thought, but kept the comment to himself.

"Your service has been right and honorable, but my son has not followed your example as I had hoped. I must now send him away, and you with him."

Kage's head involuntarily lifted, eyes flicking toward the window. Fortunately, the other man had not turned around and did not see, focused on whatever images were there for him in the darkness beyond the glass.

Chairman Shigeda was a relatively young man for his esteemed position, and believed it was important to maintain appearances. He dressed in a Western fashion, in a dark, tailored suit with a cream-colored, perfectly pressed shirt and a handmade silk tie. His collar and cuffs were long enough to conceal the *irezumi,* the traditional tattoos he wore, and his black hair was neatly trimmed and styled.

Kage considered the contrast between them, dressed as he was in a flowing armored coat, even indoors, with the close-fitting dark clothes underneath made of modern armor-cloth blends. He wore serviceable combat boots rather than imported leather shoes, and was permitted not even the tattooing of a lowly initiate, as he could not be acknowledged as anything other than what he was: Not of pure blood, but with mixed Japanese and Western features. His head was shorn, for simplicity and utility, making him look much like a dark-clad, lethal Buddhist monk, sworn to follow his path for life.

They were a study in contrasts, and yet there were things in common: a strong set of jaw, the steady gaze, the proud carriage, if you knew what to look for.

"It will be easier for you to protect him elsewhere," the Chairman said, somewhat sadly.

"To protect him from what, Shigeda-*sama*? Is there a threat I should know about?"

"There is *always* a threat, Yojimbo, but yes, I have heard rumors. Others may move against me. When that happens, it would be best if Tomashi were elsewhere."

"Yes, Chairman," the bodyguard said with a bow. It was the only possible reply.

"Go and pack what you need. I will speak to my son alone. You will leave tonight."

"Yes, Chairman," he bowed deeply and backed out of the room, the doors whispering open behind him, then sliding closed, cutting off his last view of the study and the man he had served his entire life.

Yojimbo, he was called, "bodyguard," in the old Japanese fashion. It wasn't a name, merely a title, no different than calling a chair a chair or a sword a sword. Tomashi called him *Kage,* "shadow," his ever-present companion since he was allowed out of his mother's sight, his ever-present champion. *Kage Yojimbo,* shadow bodyguard. His life was lived in the shadows: the shadows of other men, the shadows cast by the *gumi,* the Shigeda clan.

His quarters were even more Spartan than the Chairman's study: just a sleeping mat, a wall cabinet for weapons and personal items, and a small, recessed closet. Necessary displays and the like were all virtual, projected via his headware and commlink as they were needed, although they rarely ever were in here.

There was little actual packing to do: Yojimbo kept necessities packed and ready to go at a moment's notice. Still, he welcomed the order as an opportunity to take a few precious minutes to himself to gather his thoughts more than his meager possessions. He would take his essential weapons, of course: the matched Fichetti security pistols with extra magazines, collapsible shock baton, the concealable ceramic and carbon fiber blade. The Chairman hadn't mentioned the need for heavy ordinance, or else he would have provided it. Besides which, Kage was his own best weapon.

You were made to be his perfect companion and protector... The Chairman's words were truth. Kage closed the door of the cabinet and looked down at his hand, flexing it slowly as if seeing it for the first time, feeling the power of the myomer-fiber enhanced muscles, the nano-composite laced bone. He recalled the middleman's throat, held in his vice-like grasp, dangling off the floor...

"Did you fuck her?" Tomashi asked. He recalled the woman, half-covered in the forgotten sheet, all her attention fixed on him, her dark eyes bottomless pools. He remembered the gun in her hand from underneath the sheet, how easily he took it from her, stepping in, grabbing the hand holding the gun faster than the eye could follow, pinning the wrist in a vice-like grip. He could have broken it with just a twist or a squeeze, could have pushed her down, but he didn't. She didn't beg for mercy or even look away, capturing his eyes with hers. She pressed the gun into his hand instead.

"You know what you have to do," she said, and it had taken him aback. Did she *want* to die? Her tone was different, haunted. Then he saw the neural socket behind her ear, the particular glimmer to her eyes. She was *bunraku,* a flesh-puppet, her brain wired with software to make her whatever fantasy her client wanted. Was it the software speaking to him, or the true woman coming through? His hand closed around his own Fichetti pistol, alone in his room, recalling how he had gripped the gun, taking it from her unresisting hand, and stepped back.

"Do what you have to do," she said in the same tone, not looking down or away for what seemed like a very long time. It was Kage who finally broke their gaze. He turned and walked out, leaving the woman behind. Tomashi was going to be disappointed, and worse, angry at him, not only for the witness he left behind, but for the opportunity he passed up to improve the "show" for him. But Kage found he didn't care.

"Your service has been right and honorable..." the Chairman had said, and hot tears stung the bodyguard's eyes. If only Shigeda-*sama* knew. He was as much a whore as that woman, as much a puppet for the entertainment of a spoiled child. The boy Shigeda's wife adored beyond all reason, the boy the *oyabun* indulged, the boy Kage swore to protect with his life's blood. With the sim-rig, Tomashi was inside of him, as surely as if...

The sound of the gunshot had Kage moving almost before he was aware of it, a lifetime of training taking over in an instant. As he ran down the corridor, pistol in hand, there came a second shot, then a third. He counted five by the time he reached the doors of the Chairman's study and they obediently slid open for him.

Shigeda-*sama* sat behind the low desk, blood spread dark across the front of his immaculate dress shirt, his face frozen in an expression of shock, mouth open, and eyes wide. He hadn't even had time to call out.

When the doors opened, Tomashi turned towards Kage, gun held before him like a talisman, twin of Kage's own.

"Do what you have to do," he muttered, finger tightening on the trigger as he raised the weapon. He jerked and the shot went wide when the bodyguard's first bullet took him in the eye, staggered back towards the desk, then sprawled across it when another shot hit him in the chest, then another. He was laid out in front of his father, gun falling from his nerveless fingers to the floor with a clatter. The older man's head was thrown back, mouth open, as if in mourning.

Time started again. Kage took in the bloody tableau for what seemed like an eternity, dimly aware of the sounds of alarm in the house, of people shouting and running. Then awareness opened like a flower blooming in his mind and he turned away, scooping up the fallen Fichetti and letting the panel doors close over the scene. It was more than just fortunate that he was packed and ready to go. It was providence.

"You will leave tonight," the Chairman had said. His words were truth.

❀

The design of the low desk in the Chairman's office was modern and Western, its dark glass surface a standard display and touch interface. Kanaga Sato brushed aside newsfeed windows and status reports with a flick of his fingers, scattering them like neon leaves as an incoming comm window opened from the dark depths of the glass.

"It is done?" a man's voice asked in Japanese, and the *kobun* nodded. "Good. Oversee the investigation. When the dust settles, you will have my support... Chairman-*san*."

"Thank you, Shotozumi-*sama*," Kanaga said with a slight bow toward the desk. The window closed, leaving only his reflection in the dark depths.

The slow smile spreading across the *kobun*'s thin-lipped mouth froze at the press of something cold and sharp against the side of his throat. He didn't turn around, barely moved except to slide his right hand slowly over...

"Don't," came the flat voice from just behind his left ear, the pressure on the blade increased just slightly. The hand stopped, hovering where it was.

"Yojimbo," Kanaga said quietly. "You're still here."

"Was I expected to run?" the bodyguard replied softly. "Was that how it was planned?"

"I don't..." the bladed pressed again, and he stopped, swallowed.

"I know this place better than anyone," Kage continued, "well enough to know how difficult it would be for an assassin to get in without help."

"Assassin?" Kanaga said in mock surprise. "Everyone knows what happened, or soon will. After all, *your* weapons were used in the killings. Tomashi..."

"Tomashi had his bad qualities," Kage said, "but one thing he could never do was stand up to his father. He wouldn't—couldn't—have done this on his own. He wasn't in his right mind when..."

"When you killed him?"

"When *you* forced me to kill him."

"How do you know I had anything to do with it?"

"I didn't, for certain, until just now. I only suspected." Kage's free hand touched the edge of the desktop, out of the corner of Kanaga's field of vision. "*Oyabun* Shotozumi-*sama* seemed pleased."

Kanaga swallowed slowly. "And now you're here for revenge?" he asked.

"No, answers."

"To what?"

"How... and why?"

"I think you know the second one already."

"Yes... I knew you were a traditionalist, Sato, but I never thought..."

"I would take action?"

"That you would betray the Chairman," he corrected.

"He is the one who betrayed *us*," Kanaga hissed through gritted teeth, "betrayed our traditions!"

"Oh?" Kage observed. "Like the tradition of using others as puppets? How did you get him to do it, Sato?"

"It wasn't hard," the kobun replied with a slight shrug. "You made it easy, in fact."

"I ..." Kage breathed, then sighed. "The sims."

Sato smiled without humor or warmth. "Yes. A subliminal program, a viral subfeed."

"That woman..."

"A puppet," he replied. "Like Tomashi... like you."

Kage recalled the woman's intense stare, the endless depths of her dark eyes, the signs she was *bunraku.*

"Why didn't it affect me?"

"The program needed to be compressed into a tightly contained data pulse to be transmitted by the carrier's corneal emitters. It only extracts and runs in the simsense playback, and even then only during direct experience of the wet record. You would have had to replay the sim, which, of course, there was no reason for you to do. If you had, it would have served just as well. Its effect is quite limited, but profound. Fortunately, it didn't need to last long. Once I found out about Tomashi's new 'hobby,' it seemed like a prime opportunity."

"You know what you have to do," she had said, pressing the gun into his hand. She hadn't been talking to him. He thought of Tomashi, reliving that moment as the invasive program unfolded and ran through his brain.

Kage pulled the knife away from Kanaga's throat slightly. His hand was shaking and he focused to steady it, and keep it from slashing across the steady pulse of the artery there.

"So," the *kobun* said with remarkable calm. "You have your answers. What now? The man you protected is dead. The man who employed you is dead, and the rest of his men know their place and will shoot you on sight. It's only a matter of time before they realize you're here, if they haven't already. You'll never leave here alive. Do you kill me now and go out in a blaze of glory?"

He stopped when Kage drew his pistol and leveled it at him, stepping around to the side of the desk, keeping his eyes—and his gun—fixed on Kanaga.

"I should kill you," he said. "In fact, honor demands it, does it not? But you were right about Tomashi's habit being an opportunity. I've had some time to think things over while waiting for you. For the first time in my life, I'm free of obligations, free of debts, and tired of being used. That's why the sim of *this* conversation is being transmitted and stored someplace safe." The new Chairman's eyes widened only slightly, but it was enough for a moment of understanding to pass between him and the former bodyguard. "If anything happens to me... I won't be the only one to go out in a blaze of glory. Sometimes it's better to just fade away."

He stepped back from the desk towards the doors of the study, and they slid open. Kage's eyes—and the unwavering gun barrel—remained locked on the man behind the desk until he was through them and they closed in front of him.

Sato immediately opened a new comm window on the desktop.

"Yojimbo has just left my... the Chairman's office," he told the man on the line.

"What are your orders, sir?"

"Let him go. He's nothing, and no one, now." The other man hesitated, confusion clearly written on his face, but only for a moment. He was trained to follow orders, not to question them.

"Hai!" he replied, nodding sharply. Sato closed the window and sat back in the chair, his own, rather than the one Shigeda died in. He would need to get a newer one, befitting his new station, he mused. He glanced out the darkened windows; the rain had stopped, although droplets of moisture still ran down the outside of the glass.

Fade away, then, he thought to the now nameless, masterless man headed out into that empty night. *Fade away, into the shadows.* ✪

BIG JAKE

BY DAN C. DUVAL

Dan C. Duval has published more than 20 short stories, including one in the DAW anthology Cosmic Cocktails *and another in the upcoming DAW anthology* Swordplay. *A grizzled veteran of the high-tech community, Dan is happy to be leaving the supercomputers to the younger people while he enjoys life on the Oregon Coast with his cats (who complain he does not pet them enough) and his horses (who complain that he rides them too often.)*

The Spirit drifted over to the curb and eased to a stop. Paulie was an excellent rigger and one of the few I would trust to remote me anywhere, especially after more than twenty years hiding out. You get used to not trusting anyone when you have been under the radar that long.

This was stupid, in so many ways, but when Donna—probably my daughter—got in touch and told me that my grandson—probably—had been kidnapped, what choice did I have? I might be—well, over fifty years old anyway, but I still hope to live enough years that I don't want any more regrets following me around.

And, God help me, I couldn't resist being John Wayne just once in my life.

Through the windscreen, I saw the shop at the corner ahead, the last shop open in this part of Seattle at this time of night. Some of the apartment windows above the shops were lit, but most were dark, meaning either early risers or a lot of empty apartments. The streets almost looked clean, shining with the rain that had been falling all day and had just given up, probably for a short breather before starting again.

As soon as I stepped out of the little three-wheeler, the clock would start. If the kidnappers were late or if the deal didn't go down quick enough, we would all have more problems than we were ready to deal with. 4th and Pine was not the most happening part of downtown, but all of my contacts combined still gave me no hope of being able to spoof all of the cams, sniffers, ears, and other possible stuff that could be scattered all over the place here.

My best hope was that popping up unexpected, in a city far from my normal haunts in my runner days, would give me enough time to get the swap made and get my grandson out of here, before Humanis goons overran the drop point.

Frankly, I was tempted to blow it all off when the call came from Donna, but then she knew she was taking a chance of blowing my cover by calling in the first place, and the need was desperate enough that she used the one-off code I'd given her, so it had to be serious and I knew, at least, that it was her and not anyone I really had to worry about. Made a trap at least a little less likely.

About the time I dropped off the face of the Earth, she was just starting at Ares, a development manager in some lab or another, doing something that she couldn't talk about, but she probably was my daughter, so I had to leave a contact point with someone in case some of my old friends needed me. In the bosom of Ares, she was about as safe as she could be from anyone trying to pry the contact info out of her. Besides, only my really good friends knew she was probably my daughter: my name didn't appear anywhere on any of her records, so if I hadn't told someone myself, they wouldn't know. I trusted my closest friends to keep the secret and, since I am still alive, they must have.

I took a deep breath and popped the hatch. As I stepped out, I started a clock in my head. Packets were doubtless already flying and it was only a matter of time before one of those packets hooked up with a spider out in the Matrix somewhere and a whole world of crap would descend from the sky.

OK, I chose the place. Donna gave me the contact info for the exchange. Fortunately, the people who took the kid were smart enough to realize Donna had no hope of getting around Ares security, so they were willing to allow a go-between and the fact that the go-between was an old man with the beginnings of a serious belly seemed to go well with them.

Of course, the picture I let them see wasn't really me. Facial recognition software would have tied my face to my name and that would have been the game.

I patted my jacket and tapped the various pockets in my cargo pants.

And they said cargo pants would never come back in style. OK, so they were right, but all those pockets were still useful for carrying stuff. I just hoped it was enough.

I stepped on the sidewalk as the Spirit pulled back into the street and disappeared into the night. Paulie would lose it out there somewhere for a while, long enough that I would hopefully be able to crawl back into a hole somewhere before anyone could use it to track me down.

I shuffled down the sidewalk as fast as I could. Less time on the street, the less packets maybe, but any one packet could be enough.

The door of the shop swung easily and I slipped inside.

Lou's Gear-Up was just that: if you had the money, Lou had the gear. Looked like the Radio Shack when I was a kid. Aisles of stuff, from pods to comms to scanners to spy gear to just about every sort of electronic toy you could imagine. Bright, overhead fluorescents and an above-average security system. Bars over the windows.

I was here a good fifteen minutes earlier than I had told the kidnappers. I had some business to take care of first.

The guy behind the glassed-in counter was nondescript, a nobody. Early middle age, starting to bald, rounding in the belly even faster than I was, his practiced, eager-bland expression offset by a shrewd pair of eyes that looked me over carefully and dismissed me as mostly harmless.

I pulled out a credstick and stuck it under the guy's nose.

"Ten K nuyen. Crank your ECM as high as it'll go." I didn't care. Wasn't my nuyen. Donna wasn't stupid: her first call had been to Ares Internal Security. I'd asked for a half-dozen 10K credsticks and the AIS chick I worked with didn't even blink as she handed them over.

Naturally, he immediately became suspicious.

"Relax, dude," I said, "A guy is going to show up here, we're going to talk a little, then we leave. I just don't want anyone listening in, 'K?"

The little wheels in his head cranked for several seconds before he reached under the counter, came up with a packet of cheap hearing aid batteries and slid them across the counter. The guy was pretty good at this, but not good enough to keep me from seeing him snatch the 10K 'stick from my hand, palm it, and drop a different stick into the cash drawer. Good enough for the security cameras in the store, though.

He rang it up and handed me a paper receipt that showed a purchase of a whole five nuyens. The paper was brown around the edges. Must have been in the machine for a long time. No one used credsticks anymore.

Just old fossils, like me.

The guy smiled and stepped down to the end of the counter, where he tapped on the keyboard of a pretty hefty old deck. Then he nodded at me.

I didn't put a lot of DMSO on that credstick, so the rohypnol would seep into his bloodstream slowly. If I timed this right, the guy wouldn't remember much of anything but, more importantly, wouldn't be inclined to get involved in anything that was about to happen.

With luck, that also wouldn't be much, but why risk any more complications than I already had?

"Where are the personal secretaries?" I asked.

The guy had a sort of dreamy look on his face when he drifted back to my end of the counter and tapped the glass over a half-dozen handhelds on the top shelf.

"Which ones are secure?"

His hand wavered a bit as he pointed out the three at the end. I may have given him a bit more than I'd wanted. I just hoped he wouldn't pass out before the deal was done.

Now, there was a chance that just upping the security on the place was enough to trigger warning flags someplace. A chance, but who knew what sort of skull gear the kidnappers would be walking in with?

Five minutes early, an elf walked into the shop.

Nasty-looking elf. No apparent gear but what did he have in his head? He was alone and, if this was the guy, he was supposed to be alone, at least while we were in the shop. Can't say the purple hair and subcutaneous LEDs were exactly inconspicuous, but he was an elf.

I'd been underground for years. What did I know about fashion?

"You the man?" the elf asked me.

"If you got the kid," I said, "I am."

"Yeah, I got the kid. You got the stuff?"

What this was all about was something that Ares had cooked up in one of their labs, just simple corporate espionage. I give them the files, they give me my grandson. As long as they didn't tweak to the kid being my grandson, things would be just fine and very businesslike.

'Course, I'd get a bonus from Ares if I managed to get the boy back without handing over the files. And another bonus if I found out who this bunch of faeries were working for. Priority was the kid, though. Donna had apparently become pretty important to Ares and their primary interest was to keep her happy, more than anything else.

I stepped to one side and pointed out the three secure secretaries. "Pick one."

The elf looked at me like I was crazy. "Nobody uses that obsolete crap anymore."

"I do," I said, tapping the socket behind my ear. "Couple genera-tions old. You want the data, it goes into the sec. When I get the kid, you get the sec released." I shrugged. "No other way to get it out of my head."

The elf peered at the three units. "Secure, eh? Double biometrics lock and the whole bit?"

I shrugged. "Sure. It all still works. That's why they still make them."

The nice thing about these little secure secretaries is that some-one could dissect them but not before they overwrote the data ten or twelve times. The data would be secure enough for the next hour or two, long enough for me to collect the kid and get away, even if everything else went to hell.

Pointing at the Schraeder, the elf straightened up.

I stuck out my lower jaw and nodded. "Good choice. You know your gear."

Schraeder was a very minor player in the corporate world, but that meant they had to try harder. Rugged, reliable, and hard to spoof the security features. I waved the guy behind the counter over and indicated the Schraeder. He reached in and handed it over without even asking for payment.

I probably had given him too much of the roofie. Then again, he already had one of Ares' 10K sticks, so what the hey? He could afford to cover the cost of the Schraeder. Long as he didn't pass out on me.

Someone way back in the 20th Century had invented packaging that you could not open without power tools. It was good to see that they'd improved things since then. I nearly tore off a fingernail getting the damn package open.

The rear of the sec had half a dozen interfaces, none of them compatible with my old, old headware. I poked the sec under the slightly-crossed eyes of the counter guy. "What you got that inter-faces to a MD-45?"

He weaved a little but finally a hand rose up and he pointed at a rotating kiosk farther back in the store.

But first.

I rubbed my thumb on the pad I'd glued onto my belt, getting a good dose of ruffie on it. Wouldn't hurt to make the elf relax a bit. Better if he relaxed a lot.

I put my thumb on the biometric pad of the sec and waited for the beep, then handed the unit to the elf.

Secs are pretty standard stuff. Nobody wants to have to relearn a new sec, so they all work alike. Feed the biometric reader, then set up your security.

The elf planted its thumb on the pad and waited for the beep.

I took the unit back. Now I had to stall a bit. It would take a few minutes for the drug to work its way into his system.

Fortunately, I didn't have to pretend that I was having trouble finding the right adapter. I knew there had to be one but damned if I could find it the first time through or the second. I must have turned that kiosk four of five times.

Naturally, the bloody thing was hiding behind a different adapter that someone had hung on the rack in the wrong place. And this one was also wrapped in Impenetrable Plastic.

I always carry my own cable and snapped it to the adapter and felt around behind my ear for the skin pad I had had grafted over the plug to my datalock—quite expensively, if I may say so. Then it was just plug and play.

Like I said, I had been a courier back in the day. Lots of fine storage in my skull, most of it secure in a datalock. All of it obsolete.

Good enough for me, though.

I was just about as obsolete. Tried my damnedest to keep my hands from shaking.

The clock I had started in my head when I got out of the Spirit was starting to get into the yellow zone. I had to push things along.

It still took nearly a minute to download the file. I understand it's significantly faster these days but I've got too many enemies from the old days to risk anyone working on my skull anymore.

The file automatically deleted itself from my skullware when the download completed. Standard courier model. I don't have any sort of access to that memory, either.

I tapped up the first page of the file in the secretary and locked it. Then I stuck in a password to freeze the display. Only the elf and I could access the secretary now, but the elf would need my password to change the display.

Before I had a chance to hand over the sec, the elf's face brightened. "Hey, you're Jacob McCandless. I heard of you. Weren't you with Echo Mirage? I heard you were dead."

No, I wasn't with EM. I was twelve back when they were changing the world, but something I've noticed over the years is that for people these days, anything that happened before they were born apparently had all happened at the same time. That damn elf probably thought we rode dinosaurs like the Flintstones.

Plus, my original name wasn't McCandless, but for the last thirty years I had used it. I stopped the clock I had running in my head. The piece-of-crap ECM in this place had not prevented this elf from getting a facial recognition search started and no doubt that search raised flags all over the place when the search hit on that name.

The elf knew my name and had accessed the Matrix to get it. I had to run, if I was going to get out of this intact, but I could not afford to panic this elf.

Or any of the confederates he no doubt had scattered around outside.

I laughed. "You must be a John Wayne fan."

"Who?"

Yeah. One thing about elves, if it isn't that artsy-fartsy airy-faery stuff, they thought it was too much like crap to be worthy of their attention. When I was a kid, I watched all of John Wayne's movies. On a 2D TV set, no less.

"OK," I said, "I showed you mine. Now you show me yours."

I'd told him when I'd talked to him that one time, I had to see the kid, in person, alive and well, and I'd be able to tell if it was some sort of simsense chameleon program. So the boy had to be somewhere close.

I just hoped he was on this side of the street.

Time was running out and I couldn't afford to run back and forth across the street too many times.

Now the elf decides it's time to talk.

"The kid anything to you?"

I felt like I was in the movie.

"Nope. I get paid to bring the kid home in one piece. If something happens to him, I don't get paid and I become cranky."

"I'm scared. You're a real badass."

Didn't have a clue, which was just as well. He might have been more careful if he had. Fortunately, I had spent a lot of nuyen making sure that sort of data had been purged from all of the pertinent files about me. At least, the files I could find.

"Yeah. Big time." I nodded toward the door. "The kid."

The elf shrugged and led the way.

Out the door, turned right, and into a door right next to the shop. Two steps up from the sidewalk, through the door, and onto a landing with a set of stairs that went up into the darkness.

Someone had knocked out all the lights.

Damned elves can see in the dark, but not old, fat men.

Well, not normal old, fat men. I had the best artificial eyes you could buy—twenty years ago. Not to mention ears, nose, and taste buds. All with full recording capability. Better than any other receipt a courier could provide.

Inside my head, I turned up the gain on the image intensifier and the darkness turned into green shadows rather than utter darkness. I nudged up the IR gain, too, though the only significant heat source was the elf.

I still put in a couple of theatrical stumbles on the steps, just to make it look like I was blind up here.

The door at the top of the stairs could have used some paint. The stairs turned the other way behind us, going farther up. I stepped through the door after the elf. No lights in this hallway, either, though a couple of doors had light showing underneath them, enough that I could nudge the intensifier image down a bit. Might need some re-serve battery power later, so no reason to waste it.

On the other end of the hallway, I could just make out another door. Calling up a floor plan of the building from the Matrix, I saw that both sets of stairs went all the way to the roof and into the base-ment, so it wouldn't matter which I used when Escape and Evasion time came.

At the farthest door from the front of the building, the elf stopped and tapped, tapped, paused, then tapped one more time. It was one of the doors with light coming out from underneath. Could be a good thing. Maybe they weren't keeping the kid blindfolded and gagged.

As the door swung open, I saw that it was just gagged.

And tied to a chair.

With three other elves in the room.

You know, the stereotype of elves are all slender and brittle-look-ing. These three bruisers did not follow the stereotype. If they had been a little taller, a person might have been able to mistake them for orks.

They had to go.

Except for the chair, the rest of the apartment was empty. One light shone down from the ceiling fixture right in front of the hallway door. There were sockets in the ceiling in other parts of the big room and one in the ceiling of the kitchen that I could see, but rather than broken bulbs, it looked like the last tenant had taken them. Taken the plastic covers of all the electrical outlets, too. Some people.

"Let the kid go," I said. "Let me take a look at him."

The head elf looked at me for a moment, then nodded to the muscle. One of them touched the binders on the kid and they snapped open.

The kid immediately hopped out of the chair and started for the door.

Didn't get far.

One of the bruisers caught him by the back of the shirt and lifted him off the floor, legs still kicking, tossing him back toward the chair.

Got to give this to the kid, he was persistent. Three times he got caught before he gave it up. Granted, he was a kid, but given how easy he got caught each time, I'd have given up sooner. But finally, the kid stood there in front of the chair, panting, trying to pull the gag free.

"The gag," I said. I knew the kid could claw at that thing for years and never work it free.

The right touch and the gag popped free, too.

"He looks OK to me," the elf said, sneering.

Looked OK to me, too, but no reason not to make sure.

"How are you, kid? They treat you OK?"

In the John Wayne movie, the kid is dressed like a sissy but he says to John Wayne, "Sir? Are you my grandfather?" Now, I didn't really want the kid to mention that I might be related to him, but I doubted the kid had a clue—the only time I had ever seen the kid, he was barely a year old. But that "sir" part had always sounded good to me, maybe with a touch of defiance, refusing to knuckle under.

"Bite me, dickweed," the kid said.

Well, another lost John Wayne moment. At least the voiceprint matched.

Turning to the elf, I said, "Can't believe they want this back."

The elf just shrugged. "Password?"

This is the dangerous part of any such transaction. Outnumbered like this, they didn't have to let the kid go, or me either, once they had the password. In fact, if the extortion worked once, it might well work again. Who knows how many golden eggs the kid could lay for them?

I had to get things moving. Out there somewhere, some Human-is operatives were herding every asset they could get hold of in my direction.

They believed I had a bunch of dirt on them that they didn't want made public.

I did but it was well hidden because as long as I had it, I had a chance to live.

It wasn't going to go public until I was good and dead. It was that sort of information: wasn't going to expire any time soon.

Me, I had decided years before that I wasn't going to be taken alive. Not if I had a choice, anyway. One of my pants pocket contained an autoinjector full of ricin. Illegal as hell but arrest was the same as capture for me, to be avoided at all costs, so wtf.

The elf got a stricken look on his face. He looked at the bruisers and their eyes narrowed before they headed for the door. In seconds, all three of the big boys were gone.

It could have been anything but I was sure something was going on outside and I was afraid I knew what it was.

"The password," the elf demanded.

"Hogwarts," I said. I'd loved those books when I was a kid.

Where the elf pulled that pistol from, I couldn't say. I would have sworn there hadn't been any place in his clothes lumpy enough to hide it, but there it was. "I told you to come alone."

"I did. What's going on?"

"One of my people is not responding."

Raising my hands to the level of my shoulders, I said, "No clue. I came for the kid. You got your file, I got the kid, I just want to go get my money."

For a few moments, I stared down the muzzle of the pistol the elf held on me, wondering if this might be it, finally, after all these years. My knees shook.

Geez, I'd been targeted by robocannon and I can't tell you the number of times I ran down a corridor dodging bullets. I was younger then.

For sure, I thought I wasn't going to get any older, but the elf displayed that slack-faced expression I had come to recognize. The ruffie had started to kick in.

Time for my secret weapon.

If you practice long enough, you can learn to walk quite normally with something not too large—or with too many sharp points—clamped between your butt cheeks. People doing a pat-down don't usually cram a hand in there.

I let the little metal tube slide down my leg as I turned off my eyes and ears for a moment.

The flash-bang exploded when it hit the floor.

Immediately, I turned the gain back up on my eyes and I reached out my hand and took the pistol from his hand.

"What is it? What's out there?" I said, as I jammed the muzzle up under the elf's chin.

"Ghouls. Maybe two dozen."

Crap. I hadn't thought anyone could get ghouls to do anything, but apparently the Humanis people were not only able to get over their aversion of meta-humans enough to use them as operatives but had found some way to convince ghouls to cooperate.

Maybe it was just a matter of making sure the ghouls had plenty of meta-human flesh to chew on. Ghouls liked that.

I thought about shooting the elf but why attract attention? At least, any more than the flash-bang already had.

So I kneed him in the groin and jabbed my fingers into a nerve nexus under his right arm. Dropped him like a rock. Nice thing about the martial arts is that they never go obsolete.

Dropping the pistol into one of the pockets of my pants, I snatched the secretary out of the elf's other hand and stuffed it into another pocket. Another chunk of change to me for preserving Ares' data.

I reached inside my waistband and pulled out two bundles of black plastic. Harnesses. Memory plastic.

Each bundle had a fist-sized disk of metal in the middle and I held one of those disks to my chest and pulled the slider on the side downwards.

The bundle undid itself and legs reached out like a startled spider, then wrapped themselves around me, making an effective harness as the plastic folded itself into the pre-programmed shape, the "legs" gripping each other in the middle of my back.

The kid had just stood there and watched as I had disarmed the elf and done the harness thing, but when I took the first step toward him, the kid turned on his heel and ran for it. Since I was between him and the hallway door, he had no choice but to head for the darkness and gloom of the kitchen.

I stepped up the gain on my eyes so I could see the doorway on the other side of the kitchen that either led into a bedroom or to a hallway that led to the bedroom. I had no idea if there was a back door to the place, but the kid didn't even know whether the kitchen was a dead end or not. Not that he had much choice.

He also didn't have much in the way of legs. Given a bigger start, he could have gotten away. No way my old legs would have been able to keep up with him but he was close enough that I only needed two steps to reach him.

I put the disk of the second harness in the middle of the kid's back and slid the switch. In a fraction of a second, I had him by the harness.

My old fingers almost let go, though. I think if the kid hadn't been startled by the flapping black legs whipping around him, he might have been gone and away. As it was, I held on by my fingertips and hoisted the kid off his feet.

I mentioned that I had seen the kid once before, when he was a year old. Needing a place to hide out I had hunted Donna up. Big surprise for her. Stayed with her for two days, until I could use my contacts to set up a new hidey-hole.

One of those days, she hoisted the kid out of his crib and handed him to me, telling me to hold him for a second while she changed the sheets.

I am not a kid-person. Didn't know what to do with my fellow kids when I was a kid and hadn't had anything to do with them afterwards.

Didn't know what to do with this kid, either. His face was screwed tight and he expressed his unhappiness with the general state of the universe by howling at the top of his lungs. If I had not been distracted trying to turn down the volume of my ears, maybe I wouldn't have gotten nailed, but the bugger planted a bunny-suited foot right in my huevos.

I almost puked then.

Now, ten years down the road, the little bastard cow-kicked me again, square in the nuts.

I almost puked.

But I didn't have time for that.

Ghouls. Elves. God knows what else.

Time for the escape plan.

I clicked the disk of the kid's harness onto the disk of mine. They were made to mesh and once they clicked, the kid was not going anywhere without me until I reached between us and hit the release.

His feet hammered on my knees and thighs.

Old muscles and bones don't like that. These days, I bruise just by thinking about it.

That's one of the places where I had not planned well. I should have had something to put the kid out but I didn't.

So it wasn't a perfect plan. Sue me.

Rather than going out the front, I turned toward the rear stairwell. Paulie would have another car at the end of the alley between 4th and 3rd. All I had to do was get to it.

The stairwell was pitch dark. I generally approve of efficiency, but if the elves had taken out the lights in this stairwell, too, I thought maybe they were overdoing it a bit. Still, that's what light amplifiers are for. I cranked up the gain on my eyes.

And the biggest, ugliest, droolingest ghoul I had ever even heard of was there, halfway up the flight of stairs. Apparently they can see in the dark, too. Or at least this one could.

That damned elf hit me from behind right then.

You know, when a man takes one in the nuts, he should lay on the floor for a while and pray for death.

Instead, that elf either had cast iron balls or some pretty good painkiller implants.

But again, the old reflexes saved me.

As the elf barreled into me, I bent my knees and sidestepped slightly, reaching up and grabbing his arm as he tried to get an arm-bar on my throat. One good twist of my body and his momentum sent him up and over my shoulder.

Wish I could have seen his face when he got his first look at the ghoul he was sailing right into.

Both of them went down, tumbling on the stairs in a ball of legs and teeth.

I didn't hang around to see which one was going to win the wrestling match, though I think the elf probably had the most motivation. It was highly unlikely he was going to try to eat the ghoul if he won, which was not at all true of the ghoul if it won instead.

Unfortunately, I am not a twenty-something anymore and the kid's weight put me off-center enough that I went down on one knee.

Hard.

The only good thing about pain is that the worse it is, the faster the body's endorphins kick in. At least long enough for me to fumble an autoinjector out of my pocket and jab it into the fleshy part of my leg.

The pain went from flashy sparkles of color in my vision to mere agony in seconds.

I'd only bought myself maybe ten minutes, though, before that knee was going to swell and lock up on me.

At the top of the first flight, the extra twenty kilos of kid strapped to my chest combined with fifty years of muscle atrophy to make my tired old heart hammer in my chest. The painkillers probably helped with that.

I never wanted to be a courier. I wanted to be a fighter. I had the knack and I trained, when I was young, in the martial arts. When the Awakening happened, I was one of the first kids in my school tested for magic. I spent my college money learning the adept magic.

But I fell in with the wrong bunch, signed the wrong contract, and by the time I got myself out of that, my head was full of silicon.

There wasn't much left of my magic.

I was on the third floor, I was sweating like a pig, and the damned kid was beating my poor knees to pulp.

Donna loved this kid. No way she could be a child of mine. A child of mine would have drowned this spawn the first chance she'd got.

Weak or not, I needed the old spells.

Never learned to do the spells without moving my lips, muttering the guiding instructions my old teacher gave me. Then again, I never had that much need for them, so I never really learned to do it the right way. Kept telling myself I would do the work, practice, and get better. I still do. Hope springs eternal.

I felt new strength running into my legs, into my chest. My heart rate slowed a bit but I was still puffing like a bellows as I made my way up the last four flights and onto the roof.

The way to make an op work is to have a plan. That plan should include a backup plan, in case things go to hell.

If there was any justice, there would appear to be three air conditioning units on the roof. The building plans would only show two but if my people had done their jobs, there would be three. I wanted the one closest to the alley.

I also wanted my heart to either to stop hammering so hard or to just give up, have the heart attack, and let me die. The spells had helped some. I had made it to the roof, even if I felt death breathing on the back of my neck.

Did I mention that the kid was howling at the top of his lungs the whole time?

Cargo pants are a good thing. I had scooped up the gag the elves had used as I scooted out of that apartment and had stuffed it into a pocket. Before I broke the handle off the roof door, I slapped the gag over the kid's mouth.

Good gear is worth every dime. I still have that gag, by the way.

That's the second error I made in my plan. Maybe I was still caught up in that John Wayne thing, but gag, hobbles, binders: those should have been in my kit. I'd been lucky that the elves were more experienced with kids than I was.

When I eased the door open, the roof was empty. One big flat expanse, covered with crushed limestone over a tar base.

And three AC units.

The only thing better than good gear is good contacts.

The kid was still drumming his heels on my poor knees and I knew that, if I lived through this, I'd be limping for weeks, as much from the kid as that jammed knee I took on the stairs. I just needed to limp another ten meters.

This last box looked just like an AC unit, felt like one. In the old days, we'd used these boxes to hide all sorts of stuff. Good place to stash extra gear, cache extra ammo, or hide stuff you'd stolen while you beat feet for freedom. No one looked twice at an AC box.

The kid kept bracing his feet against the edge of the unit and pushing off, which pissed me off until I turned around and backed into the unit, feeling around under the edge for the release.

I found the button and pushed it. As I stepped forward, to get out of the way, the kid threw himself to one side so hard I almost fell on my face.

Believe it or not, I actually panicked for a moment, afraid I was going to fall on the kid and hurt him.

Fortunately, I caught myself, though I twisted my ankle, and my foot folded underneath. I hopped a couple of times to catch my balance again, without putting any pressure on my foot, but it felt like I'd broken every bone in my foot and torn every tendon in my leg.

I hate getting old.

Behind me, the rustle of heavy fabric and a rush of air told me the balloon was inflating. Turning, I watched it pop free and rise above it, a dozen cables holding it to the box.

They make pretty fine plastics for all purposes these days, but cloth doesn't reflect radar and, filled with helium rather than hot air, it wouldn't show a heat signature either.

The kid jerked again and I caught myself on the already-damaged ankle.

"Goddamnit, kid," I growled, my eyes tearing up from the pain. "You act like you never want to see your mother again."

He stopped struggling, just like that.

Who'da thought it'd be that easy? Kids.

Once all the lines were clear and the balloon loomed over the box, I stepped over the edge and settled down inside it. What with the helium tanks, there wasn't much room for me and the kid. The frost on the tanks warned me not to touch them. Fire-burn, freezer-burn: burn is burn and it hurts. Avoid hurt.

In the middle of the floor of the box was a handle. One twist and the box came free of the roof and off we went, rising silently into the air.

I almost dared to breathe.

Until I heard the helicopters.

Maybe they were friendly, maybe not. Probably not.

Riding a balloon is deathly quiet. Since you move with the wind, there is no sound from that. You are far enough up that you don't hear much of anything from the ground.

I sat up enough to peer over the edge of the box and saw the lights of the city creeping by below us. All I could hope for was that without radar or IR to find us, the helicopters would fly right by.

Still, I reached over and eased open the valve on the nearest can-nister. Helium hissed and I could feel the minutest rise of the balloon. The choppers will be low, looking for us, so the higher we went, the less likely they would find us.

Not to mention that having a helicopter blade slash the gasbag would change the ending of the story.

I settled back for the ride. I felt the kid shiver against my chest, and I looked down to see he had wrapped his arms around himself.

The bottom-most pocket on my right leg contained my first aid kit. Kind of silly to carry it, since most times you either got away clean or were leaving body parts behind, but I had a mylar survival blanket in the kit.

My ancient fingers almost fumbled enough to lose it but I man-aged to get it wrapped around us enough to save some heat. The kid didn't stop shivering, but the shakes weren't as bad.

My knee and ankle were both killing me, my body felt like I'd been pulled backwards through a knothole, and what I wanted more than anything else was a big glass of single malt.

But I'd pulled it off. Got the kid, kept the data.

Just needed to drift across Lake Washington and wait for AIS to pick us up.

The kid had fallen asleep against my chest, still shivering a little. But I had done it. Succeeded. Won.

That had seemed a lot more important when I was younger.

I got bored a lot of times, hiding out all these years, wishing there were some op I could join and feel a bit of that old excitement. Now, though, I just wanted to crawl back into my hole. I was way too old to be doing this stuff and whatever thrill it had had for me as a kid, it just scared me now.

Realized that I hadn't even asked the elf who'd hired him. Well, I never expected getting any name besides 'Johnson' anyway, even assuming the rohypnol would have made him talk.

I hate making mistakes. John Wayne didn't make stupid ones like that.

Could have made some use of the bonus from that, too, but I would have to settle for what I was going to collect when I turned the kid over.

All in all, though, I love it when a plan comes together.

Wish there were more of us still alive who remembered where that line came from. ✪

WETWORK

BY STEPHEN DEDMAN

Stephen Dedman is the author of the novels Shadowrun: A Fistful of Data; The Art of Arrow Cutting; Shadows Bite and Foreign Bodies, *and more than 100 short stories published in an eclectic variety of magazines and anthologies. An avid GM, he has also written for GURPS and V&V, and has been shadowrunning since 1990. For more info, check out www.stephendedman.com.*

The rain thundered down, as loud on the roof and sidewalks as hail and so thick that George White couldn't see the other side of Western Avenue through the ballistic glass panel in his door. He sighed, and wondered whether he should close early: Seattlites were accustomed to rain, of course, but he couldn't imagine anybody venturing out in weather like this to buy army surplus camping gear, or anything else he sold. He yawned, then started channel-hopping on the sports networks in the hope of finding either a good urban brawl game or a swimsuit special, until the door opened and someone hurried in. White looked up, his fat face bland as usual, and glanced at the customer. Unsurprisingly, he was wearing a long raincoat with a waterproof hood that hid most of his face.

A chiphead, thought White, or some other addict, with something to fence. And if he's desperate enough to come out in this weather, he really needs the nuyen fast. "Help you?" he asked cheerfully.

"I hope so," said the man, looking around the shop while he fiddled with the drawstring on his hood. "You sell guns and ammo, right?"

"I sell them, yes," said White, warily, as he grabbed the taser he kept under the counter. "If you have the right ID."

The man walked towards him. "I need some special stuff," he said quietly. "Mil-spec, hard to get. I heard you might have what I'm after. Didn't you used to be a supply sergeant?"

"Yeah, in the reserves. Do I know you from there? I'm not that good with faces." He looked the man up and down, re-assessing him. He seemed watchful, but not nervous, like someone who was used to guard duty. And he had weird parallel scars just above the top of his collar, as though he'd been clawed by something very nasty. No, not scars, White realized: rents. Open wounds, except that they weren't bleeding.

"No, it was just something I heard around the...traps."

White nodded slightly. "What do you want?"

"Caseless ammo for an M24A3 carbine. 6mm Gyrojet Plus. Any sort of missile launcher that works underwater. And other stuff – ration bars, inflatable boat, that sort of thing."

The merchant blinked. He had a long-standing policy of never asking a client why he wanted a particular item, but something about the man made him uneasy. "Going fishing?" he asked, his voice dry.

"You can't be too careful nowadays," came the reply. "Sea leeches, sea drakes, saltwater serpents, unicorn fish, torpedo sharks, kraken...it pays to be prepared."

The merchant relaxed. "I have a Spike in stock, heat-seeker, dual-purpose high explosive warhead, reduced backblast. I can get others, if you need more, but it'll take a few days. Same with the caseless. The gyrojet...sorry. I've never had one in here."

The man smiled. "Wrong," he said, pulling a revolver out of his coat before White could react. White barely had time to recognize the gun as a Taurus Multi-6 before the man shot him through the eye.

✖

Professor Magnusson stifled a yawn as he read through another freshman paper on magical theory. This one was a comparison of Paracelsus's description of *undina* in the *Philosophia magna* and Guazzo's classification of female water demons from the *Compendium Maleficarum* with the studies of water elementals and sea spirits by 21st century magicians. The writer, a pre-law student, had not the faintest spark of magical ability, but Magnusson suspected that if he didn't learn to summarize more concisely, he would be able to send judges and juries to sleep as effectively as if he'd used a stunball.

He was wondering how to put this politely—or at least, politely enough that he wouldn't be sued—when he heard a knock on the door. "It's open," he said, not at all unhappy at the interruption. He smiled, and closed the computer file as he saw Kenda Reyes walk in. Though her black hair, dark eyes and bronzed complexion revealed her Sioux ancestry, her presence always seemed to brighten any room. Maybe it was her powerful aura leaking through into the normal visual spectrum—or maybe, he admitted to himself, it was just his imagination. No matter. "Hi," he said, leaning back in his chair.

"Hi," she replied, less cheerfully.

"Problems?"

SPELLS & CHROME ■ 179

"I was wondering if you had any news on my funding application."

Magnusson's smile faded slightly. "I'm afraid not, but unofficially, I don't think they're going to grant you another extension. The dean says the faculty simply doesn't have the money."

"We don't need much."

"There are also other people who want to use the submarine. But I think the real problem is the liability. Some of the creatures you're looking at can be dangerous, and if anything goes wrong, it's not going to be easy getting someone out there to help you."

"Or cheap."

"True," he admitted. "Are you still trying for corporate sponsorship?"

Reyes shook her head. "Gaeatronics are the only ones who've shown any interest, and they have a backlog of applications. It could take years. If we can't survey the islands all year round, how are we going to find out about migratory species that visit them?"

Her professor shrugged. He hated to disappoint Reyes, a Sea totem shaman of considerable talent—but he also knew that the paranormal ecology of the San Juan Islands, her current obsession, wasn't considered a particularly high priority by either the School of Magic or the College of Ocean and Fishery Sciences. It didn't help that their respective deans loathed each other, and had pet research projects of their own. "Paul's out there now, isn't he?"

"Yes, on Battleship Island. We can do without the sub if we have to, but we'd still need money for food."

"I'll do what I can. Unfortunately, they don't allow influence or truth spells at faculty meetings."

Reyes smiled. "Thanks. I'll call Paul and let him know."

✖

Marcus Shawn looked down at the body behind the counter, hoping to assense some clue that would lead back to the fence's murder. "George White, also known as Picket," intoned the homicide detective. "Small time fence, bought and sold a lot of guns. No great loss: he screwed up a lot of cases for us."

"How?" Shawn asked her, without much interest.

"One gun he bought and sold was used in three murders by three different owners. You can imagine how hard that made getting a conviction for any of them. And, of course, even when we persuaded

Picket that it was in his interest to talk, his recordkeeping wasn't what you'd call helpful."

Shawn, one of Lone Star's most gifted forensic mages, looked around the store. "So not much chance of telling what's been taken?"

"Fuck-all, I think," said the detective. "He probably hasn't done a stocktake since he bought the place, and if there is an inventory on his system, it's going to be cased in enough ice to sink the *Titanic*. Same with anything from the security cameras. We'll let the hackers have a go at it, but I don't see it as a high priority. Any idea of the time of death?"

"There's no aura, and rigor has well and truly set in, so at least twelve hours. No insect activity, though, so it probably happened after sunset. It looks as though the shop was still open when it happened, so probably before eleven last night..." He opened his case and removed a rectal thermometer. "I can give you a better estimate in a minute, but I won't know for sure until we get him back to the lab."

"It started pissing down sometime after four," she reminded him, "and didn't let up much until sunrise. Visibility less than a meter. If it happened after that, I don't think we can expect much help from witnesses. Not unless they could breathe water."

✪

Magnusson, clad in an old bathrobe, walked into his combined kitchen and alchemy lab and did a double-take when he saw an attractive leather-clad woman and bald black dwarf sitting at the breakfast bar. Mute smiled slightly at his expression. "Sorry," she said. "I knocked, but no-one answered, so I let myself in."

The mage bit back a testy reply: Mute, he knew well, was an expert at not making any noise, and at getting into places that were supposed to be off-limits. "What's up?" he asked.

"We have a job," said the dwarf, "and we'd like some magical back-up."

Magnusson sighed as he filled the kettle. "I'm flattered, but I haven't been on a shadowrun in years—decades, even. Get someone younger." He glanced at Mute. "Where's that leopard shaman girlfriend of yours?"

"Denver. And she's not as good as you—well, not at this kind of thing."

"*What* kind of thing? Do you want tea? Coffee?"

"Coffee, thanks," said 8-ball. "The job's... well, it's sort of an extraction, except that we have to find him first, which is why I thought you could help. Problem is, he's cybered to the max and possibly beyond, and he's very good at hiding. One of the top scorers in Survival, Evasion, Resistance and Escape training."

Magnusson leaned back against the kitchen counter. "Who is he?"

"His name is Lucas Fletcher, but his friends call him Thresher," 8-ball answered. "He's a former Navy SEAL who volunteered to test out new Saeder-Krupp military-grade biotech and cyberware, something called Project Ultramarine. Among other things, they gave him gills, more durable than the old OXSYS implants, and cyberlegs with waterjet engines in the shins."

The professor closed his eyes. "What else?"

"Some new form of specially streamlined orthoskin. Enhanced senses, to cope with the underwater environment—sonar, thermographic vision, that sort of thing. Retractable fins. And a lot of other military grade implants—wired reflexes, adrenaline pump, digestive expansion, synthacardium, muscle mods, boosters, compensators, and possibly some headware as well. Zurich knows more about it than I do, and he's trying to see what else he can dig up."

"What went wrong?"

"What?"

"Why is Fletcher hiding?"

"He killed his wife and his lieutenant, then ran," said the dwarf. "NCIS isn't being all that helpful when it comes to details, but they've confirmed that both victims were found in the bedroom of Fletcher's house. It looks as though the wife and the lieutenant were having an affair, and the lieutenant may even have tricked Fletcher into 'volunteering' for Ultramarine just to get him out of the way for a while. Whether that's true or not, it's pretty clear that it was Fletcher who shot them: their forensics matched the rifling marks to a Multi-6 he owned. The gun safe is empty, and that had a print scanner maglock. Then he disappeared.

"They found his car in the parking lot in Gig Harbor, and they think he stole a boat there, an old Aztech Nightrunner. Disabled the RFIDs, of course, and it hasn't turned up yet.

"The navy wants him back, even though they think he's gone rogue, and so does SK, but he's been missing for nearly a week now and word has gotten out. SK is offering a reward: sixty thou, half in nuyen, half in shares. Are you in?"

"Probably not," Magnusson replied. "Why can't they track him down through his implants? Aren't they online?"

Mute and 8-ball glanced at each other, and the dwarf grimaced. "All his cyberware has a stealth mode—an override that prevents anyone hacking into any of it and taking control, or even locating it. The Navy won't tell us anything more'n that, neither will SK, but Zurich's heard that he can take himself offline any time he's conscious. That way, no-one can find him or send him false data when he's doing anything covert...but if he's wounded and blacks out, the override switches off, and the Navy can find him and bring him back in."

"What if he's asleep?"

"I'm not sure... but if he sleeps somewhere which is well enough insulated, he should be okay. Like in a Faraday cage."

"Or underwater," added Mute.

"And?" asked Magnusson, sensing that there was still more they weren't telling him.

8-ball hesitated. "The Navy thinks the implants have made him paranoid and given him a hair trigger—a worse one than he had before. And the same Multi-6 he used to kill his wife was used to kill Picket, night before last."

"Picket?"

"The fence," explained Mute. "George White, Western War Surplus. Bought and sold a lot of guns, and other gear. You never dealt with him?"

"No," said the magician, coldly. "I never needed money that badly. Or guns. And I still don't. So unless you can give me a better reason than that, count me out."

"Oh, come on, Maggie," said 8-ball, lightly. "It's never been just about the nuyen. It'll be fun."

"I helped defend the Crypt because of my oath to the coven," said Magnusson, "and I'd do it again, if necessary. But I won't do wetwork; I'm not a hired assassin." The kettle boiled, and switched itself off. He grabbed three mugs from hooks above the stove, slammed them down on the counter. "Besides, the Navy will be looking for him, so will SK, and Lone Star... and from the sound of it, so will other shadowrunners. And the first two of those will have material links for him, even if the others don't, and wagemages, and other resources. So what makes you think you can get there first?"

"He's already managed to evade them for five days," Mute replied. "I don't know enough about magic to know exactly how, but as Ball said, he's trained in SERE—and nowadays, that includes evading an astral search as well as an electronic or visual one."

"And he trained alongside at least some of the people who'll be looking for him," said the dwarf, nodding. "He'll be expecting the Navy, and probably the SKs, and maybe even Lone Star... but he won't be expecting us.

"The Navy seems to think he's hiding somewhere away from people, either in the water or close to it—somewhere with enough life to mask his aura. Saeder-Krupp think he's left the UCAS completely, maybe with the help of some of his old shipmates, which is why they've called in runners. If he *did* leave, though, he must've stowed away or paid a people smuggler, or swum, because he's too easily recognized to have caught a passenger flight. And if he's still in town, well, we know the hiding places here better than anyone in SK or the Navy. But it'd speed things up if someone could summon up a few smart watcher spirits...besides, the Lone Star forensic mage who's working the case is a former student of yours. Marcus Shawn."

The magician handed Mute her mug of tea, and spooned sugar into his own. "What makes you think Marcus is going to tell me anything that isn't on the record?"

"Because he wants to find Picket's killer," said Mute quietly. "And he knows you can help."

Magnusson sipped at his tea. "Okay," he said. "I'll call him. But that's all. I'm not going to kill, or run a greater than usual risk of being killed, just for money. I have too much other work to do."

✪

The forensic report from Marcus Shawn arrived in Magnusson's commlink's inbox while he was teaching his three o'clock class in basic conjuring. He glanced at it when he returned to his office before forwarding it to Mute and diving into a thesis on the role of different industrial pollutants on the formation of toxic water spirits. He was staring at a table of statistics when Reyes knocked on his door, but his pleasure at being interrupted was short-lived. "What's wrong?"

"I can't reach Paul. He's not answered his commlink all morning. Have you heard from him?"

"No. Could he have forgotten to recharge the battery?" asked Magnusson, who knew all too well how academics could lose track of time when obsessed with their research.

"Maybe. But I sent a watcher out to the island to find him. It couldn't."

"Isn't he in a hide?"

"Yes, but the watcher knows where it is. He said he wasn't there. He might be out in the field, but he should have taken his comm with him."

"The islands are far enough away that a watcher wouldn't have much time to do a search if he wasn't in the hide," the professor pointed out. "Especially if he was looking on one of the other islands. Or he might be in the sub."

"Possibly," she said, uncertainly. "I'll keep trying. Thanks."

❌

It was raining again when Jimmy Kaminsky returned to his tiny apartment after the end of his shift. The sunlight had been almost completely blotted out by storm clouds, and when he switched on the low-watt light and saw the dark-skinned woman sitting on his sofa-bed, his first thought was that he was hallucinating in his eagerness to get to his porn collection. An instant later, he recognized her, and his spirits deflated like a bullet-riddled airship. "What the hell are you doing here?" he asked, wishing he hadn't shut the door behind him.

Mute glanced around the room, and her nose wrinkled. "Just visiting, fortunately. I need some information."

"Blow me."

She brought her hand out from behind a cushion, and pointed a slivergun at his chest. "Would you care to rephrase that?"

Kaminksy closed his eyes. "I don't know anything."

"George White, also known as Picket. Murdered in his shop, Western War Surplus, on Monday night."

"You don't think I had anything to do with that, do you? I hardly knew the guy!"

"How did you know him? Through the Moon Traps?"

The survivalist hesitated, then nodded. "He came along to meetings sometimes. He sold us stuff cheap, that's all."

"What sort of stuff?"

"Survival gear. MREs, camo, weapons, stuff for our shelters..."

"Did he have a shelter of his own?"

"Apart from his shop? I don't think so."

"Did he know about anyone else's?"

Kaminsky bit his lip. "You think we published a guidebook or something? He might have known about a few, though we were only supposed to know the exact locations of three, in case one of us was captured and talked."

Mute managed not to smile. "What about Lucas Fletcher?"

"Doesn't ring any bells," said Kaminsky, uneasily.

"Think. He's a Navy Seal, if that helps." She reached into her pocket and drew out a photographic print of Fletcher pre-surgery, which she threw like a shuriken. Kaminsky ducked, then cautiously bent down to pick it up.

"Nope," he said, after a moment's thought. "But we weren't the only ones who did business with Picket. He had friends in the military, too—that's how he got a lot of his stuff."

"Would they have known he was in the club?"

"Dunno. Maybe. Why?"

"Lone Star thinks he killed Picket. He may have taken some stuff from the shop—ammo, weapons, survival gear—but they don't know how much. Did Picket have anything of value there?"

"Doubt it. Anything he could sell, he did, soon as he could find a buyer."

"Would he have sold a list of names and addresses? Fallout shelters, places to hide?"

"He might have," Kaminsky admitted. "He liked money. But I dunno."

"Think," said Mute, firmly, looking at him along the gunsight. "You're a survivalist, aren't you? Think of this as improving your chances of survival."

✖

Magnusson spent the evening at home, nuking himself a meal, and reading academic journals while listening to Beethoven symphonies and stroking his pet cat (not a familiar, despite rumors to the contrary). He slept badly, dreaming of surgery that turned into autopsies, and arrived at university barely in time for his first class, resorting to a makeover spell instead of a shave and eye-drops. Fortunately, he had enough seniority at the university to be able to avoid teaching on Friday afternoons, when all but the most obsessive students were thinking of better things they could be doing.

Friday night was no more restful than the night before, and on Saturday, he went to the gym for a workout, a sauna and a swim, something he hadn't done since his brief spurt of anxiety at turning fifty, a year before. He even looked in his sock drawer to make sure the Roomsweeper 8-ball had given him ten years before was still there, then removed the gel rounds and dry-fired the gun a few times to be sure his fingers remembered how.

When a tearful Kenda called him on Sunday afternoon to say that the body of a male elf had washed up on a beach on Shaw Island and that Paul's parents were flying out there to make a positive identification, he listened carefully, then phoned Marcus Shawn.

✖

"How did you know he'd been murdered?" asked Shawn as he sat down in Magnusson's office. "The body had been in the water nearly three days; after the fish and the birds finished with it, we're lucky there was enough of the head left that we could ID him with dental records. If the dart hadn't stuck in his spine, we might not have found any proof he was killed."

"I didn't know," said Magnusson. "I just...it was somewhere between a hunch and paranoia. I didn't even know him all that well; he was in one of my classes as an undergraduate, but I hardly saw him after that. But his partner—research partner and girlfriend—is one of the faculty's research assistants. Best student I've had since you dropped out."

"I didn't 'drop out'," said Shawn, slightly nettled. "I just didn't want to be an ivory tower academic. When I'm your age, maybe I'll feel different, but *someone* has to do field work!"

"I know," the professor replied. "I'm sorry...you were saying something about a dart?"

"A flechette. It took us a while to identify it: it's from an M24A3."

Magnusson looked politely blank.

"It's a special carbine designed for underwater use. Takes caseless ammo. The Navy uses them, but not many of them make it to the street."

The professor's face turned pale as he thought. "The Navy...do they know about this?"

"I haven't told them," said Shawn. "I don't know about the coroner. There are NCIS agents in town, investigating the George White case, but they're not telling us anything, so she probably won't have mentioned it. Why?"

"White sold military weapons, didn't he?"

"Yes. You think there's a connection between them?"

"I don't know," said Magnusson. That was strictly true, but he had a sinking feeling that the man who'd killed White had also murdered Santos... and that if he'd agreed to help 8-ball and Mute, Santos might still be alive.

"It's not much of a lead, anyway," Shawn replied, "Even if it is the same killer, there are hundreds of islands in that archipelago large enough for him to hide on, if he hasn't moved on, and most of them are Salish-

Sidhe territory, out of our jurisdiction. Getting permission for a search would take days, maybe weeks, and it might just be a red herring."

He looked at his former teacher's gloomy expression, then at his wristwatch. He knew that Magnusson had learned more magic on the streets than in the university, and rightly suspected that he'd run the shadows in his younger days. Unlike many in Lone Star, Shawn had nothing against shadowrunners per se, except when they created extra work for him (usually in the form of crime scenes, and corpses needing to be autopsied). "I'm due in court at eleven," he said, "have to testify in another case which might take all day. I can put this on the backburner until tomorrow, and call NCIS then, suggest that they search those islands that they can without causing an international incident. Let me know if you find anything or if there's anything I can do to help."

"I will," Magnusson promised, then walked Shawn to the exit. On his way back to the office, he stopped at the alchemy lab storeroom and picked out a collection of talismans and elemental binding foci.

❽

Zurich leaned over the gunwale of the Nightrunner and vomited. Mute, at the helm, glanced back over her shoulder and said, "I thought you were used to boats!"

"Boats, yes," said the dwarf. "Seas, no. I learned to sail on Lake Geneva."

"Oh." Mute turned to Magnusson. "You okay?"

The magician nodded. Now that the peaks of the San Juan Islands were in sight, he was busily conjuring watcher spirits and sending them to search the archipelago. The first, he directed towards the hide on Battleship Island, where Paul Santos had camped. If Fletcher had found it, he might well be taking advantage of its rather primitive comforts; if not, then much of Santos's equipment might still be there, including his cameras and computers. Magnusson dispatched another four watchers to the larger uninhabited islands in the archipelago, but without much hope: even at high tide, there were more than a hundred islands and another few hundred rocks large enough to make good hiding places, and the heavily forested areas provided good cover for astral vision as well as the normal spectrum and infrared, especially for a heavily-cybered man trained in evasion.

Mute powered down the multi-fuel engine and started up the quieter electric motor, slowing the boat down to little more than walking speed as they sailed into Haro Strait. Zurich stopped retching long enough to toss a microskimmer drone off the boat, while 8-ball stared at the 3D map on his commlink screen. "Orcas Island... Skull Island...

Deadman Island... Cemetery Island... Victim Island... Massacre Bay... Smallpox Bay... Deadman Bay... Suicide Cliff... another Skull Island... hell, who had the naming rights to this place? Edgar Allan Poe?"

"Do we know where Santos was killed?" asked Mute.

"I've run a simulation of the tides," said Zurich. "He must have been either killed or dumped in the water for the current to have carried him where it did, but without an exact time of death, all I have is probabilities. Sorry."

"Battleship Island's over there," said Magnusson, pointing at a tall pine that resembled a mast. "Could his body have come from near there?"

"From the north side... it's possible. More likely it was further east, in deeper water."

Mute nodded, and headed northeast to circle the island. Magnusson's watcher spirits returned, but none had anything to report. Gloomily, the magician asked Mute to stop the boat close to shore so that he could astrally project into the camouflaged hide and search it, and then the forest, more thoroughly: watchers, he knew, wouldn't recognize a clue unless they were given a detailed description beforehand, and he didn't want to send the water elemental he'd bound to his service on a job he could do at least as well himself. He sat down in the seat next to Mute's, adjusted his floatation vest and fastened his seatbelt; then, his consciousness flew towards the island, leaving his physical body behind.

Zurich looked at his commlink at the datafeed from his microskimmer. "Anyone else get the feeling we're looking for a needle in a couple of hundred haystacks? What if he's not even here any—" He stumbled as a wave hit the boat. "—ulp—'scuse me—" He leaned over the gunwale and opened his mouth to throw up, then yelled in pain and staggered backwards. 8-ball stared at him, and saw the finned tail of a flechette protruding from his cheek, which was bleeding profusely.

"Shit!" he yelled, as Zurich keeled over. "The bastard must—"

Mute turned around, and kicked her boosted reflexes into high gear so that the world seemed to slow down as if its batteries were running low.

"—beee riii—g"

She flung off her vest and hastily grabbed her spear gun..

"—tuuunnndddrrruuusss—"

—and dived into the sea, activating the oxygenating talisman Magnusson had given her in the same instant as Thresher's heat-seeker rocket hit the Nightrunner's engine and the explosion blew the stern of the boat to splinters.

✪

Magnusson looked around the hide—an artfully camouflaged tent roughly the size of a small van, with the cameras and other gear leaving just enough floor space for a troll-sized inflated mattress and sleeping bag. It didn't quite have the aura of a happy home, but there was no astral residue from violence or death inside the shelter, suggesting that Thresher probably had never found the place and that Santos had left it voluntarily...and probably not very long before his murder, if Magnusson was any judge. The scientific equipment still had the psychic patina of something often used with great care as well as eagerness, and even a certain degree of love. As he left the shelter, trying to follow the faint astral impressions of Santos's footprints, the professor found himself regretting that he hadn't known the parazoologist better.

He was halfway to the shore when the shock hit his astral body, sending it reeling in pain.

✪

Mute drew her smartlinked Fukubi with her right hand, and scanned the area for a heat trace from Thresher's weapons. She spotted the contrail from the rocket before she saw the well-disguised shape of her human target; Thresher had dropped the launcher tube and swum away from it, then unslung his M24A3 and fired.

A needle-sharp flechette tore through Mute's lightly armored bodysuit and into the flesh of her right shoulder. The rangefinder in her cybereyes told her that the SEAL was nearly fifty metres away, much too far for either of her weapons to be of much use; she returned fire with the Fukubi anyway, in the hope of spoiling his aim, but none of the shots came within a metre of hitting him, and they had lost most of their force before they even came close.

Thresher grinned as Mute swam towards him as fast as she could, weaving through the water like a dolphin and being careful to present the smallest possible target and squeezing off single shots in the hope of distracting him. She knew the carbine's clip held thirty shots, but she could only hope that he didn't have enough ammunition left that he could waste it. If she could just get close enough to fire the speargun...

✪

8-ball sprayed a bandage onto Zurich's face, sealing the puncture made by the flechette and stopping the blood loss, then hooked the medkit up to his friend's biomonitor before dragging him over to where Magnusson's meatbody was floating. His inflated vest kept him the right way up, but he'd had to ditch his backpack, gunbelt and most of his weapons to keep his face above water. It hadn't been an easy choice.

Unlike Zurich, the magician had been sitting far enough from the explosion that he didn't seem to have been badly wounded – the back of his seat had absorbed most of the fragments, and 8-ball had cut him free of the wreck before it sank. Magnusson was still staring sightlessly at the dark clouds above him when the rain began to fall onto his face and Zurich's, and onto 8-ball's hairless scalp. The dwarf checked the pulse in his throat yet again, unsure whether there was anything else he could do to help any of them, and sighed with relief when the magician suddenly turned to face him. "What happened?" asked Magnusson.

"He shot Zurich, then blew up the boat," said the dwarf.

"Mute?"

"Went after him. Took the power head."

Magnusson nodded. "Can you make it back to shore? We're sitting ducks here."

"I'll try. You?"

"I'll see if Mute needs help." He cast an Oxygenate spell on himself, commanded his bound elemental to sustain it, and slipped out of his lined coat and flotation vest and into the depths.

The magician's astral vision allowed him to see underwater more clearly than even the best cybereyes, though the sea was teeming with life that shone in the astral like fireflies. Thresher, by contrast, was little more than a shadow, so heavily cybered and modified that he barely had a recognizable aura; only the murderous intent he radiated made it clear that he was actually alive. Magnusson cast a stunball spell at him; Thresher, his adrenaline pump having already kicked in, remained utterly unfazed. His next shot hit Mute below the collarbone, but she continued to press on, watching the rangefinder reading superimposed on the crosshairs on her retinal display as she closed the distance between herself and her target. Thirty-eight metres... thirty-seven...thirty-six...

Magnusson cast a levitation spell on Thresher's carbine, trying to wrest it from his grasp. The SEAL managed to retain his hold on the weapon, but the magician did succeed in deflecting the gun upwards so that the next burst missed Mute, and in distracting him while she swam near enough to fire the speargun. Thresher looked towards her an instant too late to dodge the dart, and it slammed into his chest hard enough to detonate the power head. Flechettes ripped into his armored wetsuit and toughened orthoskin at point-blank range, missing his heart but tearing a hole in his left lung.

Thresher released his grip on the rifle and clapped a hand over the bubbling wound, trying to hold it shut. As Mute neared, he drew his underwater pistol and fired the last three rounds, hitting her twice. Then he drew his fighting knife while he waited for her to come within melee range—but instead of returning fire, Mute drifted down towards the sea floor. Thresher watched her until he was convinced she wasn't merely feigning unconsciousness, then activated the jets in his leg and shot up towards Magnusson, spearing him in the stomach.

✪

8-ball sighed with relief as his flailing feet finally touched wet sand. The inexpert swimmer staggered the last few meters before dropping Zurich on the shore of Battleship Island, then collapsed beside him, staring up at the sky and gasping for breath. A few seconds later, he sat up, checked the medkit screen to see whether there was anything more he could do for Zurich while they waited for DocWagon, then patted himself down in the hope of finding some weapons he hadn't discarded. It didn't take long to discover that all he had was his neck knife and a signal flare. He would have sworn long and loudly, but he didn't have the energy to spare.

✪

The force of the collision lifted both Magnusson and Thresher partly out of the water, and when the SEAL cut the power to his jets, both of their heads remained above the surface. They stared at each other, almost nose to nose, for a few seconds, before Thresher removed the knife and began to laugh. "You should've stayed home. You're way out of your depth—but me, I'm in my element."

"Maybe," Magnusson gasped weakly, "but you're in *my* elemental."

"Wha—" Thresher drew back his knife for a killing blow, and the water spirit engulfed and bound him, lifting him and spinning him around in a towering vortex far above the magician. Magnusson watched the SEAL struggle for a moment, and realized that he couldn't drown and was protected against cold and possibly even against the great crushing pressure that the powerful elemental could generate. He thought quickly, then ordered the spirit to hurl him towards the island.

The elemental obeyed: like a small but powerful tsunami, it sped across the sea, releasing Thresher just as it reached the shoreline and propelling him into the trunk of a lodgepole pine with damaging force. The SEAL picked himself up, taking two unsteady steps on his finned feet, then fell face-down into the mud. He picked himself up with some difficulty, then turned his head to see a pair of boots less than a meter away. He looked up, and saw 8-ball standing over him, brandishing a piece of driftwood the approximate size and shape of an executioner's axe. The dwarf grinned, then brought the heavy cudgel down on Thresher's head with all of his strength.

✪

When Magnusson swam ashore three minutes later, carrying Mute and assisted by the water elemental, 8-ball was sitting beside his unconscious foe. Thresher's wrists and ankles were bound together with duct tape from Zurich's pocket, and 8-ball had donned his web belt and was admiring his gyrojet pistol. He looked up as Magnusson, chanting in Aramaic to centre himself and reduce the drain of his magic use, gently lay Mute down on the sand. "Is she okay?" he asked.

The magician nodded wearily.

"You?"

Magnusson sat down, and looked at Zurich, raising an eyebrow.

"Stable," said the weapons master. "I've called DocWagon, and they should be here soon."

"You?"

"Never felt better," said 8-ball, grinning. "Just been SEAL clubbing."

Magnusson groaned at the pun, and lay down on the beach.

"Mute said you were the best," the dwarf said, more seriously. "She was right."

The magician didn't reply.

"We've got another job coming up," 8-ball continued. "Datasteal from Mitsuhama's magical research. Should be interesting. You want in?"

Magnusson stared up at the sky, then closed his eyes. He planned to secretly give his share of the reward for Thresher to Kenda Reyes so that she could continue her research, but he knew it might not be enough. "Maybe," he said. "But only if it doesn't involve any wetwork." ✪

THE GOOD FIGHT

BY MARC TASSIN

Marc Tassin was enthralled by books from an early age. He marveled that a collection of letters on a page could sweep a person away to another world, change the course of a life, or evoke any number of emotional and intellectual responses. The power of this literary alchemy is what inspired him to try his hand at writing, although it is the joy of sharing his work with others that drives him today. Marc lives in a small town just outside of Ann Arbor, Michigan, with his wife, Tanya, and their two children.

"Outta the way, grandpa."

The two gangers muscled past Kaine, shoving him aside as they struggled out to the waiting GAZ-P pickup with the decade old trid console. Near the apartment building steps, groups of people, most still in their pajamas, stood huddled together. Some were crying, some stared steely-eyed at the gang members, while others just watched in quiet resignation.

Kaine ignored it all. He shoved his hands a little further into the pockets of his battered trench and made his way past the huddled masses, up the steps, and into the decaying apartment building he'd made his squat a couple of years back.

Inside, he stepped around another ganger who had the young couple from 4C at gunpoint and pinned against the wall. They were wearing their links, and they punched shaking fingers at the air in front of them.

"That's right," the ganger said. "And transfer those trid speakers too. If any of you slots get it in your head to call Knight Errant, I want it nice and clear that you sold us this stuff."

"Can't beat the price!" shouted another ganger as he went past with an armful of clothing.

Kaine had seen this before. Gang hits a building at night, forces everybody outside, and cleans out their squats. The twist on this one is that they force all the residents to legally sell the stuff to the gangers for a song using their links. The gangers pay a couple of nuyen and walk away with a pile of stuff. And of course none of the folks they hit have enough nuyen or status to prove otherwise. Instead they just eat it and move on, saving that call to Knight Errant for important stuff, like murder. Course here in Detroit, anyone outside "the Wall" knows it's a lucky break if the Knights show up even for that. Kaine had seen a corpse rot in an alley for a week before a Knight Errant cruiser finally appeared to check it out.

Kaine made it to his apartment unmolested. An old man in a battered trench coat was easy to ignore. Granted, he was a little bulkier than most men his age, and the hard lines of his face, half-hidden in the shadows of his wide-brimmed hat, might have given the punks pause. Fortunately, gangers weren't known for their observation skills.

The door to his squat hung by one hinge, and the new maglock he'd installed a couple weeks earlier lay on the floor, twisted and bent. Frowning, Kaine stepped over the wreckage and surveyed the damage. As expected, it was his old trid he'd seen them hauling out. The soy processor was gone too, as well as the projection window he'd picked up last year. They hadn't taken his collection of turn of the century CDs, but probably not knowing what they were they'd made sure to smash the hell out of them. Kaine grimaced as he stepped over the glittering shards of his collector's edition copy of the *Best of the White Stripes*.

None of that concerned him. It wasn't the first time he'd had to start over, and it wouldn't be the last. He'd made provisions for this sort of thing and had more than enough nuyen to cover it. Even the CDs weren't a big deal. Hunting for them in the various online auction houses was more than half the fun anyhow.

Kaine was worried about something more important.

He reached the bedroom and found exactly what he was afraid of. Lying on the floor in a slowly expanding pool of blood lay Alvin. Alvin was a mixed breed, but he'd had the look and temperament of a lab. Kind, happy, a friend who would never turn on you. Not only that, but he was an honest-to-god dog. Not some vat job or Japanese clone or Chinese synthound. It didn't take a vet to tell Kaine the old boy was done for.

Kaine stooped beside Alvin and ran his gloved hand along the dog's side. Glassy, dead eyes stared up at him, the hound's pink tongue lolling out to one side and streaked with red. Kaine heard footsteps behind him.

"Watchoo doin', old man?"

He recognized the voice as that of the ganger he'd stepped around coming in.

"You didn't have to shoot him," Kaine said without turning. "He was a good dog. He wouldn't have hurt anyone."

Kaine heard the distinctive slide and snap of an MP-5 cocking lever moving into firing position.

"Shut yer slot," the ganger growled. "Grab yer link, and get out here. We got business to do."

Kaine's vision blurred, and he felt an old itch in his back that he'd almost forgotten about. He'd put up with a lot of shit over the years, but this was too much. These little bastards didn't respect anything. It was going to be the same damn thing again and again and again.

Kaine stood, avoiding any sudden moves. Instead of turning, he stepped to the nightstand.

"I need my medicine," he said, reaching for the drawer.

"Get away from there!"

Still facing the nightstand Kaine froze but continued speaking, his voice calm and low, "I need my heart medicine. If I die, who's gonna do the transaction?"

The ganger took a long moment to think about this. Kaine gave him time to puzzle it out.

"Fine! Grab yer shit, and let's go," the ganger yelled.

Kaine opened the drawer and reached inside. Turning his hand over, he reached up and grasped the Ares Predator he kept secured there with MagnoTape.

With a sharp mental command he hadn't used in almost eight years, Kaine tripped his wired reflexes. The jolt to his system was one part excruciating pain and one part ecstasy. The world slowed to a crawl as his body was ripped from the realm of normal human perception and into a place where nanoseconds stretched out long enough to make a blink a temporary blackout.

As he spun around he could see that the ganger was wired too. Most likely he had one of those new Mitsuhama rigs. Twice as fast and half the cost of the ancient hardwire Renraku system Kaine was running. The ganger opened up with his SMG, but Kaine was already dropping to a crouch. The stream of bullets perforated the wall behind him, cutting his favorite Poker Dogs painting in two. The ganger was all jitter and no jive. Like a drivers ed student behind the wheel of a Lamborghini.

As Kaine dropped he brought the predator around, popped the safety, and squeezed the trigger once, twice.

Twin thunderclaps roared. The first bullet caught the ganger square in the chest and sent his arms flying out in front of him. The second round hit right between the eyes, snapping the ganger's neck back and coating the room behind him with a design that would have made Jackson Pollock jealous.

Kaine had already crossed the room before the body hit the floor. His hat flew off, revealing the wiry brush cut he'd worn since serving in the UCAS Marines back in the '30s. The only difference was that it had faded to a steel gray over the past few decades.

Kaine stopped beside the body and looked at the corpse.

"You can steal the things a man holds dear. You can burn down his home. You can even take a man's life. But *never, ever,* fuck with a man's dog."

✪

By the time Kaine reached the apartment door, he could hear the shit hitting the fan. The gangers were shouting to one another, kids were crying, and some lady had started screaming. In retrospect he probably should have let it go. This was exactly the sort of attention he'd spent the last fifteen years avoiding.

But Alvin had been a good dog. He couldn't let that one go. Didn't make much difference at this point. His foot was well into it. Only option now was to see it through to the end.

Still in his apartment, Kaine heard footsteps coming down the hall toward his place. He shrugged out of his trench coat leaving him in jeans, a black Troika Death t-shirt, and sensible brown work shoes. He had a good build for a man of sixty, thanks in no small part to the 70% of his body that had been replaced with chrome. Not the slick "looks like real skin!" crap Runners were getting these days. It was hardcore; polished steel, exposed pistons, buff it with Turtle Wax chrome. Not even the retro-rustic crap the gangers were getting into recently could compare.

Kaine flexed feeling the rotors in his joints whirr, and he called up a status report via the HUD in his cybereyes. Everything was either yellow or green, meaning it would work well enough for what he was about to do. It felt good to fire up the old systems again. Real good.

Kaine dove out the door, rolling into the hall and coming up next to the stairs. Two gangers, both armed with old model HKs, skittered to a stop as he appeared. Before they could activate their wires, Kaine had the Predator up and firing. The first ganger dropped before he could figure out what the hell was happening. The one behind him only managed to get a single shot off before the unexpected arrival of a chunk of hot lead in his skull interrupted his concentration.

Kaine ducked in time to avoid the ganger's bullets, but they hit the banister beside him, peppering him with a hail of splinters. By the time he got to his feet, two more gangers had hit the hallway.

"What the hell?" the first one gasped. "This fucker is chromed."

Kaine sprinted towards them.

Or he would have, if his right knee hadn't gone redline. The whole mechanism locked up, his HUD squealing an alarm, and Kaine took two stumbling steps forward. Reaching out with his free hand, he grabbed one of the banister's pillars just in time to keep from falling.

In a stroke of the same good luck that had kept him alive all those years back in Seattle, the boys at the door didn't have guns. Of course, in a stroke of the same bad luck that had forced him into hiding in the first place, they were carrying something just as bad.

Monofilament swords.

He hesitated for half a second, wondering again just what the hell he was doing. He might as well put up a flag out front with his face on it. The smart thing to do would be to get out now, before things got any worse.

But damn it, Alvin had been a good dog.

As his system tried to reboot his left knee, Kaine brought up his pistol. A single shot took the first ganger down, but he knew the second would be on top of him before he could fire again. Instead, he pivoted to the side just as the ganger got close. As the ganger passed, the mono-molecular edge of the blade cut harmlessly through the air instead of slicing his arm off.

Kaine gave his wires another kick, even though he knew full well that's probably what screwed up his knee, and brought the Predator around. The ganger recovered at the same moment, and he swung his blade at Kaine. Before Kaine could get the shot off the ganger's blade sliced through the end of the Predator's barrel.

"Shit," Kaine growled, tossing the now worthless chunk of metal away.

The ganger, shocked by his own success, didn't react quickly enough. It gave Kaine the time he needed. Willing the chrome in his left arm up to full power he ripped the pillar loose from the stairs with a crack. Pivoting on his locked knee, he brought it around and jammed the jagged end of it straight into the ganger's face. The ganger dropped his blade and stumbled backward, hands clasped to his bleeding face. Kaine limped after him, and with a swift blow to the ganger's neck dropped him to the floor, lifeless.

From outside, Kaine heard shouts and cheers.

He limped down the hall to the building entrance, his damn knee still not turning over. With tires squealing, the last two gangers peeled off down the street in their GAZ-P, crap tumbling out of the back as it skidded around the corner and disappeared. Kaine's neighbors rushed to him, clapping him on the back, and shouting their thanks.

Kaine grimaced.

✪

Everyone gathered in the empty apartment at 4D. Kaine had finally gotten his knee to reboot, but it was still running on the edge of red. He sat on an empty crate, listening to the crowd of people arguing over what to do.

"We don't need to do anything," the young man from 4C insisted. "Those guys won't come back here."

A number of people nodded, making noises of agreement.

"I don't know," an older woman from the apartment above Kaine's replied. "I think the best thing we can do is move on. Find somewhere else."

A few folks mumbled their assent, but others began arguing against this. Kaine could see the argument that had been going round and round for the last twenty minutes was building up steam again. He couldn't take much more of it.

"She's right," he shouted, his hard, gravelly voice cutting through the noise. The crowd went silent.

"Didn't you see the markings on those kids?" he asked. "They're New Chamber Boys, the biggest, best-armed gang on the west side of the wall. You think those boys are just going to run home, and that'll be that? Hell, no. They're going to go back to whatever shithole they crawled out of, they're going to get a whole bunch of their friends, a lot more guns, and they're going to come back here to teach everyone a lesson."

A low murmur ran through the crowd.

"This is all your fault," a middle aged guy in a shirt and tie growled at Kaine.

"You're right," Kaine said. "This is my fault. I should have let it go, but I didn't. For that, I'm sorry. The only smart thing to do is get out of here."

"Sorry?"

The voice was soft, wavering. It cracked a bit at the end of the word, and Kaine knew it was Madam Hilda. The ancient ork woman, draped in the multi-colored crocheted shawl she always wore, shuf-fled forward. The people around her stepped out of the way, and as she passed, the gnarled stick she used for a cane rapped the floor with surprising strength.

"You're sorry that you refused to be degraded by those beasts? You're sorry that you did what more of us should do? Or perhaps you're sorry that you didn't kill them all, the only apology I'd be will-ing to accept, I might add?"

She limped right over to Kaine and glared at him.

"Look, lady. I hear you. I really do, but let's be serious. If these folks stay here, they're gonna get slaughtered."

"No way," the young man from 4C said. "I'm done being the whip-ping boy for every damn slot in this city. I'm gonna stay and fight. I've got a gun."

"Same here," rumbled the big truck driver from 5E. "I'm sick of bein' some gang's bitch. I ain't movin'."

More people spoke up, and a murmur of agreement ran through the crowd.

Kaine looked around and gave a hard laugh.

"You people are crazy. That's not how the world works. It beats you up, and if you manage to live through it, you get up and start again. Keep your head down and your mouth shut, and you just might make it. I already apologized for screwing this up, and that's all I've got to offer. Go have your little war if you want, but count me out."

As Kaine left he heard someone say "We don't need him" and the group began making plans for their defense.

Out in the hall, Kaine stopped. He heard the voice of the old, wheelchair-bound guy from 7D offering his shotgun. He heard the pretty welfare mom with five kids mention a year in the UCAS Army Reserve. He heard the skinny kid from the top floor offer to hack the building and help coordinate.

Kaine frowned. If they went through with it, those people were dead. They were brave, and their hearts were in the right place, but they weren't killers. Not one of them knew, except maybe the Army Reserve lady, what it really meant to kill. Worse, he doubted many of them knew what it meant to watch the guy next to you die.

It'd be a bloodbath, the gang would tear them apart, and tomor-row he'd read a two-line story about it, six pages down in the *Detroit Free Press* police blotter.

Kaine leaned against the wall, taking some of the weight off his bad knee. He wondered if the old lady was right. He'd spent the last fifteen years "playing it safe," and what had it got him? A long string of crappy squats in the worst neighborhoods the UCAS had to offer, a list of dead friends as long as his arm, and the pleasure of having his dog shot by a bunch of snot-nosed brats from the ass end of Detroit.

Kaine cursed himself for what he was about to do, but something sparked deep inside him that he hadn't felt in a long time. As he stepped back through the door of 4D, everyone stopped talking.

"I'm not saying you won't all die, but if we're gonna do this, let's at least get you some real weapons."

❌

A small group of them stood in the boiler room of the apartment building. Kaine reached behind the boiler and hauled out a heavy sledgehammer.

"A sledgehammer? That's what we're going to fight them with?" the annoying teenager from 2H asked.

Kaine glared at him and resisted smacking him upside the head.

"No, kid," he growled.

With a swing that sent the others scrambling back out of the way, he brought the hammer around and smashed it into the cinder block wall. The blocks cracked, and with two more swings he smashed a good-sized hole. Shining a flashlight into the gap, the thin beam revealed a closet sized room filled wall-to-wall with rifles, pistols, submachine guns, boxes of ammo, and even a small crate of grenades.

"We're gonna fight with those."

❌

He spent the next hour handing out weapons and showing folks how to use them. As he tore the plexiwrap from an Uzi III and handed it to a kid that couldn't have been more than fifteen, the kid asked "They're still in plastic. Are they brand new?"

"No, I sealed them so they'd be ready to fire without prep if I needed them."

"How long have they been down here?" the kid asked.

"I don't know. Ten, eleven years?" Kaine said, pulling the last of the plexiwrap from the next weapon.

"But you only moved in here two years ago," the kid said.

"Fer cryin' out loud, kid. what are you, trying out for the Knight Errant investigative squad?"

The kid looked at his feet and kicked at the dust.

"I'll admit," the young guy from 4C said, holding a Defiance T-250 shotgun like it would bite him if he grabbed it too hard. "I'm kind of curious about that too."

Kaine sighed.

"Before I retired, it was useful in my line of work to have places where you could run if things went bad. When I was looking for a squat, this just seemed like a decent place to settle."

The kid waved the Uzi toward the hole in the wall and said, "So you hid all this stuff there back in the 60's? That's cool. It's like *Prime Runners*."

Kaine glared at the kid, reached out, and pushed the barrel of the Uzi, which was currently pointing straight at him, down toward the ground.

"Yeah, and they're all freakin' loaded, so do me a favor and keep it pointed away from me."

❏

About an hour later they had gathered in the empty apartment again. The crowd was smaller this time. The one bit of sound advice Kaine's neighbors *had* listened to was to send the families with young kids away. The only exception was Elise, the ex-army reservist. Her mother took the kids, and Elise stayed behind. Kaine wouldn't say he wasn't pleased. It would suck if the kids had to grow up without a mom, but he needed anyone who actually knew what they were doing with a gun here.

He turned to the trucker and a couple of his big buddies.

"Let's go over it again. You three are on the front door. You gotta keep them from breaking through, and if they do you need to hold them until we can regroup on the main floor."

The men nodded, readjusting their grips on their weapons. Kaine had given them the two mono-blades from the dead gangers and a shock baton from his own collection. They looked like they could fight, but if the gangers were carrying anything heavy they'd be little more than a speed bump. Of course they didn't need to know that. He turned to the next group.

"You eight are going to take positions in the upper story windows. Four front. Four back. Even if it looks like we're getting hit heavy from one side, I want two of you to hold to your side at all times. Let's not get fooled by a feint. When firing, never take more than three shots from any position, then move to the next. It'll make it hard for the gangers to know how many we've got and where to shoot."

He turned to Elise.

"Elise. You're my second. I want you on the roof where you can perform physical overwatch. I also want you to take the grenades. You'll be our air support."

He turned to the rest of the group.

"What Elise says is law. Like I told you up front, you need to do exactly as you're told if this is going to work. You go running off on your own or playing this like some Neil the Ork Barbarian sim and we're all dead. The only chance we have of making it through this alive is if we work together. Got it?"

Everyone nodded.

"What's our status, Darius?"

The skinny kid from the top floor was swiping wild patterns through the air in front of him, his eyes twitching between AR windows only he could see.

"It's Shadowpanther," the kid corrected him, never taking his eyes off his virtual displays.

Kaine sighed. Darius had informed him that Shadowpanther was his Shadowrunner name. Ever since the trouble started he'd insisted that everyone use it. "Whatever, kid, Just give me a damn status report."

"They're three blocks off but moving slowly. Looks like they're stopping to pick people up along the way."

"How many?"

"Twenty-three, no, twenty-four now. Five cars. Almost everyone has guns."

Kaine didn't show any sign of it, but he was impressed. The kid's old link had been decent, but not up to the sort of matrix work they needed. Kaine had hauled an old deck out of his cache. It had belonged to Spindle, a decker he'd run with in the 50's. Last he'd heard Spindle went down with all the other unlucky bastards in the crash of '64. Kaine figured Spindle wouldn't mind if the kid cannibalized the deck and its software.

Despite the age of the stuff, the young hacker had managed to cobble together a decent set of cut and control apps, certainly better than what he'd been using before. In less than an hour the kid had hacked the local sec-net, giving them a blanket view of the surrounding neighborhood. Shadowpanther *definitely* had potential.

"O.K. We've got less than twenty before they get here," he said, looking at the dozen or so people he hadn't addressed yet. "I want three of you with Elise on the roof. The rest of you run support for the other positions. Keep moving. We don't want anyone getting pinned down. And if things really go south, use the holes we cut through the walls to the other buildings to get the hell out. No one goes down with this ship."

The people nodded, sweat beading on foreheads, hands gripping and re-gripping the weapons they carried.

"All right," Kaine said, wondering how the hell they'd pull this off without everyone getting killed. "Let's get into position."

There was the soft sound of someone clearing their throat in the back of the room, followed by a familiar: *shuffle, thump, pause, shuffle, thump, pause.*

"And where should I be?" Madam Hilda asked as she stepped into the light.

Kaine grimaced. He'd personally put her on the step-van that had left with the last load of kids and parents.

"Crimeny, Hilda. What are you still doing here?"

"This is my home too, young man. I intend to defend it."

Kaine walked over to her and kneeled so he could look her in the eye. In reality he was probably ten years older than her, but the biological clocks on orks tended to run fast, making an ork "fifty" equivalent to a human "eighty." Still, somehow, she seemed to have already gathered all the wisdom an extra thirty years would have granted her. It made him all the more frustrated that she was still there.

"I'm not going to sugarcoat it, Hilda. You're not going to help. If anything, you're going to be a liability. Now I have to give up a couple of our fighters to get you out of here."

For a second her face hardened, and it seemed that fire flared in her eyes. The shadows around them grew darker, and Kaine felt a chill run down his spine. He knew the feeling, something he hadn't felt since he'd run with Eagle, a shaman out of the NAN.

The strange sensation faded.

"Judge me not by my size," she said, a mischievous grin on her face.

"You old buzzard," he chuckled. "You've been holding out on us. All right, you take the roof with Elise and Shadowpanther."

He turned to the assembled group and shouted, "Let's go people! Move out!"

Looking around as his neighbors hurried off to their positions, Kaine wondered if they might just pull this off after all.

✪

Kaine had a clear view of the ganger army from his vantage point on the roof. Over thirty of them, armed to the teeth and mad as hell. When they'd waltzed up to the front door, a volley of fire from the building had sent them scurrying back behind their vehicles. They clearly hadn't expected that, although Kaine had to remind his people to be careful about ammo. Wouldn't do to empty their mags before the real fighting even started. In the meantime, it forced the gangers to fall back and come up with a new plan.

Kaine mentally adjusted the telescopic sights on his cybereyes to zoom in on the gang's leader. He was a troll, nearly eight feet tall, his horns sawed off to stumps. Kaine was certain the GE minigun sitting in the back of the GAZ-P belonged to him. Even the concrete walls of their building wouldn't be a hell of a lot of protection against that thing.

With a mental command, Kaine clicked on his comm and sub-vocalized, "Spot the troll hiding behind the GAZ-P. He's got cover right now so don't waste your ammo, but you see him reach into the back of that truck, unload on him with everything you've got."

Lights blinked in the AR in front of Kaine as the others acknowledged his orders.

"Sir! I'm still concerned that I can't get your link on the overhead," Darius whispered behind him.

Kaine flicked off his cybereyes and turned to face the nervous hacker.

"Listen, kid. I keep telling you, I like to stay under the radar. I've got fifty nuyen that says they've got at least two hackers running overwatch and trying to pin us."

Elise moved over next to them.

"So they must know how many we've got in here and where we are," she said.

Kaine shook his head. "No. That scramble script Darius pulled from the deck is old but damn good. To anyone outside, this building'll be nothing but a big black box. But when I go out there I don't want them to see me coming."

"You're going out?" asked Elise, her eyes wide.

Kaine flagged two red blips on the exterior overhead that showed where the gangers were, and he transmitted it across the LAN to her.

"See those two? They're mages. If anyone is going to screw things up for us, it's them. They're not going to stick their heads out where we can get a shot at them, so somebody has to go out and get them. I'd rather they not know I'm coming until the bullet hits them."

"They're forming up!" one of the lookouts hissed through his link.

"O.K. folks, showtime," Kaine called back.

Looking over the edge, he saw the gangers spreading out and gathering into small groups. Suddenly, two groups that had been hidden behind the cars popped up, weapons at the ready.

"Everyone down!" Kaine shouted over his comm, dropping behind the short, concrete wall that ran along the edge of the roof.

Thunder exploded as the gangers opened up. Bullets screamed overhead, smashed through windows, cracked against the walls. It seemed like minutes went by, and the firing didn't let up.

Kaine signaled to Elise. She nodded and lobbed a pair of grenades over the edge. The firing stopped, followed by two ear-pounding booms that echoed between the buildings.

"NOW!" shouted Kaine.

All around him, the fighters on the roof popped up and started firing. Below them, gun barrels appeared in half the windows of the apartment and opened fire as well. Kaine, meanwhile, dashed toward the back of the building. Hilda was there, waiting.

"If you're gonna use some of that juju, grandma, now's the time."

"Who you calling grandma, *old man*," she said, giving him a sly grin.

Kaine gave her a half smile, shook his head, and kept moving to where he'd secured a length of rope to a pipe. As he grabbed the rope and hopped over the side he heard Hilda chanting followed by the sound of roaring flame. Looking up he just caught a glimpse of a large, humanoid shape made completely of fire.

He was suddenly very glad she was on their side.

Drawing on skills he hadn't used in ages, Kaine rappelled down the side of the building in perfect silence, touching down on the pavement without a sound. The alley was dark. Nothing moved. Nevertheless, Kaine doubted he was alone. Gangers weren't the smartest guys around, but they weren't stupid. The stupid ones didn't last long.

Kaine thanked his lucky stars he'd managed to squeeze into his old stealth suit. He wouldn't call the fit comfortable, but the matte black fabric with its heat canceling mesh made sure that he stayed hidden, even from thermographic vision.

Assuming he wanted to stay hidden. He rapped his hand on the side of a dumpster, and ducked back as the expected burst of gunfire erupted from the other side of the alley. Bullets whistled and clanged off the metal. From above, he heard shots fire. He was pleased. The men at the rear had followed his instructions and held their position, although he doubted they would hit anything. It was too dark, and they were too inexperienced, but he had the necessary cover fire to get past the rear guards. Kaine dashed down the alley, little more than a shadow in the night. Firing his reflexes up to full, he sprinted away at superhuman speed.

"Report on the gangers in the alley." Kaine subvocalized.

"Holding," Darius' voice rang back over the AR.

He'd gotten past undetected. The easy part was done. From the front of the building he heard what sounded like a war. Hell, it was a war. Automatic weapons fire, the boom of shotguns, the reverberating thunder of grenades, and a high pitched screech of something not of this world tore the night air.

A strange calm fell over Kaine. For the first time in ages he felt like he was where he belonged. He knew who he was, what he was supposed to do. A smile crept across his lips as all the excuses he'd told himself back in '57 about why he had to go into hiding melted away.

Everybody makes mistakes, he thought, still grinning. *Time to make up for lost time.*

✪

Emerging from the alley at the front of the buildings, Kaine got his first clear view of the battle. The gangers were pinned down behind their vehicles. The gunfire coming from the building was light but constant, exactly as he'd instructed. Now and then, Elise dropped a grenade into the middle of it all. The goal at this point wasn't to take the gang out, just make them think really hard about whether rushing the building was a good idea.

Of course the main attraction was the elementals. Hilda's enormous fire elemental was locked in combat with an earth elemental and an air elemental. The air elemental spiraled around the battle like a tiny tornado, tossing dust and debris and taking an occasional swipe at the fire elemental. The earth elemental grappled directly with the fire elemental, trying to force its way past the fire spirit to the building. As the fire elemental batted the earth elemental back, Kaine whistled under his breath. Hilda had some serious mojo.

Scanning the gangers and matching them to the overlay Darius was transmitting, he re-tagged the shamans. If he could get across the road, he could get behind their line. The problem was the streetlights.

"Darius. Kill the streetlights on the west side of the building."

"Um, I'm not sure how to do that. I can brighten them and dim them and stuff, but I don't think I can turn them off."

Kaine cursed and wracked his brain, trying to remember something that might help. He remembered a run his team had done on a Renraku research center a long time ago.

"O.K., don't worry about turning them off. Just crank them up. All the way. Past redline if you can."

The lights flared, and Kaine's cybereyes worked overtime to compensate. After a few seconds of blinding, white light, the bulbs started to blow. Moments later, the street was dark.

"Nice work, kid."

"Whoa! That was awesome," Darius replied.

Kaine didn't wait. He dashed across the street. Halfway to the other side a beeping alerted him that his knee was hitting red again. Kaine cursed the old hardware, but he didn't stop. He reached the other side, apparently without drawing attention to himself, and crouched behind some trash cans. Peering over the cans, he saw the gangers. They were focused on the building.

He spotted one of the mages sitting behind an old Ford Americar, his back against the front tire. The mage's eyes were squeezed shut, and he was rocking and muttering. Kaine knew that look. The guy was struggling to keep his elemental under control. Looking up, he saw Hilda's fire elemental getting forced back. The ganger mage might not have full control over his elemental, but the tide was definitely turning against Kaine's people.

Not ready to reveal his position just yet, Kaine weighed his options. Even with the battle raging, gunfire coming from behind the lines might grab somebody's attention. Reaching behind his back, he popped the mini-crossbow he carried from its mount and pulled a bolt from the pocket on his thigh.

Doesn't need to be state of the art to kill ya, Kaine thought.

He raised the crossbow, his cybereyes' smart assist locking onto the mage, and he squeezed the trigger. With only the slightest whisper, the bolt flew through the air and made a little pop as it embedded itself in the side of the mage's head. The mage slumped over, and when Kaine looked under the car again he saw the air elemental blow away like smoke on the wind.

One down, he thought. *And not a moment too soon.*

With a scream and a sudden stench of sulfur, Hilda's fire elemental exploded. The earth elemental had plowed straight through it. Fire swirled around the stone creature for a moment, and then wicked away in a shower of sparks. The gangers let out a cheer, and with a command from their leader they charged. The earth elemental headed straight for the door.

Kaine was thankful that he'd outfitted the door guards with the hand weapons. They weren't much, but it was a hell of a lot better than fighting that thing with their bare hands. Eagle had once tried to explain to Kaine why normal weapons didn't do much against elementals, but Kaine had gotten bored and dozed off. He didn't care about the ins and outs of it. He just needed to know how to kill the damn things.

With any luck, Kaine might take out the other mage, and thus banish the elemental, before the monster managed to do too much damage. Kaine rechecked the second mage's position and started creeping along behind the gangers' cars. Except for a few wounded, the rest of them had rushed the building.

Check that, Kaine thought. *Almost all the gangers.*

Just as Kaine was about to round the bumper of a rusty Hermes delivery van, he spotted the massive troll leader with two other gangers. As the troll watched the battle, the two gangers worked furiously to mount the troll's mini gun on him. Kaine peeked under the Hermes and saw the earth elemental crushing the front door of the building. A stream of gangers poured in behind it.

Shit!

There was no real choice. He had to take out that minigun and hope to hell that those boys inside could handle the elemental. Dropping his crossbow, he drew his matched set of Cavalier Deputy pistols.

Kaine popped his reflexes and stepped out from behind the van. He cursed when he found that he didn't have a clean shot on the troll. His cybereyes locked on the two gangers helping their leader instead. Via the smartlinks on his pistols and palms, his arms and weapons snapped up into perfect firing positions. He squeezed the triggers, felt the rounds spiral down the barrels, and heard the pop as twin silver bullets cracked through the sound barrier and exited the gun. A nanosecond later two wet, red holes appeared in the foreheads of the gangers, and they dropped to the ground.

The troll, his minigun already in its harness, spun to face Kaine and pulled the trigger. Kaine winced when he saw that the barrels were already spinning. He knew what was coming. The angry squawk of a couple hundred rounds exiting the gun almost simultaneously echoed in the night air. Kaine barely rolled back behind the van in time.

The screech of his AR alarms was the only notification Kaine had that he'd been hit. Praying the readout was wrong, he looked to his left. It wasn't wrong. The stream of bullets had sheared his left arm off just below the shoulder. The glittering chrome appendage lay twitching on the ground, one of his Deputies still gripped in the hand.

The troll laughed, a rough, awful sound as hard as the minigun's bullets. At the same time, a cacophony of shouts and screams blasted through Kaine's comm. Over the chaos he heard Elise shouting orders while Darius cried out positions. Kaine shut it off. There was nothing he could do for them now.

"I don't know who you are, *omae*," the troll called out, "but you do *not* fuck with the New Chamber Boys!"

In the background he heard the whir of the minigun's barrel still spinning, ready to spew forth another stream of pure death.

"Fuck you," Kaine spat, still crouched behind the Hermes. Conversation under fire had never been his strong suit.

The minigun squawked again. The screech of rending metal filled the air, and a shower of sparks rained on Kaine. When the noise stopped, Kaine looked up and found that the troll had cut the back side of the van in half with the gun. Had he been standing, he'd already be dead. From across the street he heard an explosion detonate inside the building.

Kaine growled. There was no way in hell he was going down cowering in the shadows. He'd already spent the last fifteen years doing that.

Bypassing the failsafes, Kaine popped his wires into full overload. The burn that raged through his nerve endings was agonizing, and he smelled the sizzle of flesh as the wires went into meltdown. Kaine launched himself from behind the van. The troll was ready, and Kaine watched as in slow motion the huge metahuman squeezed the trigger on the minigun. The bullets streamed toward him like a glittering ribbon of mercury.

Kaine brought up the Deputy. At this speed, even his smartlink wasn't keeping up. He ignored it and lined up the shot along the gun's iron sights. He pulled the trigger, and the big pistol bucked in his hand. The cybernetic muscles in his arm locked down and compensated for the recoil. The stream of lead from the minigun sliced through his shoulder. Pain dampers shut down all sensation, and Kaine squinted through the mist of blood that sprayed off the wound.

Kaine squeezed again. A second silver bullet roared out of the pistol, riding the wake of the first.

Without warning, Kaine's AR went solid red, and the world exploded back into real time. He slammed into the ground on the stump of his left arm and skidded across the pavement. A shower of mortar and concrete rained down on him. Through the dust, he caught sight of the troll reeling backwards, still clutching the minigun's trigger and spraying the building behind them with bullets as he tumbled over like an oak tree in a windstorm.

As the troll's lifeless body slammed into the ground, the minigun finally stopped screaming. Kaine rested on the ground for a second, catching his breath and listening to the slowing whine as the minigun barrels came to a stop. He clicked on his comm, one of the only systems he had that was still functioning.

"ALL AROUND US..."

"...get back to the..."

"...GEEAAAAH..."

"...Hilda won't come with us..."

"Run! Run!"

Kaine let his head drop to the concrete. He couldn't let it end like this.

He struggled to get to his feet but slipped in something warm and wet and fell back to the ground. His head spun and black spots were forming before his eyes. Looking down, he saw a pool of blood under him. At first he thought it was from one of the gangers he'd taken out, or maybe the troll. As an afterthought he looked at his own body.

A jagged saw line cut from his shoulder down a few inches into his chest.

"Fuck," he gasped, and collapsed.

✖

Kaine was surprised when he woke up, more by the fact that he woke up at all than the events going on around him. Not that what he woke up to wasn't surprising. He was still lying on the street it seemed, soaked in blood, but he felt a strange sense of calm. It took him a minute to realize that it wasn't a natural calm but rather the result of a shit load of drugs pouring through his system.

Looking around he saw two medics in white coveralls leaning over him, wielding strange instruments and shouting things like "lung is collapsed" and "I need blood over here, *now*." Kaine tried to sit up, but one of the medics pushed him gently back.

"It's alright, sir. We're from DocWagon. You're going to be O.K."

DocWagon? he thought. Then he remembered the DocWagon contract he signed up for all those years ago. He smiled, remembering when Spindle told him he should pay better attention to his bank accounts. Apparently he'd still been paying for the damn service all this time.

The scent of antiseptic was heavy in the air, but there was another, stronger odor; the chemical stench of a burning building. He turned his head and spotted his apartment building between the gangers' ruined cars. It was wrapped in flames, and black smoke billowed into the night sky.

Off to the side, he spotted a small knot of people gathered, watching. There was Elise, and the young couple from 4C, the big trucker, and a few other folks he'd never really gotten to know. And Darius.

Shadowpanther, he thought and smiled.

Maybe it was the drugs, but the strangest thing struck him. As he looked at them, he didn't see looks of defeat on their faces. It wasn't even pain, or loss.

It was pride.

The sort of pride a person feels when they aren't anyone's slave. When they no longer have to bend over and take it from any asshole that wants to keep them down.

The sort of pride that keeps a person human.

Darius still punched at the air in front of him. Suddenly Kaine heard a screech, and an avatar that looked like a panther-man version of Darius popped up in the air in front of him.

"Found you," Shadowpanther said, grinning like a kid who just beat his dad at Virtuaball for the first time.

"Nice work, kid," Kaine whispered, smiling back at him.

"We just wanted to say thank you, Kaine. From all of us."

"No, kid," Kaine whispered. "Thank *you.*"

"He's delirious," one of the medics shouted. "Vitals are weak—let's get him on the chopper."

"Good-bye, Kaine," Shadowpanther said, and faded away.

"See ya kid."

The DocWagon med techs lifted Kaine onto a stretcher, and a

moment later they wheeled him into the stark white interior of some sort of medevac chopper. As the chopper lifted off, and one of the med techs slid the side door shut, Kaine caught one last glimpse of the inferno that used to be his home.

And he could just make out a small group of silhouettes, standing tall before the flames. ⊗

SNAKE IN THE CITY

BY JENNIFER J. HARDING

Jennifer Harding has contributed to many of the SR4 sourcebooks, including her favorite sourcebook so far, Feral Cities *(featuring Lagos). She has a degree in Creative Writing from Linfield College. A long time fan, she began shadowrunning in 1995 and still manages to fit in a weekly game–although these days, her gaming group all have mortgages, careers, and children who occasionally eat her lucky D6.*

"I said *no*," Mamba said to the four orks surrounding her, each radiating swaggering machismo. The Igbo gangers ruled the streets of Lagos, but she'd already paid out all the *naira* she had buying information. She had nothing left for the gangers' bribe—at least, nothing she was willing to barter with. *Stupid, stupid, stupid.*

Two of the orks moved to flank her, kicking her instincts into high gear. She didn't like feeling crowded. She didn't like loud, ham-fisted men. And she *really* didn't like being seen as helpless.

"No *naira*, no problem," said the biggest ork, the one Mamba already had pegged as the head of the group. "We make other deal, eh, boys?" The other three laughed. The street was crowded, but the people, always wary of the gangers, had left a clear space around the four burly orks and the one petite woman. Mamba coldly figured the odds; they had AK-97s, but they weren't bringing them up. Either they were confident they had their prey outgunned and intimidated, or they hoped not to kill her *before* they'd had their fun. They had the advantage in reach and muscle mass, but she had invested a lot in bioware; what she lacked in size, she made up for in quickness and agility—not to mention her forearm blades. If they continued to press her, she'd show them just how stupid—

The Igbo to her left reached out one huge hand and slapped her on the ass. In an instant, her cold calculation disappeared. Mamba didn't even blink as she sprung for the leader. She punched him in the throat with a fist made stronger than any normal human's, the dense bones of her hand crushing his windpipe before any of the four could react. He dropped his AK-97 to reach for his throat; already dead, but too stupid to realize it. Mamba spun and dropped, kicking out to shatter the knee of the ganger to her left. As she completed the movement, she tensed her forearms in a carefully-trained reflex, flicking out her forearm blades, and swiping out both arms to slice the third ganger, who was finally bringing his AK up. One cut went directly through his wrist, his hand flying off, still holding the assault rifle, blood spraying the air in a steaming arc. The other cut sliced him open across his gut, intestines spilling out into the filthy, red dirt of the road.

With a howl, the fourth ganger fired, forcing Mamba to dodge, augmented reflexes screaming into overdrive as she dove between his legs and leapt back to her feet. As he spun to track her, his gun sprayed bullets on the crowded street and screams erupted as men and women dropped. The ganger was still roaring, and Mamba stabbed at him. The ork was quick and her strike missed his vitals, but the blade sliced through his hand—taking a few fingers with it—and locked behind the trigger, forcing the gun to go silent. With one of her hands trapped, the ork gave a feral grin, and he pulled out a large machete with his left hand, arcing it towards her.

Parrying the machete with her own slim, left-handed blade, Black Mamba's 'link buzzed an incoming call. She didn't answer, but it didn't matter; her 'link opened the connection anyway.

"*Mamba, you're late,*" a women's voice said into her ear.

The ork swung at her again, making her arch into a back-bend to avoid him, dragging the gun they both stubbornly held onto down to put him off balance. Two more Igbo ran through the crowd, AKs ready. They couldn't fire at her without risking hitting the other ganger, so they slung back their guns and pulled out wicked-looking knives. Damn Igbo. They were like vermin out here, coming out of the woodwork.

"*Mamba, did you hear me?*" the woman continued.

"Shit, Pharisee, kinda busy here," Mamba sent through her 'link, panting, dancing over a dead ork. While the other two entered the fray, the ork she was entangled with came at her again. She retracted the forearm blade stuck in his AK and sidestepped his latest attack. He half-fell, unbalanced by her action, and she used the distraction to face the new orks, parrying with her remaining blade as one struck at her. The other ork swung at her, and she dropped back, barely avoiding having her guts spilled into the filthy street. Her right forearm blade flicked out again and she brought it up.

"*What's going on? Damn it, why'd you take off your AR glasses?*" Pharisee demanded. "*I knew I should have gotten you the AR contacts.*"

Mamba parried another blow, using the man's own strike to slide her blades up his own and spear him through the hand. Blood welled up, and as she pulled out her blade with a wet, sucking sound, it began to fountain. She twisted around him and followed through by slicing his throat so deeply she almost cut his head off. His body toppled. The two gangers still standing looked at her, blood splattered, dual blades running red from their companions' blood. Mamba flicked them at the ground to get rid of the worst of the gore. At that, one ganger turned and ran through the screaming crowds. After a second's hesitation, the other followed. Mamba stood, gasping, the acrid Lagos air burning her throat and bringing tears to her eyes. She hated this city sometimes. She stepped over the bodies and to the man who'd dared to touch her. He was holding his shattered leg, white bone showing through the ripped black flesh and flowing red blood. He whimpered as he looked up at her.

"I said *no*," she said, then slit his throat.

She took a second to look around. People were screaming; some, no doubt, injured or killed by the Igbo's indiscriminant aim.

"*Mamba*," Pharisee shouted into her ear. "*What the hell are you doing?*"

"Sorry, Pharisee," Mamba panted, suddenly breathless. "Ran out of money. Be right there." She quickly flipped through the dead ork's pockets, sparing just a second to grab a handful of *naira* tokens. The crowd around her was still in chaos, wounded people still screaming, not realizing the danger had passed. Mamba slipped into the crowd and began running.

The slums of Lagos were crowded with pedestrians, dark faces showing the stamp of a dozen different tribes, most dressed in colorful fabrics, men peddling their wares in the crowd, women clustered together for safety. Modified motorbikes wove through the people, while dozens of cars crept along, children and grown men alike attempting to sell the passengers anything from bags of water to electronics. Hemming everything in, squat cinderblock buildings stood two stories over the dirt streets, covered with a grimy coating of red dust from the harsh December winds that plagued the city. Everything stunk of rot, garbage, and the acrid smoke belched out from the factories.

The hovel she'd secured was just a few streets over. Frustrated with the crowded streets, Mamba cut through tight alleys, balancing on narrow boards that lay over the thick muck of the alleys. Part swamp mud, part garbage, and part human waste, the stench from the black muck was overpowering. Mamba had left her breather with Pharisee, not wanting to look too much like an *oyibos*, a foreigner. Unfortunately, the disguise she'd taken for this job had been enough

216 ■ SPELLS & CHROME

to peg her as one anyway, and a target for every opportunistic ganger on the streets. Her normal ebony skin wouldn't have drawn attention, but the exotic Native American face and chestnut-colored skin of her stolen identity stuck out in the Lagosian slums.

"Pharisee, you better be packed and ready," Mamba said into her 'link.

"What have you done now?" the technomancer asked.

"Cut down a few Igbo," Mamba sent as she worked on managing her breathing. Even her bioware enhanced muscles needed clean air to function properly. *A tracheal filter would be useful, if I ever manage to salvage my rep from this fucked-up job.*

The guards at the front of the squat "hotel" looked at her askance, but she brushed past them without a word. No doubt, the Igbo would start looking for the *oyibos* woman who'd hurt their gangers. The way the Area Boy gang had their network of informants, it wouldn't take long. She had to get Pharisee and move out... fast.

"We're leaving," Mamba announced, when she got to Pharisee's room. "I just need to change."

The Egyptian woman looked over at Mamba, then shook her head.

"I *thought* you were going shopping," she said, but Mamba had already brushed past her, into her own tiny room. Calculating the time, she stripped out of the bloody clothing, then used a ratty cloth and lukewarm water from a bottle to wipe away the blood on her face and hands. With more care, she cleaned her forearm blades. Luckily, Mamba had a few more outfits in the luggage she'd stolen, despite her general distaste for the clothing. Armor would've been nice, but not with the ID she'd stolen. God, she hated playing this part.

Once she was mostly clean and dressed, Mamba felt the wave of nausea coming. Sweating, she fought it down. A flashback hit her; a crowd of men, the smell of sun-baked clay, the pain of her cheek shattering under a huge fist. Mamba closed her eyes, forced herself to visualize the four Igbo today, bleeding, dead, helpless. Forced the flashback away with the image of today's fight, the feeling of their blood spilling over her hands. *I'm not helpless anymore.*

"Mamba?" Pharisee was standing in the doorway, a backpack slung over one shoulder, her fingers gripping the blue hand amulet at her throat. "You okay?"

Mamba took a deep gulp of air, felt it scour her throat. "Yeah."

✪

The trip to Lagos Island involved getting an *okada*, one of the narrow, modified motorbikes common to the feral city. Mamba dealt with this with cool practicality; she stole one, leaving the driver lying in the street with a broken nose. Pharisee sat behind her, arms clenched around Mamba's waist, eyes closed as she skillfully wove through the thick traffic, cutting through pedestrians and zipping down the narrow, stinking alleys when the vehicle traffic grew too slow for her taste.

"Our employer wants to talk to you," Pharisee said after Mamba had come to a stop on the Eko bridge. The Eko was one of two ways onto the secured enclave of Lagos Island, and even the modified motorbikes couldn't get through the packed traffic clogging it. The heavily guarded gates on the island side of the bridge were clogged by the jam of Lagosians who wanted on the island enclave. "He's been calling for the last hour."

Mamba jerked her head. "You talk to him." She'd replaced her AR glasses and breather, part of her *oyibos* disguise that would prove valuable on the island enclave. For once, the damn disguise would come in useful: as a foreigner, she'd be able to get past the guards with few questions. Unfortunately, the Eko bridge was a heavy spam site. Clusters of garish ads—everything from bridgeside vendors selling palm wine to whores advertising their services—cluttering her view.

Pharisee made a rude noise. "What am I supposed to tell him?"

"Tell him the job's screwed six ways to hell, that asshole Nubian stole the artifacts, and there's no fucking way we can rob Lekan's mansion with just the two of us. And I want my face back."

Mamba heard Pharisee swear in Arabic, then suddenly a connection was opened in Mamba's AR view, the Johnson's very annoyed icon staring at her in the AR window. Behind the translucent man, Mamba saw the packed bridge and the crowds of Lagosians. Pharisee had done some techno thing to get all the spam to drop out of sight.

"Damn it, Pharisee," Mamba muttered, as the AR image sprung to life in her view. "Stop hacking my 'link."

"Buy a better firewall," Pharisee replied. Mamba snorted. "Sweet goddess, was that a laugh?" Pharisee asked.

"Black Mamba," Mr. Johnson's icon said. "I've been waiting for your report."

"Well, fu—" Mamba felt Pharisee jab her in the ribs. She cleared her throat. "We've continued onto Lagos to finish the job, sir. I should have more to report later."

"And the artifacts? My *gift* to the Yoruba king, to gain me admittance to his auction next month? You have them?"

"Ah," Mamba stared straight through the translucent icon, to the gleaming highrises of Lagos Island. The land of promise for much of West Africa. "Unfortunately, we lost the trail on the artifacts. We're exploring other options."

"*In other words, after you'd stolen them, someone else knocked you out, took the artifacts, and left you high-and-dry in the middle of the desert,*" Pharisee interjected. "*You want to tell him how I came to the rescue when those Apep goons realized you weren't Dr. Madeira?*"

Mamba gritted her teeth.

"Black Mamba, your reputation is excellent. I'd hate to find my trust in your abilities unwarranted," Mr. Johnson replied. The warning was clear. In the shadows, you lived and died by your reputation.

"Understood," Mamba replied. Mr. Johnson cut the connection. Mamba's AR view was once again flooded with spam.

As they moved slowly through the traffic, Pharisee asked, "So, do you have a plan? Or are we really screwed?"

"Six ways to hell," Mamba muttered.

✪

She left Pharisee at a tiny park on the exclusive Victoria Island. The Egyptian woman would be safe enough there. Polite and well-armed guards patrolled the island enclave, and anyone bothering an *oyibos* woman would find themselves facing a squad of security goons. No one would bother her as she did her techno thing and hacked into the mansion of the Yoruba "ambassador" to Lagos. The very foreignness which made the women so vulnerable in the feral slums of mainland Lagos was a magic charm here. Even the air was cleaner, the streets made of well maintained pavement, the buildings sparkling with thousands of reinforced-glass windows.

A completely different world.

The mansion was in the quiet suburban area of Victoria Island. Masses of well-tended, flowering vines grew on every wall lining the streets in the upscale neighborhood, scenting the hot air with a sweet, floral fragrance that covered the stench of the city beyond. Vehicle traffic was light and orderly, pedestrian traffic heavier, but just as polite as they walked down sidewalks shaded by trees and vine-covered walls. The walls all stood two stories tall, pristine white showing beneath the thick greenery. Wide iron gates forged in fanciful designs were guarded by heavily armed men, sweat rolling down their impassive faces as they stood statue-still in the hot December sun, unaugmented eyes hidden by dark glasses. No AK-97s here; those were the guns of the slums, the gangers and the common masses. These guards—and by proxy, their masters—played a blatant game of one-upmanship. If one house was guarded by men with chromed Colt Cobra TZ-118 submachine guns, their neighbor would have up-graded HK Urban Combats with pearl handles and gold-alloy chas-ing. It was an arms race for the pampered wealthy, an amusing game, nothing more.

Black Mamba thought it was sickening.

The guards ignored her as she leisurely walked down the clean-swept sidewalks, passing within arms' reach of them. She wore the perfect camouflage for the island enclave: an embedded RFID chip that proclaimed her ID, a commlink broadcasting a valid SIN—even if it wasn't *hers*—and skin dyed chestnut, with a face shaped to mimic Sioux heritage. Had she looked like *herself*, they'd have watched her behind those dark glasses, and no doubt one or two island guards would have followed her as she meandered along the streets, ready to hassle her if she paused too long in any one spot.

Her AR glasses served a dual purpose, blocking the harsh sun while they displayed images. The map she'd bought for a thousand *naira* from a Festac Town hacker was displayed in her lower view, a birds-eye view of the streets she was navigating. There were lots of maps of Victoria Island available to purchase legally, but none of them listed who lived in each walled-off mansion. And none of them mentioned that Olabode Lekan lived behind the vine-covered walls of 12 Adua Street.

I'm in the system, Pharisee messaged Mamba, the text scrolling across her AR view. *Cameras embedded in the walls. I can see you now. You forgot to brush your hair, by the way.*

Mamba scowled, but ran a hand through the tangles. Luckily, Dr. Madeira had chosen a very short cut for her silky, black hair.

Six guards stood outside the wrought-iron gate at 12 Adua Street, each holding an Ares HVAR with military precision. The gate itself had a clever arrangement of garden-soil filled boxes attached to its base, supporting verdant twining vines, heavy with scarlet flowers, on the gate itself. It was an attractive way to block the only view into the inner courtyard from the street.

Mamba gritted her teeth and continued to walk down the street, pretending to admire the colorful flowers draping the walls. A flock of bright mini-parrots started to squawk in a tree two houses down from Lekan's mansion. Mamba paused beside the tree, pretending to take a video of the birds with her commlink. Surreptitiously, she continued to scan Lekan's walls, looking for a weakness.

Pharisee transmitted the inner view of the courtyard and mansion. Mamba saw a dozen more guards standing at attention inside the gates.

Looks impossible, the technomancer texted. *Sensors in every wall. No drones, but I see where they've got some caged beasties. Probably use them to patrol at night.*

"Shit," Mamba muttered, staring back at the place. Olabode Lekan had the invitations to the auction in his mansion; she'd bought that information dearly enough. Goddamned *physical* invitations. Without the two ancient, sacrificial knives to buy his goodwill, they'd have to steal an invitation for their employer. Mamba analyzed the data Pharisee was sending her while she inspected the neighborhood, trying to find the weak point. She didn't see one.

If she hadn't had been watching so closely, she'd have missed the man standing a block down, watching the same gates. As it was, her gaze passed over him once before snapping back.

His face was mostly hidden behind oversized black glasses and a fashionable breather, but she recognized him from the cocky way he stood, the breadth of his shoulders under a bright red shirt. When he turned his head, the line of his skull, under the tightly braided rows of black hair, triggered her memory.

Pure rage had her taking a half-step towards him before cool logic overrode her instincts and had her turning away.

Slipping into a group of women, Mamba crossed the street and worked her way past where the Nubian stood, keeping him in her sight. Screw breaking into Lekan's mansion. If Medjay was here, then perhaps the knives were, too. And if they weren't, well, he'd know where they'd gone, wouldn't he?

Mamba? Pharisee asked, *Where are you going?*

"I found someone who needs to die," Mamba replied, baring her teeth.

What? Who? Mamba!

Mamba ignored the technomancer.

After a few more minutes, Medjay turned back down Adua, going towards the island's busier commercial center. She shadowed him, using every bit of her skill and inborn abilities to blend into the crowds of shoppers and upscale residents. The Nubian wasn't a beginner at this himself, and Mamba found herself reluctantly enjoying the challenge of shadowing a professional.

Eventually, he ended up on Anmadu Bello road, the main thoroughfare, where the streets were packed with residents and foreigners alike. When Medjay walked through the gleaming front doors of the Federal Palace hotel, Mamba paused at a street vendor selling iced drinks.

"I'm at the Federal Palace hotel, Pharisee," Mamba told the technomancer. "I need you to hack the hotel."

"*I'm on my way,*" Pharisee replied. "*Don't do anything stupid before I get there.*"

The busy AR signage on Anmadu Bello overwhelmed Mamba's view for a second, until she reset the stupid 'link to weed out the spam. The frozen-drink vendor had a brightly colored menu available in AR; Mamba picked a frozen limeade and made the 5 nuyen transfer. Drink in hand, she settled down on a bench under a shade tree and pondered the hotel while waiting for Pharisee. To drink the iced limeade, she had to unclip her breather. The air was harsh, gritty from the hot *Hamattan* winds, carrying a faint hint of the stench of the lagoons: putrid vegetation, stagnant water, and rotting fish. The iced drink tasted like heaven by comparison. The hotel had several public AROs broadcasting and she began to browse them idly as she enjoyed her drink. The prices were high, as she'd expected for a hotel on the exclusive Victoria Island enclave, and the history was boring as hell. She browsed through the hotel's amenities for a few minutes, clicking open panoramic AR views of various hotel suites and even the hotel's layout. Security procedures looked standard, with MAD scanners at the front doors. Mamba sighed. When no one was watching, she slid off her forearm snap-blades and stowed them under a dense, flowering bush. Idiot wageslaves didn't see a thing. Mamba had finished her drink by the time Pharisee arrived, the plump Egyptian woman puffing from the long walk and the heat.

"Are you in the hotel's system?" Mamba asked her, as the woman stared longingly at the frozen drink stand. When the technomancer nodded, Mamba stood and strode up to the hotel. Pharisee reluctantly followed.

Armed men stood in a line by the front door, wearing snappy blue uniforms with gold pin striping and matching breathers. Even their Ares Alphas were the same bright blue; obviously someone's idea of a well-coordinated security team. Mamba rolled her eyes as she stepped through the revolving door and into the blessedly cool lobby. Gold-veined marble floors were topped by plush blue carpets, while teak tables held massive urns of star-gazer lilies, their scent almost overpowering. Mamba looked around, didn't see Medjay anywhere in the main lobby. She glanced casually into the dimly lit lounge to the left, but it was almost completely empty. She didn't remember him as being the bar-type, anyway.

"What exactly are we doing here?" Pharisee asked.

"Human male, one-point-eight meters tall, black skin, black hair in braids. Red shirt over tan pants, silver breather, black glasses. Just came in a few minutes ago. Can you find him?" Mamba asked, scanning the lobby.

"Um..." Pharisee got that far-off look, the one Mamba associated with her hacking. "Mr. Marius Jay, room 804," she said, after a few seconds. "Why?"

"Bastard's the one who narcojected me at the Apep dig, stole the knives, and left me to take the blame," Mamba muttered.

"The knives you'd just stolen yourself," Pharisee pointed out, with a raised eyebrow. "After you'd *killed* Dr. Madeira and taken her place at the dig."

"Details," Mamba replied, waving her hand. "Let's go."

They didn't have a pass for the elevators, but the doors still slid open when they approached. Normally, Mamba didn't like working with other people. Still, a hacker—in this case, a technomancer—could be damn useful at times.

Medjay used to take care of the hacking when they'd worked together.

Pharisee directed the elevator to take them up to the eighth floor.

The hall was carpeted, the walls covered with brocaded wallpaper, gilt-edged mirrors reflecting the light from crystal wall sconces. Mamba sneered at the luxurious indulgences of the rich, blocking off any slight longing she might have otherwise felt. Luxury made you soft. Weak. Easy prey.

Room 804 had a wood-paneled door with a maglock. Mamba raised an eyebrow, and Pharisee shook her head.

"*Are you planning on killing this guy now?*" the technomancer asked, piping the question over Mamba's 'link and into her earpiece.

"*Stop hacking my commlink*," Mamba replied. "*And stand back when I open the door.*"

Pharisee stared at the maglock, concentrating. Mamba tried to imagine Medjay, what he would do. Would he recognize her? With a different skin color and silky straight hair, her eyes hidden behind the dark glasses, most people wouldn't see anything other than a Native American woman.

The Nubian wasn't most people, however. Still, Mamba unclipped her breather and popped out her earpiece, then handed both items and her AR glasses over to Pharisee. The technomancer gave her a startled look.

The light on the maglock flicked from red to green. Mamba put her hand on the door knob, took a breath, then slammed the door open.

The Nubian was just coming out of the bathroom, and for one shocked second, he stared at the unfamiliar woman bursting into his room. The shock didn't last. He had the same lightning quick reflexes she did. Hell, they'd gotten their synaptic boosters at the same clinic, at the same time. By the time Mamba was through the door, Medjay had dropped into a crouch, ready to engage.

She came at him cautiously. She prided herself on fighting with cold calculation, not hot rage. He didn't have any weapons on him, unless they were hiding under the towel he'd tied around his waist.

Mamba's own blades were tucked under a bush outside the hotel.

A matched fight, then.

Mamba acted first. She kicked out, spinning, her foot passing a hairsbreadth away from his face. Medjay sprung back, landing on his hands, his feet kicking out and hitting her in the thigh. Mamba took the hit and spun with it, using the momentum to snap a kidney punch at his exposed right side as he sprung forward and back onto his feet. He blocked her shot almost effortlessly, then snapped his left arm up barely in time to block a second jab.

"Dr. Madeira?" he said, puzzled, and Mamba felt her rage kick up, infuriated that he didn't recognize her, hatred of her assumed face pouring out as she attacked him. Her cold calculation dissolved under her fury and impotence. She made a quick jab to his throat, which he blocked, using the motion to slam her shoulder. She fell back with the hit, using the energy to spin around him, punching at his face. He dodged left and back, coming up against the wall. Mamba's momentum had her fist blowing past his face and into the wall, hard enough she felt the plaster crack. Her body slammed against his.

Pressed together for one startled moment, she felt Medjay tense, knew the moment he realized it was *her*.

She followed the revelation with a solid punch to the gut, but pressed so close, there was no real energy behind the blow. He slid out and away, spinning and swinging out a foot to crush her knee. She foiled him by throwing herself to the right almost too fast to see.

He countered with a lightning quick blow to her face. She jerked her head to the side, not quite quick enough, and his fist connected with her cheekbone, a burning sting of pain. She punched him solidly in the shoulder, but he turned with the blow, using the motion to twist her arm up and behind her, sliding his other hand down her free arm and pinning it, too. He jerked her close to him, her back pressed against his chest. His breath was hot against her aching cheek. For a heartbeat, two, they held the close embrace.

"Sweet Mamba," he said in his rich whiskey and cream voice, just a trace of London accent left after all these years. "The face is new, but the moves are the same."

"Asshole," she spat at him, as she strained to break the hold. "You poached, stole my score, and left me stuck with this face."

"Just a job," he said, taking a kick to the shin that would've crippled an unaugmented man. "Isn't that what you always say?"

In answer, Mamba slammed her head back, cracking it against his collarbone, felt the old injury give a little. Surprisingly, Medjay dropped.

Mamba spun to finish the fight, but Medjay was sprawled on his back, his brown cybereyes glazed over, limbs limp. She looked up to see Pharisee standing with her back to the closed door, a small pistol in her hand.

"Gamma-scopaline," the technomancer said, as Mamba shot her a murderous glare. "Sorry. You two were starting to embarrass me. Maybe I should've just gone out and put up the 'do not disturb' sign?"

Mamba was still flushed with hot, bubbling anger. She hoped it was anger. "Shut up," she managed.

Pharisee just raised an eyebrow. "*Sweet* Mamba?" She waited a second, to see if Mamba would rise to the bait. "I take it you know each other?"

Mamba shook her head, attempting to clear out the heat, to find her cold, rational center.

"He's the one who stole those knives. If he doesn't have them in here, then we'll just wait, ask him who he gave them too," Mamba said. "And hope they weren't for his master," she added under her breath.

Mamba began to search the room, methodically going through the Nubian's things. The technomancer stood over his limp body.

"He smells nice," she said, as she fastidiously draped the towel—which had fallen off in the flight—back over his hips. "Easy on the eyes, too. What's the story?"

"No story. We worked together a while back. On a job. After the job, we went our separate ways," Mamba said, dumping out his small valise and ripping through the lining.

"What's his name?" Pharisee asked, curious. Mamba hated how curious the damn woman could be.

Mamba shrugged. "Don't remember."

"Mm-hm," Pharisee replied. "Right."

Mamba looked at the Egyptian woman, her eyes cold. "He's a Knight of Rage. Heard the term?" Pharisee narrowed her eyes, looking down at the unconscious man. "Exactly. He's loyal to his master, and no one else. I wasn't willing to be recruited," Mamba sneered. "Didn't want to be a bitch on Celedyr's leash," she said.

Pharisee didn't reply to that. Mamba turned her back on her partner to search through the hotel room. After Mamba had finished ransacking the room, she stood, her hands on her hips.

"Nothing. Damn it," she said.

Pharisee was relaxing in a chair, legs crossed. She looked around the trashed room. "Feel better?"

Mamba shot an annoyed glance to the technomancer. "I was doing my *job*," she said through gritted teeth. "Looking for the *knives*. Remember those?"

"Oh, is that why we're here?" Pharisee asked snidely, looking back down at where the man lay, paralyzed and barely conscious, his black skin stretched taut over his muscles. At the look Mamba shot her, she cleared her throat. "Then why didn't you check the safe first?"

"Safe?" Mamba asked, narrowing her eyes.

"Oops. Did I forget to mention the safe?" Pharisee pointed to a flat section of the wall, where a small mirror hung. Mamba went to it, stared for a moment, then saw the tiny switch. Physical, not wireless. Only in Lagos.

She flicked the switch and the mirror slid aside. A small biometric palm print reader made her swear. She glanced back at Pharisee.

"It's not wireless," the technomancer said. "And I don't have my electronics kit here. You *sold* it, remember?"

Mamba looked back to where Medjay was stretched out on the floor. She'd already tucked one of his knives—conveniently stored beside his bed—through her belt. Mamba walked back over to the man. His hands were long-fingered, elegant. Like an artist's, she'd thought once, not like the fat fingered hands of the men she remembered from her broken childhood. She knelt beside him.

Pharisee watched in mute horror.

Mamba picked his left hand up, slid the knife out of the sheath, and set it against his skin. His hand was warm, the fingers callused. She had a brief flashback, a memory of his clever fingers stroking her cheek, of her turning her head to place a kiss on his palm. The memory came with a stab of some unexpected emotion. Guilt was an uncomfortable feeling, longing even more so. Black Mamba dropped Medjay's hand as though it had burned her, singed her with things she didn't want to face. She scowled up at Pharisee.

"I swear, if you ever tell anyone about this, I'll kill you," she said, setting down the knife and awkwardly grabbing the man, grunting as she lifted his limp weight. She supported his weight and shoved his hand against the palm reader, then dropped him unceremoniously to the floor. The safe popped open with a little click.

Inside, the small plastic case was waiting for her. She slipped it out, opened it. The two ancient knives were snug inside, nestled in the soft velvet lining. Mamba snapped the case closed again, slid it under her shirt, against her back.

"Let's go," Mamba said to Pharisee.

"What about—"

"Let's hope we can get off this damn island before he wakes up," Mamba replied, curt. Without a backward glance, she left the room. Another minute to wait for the elevator, then down to the wide lobby. Before they went through the doors, Mamba looked over at Pharisee. "How'd you get your little gun through the MAD scanner?" she asked, curious.

Pharisee just raised an eyebrow, then walked through the scanners and back out into the harsh December winds.

Mamba followed. "Stay here," she ordered the technomancer, pointing to the bench outside the hotel. Mamba took back her breather, earpiece, and AR glasses. "My blades are under that bush. If things get ugly, bring them to me. Otherwise—"

"I know, I know, don't hack your 'link," Pharisee muttered, "As if you could stop me," she said under her breath as she went towards the iced drink vendor.

Mamba shook her head at the technomancer's back. Pragmatically, she snapped her breather on and retraced her steps back to Adua Street and Olabode Lekan's well-guarded mansion.

The drug would last an hour, maybe two at the best. She planned on being off Victoria Island well before then. She was already regretting the impulse that prevented her from killing Medjay, or at least maiming him. *Stupid, stupid, stupid*, she told herself. She shied away from thinking about *why* she'd left him alive and whole in his hotel, and as a result, was feeling more than a little pissed when she stopped in front of the guards at number 12 Adua Street.

"I'm hear to see Lekan," she said, curtly, to the man closest to the gate. He was Yoruba, so she repeated herself in his language. Sometimes playing the foreigner card worked, sometimes it didn't. In her current mood, she'd be just as happy taking his gun and mowing all them down before they could react. Carefully, she tamped down the anger. Emotion got you killed in this line of work. There was no room for *moods*.

The guard just stared at her.

"Tell him Dr. Sierra Madeira is here," she said. "He'll want to see me."

The guard didn't speak, but Mamba bet he was sending a message via his 'link. After a moment, he nodded to her, his expression slightly more polite. A clever, meta-human sized door swung open in the center of the vine-covered gate. The guard in front of it stepped to the side, and with a jerk of his head, motioned her through.

She went in.

The courtyard was laid out in muted red bricks, in a concentric circle around a large reflecting pool. Trees cast some shade, but there was little in the way of gardens or bushes. *Nowhere to find cover*, a portion of her mind observed. More armed guards, decked out in full security armor, stood around the courtyard. The mansion was set back, a square building that glowed white in the harsh sunlight. Windows glinted, like crystals, and the entire building was sparkling clean. That, more than the size of the building or the small army of men, spoke of real wealth in Lagos. A human man in dun-colored robes approached her, followed by two heavy-set orks in military grade armor.

"Dr. Madeira? If you'll please follow me," he said in English, then turned back towards the broad, double door of the mansion. She followed him up some shallow steps to the doors. Once she'd stepped through, the two orks slid the doors shut with a quiet click.

The man in the robes paused once they were inside the cool building. "I must ask you to relinquish any weapons," he said, politely. The two orks beside him gave unspoken force to his words.

Mamba slid out the plastic case from under her shirt, using very slow and deliberate motions.

"These aren't weapons," she said, flicking the case open. "But something I believe Lekan would like to see."

"If I may?" the man replied, holding out his hands. Mamba reluctantly handed over the case. She'd already lost the damn things once. Now, she was *this* close to finishing the job she'd given up as a lost cause. But she felt the press of time. Every minute that passed, Medjay would be closer to recovery. He was an able enough hacker, when he used those damn skillsofts. How long would it take him to track her down?

And why hadn't she thought of that when she had the opportunity to slit his throat? Why hadn't she at least left him tied up? She shied away from acknowledging the answer to that question.

The man in the robe took the case, then smiled and led her though the soaring three-story entrance hall, down a dimly lit hall, and into a richly appointed office.

A human male, with wrinkled black skin and a tight cap of snowy white hair, sat behind a large, polished wood desk. He wore richly textured woven robes, in a variety of bright colors. Olabode Lekan looked every bit the distinguished statesman, and nothing like the warlord he really was.

Once Mamba was in the room, the man in the dun robes carefully handed Lekan the plastic case, then left, closing the doors behind him. The two orks remained in the room, standing at attention. Two more guards, trolls that Mamba could tell were cybered to the gills just by watching them twitch, stood behind Lekan.

Lekan opened the case without speaking to her. He raised one white eyebrow at the two ancient knives, then clicked the case closed and sat it on the desk in front of him. He looked Mamba over.

"Dr. Madeira has been reported missing by the Apep Consortium in Cairo," he began. His voice was rich and full, almost too robust for the small office; a voice meant to be giving speeches, not addressing low-life shadowrunners. "And at the same time, rumors are that an unnamed Apep dig site was hit by thieves. This, coupled with the fact that Dr. Madeira has no biological augmentations, certainly not to the level and quality of your own, presents an interesting mystery."

Mamba inclined her head. "I've been employed to bring those artifacts to Oni Adegoke," she said. "My employer heard about the Oni's upcoming auction, and wanted to—" she struggled to phrase it politely. "—to send a gesture of good-will."

Lekan tipped his head, considering her. Black Mamba wondered if he was using a spell, emotion mapping software, or just his judgment. She *hated* losing control of a situation.

"I see you appear truthful," he said.

Mamba let out a breath.

"Very well. I'll accept this gift on behalf of the Oni. In exchange, I'd be happy to offer you a gift for your employer." The old man stood, more graceful than his age would lead her to believe, and went to a small safe at the back of the room. When he returned, he dropped a small stack of ivory disks on the desk. "Tokens," he said, gesturing to the disks. "Each one will admit one person to the auction. Your *employer* can contact me directly for more details, if he—or she—wishes." He said it with distaste. The message was clear; *don't send any more shadowrunners.*

Mamba picked up the small disks. There were five. She nodded to the old man, but he'd already dismissed her. Mamba bristled, but the odds were still against her... and she did have a job to finish.

She was escorted out of the mansion, back out to the street, the vine-covered gate closing behind her.

It'd been just over an hour since they'd left the Nubian in his room. He was probably awake by now. Or would be soon.

Mamba began walking back to where she left Pharisee.

"Everything's frosty," the technomancer said. *"I watched through your AR glasses' camera. I can't believe we did it."*

"Stop hacking my commlink," Mamba retorted. "And we still have to get these damn tokens back to our employer. Hell, we still have to get out of Lagos. Before Medjay catches us."

"Oh, is that his name?" Pharisee teased.

Mamba ignored her, her mind already calculating, planning the next move. She was in control again. Catch an *okada* to the mainland, and from there to the airport. Getting through Lagos without tangling with the Igbo—who were probably still out for her blood—would be challenging. Getting out of Lagos before Medjay found her would likely be even more impossible.

Without realizing it, as she walked down the manicured streets and back to the dangerous blight of the feral city, Black Mamba smiled. Out of civilization; back to her comfort zone.

And towards a good fight. ✪

DEAD NAMES

BY WILLIAM H. KEITH

So far, William H. Keith has published over eighty novels, including military novels, geopolitical spy thrillers, and science fiction, writing under his name and several pseudonyms. As "H. Jay Riker" he wrote the long-running SEALs: The Warrior Breed. *As "Ian Douglas," Keith wrote the* Heritage, Legacy, *and* Inheritance *military-SF series, following the exploits of the U.S. Marines into the far future. Most recently, he's been writing spy thrillers in collaboration with best-selling author Stephen Coonts. Bill currently lives and writes in the mountains of western Pennsylvania.*

I have to say right up front that I didn't believe our Mr. Johnson. I mean, I've seen some freaked-out scat in my time, but this was just too hardwired weird for school.

"What?" I yelped at the guy. "You're doodoodling me, man, right?"

We were sitting in the High Tox, the bar I'd chosen for the face-to-face. I guess I yelped a bit too loud when I heard what the op was, because I noticed Tony surreptitiously reaching for the scattergun he kept behind the bar. I met his eye, shook my head a little, and he relaxed.

But it was good knowing I had back-up with this bozo. He just meatjackin' *couldn't* be cruising the Real!

"I'm very serious, Mister, er, Faceman," my contact said. "Roger Nakamura is supposedly paying forty million nuyen to Zayid if he can pull this off. My sponsors wish to intercept the ... ah ... package. At the source."

I leaned back in my chair and sipped my drink. A banzai boomer, neat, bitter, the way Tony knows I like it. I needed to think this through. The Johnson *had* to be scamming us, *had* to have an angle.

The thing is, I'd worked for *this* Johnson before, and he'd always been a straight burner. He'd been the one who leveraged the Yokahama smartdust deal for us, and that had been pure sugar, a quick in-and-out that netted each of us forty-K nuyens, easy money.

And it had been a while since our merry band had scored. This time, our Mr. Johnson was offering us 200 K. We needed the money, and it wasn't like we could afford to be picky.

The bastard was grinning at me. "You don't believe me, do you?"

"Truth?" I asked. "Hell no. I think someone's playing with your head, man." I didn't add that I was still trying to see how the Johnson might be trying to scam us. This thing just wasn't adding up.

"Ah. But if it's true. If Zayid has found the Gate ... *think* of what it might mean!"

"Look," I said. "It's reality-check time, okay? Has anyone told your sponsors that this thing isn't real? It's a freakin' work of *fiction*, for the gods' sake!"

"That," Mr. Johnson said, "is a matter of what you believe, isn't it?"

"Aw, c'mon, Slick! The effing *Necronomicon*? Get real! Lovecraft was a *writer*, okay? He invented the thing for his damned stories!"

"And if enough people believe in a thing, Mr. Faceman, it takes on a certain amount of hard-cache reality. *You* know that."

Of course I knew that. Everybody since 2011 knew that. But, damn it ... this was *fiction*!

H.P. Lovecraft. The guy was all but unknown when he was alive, a minor horror writer in the pulp magazines of the day. He acquired quite a following in the years after his death, though, spawning a sub-genre all his own, populated by monstrous gods or godlike monsters that cared nothing for humanity save how they were going to eat us for dessert. Nyarlathotep, the Crawling Chaos. Hastur the Unspeakable. Azathoth, the daemon sultan bubbling and blaspheming at the center of infinity. And, of course, Great Cthulhu himself, lying dreaming in sunken R'lyeh.

Jesus. All those stories from the 1920s and '30s, set against a backdrop of hopelessness, nihilism, madness, and despair. God doesn't love you; He's going to squash you like a bug. Or better. God *loves* you, because you taste great with a little BBQ sauce. Maybe that's why old HP was so popular with the younger set, even now, a century and a half later.

And Lovecraft had invented the *Necronomicon* as a singular plot McGuffin, an ancient tome of dark magic replete with forbidden knowledge, including the incantations and formulae necessary for calling forth dread Cthulhu and his kind. It was supposed to have been written by Abdul Alhazred, the Mad Arab. Hell, anyone who speaks Arabic ought to get a clue right there. No Arab would *ever* be named "Abdul" in real life. That's Western racist ignorance. It means "slave of—" and needs to have a name tacked on at the end. "Abdullah," for instance, "Slave of God." Do you understand? *Lovecraft made it up ... and he got it wrong*!

"Let me get this straight," I said after a moment. "Nakamura has hired this Arab magician or technomage to open some sort of a gateway to ... what did you call it? An alternate reality?"

"Or a parallel dimension, if you like."

"And this Zayid character is supposed to find an actual, physical copy of the *Necronomicon* and bring it back."

"Exactly."

"And you want us to hijack the book before Zayid passes it on to his boss."

"Just so. Can you do it?"

"Not if the book doesn't exist!"

"Ah, but it *does* exist. It *must*. Don't you see? For 150 years, millions of readers, the fans, the *devotees* of H.P. Lovecraft, have read those stories, and they have believed. *Believed!* Did you know that fifty years after Lovecraft's death, libraries at places like Harvard and Oxford were *deluged* with search requests for that book? Perhaps a dozen works were actually published under that title, adding to the confusion."

"You ... you're saying that because a bunch of losers believed the *Necronomicon* was real, it *is*?" I looked him up and down. "That's just whacked! You been doing too much BTL, man?" I was serious. Folks jazzed on better-than-life sims could pick up some weird delusions, sometimes.

"I assure you I'm completely rational," Mr. Johnson said. "And in earnest. Belief is *everything*. So, will you take the job?"

Belief? Was that all it took to create reality from fiction? *Belief?* Nah. . . .

But we did need the nuyen.

"Okay," I said. "We'll take it. But half up front. And it's nonrefundable if this turns out to be a goose chase."

"Uh-uh," Mr. Johnson said. "Fifty-K up front. *And* you wear nannies."

"Shit. Why?"

"So my people can peek over your shoulders, as it were. What you see and hear, they'll see and hear. And they'll know you're not ripping them."

"Hey! You've hired us before! When did we ever scam you or your clients, huh?"

"Never. And you *won't*." He shoved a plastic bag across the table at me, with a tangle of equipment inside. "Besides, there's one thing more."

"What?"

"If you can't get the ... merchandise, my clients want to be sure Nakamura can't get it either. These will help verify that."

"Makes it more complicated, man," I told him. "Seventy-five kay up front."

He hesitated, then nodded. "Done."

An hour later I was on the streets of Pittsburgh, my collar and hood up against the thin drizzle of acid rain, shouldering through the muggliemasses beneath the neon wink-blink of come-hither signs in twenty different languages, beneath the five-story buildingboards with their smiling, naked women and sleek cars and mindless MadAv babble. Megacorp massage, direct to you from the nuyen necromancers. An alien world, Slick, a billion klicks from the streets.

In my belt was the bag of nannies, plus a credstick worth 75,000 nuyen. Not bad for a morning's work.

I didn't know who our Mr. Johnson worked for, of course. Shadowrunners generally don't. But the guy had the fashion sense and street-cred trust-me feel of a Fed, and I was pretty sure our employers were the good old UCAS.

Nakamura, of course, we knew. Roger Nakamura was Pittsburgh's grand high Pooh-Bah of Mellon-Mitsubishi, itself a branch of Renraku Megacorp.

The team was waiting for me at the Eat 'n' Meet at Fifth and Forbes, almost in the shadow of the M&M Tower. Boy, they were just gonna *love* this. . . .

○

I'd been working with them for maybe three years, and loved 'em all like siblings. Better, maybe, in Cammy's case. I never banged my sister.

Her name was Camilla Gonzales, but we all called her Cammy. The name fit. She was a weapons specialist who had this way of blending into the background so perfectly you'd never know she was there. And Thud's name fit too. I never knew what he called himself, but he was eight powerfully muscled feet of rather dim attitude, and those curved ram's horns growing from the sides of his skull gave him a certain in-your-face presence, you cop? Then there was Scooter, our pimple-faced magician, our very own wizardry whiz. And Dee-Dee wasn't just a hacker. She made computers speak, roll over, and sit up and beg.

And me? Well, never mind what my birth name was. Cam, Thud, Scoot, and Dee all just called me Fixer. I was the team's face, the one who talked nice to the Mr. Johnsons and brought in the gigs.

"We're supposed to do *what?*" Cammie said after I'd laid out the deal.

"I know," I told her. "Sounds a little over-the-top ..."

"Over the top? It's not even in this galaxy! Hey! Earth to Fixer! Comm-check!"

"Did you tell this clown the difference between fiction and reality?" Dee-Dee asked, grinning.

"Of course. He told me belief is everything."

"He's right, you know," Scooter said. "Belief is what makes the world we know."

Scoot was using The Voice, and that made us all take notice. Normally, he's got this adenoidal whine that makes him sound like an annoying teen fanboy, but every now and again the adenoids vanish and his tone drops about two octaves. It's what he calls his magical voice, and when he talks that way, you know *he* knows what he's talking about. Cammie calls it speaking *ex cathedra*, which sounds like she thinks he used to be a church.

"Scoot," See said, shaking her head. She reached out and rapped the tabletop with her knuckles. "*This* is real." She tapped the side of her head. "*This* is imagination. . . ."

He cocked his head to one side. "So ... when you run the Matrix, it's not real?"

She scowled. "Of *course* it's real."

"But it's all in your head."

"No it's not!" She waved vaguely in front of her face. "It's ... it's out there. . . ."

"What you keep forgetting, Dee-Dee, is that according to the well-known laws of quantum mechanics, *we create* reality. In effect, there is no 'out there' out there."

I'd heard this argument before. It was popular with some hermetic magicians, I knew, though it wasn't at all mainstream. Not yet.

"You're talking about the Awakening, right?" I asked.

He nodded. "And a lot else. But we brought the Awakening on ourselves."

"Nonsense," Cammie said, but she was frowning. "That was just ... just magic."

"What do you think magic is, but the use of *belief* to change reality?"

I glanced at Dee, at her delicately pointed ears, then at Thud, who was sitting there sharpening the tips of his horns, apparently not even listening, massive as a mountain, with fangs protruding two centimeters up from behind his lower lip.

An elf, a troll, and two humans. A hundred years ago, it would have been four humans. So where did the metahumanity come from?

Oh, yeah. We did it to ourselves. At least Scoot and a few like him thought so, and I had to admit the theory made as much sense as anything I'd ever heard. Seems that back at the end of the 20th century, and through the first decade of the 21st, we had all kinds of belief in the Big Changes coming. Cop it. The fundy Christians were so certain that Armageddon was right around the corner, with all the hosts of Satan ready to rise up and follow the Antichrist. And the fundy Muslims, the Shiites, anyway, were invested in the coming of the Mahdi and the creation of Allah's New Order on Earth. Even the New Agers got into the act, focusing on channeled messages of coming Earth Changes, and the ancient Mayan prophecies that the Fifth Sun was coming to an end in 2012.

With that much pure, raw belief gnawing at the foundations of Reality, man, something *had* to give.

And it did. It's tough to remember sometimes, sixty years later, that the Old World Order was all human. No trolls. No orks. No elves. No dwarves. And no *magic*. None that worked reliably, at any rate.

We called it the Awakening when the Old Order fell. Hidden away within the human genome were all of the metahuman racial types, it turned out, and suddenly Black and White and Latino and Asian didn't matter anymore. We were all humans, and we were sharing the planet with the stuff of myth and legend. Magic worked and dragons were real and Civilization itself was crumbling around our ears.

So, what the hell? Maybe old H.P. Lovecraft's little nightmares could have something to them after all. The potential of becoming real, if enough people closed their eyes and thought about it *real* hard.

"What do you think about all of this, Thud?" I asked.

"Don't think," the troll rumbled. He sounded like a good-natured earthquake. "Just *do*. Long as the nuyen're there."

Thud could be remarkably down-to-earth about things.

"We got our advance," I told them. "Look, at the very least we clear better'n eighteen-K apiece, right? We go in, show 'em it can't be done, and get out. Simple."

"Yeah? What if it *can* be done?" Scooter asked. The Voice had gone, and the annoying fanboy was back.

I shrugged. "Then we get fifty-freakin'-K apiece. How hard can it be?"

"Don't say that, Fix," Cam told me. "Don't *ever* say that. Somebody might be listening."

"They will be." I chuckled, and held up the bag of nannies. "Count on it."

"We really need to wear those things?" Dee said. "I don't like it."

"Me neither. But it's just for the op. They won't be watching you shower."

"It's just upgraded RFID," Dee said. "No big deal."

She used the streetslang pronunciation, "ar-fid." Radio frequency identification devices are everywhere—those little tags that control shoplifting and inventory, keep track of the kids, and let you dial in to the local net to get the name and number of the pretty girl you're chatting up on the street. They work by broadcasting a limited chunk of data that you can read on your commlink from like thirty or forty meters away.

Nannies are the same, but with more bandwidth, and with audio and vid channels. You wear the little flesh-colored dot on your forehead. It sees everything you see through an ultra-small nanocamera, and hears what you hear through a microphone the size of a large protein molecule. The range varies, depending on whether it's a government or a corporate model, but it's a lot farther than forty meters … and it can get through almost any of the usual RF barriers. Mr. Johnson's people really *would* be watching.

❂

It took Dee three days to hack the system, but we got what we needed to make the strike. Mitsubishi-Mellon had all kinds of defenses up, of course, but there are *always* cracks in the walls. We'd snuck into tougher places.

The biggest problem was that we were operating under deadline. Our Mr. Johnson had provided us with a few details. Seems he had a pipeline into this Zayid character's inner sanctum—a circle of twelve that was doing the heavy lifting for Zayid's major working. A street shaman named Shifter hadn't liked what he'd seen, and he'd made contact with our Mr. Johnson's people, whoever they were.

So, courtesy of Shifter, we knew Zayid was doing a series of incantations every night of the waning Moon, and that it was all coming to a head at midnight on the night of the new Moon—the 5th. And that was three days from my meeting with the Johnson.

But Dee found us a way in that ought to bypass the defenses at the front entrance, at least. We'd need to jimmy a lock to get us into an infrastructure service tunnel two blocks from the M&M building, then follow the fiber-optics and water pipes into the tower's basement. At that point, Dee would have to hack the building OS to take down certain surveillance cameras and the pressure sensors in the floor, and there would be guards outside the staff elevator.

From there it was up sixty-eight floors to where Zayid was doing his thing.

Simple. What could *possibly* go wrong?

✪

What indeed?

How about the extra SWAT-rigged security facing us as soon as we stepped out of the service tunnel?

I still don't know what the hell went wrong. Maybe Dee missed a security line when she hacked in. Maybe the whole op was compromised from the start. Hell, maybe we were set up. But Cammie stepped through that door, muttered a heartfelt oscar-sierra over her comm, and rolled for it as the bullets started slamming into the wall.

Scoot spat something under his breath, and a guard three meters away snapped backward, arms pinwheeling as he slammed into a wall. Thud reached out with two hands the size of large turkeys and grabbed a couple of other guards by the throats, hoisting them off the floor and giving them a hard shake as a pacifier. I stepped out from behind him with my Predator IV in both hands, squeezing off one shot after another into the mob of black-suits in front of us.

I don't know if it was Scoot's stunbolt, the sight of the Predator, or Thud's enthusiasm, but the rent-a-cops still standing bolted for the cover of a bend in the hallway. I pulled out a bouncy-boom, squeezing hard to arm it. I tossed it hard, aiming to bounce off the floor, hit the back corridor wall, and ricochet behind the corner. On the third bounce, it detonated with a serious ear-ringing wham, and corp-cops were spilling back out into the opening, hands clutched to bleeding ears.

"Put 'em to sleep, Thud-boy!" I called. I didn't like killing the local security, even if a second ago they'd been trying to kill *me*. After all, their only crime was trying to earn an honest credstick ... unlike yours truly.

They'd have headaches when they woke up, after Thud finished with them, but probably no broken bones. *Probably*.

The elevator required an electronic passkey. Dee could have finagled it ... but one of the guards was nice enough to furnish us with one. We crowded inside—it's always a crowd with Thud present—and told it we wanted the 68th floor.

Of course, we *weren't* born yesterday. Thud had the maintenance hatch in the car's ceiling open with one, heavy-fisted bam, and we were already scrambling up through the opening and on top the roof when the car came to an abrupt and unscheduled halt between floors 64 and 65. When the gas came hissing into the car beneath us, we were already on the maintenance access ladder and climbing.

Cammie paused long enough to drop an RFID gas sensor down the open hatch in the elevator and check the result on her commlink.

"Shit!" she said, pocketing the comm and starting to climb. "Neurotox! One-whiff deadly! *Climb*!"

Hell, that just sucked big slimy ork toes. The corp-bastards *could* have used sleepy-gas. These guys were trying to kill us!

At the sixty-sixth level we let ourselves in through a maintenance hatch, and quietly slipped into a nearby stairwell. We were two floors from our goal and well ahead of sched. We didn't have the luxury of much time, though. It would take them maybe ten minutes to ventilate the elevator, and then they'd know we'd stepped out. And *up*.

Scoot used another of his bolts to slam an armed and armored guard in the stairway senseless, and Dee tripped the maglock on the door to the 68th floor. We were in.

But I scowled at my watch and signaled for the others to wait. The toughest part about this op was the timing. We knew from our informant that Zayid expected to get the "merchandise" at midnight tonight ... and we were running about four minutes fast. If we burst in on the chanters now, we might interrupt the circle, keep them from opening the gate ... which, of course, meant we couldn't get the merchandise either.

Assuming there was any merchandise to get. I still couldn't make myself believe that we were going to find the storied *Necronomicon* when we broke up Zayid's little party.

But we waited, waited as sweat prickled at our necks and backs, waited as Scooter psychically scanned for approaching trouble.

The nanny on my forehead itched. The thing drew power for the cam and mike set from my skin. The larger transmitter on my belt had a built-in power unit all its own. I hoped our unseen employers were getting an eyeful; we were counting on them to airlift us off the roof after we'd completed the hit. It was better than trying to fight our way all the way back down the M&M Tower to the street.

Time.

I looked back at Thud, who crouched behind me with his usual patient mountain-presence. His forehead sloped back so sharply between his massive horns that we'd placed his nanny on his throat. Otherwise, our peeping Toms would've seen nothing but the ceiling through his minicam. "Get to the roof," I told him. "Clear it and wait for us. Got it?"

"Got it," he rumbled. He unslung the autocannon he'd been wearing over his shoulder and gave it a friendly pat. "I wait for you."

So now it was just the three of us, stepping through the stairwell door and moving along the passageway looking for Conference Room 68-4. That was where our informant had said Zayid was casting his circles. It ought to be just ahead.

And we could hear it now ... an eerie, droning harmony of male voices. We couldn't make out the words, but we could hear the tones easily enough, moaning and buzzing and humming from the next doorway down the hall. There was another guard standing there, but Scooter was muttering under his breath again, throwing up a stealth spell around us as we closed in on him. He saw us ... but too late. He went down as Dee burst-fired three silenced rounds into him from her Ingram Smartgun.

The door beside the body was locked, and the passkey on the body didn't work.

By now, the building's defenses must be fully alerted to our presence. We had minutes now, at most, before a small corporate army converged on the 68th floor.

Midnight. Now the only question was whether Zayid's people were on time inside that conference room. I considered waiting another minute ... but a minute is forever on a run, and I didn't much care to hang around in a corporate hallway waiting for the M&M goons to show. I nodded at Dee, and she went to work on the lock with a sequencer.

I could hear the chanting much more clearly now. Funny words ... incomprehensible, like people trying to gargle and cough at the same time.

"*Ph'nglui mglw'nafh Cthulhu R'lyeh wgah'nagl fhtagn. . . .*"

The maglock hummed and opened and the door slid aside. A cloud of pungently sour incense wafted out as we plunged into darkness.

The room was huge, and seemed larger with the lights off. An oval pool of light marked the center twenty meters up ahead, where robed figures stood in a circle filled with a shifting, auroral glow.

"*Ph'nglui mglw'nafh Cthulhu R'lyeh wgah'nagl fhtagn. . . .*"

Twelve men with raised hands continued the eerie chant. That could only mean that the thirteenth figure, robed and hooded and standing at the circle's center, hadn't yet managed to establish the astral gate.

I hesitated, unsure, now, as to what to do.

The chant faltered as we stepped into the room. "*Keep going!*" the central figure shouted. "*Keep the chant going!*"

"*Ph'nglui mglw'nafh Cthulhu R'lyeh wgah'nagl fhtagn. . . .*"

The guy in the center had to be Zayid, and he seemed flustered. Good, because that gave me my chance to take control of the situation. "Good evening," I said, and I walked forward, keeping my Predator aimed at Zayid. "Hope you'll excuse the interruption. Don't move—and don't try any magic on us—and no one gets hurt."

Sure, it was trite. But I wasn't thinking real clearly at the moment.

"What are you doing here!" Zayid snapped. "You have no business here!"

"On the contrary. I have some very important business here."

Zayid was a big man, hooded and robed like the others, but I saw his eyes glaring at me from beneath the cowl. Behind him was an altar, with a sword, a chalice, a bell, and a clutter of less readily identifiable stuff. A couple of six-foot candle stands to either side cast most of the physical light ... but that weird aurora shifted and danced in the air around them.

"You do not understand what you're dealing with here," Zayid said. "You have no possible conception! I recommend that you and your people turn around and quietly leave. Now."

"Thanks, but I think we'll hang for a while. This looks interesting."

I was taking in the chalked-out marks on the floor surrounding the thirteen magicians. They'd drawn your standard nine-foot circle— a double circle, actually, filled with your standard arcane occult sigils, signs, and squiggles. Just outside the circle, touching it at one point, was a chalk triangle three feet across.

"How about it, Scoot?" I asked.

Scooter had his hands up, facing the circle and the chanters in a kind of magical stand-off. They outnumbered us, but they were penned inside their protective circle. I *hoped* that meant they couldn't flame us from in there, or worse. And Scoot was working some protective spells, just in case.

"Looks like an ordinary Hermetic ritual," Scooter said, his brow furrowed with concentration. He was using The Voice. "Complete with a triangle of evocation. The circle protects the magicians inside. The triangle is where whatever you're summoning is supposed to appear. Now *don't* break my concentration!"

I stepped closer, keeping my Predator aimed at the black-robed bunch inside the circle. I was pretty sure that whatever protection those chalks marks conferred on the chanters, they were more effective against spirits and beings and forces coming out of the astral than they were against copper-jacketed slugs with a muzzle velocity of 400 meters per second.

"Ph'nglui mglw'nafh Cthulhu R'lyeh wgah'nagl fhtagn. . . ."

That droning chant was getting inside my head. I felt a bit dizzy, though I was putting that down to the adrenaline rush of combat.

"Careful!" Scoot warned. "Don't break the triangle!"

"I'm not." I peered inside.

And ... *Dunkelzahn*! There was something *in* there!

It was tough to see clearly. There was something ... *wrong* about the space above and inside that triangle, something that made my eyes ache as I tried to follow the shifting blur of fog and cold light moving inside. But I could make out one solid shape within the haze—a book. A very *large* book.

And it was speaking to me.

"Ph'nglui mglw'nafh Cthulhu R'lyeh wgah'nagl fhtagn. . . ."

Okay. I'm not a magician, but I'm *not* stupid. I know a little about the astral.

Part of the Awakening, you see, was the opening of channels between what we were always so smugly pleased to call the "real world," and the astral, a kind of parallel universe "on the other side" whatever the hell *that* might mean. The astral is the realm of spirits, demons, elementals, and other occult entities, and it may be generated by all life here on Earth. Magicians go up onto the astral all the time to read auras or taste the emotional or magical imprints lingering on material items.

Beyond the astral are the metaplanes, other worlds, other realities accessible only to highly trained initiated magicians ... and even the best mages have limits to where they can pass.

This was not the astral I was looking into within the triangle ... nor was it one of the more usual or accessible metaplanes. This was something decidedly else. . . .

The *Necronomicon*.

It was fiction, damn it, a myth, a literary *gimmick* created by a hack pulp-writer to spice up his story submissions to *Weird Tales* a century and a half ago.

And yet I had no doubt whatsoever that what I was seeing within that luminous aether was the fabled tome of dark magic itself—bigger and thicker than an encyclopedia, bound with iron hasps, with a binding of some brown, leathery material heavily wrinkled and cracked. As I stared at it, one of the puckers in the leather opened, revealing a still-living eye, an eye staring up at me with what might have been a keen and analyzing intelligence ... or stark, shrieking madness.

"*Ph'nglui mglw'nafh Cthulhu R'lyeh wgah'nagl fhtagn. . . .*"

According to the mythos, the thing had started out as the *Kitab Al-Azif*, written in Arabic by the Mad Arab with the impossible name somewhere around 730 A.D. Two centuries later, a Byzantine scholar, Theodorus Philetas, translated it into Greek, and called it the *Necronomicon*—the Book of Dead Names. . . .

I holstered my Predator, and took another step toward the triangle. The air was bitingly cold.

"*Fixer!*" Dee-Dee screamed. "*No!*" Cammie was lunging at me and Scooter was just starting to turn, trying to block me ... but I reached into that ethereal light with both hands, grasped the Book, and pulled it out.

No, I *didn't* know what I was doing, so don't ask! It felt like a dream, really, distant and insubstantial, like I was watching something happening to someone else. I saw the chanting magicians relax, though, and I saw Zayid throw back his head and give a wild and shocking laugh.

"*Thank* you, my impetuous friend!" he said, and he sounded almost relieved. The auroral light was gone, now, the chamber illuminated solely by the flicker of the candles.

"*Fixer!*" Thud's voice was bellowing in my ear over the commlink. "Fixer! It's a trap!" Over the link I could hear the whop-whop-whop of a helicopter, the stuttering crackle of automatic weapons. "*Fixer!*" Thud bellowed again from the roof. "*It's—*"

And the channel went dead.

At the same instant, Dee-Dee and Cammie both raised their weapons, aiming at Zayid ... but there was a crack and a flash of lightning, and both women were tossed backward in a sharp, actinic glare of magical light. Scooter was screaming, clawing at his eyes, dropping to his knees. . . .

"You may place the book on the floor *outside* of the triangle," Zayid told me, "then step away with your hands high above your head."

I was aware of doors opening, of light spilling through from outside. M&M security people were spilling in, and I heard the click-clack of their weapons as they took aim. They killed poor Dee first, shooting her down as she tried to rise. Gunfire echoed through the chamber, cutting down Scooter and Cammie both.

My whole team, wiped out in the space of three seconds. . . .

Cammie ...

She was curled up in a bloody fetal curl, whimpering. Scooter was dead on his back, arms outflung, blood pooling beneath his body.

"Place the book on the floor outside of the triangle, Mr. Michaels," Zayid said. "Slowly and carefully."

I met his eyes. How in hell had he known my birth name?

I looked at the others, all watching me expectantly from the depths of their hoods. One of them, I knew, must be the one called Shifter, our informant. But if they knew my name, Zayid and those working for him must have done a hell of a lot of digging to find out about me. This whole miserable op had been a freaking *set-up*, for Christ's sake. We'd been suckered here specifically to get this book.

And maybe it made sense, in a weird, puppet-master kind of way. The protective circle was inviolable. Zayid couldn't drop it or break it without risking some rather nasty metaphysical consequences. Someone outside the circle had to come in and actually lift the *Necronomicon* out of the triangle, out of the metaplane where it had manifested.

I suppose they could have hired some poor schmuck to do the grabbing, some rent-a-cop or clueless middle-management corpie ... or maybe the spell required an outsider, or even an enemy, someone with his own will, doing his own bidding, doing it *voluntarily*.

For whatever reason, the bastards had sought out our Mr. Johnson and, through him, hired us to do the actual grab from the metaplane. And now they had what they wanted. I could feel all those guns aimed at me from around the room, feel the eyes and the sharp magical focus of the chanters, feel Zayid's mad delight.

I felt that single, nightmare eye peering out from the cover of the book in my hands, looking up at me with its glare of malevolent madness. It whispered to me, in my mind, whispering blasphemous things about God and power and life. Hideous things, things so terrible I can no longer remember the words.

But I remember their *feel*. And the fire-charred and worm-eaten and ichor-slimed malevolence behind them.

"Don't be foolish, Mr. Michaels," one of the chanters said. He brushed back the hood of his robe. I recognized the face—Roger Nakamura. "Put the book down. You will come to no harm, I promise you. Your friend there needs medical help. And you have no place to go."

"Maybe not." My voice cracked. *Cammie! I'm so sorry I got you into this!* "But *you* can go straight to hell!"

I dropped, falling into a knee-bend crouch, and as I did so, as a dozen fingers tightened on the triggers of those aimed weapons behind me, I snapped out with my right leg, the sole of my combat boot on the floor inside the now empty triangle, and swept in a sharp turn to the left, dragging my foot across the chalk marks, scuffing a gap between triangle and circle where they'd touched.

Then I lost my balance and fell flat on my face, and that might have saved my life as full-auto gunfire cracked and reverberated through the conference room.

A few of the bullets meant for me chewed through black robes and thrashing chanters. "*Don't shoot!*" Nakamura was screaming. "*Idiots! Don't shoot!*" One of the magicians sprawled back against the altar, knocking the table and both candle stands over. The flames flared, then winked out.

But there was still light. . . .

Flat on my belly, the *Necronomicon* clutched beneath me, I couldn't see what was happening very well, but I could see that that cold and sickly illumination was back, all shifting blues and greens, and as I looked up I could see the look of sheer, brain-curdling terror on Zayid's face as *something* like a sinuous shadow stretched past and over me, uncoiling to reach from the unplumbed depths of that hellish triangle to encircle and grasp the shrieking Arab mage.

Gunfire continued to bark, but it wasn't aimed at me. I rolled over onto my back, still clutching the evil book to my chest, and looked up into sheerest Nightmare. . . .

People nowadays think they understand magic. They think they understand the Awakening. Orks. Trolls. Elves. Astral spirits. Elementals. Magic circles. Mystic incantations. It's all frou-frou, man. Fluffy-bunny Halloween dress-up make-believe, robed in black and pretending to be all about *power*. I looked into the face of that ... that *thing* emerging from the triangle of evocation and I knew that our magic-obsessed and technically adept modern reality was nothing, *nothing* compared to the eldritch Horror writhing and gibbering at Reality's gates.

Five of the chanters inside the circle were hanging in the air, now, shrieking and struggling as near-invisible tentacles slowly but inexorably squeezed. Nakamura was among them, his eyes bugging from his face in agonizing, mind-rending terror. The rent-a-cops were running, but the Thing had reached out from the triangle and grabbed two of them as well.

And tentacles were reaching for me.

"*Here*!" I screamed. "*Take it*!" And I hurled the heavy book at the monstrous chaos emerging from the triangle's rift. The tentacles hovering above me snatched the book from the air, and by then I was scrambling to Cammie's side, scooping her up in my arms, and running, *running* like Doomsday itself was descending upon us.

And for all I knew, it was. The entire building was shaking and swaying, as though its century-old structure was barely containing the unimaginable force emerging from that alien plane. Ceiling panels and overhead lighting tubes burst and fell in a shower of glass and plastic. The floor danced and shivered, earthquake-wracked, and I heard shatterproof windows outside the room shattering, the crashes like gunshots.

It sounded like the whole damned building was screaming. . . .

I reached the nearest door, pausing just long enough for a quick glance back over my shoulder. Maybe the Thing had what it wanted. One by one, the shrieking, squirming men suspended in the air vanished, though I swear I could hear their fading screams long after they'd gone.

I could still hear them as I descended the stairwell.

✪

The surviving guards had rushed out ahead of us, mingling with the late-night crowds downstairs who wondered what the commotion was up in the penthouse. I was stopped a couple of times by white-faced security people, but got by each time by saying, "Special security, with Roger Nakamura! I've got *wounded* here! Get the hell out of my way!"

Somewhere in all the confusion, I'd lost my nanny ... and I'd peeled Cammie's off her blood-splattered face. They wouldn't track us. The *humans* wouldn't, anyway.

Gods of all the Metaverse ... what did I *see*?

It still haunts me.

It wasn't a mouth that got Zayid and Nakamura. I don't *think* it was a mouth.

Is it true that our thoughts create Reality? That imaginal beings and places and nightmare horrors all somehow take shape and form and mass and seething, malevolent will in some other dimension, some other metaphysical plane?

Our myths may have more reality than we can credit. Beelzebub and Lucifer. Dark Hecate and Ammit, Eater of Souls. Yog-Sothoth, Keeper of the Gate, and Great Cthulhu, dreaming in the depths until the stars are right.

Perhaps whatever *can* be imagined is *real*, somehow, solid and fully manifested, residing just beyond the insubstantial gauze veils of Reality rising around us. Perhaps evil, true evil, arises from the light-less corners of our own hearts and minds. Perhaps even our darkest nightmares take shape and will, gibbering at the gates.

I have nightmares, now. Nightmares about Dee-Dee and Scooter and patient Thud. Dead names, now.

The nightmares where I again see the Thing are the worst.

And at night Cammie takes me in her arms and whispers soothing words in my ear and holds me close and tells me it's all right.

But it's not.

I can still hear the screams, the terror-maddened shrieks of souls dragged down into darkness. I still hear the despair. The wrenching agony of dying souls.

And I can still hear the blasphemous whisperings of the Book.

The Book of Dead Names.

Oh, gods! Gods in whom I've *never* believed, help me! ✪

THE ART OF DIVING IN THE DARK

BY ILSA J. BICK

Ilsa J. Bick is an award-winning, bestselling writer of short stories, ebooks and novels as well as a child psychiatrist, film scholar, surgeon wannabe and former Air Force major. (She is also fairly peripatetic and easily bored, but no fair diagnosing her until she's left the room.) She has published extensively in the Star Trek™, BattleTech™ *and* MechWarrior: Dark Age™ *universes, as well as original science fiction, fantasy and mystery.* The Key, *a supernatural murder-mystery about the Holocaust and reincarnation, was named "distinguished" in* The Best American Mystery Stories, 2005 *(edited by Joyce Carol Oates); a novelette-length sequel,* Second Sight, *has just been released in Crime Spells (eds. Martin H. Greenberg and Loren L. Coleman);* Locus's *Rich Horton calls the novelette " the best (in the anthology) ... heady and involving."*

Forthcoming are two young adult novels, in hardcover, from Carolrhoda Books: Draw in the Dark, *a paranormal mystery* Publisher's Weekly *called "inventive" and "riveting," which also made the semifinals of the 2009 Amazon Breakthrough Novel Award (as* Stalag Winter*); and* The Sin Eater's Confession, *revolving around the murder of a gay high school student in rural Wisconsin.*

Currently, Ilsa and her family live in Wisconsin where theirs is the only mezuzah in town.

–Küpau wau i ka manö ka manö nui ka manö nui küpau wau i ka manö:

I am finished to the big shark, all consumed by the big shark, I am finished.

(Old Hawaiian saying)

Somewhere off the Kohala Coast, Hawai'i
May 9, 2070

Something wrong.

A beautiful day, a light breeze, the sea placid as blue glass, the auras of dolphins shimmering like comets screaming to earth.

But something was definitely wrong. A distant hiss of evil whispering from the depths like a murder of crows muttering on a naked limb above a newly-turned grave. The water's fingers stroked the hairs along his arms and neck into stiff hackles through his drysuit. Something snagged the meat of his brain like the set of a hook. Reeling him in ...

Knows we're here. Maybe that's what it wants. Beneath his vest—definitely not standard-issue—a cold sweat pearled his chest. A new and more troubling thought: *Jesus, can its magic reach this far? Can it see what I think?*

Not good. He'd have to watch himself. No use tipping it off ...

These are the demons. Daniel Ben-Yusuf raised a finger to his throat. Rachel's mezuzah hung around his neck—a focus, or simply a protective amulet of silver and amethyst, he was never sure—but his gloved fingers met only chilled trilaminates and butyl rubber. *These are the princes of enmity dwelling in the abyss ...*

With the sleds, the light went fast, turning thin and watery at twenty meters. There were still plenty of fish—a rainbow of gobies and triggerfish and angels—darting in and around dense pinkish-white forests of elkhorn coral and the bristly quills of sea urchins. By the time his HUD said he was at twenty-five, the water was a weird blue-gray, and by thirty, as they stopped to purge their low-pressure lines and switch out to heliox, the reef was completely vertical, the fish petering out, the anvil of water palming Daniel's body dense and heavy. Far below, the sea was a very cold cobalt blue, the color of a lost day slipping inexorably toward night.

At sixty meters, they tied off their bail-out tank, double-checked their spare air canisters. (Hey, call him a cockeyed optimist, but if something went wrong at depth, the spare air might get one, or both of them to the bail-out.) At ninety-seven meters, a click sounded in his full facemask, and Alana's voice fizzed through, tinny and flat because of the depth: "Oh shit. Look down, your two o'clock."

The maw of the cave—a dead, unknown undersea volcano between the Big Island and Maui—yawned deep and fathomless, a nearly perfect circle as black as an empty eye socket. Just below the rim, a pair of motionless dive sleds was suspended on tethers.

But that kind of paled when you considered the sharks.

A school of white-tip reef sharks spooled up in a silent swirl, their auras ghostly, nacreous penumbras as insubstantial as cobwebs.

"Oh my God." Alana's voice was shaky. "Daniel, what ... ?"

"I don't know. Take it easy." He watched the phalanx of animals ascend, saw them veer as one toward Alana.

"Daniel?" A note of panic now. Her hand moved to her dive knife.

"Alana, no. That's a fight you don't want and can't win." Her aura blazed in his astral vision: a fierce, fiery orange-red sunburst, a supernova. He watched as the sharks angled right and began to circle the woman in a stately clockwise procession, maintaining their distance, never closing, never peeling away. "Honey, listen to me: It's *you*, don't you see?"

"Yes, yes, kayn." For the first time during the dive, the Rebbe's voice sizzled through his aural implant. A novel design, the implant could penetrate at depth and halfway around the world if need be. *"It is the only explanation."*

"What?" She was startled. "What are you talking about?"

"It's like the petroglyph. You're calling them somehow." He had an idea, a theory and the Rebbe echoed his thoughts: *"She's a latent. The tooth is a focus, kayn? But it's old, there is DNA ..."*

Daniel said, "Alana, were they here when you and Harriman ...?"

"No. I don't know. The only thing I remember is the descent and ..." She drew in a sudden sharp breath. "You *feel* that?"

He did: a tug. Not like the touch of magic this time but palpable, a swirl of current grabbing his body, first gently and then with more insistence like the subtle rush of water upstream that signaled the beginning of rapids just around the bend.

Something else homing in on her ... on us ...

The sharks felt it, too. They closed, their circle tightening round Alana, but he didn't think that would do any good.

"Okay, here's where you get gone," he said. "I'll take it from here."

"Lo, lo!" The Rebbe hissed. *"No, what are you doing? You must replicate the conditions of her encounter* exactly."

Yeah, yeah, yeah. At that moment, he wished like hell that the Rebbe was psychic instead of eavesdropping. *You're way the fuck in Israel. We're the ones on a one-way trip to hell.*

"Not a chance," said Alana. "We go together. Lee's still in there."

"That wasn't the deal."

"No, lo, take her. She's ..." the Rebbe began but then abruptly cut out.

What the hell? Then he felt it: how the sea went turgid and thick, the pressure fisting his body. Instead of rising, Daniel's bubbles hung in shuddering silver pearls, caught in a pocket scooped out of time.

Oh shit ... "Alana!" His voice came out as a wheeze, barely audible. His body felt gluey, like a fly upended on its back in a puddle of honey. "Alana, go, swim, take your sled, *go!*"

Too late. Alana gasped, and then her body gave a great, convulsive jerk as something clamped round her ankles and yanked, hard. As one, the sharks knotted in a swirl, but they were creatures that must always move, or die and so there were gaps, and he saw what would happen before it did.

No, he thought frantically, *take me!* I'm *the one you want ... !*

"D-Daniel!" Alana wailed. "Help ... h-help me!"

No, no! He wanted to scream, he wanted to hurl something killing, banish her someplace safe—and he should've while he had the chance and damn the drain; what a fool! But too late now: He couldn't move. Blood pounded in his temples. Blackness ate at the margins of his vision. He fought to clear his head, looked down at the seamount—and his heart nearly died in his chest.

A swirl of astral energy, livid as a bruise, spiraled up from the maw of the cave, twining round their bodies like the sticky weave of a spider's web. At its touch, the sharks writhed, and their formation faltered.

"N-no!" Alana's hands flew up, her wrists pinned together, and her back arched in a sudden, agonized rictus. Her sled spun away, and then her screams filled his ears as the astral web drew her down, down ...

The web closed round and then he was hurtling, the water roaring, the ring of sharks flying apart and blurring at his passage ...

And then the darkness took them both.

✪

Four Days Earlier
Kohala Neuropsychiatric Institute, Hawai'i
May 7, 2070

The psychiatrist's voice, brisk, officious: *Let's try again, Alana. Go back to the beginning and maybe we can push through some of your ...*

Denial? The word was muddy and Daniel thought that, yeah, she'd been medicated up the yin-yang. Understandable, though. The emergency evac records indicated that Alana Kamakua had been distraught, disoriented: her hands pulpy, drysuit in tatters after her mad scramble over knife-edged lava. She hadn't wanted to leave the beach, insisting the evac unit rescue her lover ... As if the bits of drysuit washed ashore in a swirl of purple water belonged to someone else.

Given that, who wouldn't be, well, a little upset?

I've told you: I remember going into the caves. Alana's voice seethed with frustration. *Then our lights went out–and then I don't remember. The next thing I know, I'm on a stretcher ...*

The doctor paused the recording. "Her thoughts get pretty derailed after that. She goes on about some old Hawaiian myth, or family story, I don't know, something she says her umptity-ump great-grandmother passed down. Even if I believed in psychoanalysis, I'm not sure you'd find much symbolism in an old Hawaiian legend of a fair maiden and a shark."

"Don't make the mistake of accepting his presumptions." The Rebbe's rich baritone was a faint faraway hiss, like the fizzle of a commlink tuned to a dead channel. *"Besides, he's a* tachat.*"*

No argument there: The doctor *was* an ass. Daniel said, "But didn't the police think Harriman was attacked by a shark?"

"Who the hell knows? Maybe *she* did him in."

"You believe that?"

"Hey, call me a cynical bastard, but I'm always suspicious."

No, you're just a bastard. His thought, not the Rebbe's. *"Yet many stories have personal valence. Maybe the myth means something."*

"Uh-huh." A pause. "Look, Mr. ... uh ..."

"Fehrmacht." The alias, the well-doctored background information, and the vague implication that he worked for Saeder-Krupp, with the hint that Lofwyr might be, well, *interested*, opened a lot of doors. That, and plenty of nuyen. An Israeli Mossad agent, even one in semi-retirement and with more than a little bit of a death wish, had a lot of tricks up his proverbial sleeve. It was one of the reasons why the Rebbe had chosen Daniel in the first place.

"Yeah. Well, look: I don't do stories. I'm not into magic. I'm a shrink, and I practice without the voodoo, thanks."

Okay, so the doctor was also a self-righteous little prick. Daniel was jet-lagged, nearly dead on his feet from the long flight, first from Tel Aviv to Sydney and from there to Honolulu International and *then*, finally, a hop to the Big Island. He'd been stewing in the same clothes for the last two days. The last thing he was interested in was playing footsie with a tin-pot dictator. "You're not prejudiced, are you, Doc?"

The Rebbe: *"Lo, Daniel, don't provoke him. We need his cooperation."*

"No, I'm pragmatic," said the doctor. "Now, I'm willing to entertain the theory that there were earlier metahuman ages—"

"Theory?"

"Daniel ..."

The doctor ignored the gibe. "And I'm happy to consider that our mythologies, and that includes those of the various religions, reflect those earlier epochs. Every culture and religion has its little people and boogeymen, its magical amulets and taboos."

Okay, Daniel considered, that was true. He was suddenly conscious of the weight of Rachel's silver and amethyst mezuzah that hung from his neck beneath his shirt. A ward against evil, yes; a focus, perhaps. So why had she left it behind ... ?

He said, "So you're sticking with traumatic amnesia." When the doctor nodded, Daniel went on: "Will her memory return?"

"Maybe *sí*, maybe *no*." The doctor steepled his fingers the way a professor does when lecturing to the dumbest kid in class. "The head injury's legit, but not *that* bad. But you tell me: Just how likely is it that *six* lights malfunctioned? That their directional guidance beacons failed? That Lee Harriman's cyber-eyes chose that moment to go completely black? If we believe her story, every single artificially-powered system—from communications to propulsion to dive computers—went on the fritz. So tell me this: How did she get from depth to the surface without a dive computer calculating her decompression stops? Hell, how did she get up without *air*? All she had was a drysuit. No gear at all."

"Maybe it was magic." He meant it as a dig, but the doctor frowned.

"Trust me, she's a mundane. No bioware implants even. The CSI team had an adept check her over, and he found nothing: no astral signature, nothing in her history to suggest a latent ability. As for the whole systems' failure stuff, land-based monitoring systems didn't pick up a single communications hiccup or Matrix glitch that entire day. So, all we've got is her story and pieces of a dead guy's suit."

"*Eifo?*"

"Where did it happen?" asked Daniel.

"She either doesn't remember or isn't saying. The evac team touched down about a half mile west of Waipi'o Valley. There are, maybe, fifty people in the place and about half are named Dave. Anyway, the Menehune have claimed the whole place. Nasty little buggers."

Privately, Daniel doubted that anything could be worse than a *shedu* and although the beings that oozed into this world bore little resemblance to the "no-gods" of Jewish lore and mysticism, their malevolence was identical. (Well, all except stories about the ones who studied Torah and followed the commandments ... but those must be exceptionally *good* shedim. He'd never met—or bound—any of *those*.) "Anything on her boyfriend, Harriman?"

"Nope. Did a lot of tech diving, sometimes hired himself out to places like the Atlantean."

"A relic hunter."

"Not by choice. I got the impression that it was mainly contract work, but Harriman wasn't working for anyone that we know of, and he wasn't a shadowrunner."

Daniel didn't bother pointing out that if you knew a shadowrunner when you saw him, the guy either wasn't very good or *you* were three seconds away from a morgue slab. "So, back to either a lie, or an accident."

"Or a little of both. *He* could've gotten into trouble, and *she* might've panicked. But the police have closed it, and I've got enough work to do. So." The doctor yawned and stretched. "We're pretty much done here. She can leave whenever."

"Tov, tov, good. Get her away from this godforsaken place. We don't have that much time, Daniel. You must find it before—"

"So you have no objection if I speak with her," said Daniel.

"Hell no, knock yourself out." The psychiatrist eyed him curiously. "But what's S-K's interest in all this? I mean, she's an *archaeologist*, for Christ's sake."

Daniel scraped back his chair and stood. "You've been very helpful, Doctor. A pleasure." A lie, on all counts. "I'd like to see her now."

The doctor might be a jerk, but he wasn't an idiot. His face smoothed into a mask of professional neutrality. "Sure. I'll have someone bring her to an interview room."

"Lo, get her out of there."

"Actually, if you don't mind, I had something a little more comfortable in mind. Something outside the hospital," said Daniel.

"What makes you think she'll go with you?"

Daniel said nothing.

The doctor thought another moment then said, "Well, there's the little problem of her expenses ..."

Daniel was already punching up numbers on his commlink. "How much?"

✪

It was late afternoon by the time they stopped in Hawi at a little restaurant, an old hotel converted into a popular eatery still going strong after a hundred and fifty years. Their waitress, a cheerful woman as round as a raspberry named "Auntie," recommended the macadamia-encrusted ono with jasmine rice.

They sat over sweating glasses of passionfruit iced tea, Daniel still a little ... unsettled. When the psych tech led Alana into the doctor's office, he'd done a double-take, his heart suddenly twisting in his chest.

Because Alana looked *that* much like Rachel: petite and bronzed, with high cheekbones, the same widow's peak, the identical set of jaw; a narrow, aristocratic nose though Alana's was a little off-kilter, like she'd broken it way back when. Her aura was strong: a scintillating blood-orange.

(Had Rachel's been the same? He couldn't remember and that made him sad.)

The main difference between the two women, though, was in the eyes. Rachel's had been an arresting hazel flecked with green, vibrant and alive. Alana's were dusky black pearls, haunted and drawn.

"Tell me something." Alana traced a finger in the dew of her glass. "Why do you keep staring at me?"

"Am I? Sorry. You remind me of someone, that's all. Your aura is ... interesting."

"I see." Pause. "Did you love her?"

Daniel blinked. A sudden talon of grief dug at his chest, and he recognized it as the danger signal it was.

The Rebbe, silent for the last two hours, sensed his distress because he broke in: *"Careful, my son. Focus on getting the information. The rest is ..."* But even *he* didn't finish the thought.

"Very much." Daniel tried a smile that he knew failed. "You don't waste any time."

"I'm sorry." She touched the back of his hand. "It's just that your eyes are so sad and ... hungry."

"So what made you come with such a mad and melancholy man?"

"The shrinks weren't helping. I didn't like being treated like a criminal."

"Well, shrinks are paid to be skeptics." He should know. Mossad's psychological screening included an exhaustive battery of tests, interviews and neural scans. Not pleasant to have someone finger-walking then dissecting your thoughts and dreams. And, of course, after Rachel had disappeared and his handler tracked him to that safe house where Daniel had been considering the merits of a well-placed bullet to the brain ... then he'd had to see another shrink, a dyspeptic shrew who seemed to get off on his suffering.

"Please. Did you spend any time with that doctor?" A fleeting spasm of her lips as she tried for a smile. "A good thing he kept me kind of dopey the first couple days, or else I'd have broken his nose. He thought I was faking, the asshole." Her shirt was open at the throat, and her fingers crept to a shark's tooth dangling from a black cord. The tooth was perhaps five centimeters long and tawny with serrated edges. She played with the charm. "But it's the *truth*."

"I *know*," said Daniel, gravely. "That doctor *is* an asshole." She laughed out loud this time, a good sound, and he grinned. "That's better."

"Yeah." But she sobered, the smile leaking away. "You think you're never going to be happy again."

Their salads came. As he stabbed arugula and mango, Daniel chinned in the general direction of her necklace. "That looks pretty old."

"This?" Chewing, she glanced myopically down, swallowed, said, "My gran claimed that it came from an extinct great white, but who knows. I've never bothered getting it dated. It's supposed to have big-time mojo, but since no Menehune ever appeared and I still had to study my ass off to defend my dissertation ... Anyway, the story goes that all the first-born daughters in my family are supposed to wear the tooth and pass it on, etc., etc. We even get a tattoo." Thrusting her left leg from beneath the table, she pulled up her jeans to reveal a circlet of black-inked wedges lacing her ankle. "Not quite the same as the petroglyph for shark, but close."

"That the story you told the doctor? The first-born stuff?"

Her skin flushed copper, and she found something intensely interesting on her plate. "You heard that. God, I'm so embarrassed. He was just such a ... It's just a myth, a kind of Romeo and Juliet thing: the daughter of a chief falls in love with the son of a rival chief; he gets killed; she tries killing herself. In ancient Hawaiian tradition, bones are sacred and have a lot of mana. Sometimes they were distributed to chiefs and other important people ... that's what happened to Captain Cook, actually."

"You're kidding."

"I kid you not. Somewhere on this island, someone's got a jaw-bone; someone else has a couple fingers. That's how they did it. More often, though, the bones were wrapped in tapa and slotted into hidden niches along high cliffs. The way they used to do it, a volunteer was lowered over the side and placed the bones, and then the *kahuna* cut the rope."

"Ouch. Talk about taking a secret to the grave. Let me guess: the daughter changed places and went over the cliff with her lover's bones."

"And cut the rope, yup. Only she didn't die on the rocks. She started sinking and then all of a sudden this huge shark appears, grabs her ankle and tows her far down the Kohala coast. Lets her go near Pelekane Bay. When she tries wading back out, the shark won't let her and she goes ballistic. The shark finally says: *Don't you know me? It is I, Kimo, your dead love, and I tell you now that you are not done with life. Let go of my bones, my love, and live.*" She gave a rueful smile. "Silly, right?"

"I don't think it's silly at all. Did she? Let go, I mean."

"Yeah. Anyway, the shark disappeared. Later, she discovered it had left a tooth embedded in her ankle." She tapped the charm around her neck. "At least, that's the claim. Afterward, she ordered that a shark *heiau*, a special sacrificial altar, be constructed in the bay to worship the shark-god. The altar's gone now but wearing the tooth, having the tattoo ... makes me feel connected, you know? To history, to the land."

Their food came. The fish was very good—snowy-white, firm and juicy—but in his fatigue Daniel only managed a few bites. Alana forked up the last of her rice and fish in about three minutes, looked at his plate, said, "You going to want all that?"

It was something Rachel would've said: *"Daniel, sharing food's a sign of true love." "Bullshit, you just want my French fries."*

"Please." He thumbed his plate toward her. "Don't be shy on my account."

"I'm *hungry*. You ever had hospital food?"

"Not in recent memory." He waited until she'd slowed down then said, "When are you going to ask?"

She looked up, jaws working. Held up a finger. Chased her food with the last of her tea, then said, "I figure you'll tell me when you're ready. Or ask me, or whatever ... So." Wiping her mouth, she crumpled her napkin, let it fall to her plate. "Shoot. You want to know what happened, right? Well, I don't remember. What's your interest, anyway?"

"It's my job."

"And what—" she began, but Auntie trundled over, gathered their plates, inquired if they wanted dessert. He said, no, just coffee, and when Auntie was gone, Alana folded her arms on the table. "What's that?"

"I'm a kind of investigator."

"Police?"

"A private concern."

"Occult?"

He waited for the Rebbe to interject something, but his brain was, mercifully, silent. "You could say that."

"But not exactly." When he nodded, she said, "Why would what happened to me be of interest to ... well, I guess you'd say, your employer, right? Saeder-Krupp? Why would Lofwyr care?"

"Does it matter?"

She stared at him a good ten seconds then shrugged. "I guess not." She scraped back her chair and stood. "I've got to pee. Get the coffee to go and let's blow this crackerjack joint."

"And we're going ...?"

Her smile was tight, with no humor in it. "To the Land of the Dead."

✖

The access road into Waipi'o Valley could only be reached from the east, which meant they had to backtrack, dropping out of the high country into Waimea before turning northeast toward the coast. Ten klicks shy of Honokaa, they headed west, following the main drag all the way to a very abrupt end. By then, the sun was slipping away, but Daniel had seen enough on the approach to realize that they were headed into a region of soaring, nearly vertical cliffs and deep, impenetrable valleys.

"Jesus, you weren't kidding when you stressed that *dead* part." He eyed the faraway ribbon of a waterfall. A three-hundred-meter tumble, easy. "You can't be serious."

"As a heart attack. The ancient Hawaiians called the valley *Milu* after an old chief who was the king of the dead. The valley's one of two places on the island where you're supposed to be able to access the shadows. Those cliffs are where a lot of the kings are buried, right in the rock. See that beach down there?" She indicated a crescent gash of black sand two kilometers long. "Water's like glass, but the undertow and rip currents'll kill you."

"If we don't peel off the road. That's almost straight down. I'll burn out my brakes. We'll never get back out."

"This is a rental, right? So, let them worry about it. Trust me, you burn out the brakes, and they'll leave the thing where it dies. Costs a small fortune in nyuen to tow anyone out. Anyway, it's only a twenty-five percent grade, most of the way."

"Only, she says."

"Well, some of it's forty-five." She gave him a tight grin. "Look, the answer's down there. I'm offering to show you."

"Why are you being so good to me?"

"Because I like you. Besides, I want to go home, and you're my ride. It's either that, or I take a horse."

"The shrink said that only about fifty guys live in the valley."

"Yeah, yeah, and they're all named Dave." An eyeroll. "So, you want to see this, or not?"

Personally, he was tempted to suggest astral projection, but she was a mundane, so ... "Shit." He dropped the four-wheel drive into low and first. "This had better be good."

The road was short but fabulously steep: a single serpentine lane for most of the way, and in rotten condition. Worse, just as he lipped the edge, Alana said that this was one of the only places on the Big Island where you couldn't access the Matrix: "No nodes within spitting distance."

"And you *live* down here?" He was sweating, resisting the urge to ride his brakes. "What do you do? Hunt with a bow and arrow?"

"I like the quiet."

"I thought the Menehune weren't exactly the welcoming type."

"I guess I'm just special," she said.

✪

There were no lights at all, no houses he could see. To his right, he had the impression of a vast drop-off, and he heard the distant growl of the sea thundering against the shore. When the road finally leveled out, he let go of a breath he hadn't realized he'd been holding. Sweat plastered his shirt between his shoulder blades.

But that's when he noticed something else: the slight fizz in his ear was gone. *No nodes.* The silence was jarring, a sound all its own.

She studied him through the gloom. "It hits everybody the same way first time around," she said. "Lee was really restless for awhile, like if he couldn't check his e-mail every five seconds, he didn't know what to do with himself."

"Uh ..." Inwardly, he was irritated that she read him so well. Never could fool Rachel either. "I'm fine."

She gave him a look that said she thought otherwise, but instead she unbuckled. "You got a flashlight in that pack?"

✪

He had two, as it happened—with a great deal more specialized gear she didn't have to know about.

✪

The day disintegrated ten minutes after they left the rental. The night, choked with stars and a crescent moon, washed over the sky in a black tide. Their path through the woods was virtually nonexistent, a narrow cut that turned and twisted through thick stands of eucalyptus forest, thickets of wild ginger and lush hapuu ferns. He smelled water and the sweetness of lemon and strawberry guava, and when he followed his light over a suspension bridge fording a swift stream, the churn of water over rock threw up a fine, cool mist. The auras of the plants, a chorus of tree frogs, the inexorable rush of water—so much mana gathered together in one place ...

Dear God, it's like discovering Gan Eden. His fingers toyed with Rachel's mezuzah, its metal too warm, its energies awakened to the mana infusing the valley. And for the first time in what felt like forever, he heard the whisper of a voice that he recognized as Rachel's: *Because, my love, this is what it would be like to be free ...*

His breath hitched in his throat. *Rachel? Are you ... ?*

"Daniel?" Startled, he tore his astral gaze from the trees—and there she was, right beside him, the fiery sunburst of her aura like a beacon in the long night of his soul ...

Alana touched his arm, shattering the illusion. "Hey, you okay?"

"Fine," he said, drawing in a long shuddering breath. He banished his astral sense and the mundane sprang up around him again. "I'm just tired. How much longer?"

"We're here." She stabbed her light at a hummock of red and brown rock. "There was a huge tsunami in 1946. Steamrolled everything in the valley. Before then, this place was a major breadbasket. Taro fields, guava, mango, you name it. After the tsunami pulverized everything, the people just never rebuilt. The major temples were reduced to the functional equivalent of anthills. You want to see anything approaching what they were, you have to go further south to the Kohala Coast. But the tsunami also uncovered this *heiau*—at least, that's what I think. It's not in any of the historical or academic literature, and the Menehune know nothing about it."

He stepped carefully, playing his light over rough-hewn rock walls that rose twelve meters at their highest point. The structure was roughly rectangular at its base but sloped inward as it climbed. More like a crude representation of a volcano than a pyramid, he thought, which made sense.

Nimble as a goat, Alana led the way up a scramble of boulders. He followed, negotiating a three-meter drop at the summit to what he saw was an open expanse marked by more rock mounds.

She pointed her light at the rock below their feet. "That's coral, which is kind of weird this far inland. The way these things were built, slaves would've passed the rocks and coral in one continuous line from the ocean. If a rock were dropped or touched the ground, the slave would be sacrificed and the rock dropped far out to sea."

He calculated they were maybe six klicks inland and whistled. "That's a lot of slaves."

"Several thousand. We're on the west side, and so this—" her light picked out a rock tumble that rose to chest height, "—is probably the *tele*, the altar. But that's not what's so weird. Look at the rocks."

He did, and realized that what he'd thought were marks weathered into the rock by time and the elements were something else entirely. He touched a divot with tentative fingers, tracing a design of a vertical gash crisscrossed by two horizontals and surmounted by a small round divot. *Head, arms and legs ...* "It's a man. Rock carvings."

"Petroglyphs, yeah, but here's the truly weird thing. The stones were supposed to be pristine. Yet every stone—and I mean, every single visible stone—is marked. This temple is one of a kind. And look here." She swung her light at a tall pillar standing east of the altar. The gleam playing over its etched surface was weird and smoky.

"What *is* that?"

"This," she said, running a reverent hand over the pillar's surface, "is an oracle tower, an *anu'u* and no, I don't know any like this and especially none made out of a single piece of pure obsidian, solid volcanic glass. And look at these carvings. They're so delicate. Can you imagine how long it took, how much care was involved?"

Years, he thought, but he felt no special power emanating from this stone, saw nothing to indicate this was a focus, or that there might be something else hidden in its crystalline matrix. (He'd heard of such things: legends of skilled adepts able to detect the aura of the tiniest of insects entombed in amber. The theory went that since, by definition, DNA was organic and all organically-based organisms channeled mana, not only an aura but the flush of a metagenome ought to be present.) But there was nothing here. On the other hand, his talents didn't run that way.

He said, "Okay, so what does all this have to do with you?"

"Here." She circled around the pillar then angled her light halfway up the glassy surface to pick out a faint, egg-shaped blotch riddled with small pits. "That's the sign for the Big Island and this big one with that sketchy pyramid is Maui with Haleakala, which would be visible from the western rim of the valley."

Frowning, he pointed to a scatter of distinctive triangular wedges arrayed like the numerals on a clock. "What are these things between the islands?"

"*That* is a location. Those wedges are the signs of the shark."

"Like your tattoo."

"You got it. Each island has its own shark-god. For example, the Big Island's is Ukanipo. But I've never seen petroglyphs arranged quite like this and *these*." She indicated two concentric circles as wide as Daniel's hand just below the shark petroglyphs. "Look at what's chiseled in the center."

He did—and his jaw fell open. "Oh my God."

"Uh-huh. The Hawaiians carved a lot of weird shit," she said. "But never, ever a dragon."

✪

"You went looking for a rift in a seamount." They sat in a bed of *hapuu* at the base of the ruined temple. He studied her profile in the dim light of the crescent moon, but a fan of her hair hid her face. "You said you didn't remember what happened."

"I don't, not everything. But no one ever asked me *where*."

"Split hairs often?"

"Look, I'm an academic. This is huge. The only dragon we know of to come through a rift is Ghostwalker. But if I can prove other dragons came through other rifts ... It's the discovery of a lifetime."

"And it cost a man *his*, someone you said you loved."

"Don't you fucking judge me. I don't need a guilty conscience; I've got one, thanks." She blew out an angry breath. "I've kept my end of the bargain. Now you keep yours. Why the fuck are you here?"

So he told her—some of it. She listened without interrupting until he fell silent, and then said, "Your people want to close it?"

"That's right. I told you: We *repair* the world. *Tikkun olam.* Yeah, okay, Ghostwalker came through, but so do shedim. If it's there, even if the rift's intermittent, it's my job to seal it. I guess we use what you'd call magic, but for the Rebbe, it's a gift, a channeling of energy from someone, something else."

"God?"

"Call it whatever you want. Mana, life force ... When we invoke that kind of power, it has to be for the right purpose."

"Read: godly, right? Great, a religious nut."

"And what you did wasn't a little nutty?"

"That was my *job.*"

"This is mine."

"But don't you see? You're no different from the guys who want all the metahumans to crawl back under a rock. Who are you to decide what should be in this world, and what shouldn't? How do you know this isn't the way the world is supposed to be? Hell, didn't angels talk to people all the time? Weren't there miracles and giants and demons?"

"And the First Born of Man gave to him the names of the djinns and lilin and the shedim gave them iron to bind spirits and their letters for protection, so the remnant concealed themselves in the remotest mountains and in the depths of the ocean," he said. "That's from an old Hebrew legend, a Midrash."

"Meaning?"

"That evil is all around and contained, but that sometimes it breaks free. It's my job to bind it again."

"Don't dodge the question. What gives you the right?"

"We have a code."

"So do hired assassins." She snorted. "Who is this rabbi of yours?"

"He's ... Well, he saved my life. Or maybe he helped me see that we're all broken in one way or another, just like the world."

"Take a good look around. Does this valley look broken to you?"

A flare of anger. "Listen, don't give me any of your self-righteous bullshit. You can't imagine my life, what I've done, how it was after my wife vanished. My world changed just like that. One second you're having coffee and the next, everything's gone."

She wasn't cowed. She was a brawler, like Rachel. "So you and your people go around fixing the world, repairing the breaks, sealing rifts—but it'll still be the same old tired Earth, right? Just one with a lot of bandages. It's like trying to reverse time, wake up in

SPELLS & CHROME ■ 265

the morning younger than you were when you went to sleep. You can't do it. If I was a shrink, I'd say that you guys are trying to fix yourselves. Frankly, that sounds pretty damned futile. There's always more pain."

"Sure, but you got to have hope. You said it: You think you're never going to smile again. One day, you do—or you trick yourself into thinking you can. Maybe ... I don't know, maybe it's the same damned thing. But I can't just do nothing. If I sit around accepting the world the way it is, I might as well have put that bullet into my ..." He bit off the rest.

They said nothing for a time. In the quiet, the wind stirred eucalyptus with a papery rustle. Finally, she murmured, "Do you remember the day you did? *Really* smiled again? Felt like, okay, this is good, I can go on?"

No fight in her voice now. His chest burned. "Yeah, I do."

"When?"

"Today. Now." The words were out before he could recall them—or maybe he didn't want to. He saw only her aura now, so bright and alive, and his Rachel was dead and there was nothing he could do to bring her back. Yet there was this woman and this place and no one—not even the Rebbe—listening, and the need for her hummed in his veins. "Here. With you."

When she didn't respond, he felt like an ass. "Fuck, I'm sorry. I'm tired. I shouldn't ..."

"Shut up," and then he felt her warm breath slant across his neck. She lifted her face and he sighed into her mouth, and when he dropped his hand to the swell of her breast, she made a sound deep in her throat.

A little later, when she cried out and called him by another man's name, he was past caring.

✪

She lay with her head on his chest. "How did she die?"

He massaged her scalp. Her hair was silken, her scent spicy. "The plane vanished. No wreckage. No bodies. Nothing."

"A rift?"

"I'd like to think so because then she could still be alive on some other metaplane, but ..." He paused. "You remind me of her. It's weird."

"Yeah, tell me about it." She pressed her head against his chest again. "When I saw you, I thought: Lee. How strange is that, that we both have the same experience?"

"Strange." He laughed. "You're talking to a guy who does magic."

"Like, all kinds?"

"Some, but I'm also kind of specialized. I ... *bind*. Sure, I can conjure—banish, hurl a couple energy bolts, stuff like that—but the Rebbe recruits us for our special talents. Binding is mine. I pull and contain wild or free spirits."

"Exorcism."

"Sort of. The process has its roots in old Torah mysticism. I *bind*. Most often it's a spirit, but sometimes it's binding as in sewing, or knitting rips between one metaplane and the next. That legend I told you? Same principle: The Kabbalist literature's riddled with stories about shedim bound in mountains, or deep in the oceans."

"And you guys put them back? But how do you *contain* it until you can ...?" Abruptly, she pushed up and stared down into his face. "You. *You're* the vessel. You're the bottle they put the genie into."

"For a while, yeah. You know, it's really not as horrible as you think." That was a lie; it was awful, like being pregnant with some kind of beaky monster gnawing at his insides. Only the Rebbe had the power to dispel, so until Daniel returned to Safed, he endured. Every encounter depleted him, left him weak as a kitten and his mana stained by evil. The Rebbe said that he was a living embodiment of a *quelippah*, the shell within which evil might be contained and then purified. Daniel's life with Mossad, the secrets he'd carried and the people and metahumans he'd killed, had toughened him—or marked him, he was never sure, and he still suffered. Given his past, maybe that was okay.

"What about reincarnation?" she asked.

"What about it?"

"Do you believe in it? Because I got to tell you, what you do, this binding stuff, taking in spirits ... it feels the same."

Was it? He had never *summoned* a spirit, though he knew the *mashiva*, the summoning incantation. But summoning was forbidden to him as it was to all the Rebbe's followers. Not that spirit possession was undesirable: He knew many in the Rebbe's circle who continually strived to make themselves pure enough to become *ibbur*, to host the soul of another. There were stories from long ago of acolytes who dug shallow graves alongside the tombs of the righteous and prayed to be so invaded if only for a short time. But the Rebbe was clear: Their job was to repair the world, to perform *tikkun olam* using the one, true Kabbalah and not the bastardization of the tradition practiced by the *goyim*.

Besides, he would never be pure enough. Not after all he'd done.

He said, "Well, I get what you're driving at, but it's totally different. My tradition calls it *gilgul*. But that can only happen to the very good and if the host spirit is willing to give up its place in the body. I'm not very good."

"But look at us. We've both lost people we love, and we've been drawn together to this place."

"Alana, I'm not Lee. There's only me in here."

"I know that. I'm not asking you to be Lee. I can never be Rachel. But there's something between us. You feel it, right?"

He gathered her in his arms. "I feel *you*. Has it occurred to you that we're seeing the reflection of what we *want* and not what's real?"

"*This* is real." She brushed her lips against his. She pressed his hand to her breast. "*I'm* real. Maybe *this* is our fate—to be here, to be together."

"Alana, I can't ..."

"Why not? If the rift's there, it's *been* there off and on for centuries. Millennia. You could stay here. *We* could."

He was tempted. To be free of the ever-watchful presence of the Rebbe, even if it was a shackle he'd donned willingly. (Had he? Could any man a hair's breadth from suicide be said to be in his right mind?) Free of the world and its demands. Just ... free. Could the Rebbe even project into this valley? He didn't know, though he thought not; surely, the Rebbe would've come looking for him already and since he hadn't ... God, he deserved some happiness. He was so tired, but ... "I'm sorry, but I can't." He took her face in his hands and kissed first one cheek and then the other, and tasted salt. "You know I can't. Don't you see? I'd be exchanging one prison for another. We could never leave. As soon as we're within range of a node ..."

"Shadowrunners do it."

"What kind of life is that? Alana, I have to finish what I've begun."

"No, you don't have to. You *want* to." She straddled his body, her hands flat on his chest. Her shark's tooth was an ivory teardrop in the hollow of her throat. "There's an old saying amongst my people: *Kūpau wau i ka manō* ... I am finished to the big shark, all consumed by the big shark, I am finished."

"Your people celebrate becoming dinner?"

She twisted a handful of his chest hair. "Don't be a smart ass.

Sharks are single-minded, they don't stop. You're like that. You're consumed. You've given yourself over to this Rebbe of yours ..."

"Yes, but not for tonight," he said, and held her close. "Tonight I give myself to you. I give myself to *us*."

"Then stay with me as long as you can," she murmured into his mouth, "and love me. Love me."

✪

May 9

He was cold. His head hurt. His chest felt like he'd broken every single rib in maybe three places. He tried pulling in air. Had a panicky instant when nothing came but then did, only hard, like he was sucking air through a straw. Jesus ... His brain was woolly, his thoughts mushy ... was he running out of air? How long was he out? A lancet of pain, and he moaned.

"Easy." A man's voice. "Take it easy."

"Daniel?" A woman. Far away, like they'd stumbled onto a bad bandwidth. "Daniel?"

"Ungh," he croaked.

"Daniel." Then to someone else: "What's wrong with him?"

The man: "He clocked himself pretty good. Still bleeding."

"Oh God." Alana pressed her hand to Daniel's head just behind his left ear.

"Ow," Daniel said.

"Hey now," said the man. "That's better."

Speak for yourself. Daniel's eyes slowly cranked open and for a second, he thought maybe his head injury was way worse than he thought because, except for a single ball of excruciatingly bright light spiking his eyeballs, everything was shadowy, inky black.

Then he got it. They were still in the water. In a cave. Well, a lava tube. Same diff because they were still screwed.

"Get that fucking light out of my eyes before I break your arm." He was appalled by how he sounded: weak and sick.

The light angled down, and then Alana said, "Daniel, you hit your head pretty hard. There's a rip in your suit, and you're taking in water."

"Uh-huh." Talking made him dizzy, and trying to move made him want to throw up, but he let her help him sit up. The lava tube was cramped, with just enough room to hunch and turn but not much more. His buoyancy had changed now that his suit was heavier, and every movement made the darkness spin. Thank God his vest was waterproof ...

The man, again: "How are you feeling?"

"Like shit." He slicked his lips, winced as a squirt of fresh blood coated his tongue. His stomach lurched, bile burned the back of his throat, and he thought: *Fuck, no, not into my facemask.* He swallowed back a mouthful of puke, grimaced. "Who are you?" He answered his own question: "Harriman?" He threw a glance at Alana, regretted it when his stomach rebelled at the sudden movement. "You've got to be shitting me."

"No bullshit." She touched the other man's arm, and Daniel's chest went just a little tighter. "I didn't believe it at first either."

"I don't," he said flatly. But when he viewed Harriman with his astral sense, the man's aura was there. Not real *bright*, but ... He said, not very charitably, "You ought to be dead."

"Tell me about it." Harriman sounded both flustered and relieved.

"No, why don't you tell us?"

"Stop bullying him," Alana said.

"You don't think this is a little fucked up?"

"Of course, but before you go around slinging accusations, look at your dive computer."

He did, asking for his HUD. He expected his air to be low; it felt like it should be. Maybe a half hour left, max (which, no, wasn't good). But his HUD said his fill was virtually unchanged from when they'd arrived at the seamount: a couple hours' worth.

That wasn't right. How much time ...? He scanned the readout, looked at the elapsed time ... and then looked again. Told his computer to do a systems check and read the impossible.

When he didn't say anything, Alana said, "See? Time's slowed down. For all intents and purposes, time has stopped."

"That's crazy." He wasn't a physicist, but ... "Even if we're trapped, time should be passing normally within the bubble."

"Well, it's not." Lee Harriman wore a drysuit as well, and a full face mask. His cyber-eyes were silver-blue and very bright. "It's been, what, two weeks? My fill's only gone down an eighth."

"Yeah, but what are you eating? What are you drinking? Why haven't you died of thirst, or hunger?"

"Daniel," said Alana.

"Alana, they found pieces of his *suit*. They said *sharks*." He thought of the sharks above the seamount. Christ, what if *they* had gone after Harriman to protect *her*?

Alana was saying: "We don't know that it was Lee's suit they …"

"Fuck this." Harriman broke in, his voice edgy. "Alana said you're a practitioner. So either I've got an aura, or not, right?" When Daniel didn't answer, Harriman said, "Right. So back the fuck off, okay? I don't know why I'm not dead, but I'm not real sorry to disappoint you."

"Bullshit." Daniel couldn't read Harriman's eyes, but he hadn't spent time reading body language for nothing. "You *do* know, or you've got a pretty damn good idea."

"Lee?" Alana was a small woman, and light—and for the first time, Daniel noticed that she was riding a little high and something dinged in the far reaches of his brain, but he couldn't chase the thought down. Alana reached a hand to her lover then seemed to think better of it. "Tell us."

Harriman was staring at the virtually featureless curve of lava arcing over them, his weirdly blue eyes clicking right then left. Finally, they settled on Daniel's face.

"I don't know for sure," he said. "But I think it's been waiting."

"Waiting for what?" said Alana.

Harriman stared at Daniel. "You."

❌

Harriman led the way, following a guideline through a maze of narrow lava tubes that led into the guts of the dead volcano. Daniel had visions of the tubes crumpling under the pressure, the full force of the seamount crashing down. His breathing was shallow; he was hyperventilating but not getting much air. His headache was worse, and his chest was one continuous burn.

Calm down. He tongued salt from his upper lip. *You've been in way worse situations.* The fact that he couldn't think of any off the top of his head wasn't reassuring. This was like something out of a childhood nightmare: visions of being trapped underground, in the dark, where going up wasn't an option.

And something else: He'd never wished for the Rebbe to find them quite as much as he did now. Some kind of irony there.

"How … how much … further?" Alana sounded as winded as he felt. He craned his neck but could only manage a few degrees: enough to see her laboring in the glow of his headlamp. Her tanks clanked rock.

"Not much." There wasn't enough room for Harriman to turn around. "Just another dozen meters or so."

It was less. Inching along, and then Daniel felt the roof of the lava tube soar away, had the sense of space opening before them. He switched to his astral sense; saw Alana's orange glow—washed out, weaker than before, like a sunset bled of color, on the cusp of night. Harriman was even dimmer, just a silvery wisp.

But now above and beyond Harriman, an immense space in which something pulsed and glowed now white, now purple, now green ...

The tube spat them out and the sudden drop was like tumbling out of an airlock into outer space: nothing above, and a long way—forever—down. He was having trouble with his buoyancy, the added weight of the water dragging him down and he scuttled back, kicking until his tanks banged rock. Grappling for a handhold, he hung—and stared. He'd seen pictures of the Watergate's Great Rift and of course, he'd seen—and repaired—much smaller tears in the fabric between metaplanes. Still, he wasn't prepared.

Ragged, gaping, the rift was easily ninety meters long, fifty meters wide. It undulated like something alive; gossamer-thin tendrils of mana coiled in its depths, glimpses of an adjoining metaplane. Bolts of light fitfully pulsed between its shredded, swollen lips, like blood spurting from a wound hacked into the skin of the earth. Something moved in the rip. Not mana. He squinted. The effect was like peering through a flawed pane of milky, runny glass. He could make out shadows, silhouettes and as he watched, one pulled together, solidified—

Oh shit ...

A shedu.

"What *is* this, Harriman? What ... ?" He swung his head toward the other man and his voice died in his throat because he saw two things: Harriman—and Alana, hovering at an angle, her feet higher than her head, working hard to keep from drifting.

God, no ...

When a diver's tanks empty, the paradoxical happens. Compressed air, trimix, heliox are all heavy. As tanks are depleted, a diver usually dumps air from her buoyancy compensator, or expels air from her lungs in order to maintain her trim. Only when a diver's air is completely gone and the lungs filled with water will the body sink. The only reason a dead person floats is because of tissue bloat from gases released with decomposition.

Alana, an experienced diver, was having trouble with her trim and the only reason for *that* was ...

"Alana." Each breath was harder and harder, but now he knew why. Cursed himself for not having thought of it before. Wondered if the same force that had fooled their senses also clouded his judgment. "Alana, honey, I need you to come over here."

"What?" Her labored breathing rasped in his ears. She sounded dazed. Her face shone with sweat.

"Alana, it's an illusion. This whole time ... we've been ... running out of air." Now that he knew for sure, he could sense the seconds ticking off his life. "Your buoyancy ... " He gulped down another thin lungful. "Headache ..."

"Carbon dioxide." He heard the sudden fear in her voice. "But ... but Lee ..."

"Alana, look at him." He swallowed, slicked his lips. "No bubbles. He's got no air ... "

"Oh my God." Her voice quaked with terror. "Lee? LEE?"

"No." With a huge effort, he kicked, closed the distance between them and wrapped a hand around her bicep. "Stay away, just ... Ah, God."

He saw now that Harriman's suit was in tatters; half his chest was gone and a chunk of his left thigh; his facemask was shattered, open to the water. A yellow stalk of nerve wormed from one empty socket. Harriman's puffy face went slack all at once, like a marionette whose puppeteer has stepped out for a smoke. His color leeched away; his head lolled; and then his lower jaw sagged. A convulsive shudder wracked his frame; something bulged and heaved in his throat.

Alana screamed.

Harriman vomited something slick and mucinous and gray. It had the undulant consistency of a jellyfish, the same translucent milkiness and yet it was also muscular, like the rope of a serpent's body worming in a gurgling, unctuous coil. Emptied of its cargo, Harriman's savaged body drifted away, spinning in a slow, lazy spiral.

Give me what I want. The shedu's voice was sibilant, gauzy, curiously tender. *This one was weak; he let her get away and then he smashed his own facemask and he died, and for what?*

And yet, Daniel thought, the shedu—clearly a Master to have manufactured such an illusion and held open this gateway—had not used Harriman's body to escape. Why?

The Master, seeping into his brain: *I require a vessel able to contain me.*

Something like him. a binder, who could hold all that monstrousness for all time, if need be. Someone whose shell would not decay. A kind of shedu-esque Dorian Gray. Well, that was his talent, wasn't it? Had the Rebbe known? He thought of the legend, that the shedim were locked away in mountains and in the depths ...

The Master: *Who do you think imprisoned me here to begin with? You are a pawn, nothing more, but I offer you power. I offer you life.*

Something had gone wrong here, Daniel knew. He was surprised at how calm he felt, as if he'd always known that *this* was his destiny. All his sins, the stains of his past ...

So. This prison had weakened, or the Master found some way to break through and now there were others, waiting to come through ...

But why Alana?

The Master, again: *Without her,* you *would never have been drawn here. Submit freely, and I will let her go again.*

A lie. He knew that. But he would have to very careful now.

"What," Daniel sucked in a mouthful of air but couldn't fill his lungs. "What ... guarantee?"

"Who ..." Alana gulped. "Who ... are you ... talking to?"

No guarantees, but I will not interfere. A pause. *You do not have much time. Soon your air will be gone and you will die. Submit. Open yourself and live.*

"Go." Chest working, he ripped off his spare air and thrust it at her. He spoke in bursts, trying to get it all out while they still had time. "Get out. Guideline. Let you go once. If I stay ..."

"N-no." Her skin was a sick, dusky blue in his headlamp. "No ... I'm nearly out." The whistle of her next breath. "I won't make it." Another gasp. "Not leaving ... without you."

"GO!" Pushing the canister into her arms, he shoved her, suddenly, very hard. The effort blacked his vision for a second, and the world tilted wildly. Then his vision cleared, and he saw that she was flailing, one hand still holding the canister, the other trying to right herself.

She wouldn't go, she wouldn't *go!* But he couldn't spare a lot of energy; if he were too depleted, they were both dead; and he certainly didn't have much time. Still, he had to give her this chance because there were no more options. Gritting his teeth, he focused his will, marshaled his mind, harnessed the power of the mana radiating from the rift, conjured up the image of the crater's maw and thought: *GO.*

For an instant, nothing. Then, he felt the energy cohering around her, the crackle sizzling through the water, and when he looked, a electric halo closed round her body the way arcs of electricity dance from an antique Van de Graaf. She stiffened, and he caught her look of first confusion and then comprehension; and she reached for him, had time for one last word: "DANIEL!"

And then she was gone.

○

And he was dead.

○

Foolish. The Master draped over him, a softly deforming ooze. *She has no chance, and you have wasted precious energy. You'll truly die if you don't take me into you. You'll suffocate, or drown ...*

Daniel felt his consciousness slewing, bit down as hard as he could on the soft flesh of his cheek. The shock was like a slap in the face, but his head was roaring now, the pain battering his skull, pulping his brain.

He couldn't wait. He wanted to give her more time. And he wanted to live so much now, more than he ever had since Rachel.

"Go," he whispered, "go, Alana, go, go ..."

Stop wasting air. Submit.

Now.

"*Shevi min hayom v'machar v'leyolam,*" he croaked: *This is the bond from today and tomorrow and forever ...*

YES. The Master closed, cocooning Daniel's body. Its tendrils wormed through the rip in the back of Daniel's suit, then slithered along his neck, streaming along his arms, twining over his chest in a kind of ecstasy. *YES.*

"*Mumah anah umishveh beshem SHEDU HA-GADOL,*" he chanted, the Hebrew flowing from his lips, riding the last dregs of his air. "I make an oath and bind in the name of the Master who sits in *Tehom* whence all evil comes ..."

He drew a breath to continue—and got nothing. Tried again, and failed.

Out of air. But it didn't matter.

Once invited, the Master would never leave, and it was in his mouth now, gargling off the last of his breath, flowing into his lungs, leaking into his blood, running in fingers over the crevices of his brain ... . Daniel felt his mind dimming, the final remnants of who he was slipping away. But he could still move—fitfully, in tiny starts, like a child's toy whose battery's run out—and his arm responded, his fingers crawling along his wrist. Now, it had to be now because if he waited any longer, the Master would have him for all time, and all this would be for nothing.

Would Alana know? Feel it? No. They were too far underground. He had done what he could.

Go, Alana. Go and live ...

With the last of his strength, Daniel punched at his wrist—

✪

As the Master suddenly sensed his intent: *WHAT HAVE YOU* DONE ...

✪

And now Daniel was swooning into oblivion: *Rachel, I'm com ...*

✪

The water flared into a bright burning rose as Daniel's vest blew.

✪

One second she was floating above the rift; the next she was staring up at an oculus of cobalt blue against black, clutching Daniel's spare canister to her chest. She was back at the seamount's maw.

She allowed herself one instant of anger—Daniel had the power to get them out all along but hadn't used it, why? Then she inhaled, got nothing, tried again, got more nothing. Thought: *Shit.*

Working fast, she stripped her full facemask, tried not to panic as the water slammed her face, located the mouthpiece of Daniel's spare canister, jammed the regulator into her mouth, hit the purge button, and inhaled. Cool air flooded into her burning lungs, and she had to fight to not suck the canister dry. The auxiliary canister was designed for depths above forty meters, and she was two hundred feet below that. The increased pressure would make her use up her air more quickly and besides, this wasn't trimix. She'd get narced pretty damn quick.

She had to get out, fast. No telling when that thing would come after her. Yet she had this feeling Daniel had one more trick up his sleeve ...

Then she saw the sleds she and Lee had tethered to the crater's rim what seemed years ago.

Please. Swimming to one sled, she punched the starter. Nothing. Not even a click. The battery was dead. *Nonononono ...* Seconds ticking away ... She was almost afraid to try the second sled. Jabbed the start button and listened to a whole bunch of nothing.

No, no, damn *you!*

Desperate, kicking at the sleds, she pivoted, pulled water. Saw the sharks whirling high above.

Oh shit. She'd forgotten about them. She watched as they knotted, bunched and then, as one, headed straight for her. Well, hell, it didn't matter; she couldn't afford to pussyfoot around. If they came after her, they came. She probably wasn't going to make it anyway, no matter what.

She swam, kicking hard, pulling as fast as she could. She shot out of the crater and now she was passing the sharks, swimming for all she was worth.

The sharks changed course, and closed.

Her heart crowded into her mouth, and she could only watch as the sharks swirled around, bottling her up, getting closer, so close she could see the jostling of spiky teeth. Close enough that she saw the roll of their dead eyes: doll's eyes, eyes that were black and flat with absolutely no whites. Close enough that, now, they bumped her, bottled her up, and when she kicked, she actually hit one with her fin. Recoiling, she almost screamed, remembered the regulator, pushed the scream back into her chest. Breathless with fear and exhaustion, she looked down—

And saw the ocean move. Felt the rip of an explosion sear her mind, her heart—and she knew: Daniel was dead. Truly, completely, irrevocably.

No. Blinking against the salt sting of the water, she tried to focus— and then a tidal wave of fresh terror roared over her.

Because the ocean was still moving. Right. For. *Her.*

✪

Something coming: huge, a dark benthic blue, as if the ocean floor were levitating ...

And that's when she felt something else: a sudden rush of heat at her throat. Her skin prickled and she thought: *Necklace ...the* tooth ...

The massive shape cohered, pulling together like something woven from mist and nightmares—and became a megalodon.

Oh my God. The beast was enormous, a good sixteen, seventeen meters, maybe twenty. It was headed straight for her, its huge dorsal fin scything the water. Its mouth unhinged and she saw the maw bristling with teeth, and something went a little loose in her mind.

I'm not seeing this. She watched it come, helpless as a bug hanging in a spider's web. When the creature was twenty yards away, the school of sharks hemming her in place splintered, each animal veering off to make way. The megalodon slid beneath, actually bumped up against her. Its dorsal fin glided past, and—almost as if in a dream—she hooked her hand round the fin.

And the beast climbed. Its tail swept the water in powerful, even strokes, and she let the animal pull her. The water rushed past; its color began to lighten, and she looked up, expecting to see the bailout tank—and did: hanging exactly where she and Daniel had left it.

But she also saw something else that made her blood chill.

Hovering in the water was the glowing imago of a man: very old, almost wizened, with a flow of snowy-white beard and intense, completely black eyes rimmed with no white whatsoever. A shark's eyes.

No. Her thoughts were panicky. *No, I'm not seeing this; I'm a mundane ...*

A small voice, one she recognized as her own, sounded in her mind: *Yeah, right. Sweetheart, you got yourself a magic tooth with a heap of mojo and you've hitched a ride on a* megalodon ...

The old man studied her carefully, closely, and she had the sense he was memorizing every detail. They stared at one another: she on the back of this great beast, and he nothing more substantial than a dream. Then he—his projection—pulled apart in a sudden ripple, and vanished.

And she thought: *Rebbe ...*

Coming after her? She sensed that might be right. So she would have to find a way to disappear. Back into the valley for a while. Then ...?

That small voice again: *Sure, you can hide. You can run. But remember: That old asshole sent Daniel on a suicide mission. Repair, my eye. Blow yourself into little teeny, tiny pieces just like Humpty Dumpty is more like it. But that rip is still there; those shedim are there and that old fart's got to be involved. Now, you gonna let that stand?*

Somehow, the megalodon knew to slow at the bail-out tank, and she wondered if maybe it was simply attuned to her needs, or could there be something else ...?

She'd think about that later. First things first: She purged the regulator of the bail-out tank and simply breathed. Beneath her, support-ing her, the megalodon moved in small, slow circles, waiting until she was ready, until there was need for its services.

Oh Daniel ... She fixed her eyes upon the light of the world above, and her resolve firmed.

No. All this would *not* stand.

Not if she had a say.

✪

Halfway around the world, an old man inhaled a sudden breath and came back to himself, and muttered a prayer: *"Modim anah l'fanehcha, melech chai v'kahyam ...* I gratefully thank You, O Living and Eternal King, for You have returned my soul within me with compassion."

"Rebbe?" An acolyte glided to his side. "Is Daniel ...?"

"Daniel's gone," the old man quailed. The projection left him weak and feeble as a baby. In the next few hours, he would be fed, bathed. He would sleep—but not before he gave one more order.

"Find her," he whispered. "Find her." ✪

BETTER TO REIGN

BY MICHAEL A. STACKPOLE

Michael A. Stackpole is a New York Times-*bestselling author, an award-winning novelist, editor, game designer, computer game designer, comics writer, an podcaster, and screenwriter. As always, he spends his spare time playing indoor soccer and now has a new hobby, podcasting, as well as working on ideas for a half-dozen other novels. To learn more about Mike's podcasting, please visit www.tsfpn.com (the website of The SciFi Podcast Network). Michael's* Better to Reign *takes you back to the turbulent gang wars of 2053 Seattle.*

They stared at me as their bikes came to a halt, furtively assessing what level of threat I might represent. Then, starting with one Ancient who quickly infected the rest of the bikers, they snickered, cackled, and roared at some hilarious private joke.

I felt my cheeks flush with shame, though I fought for control. At first, I could not understand their scorn. Like them, I was an Elf and looked no different. Besides, I had gone to great pains to outfit myself appropriately. Silver chains dangled from my black leather jacket and razored spurs gleamed in the half-light on the toes of my boots. My fingerless gloves bristled with gleaming metal studs, and I'd even gone to the ridiculous length of affecting a purple and green mohawk hairstyle so I would fit in. Even the antique Harley I rode matched their chosen steeds of steel.

As the group continued to clutch their sides and whoop out new peals of laughter every time one of them looked at me, the truth finally dawned. Everything about me was perfect—too perfect. In this noble gathering of Elves, my clothes were just too new. My studs and spurs showed no tarnish of blood residue and my fingernails lacked the telltale oily grit from working on a bike. These details and many more revealed my true nature.

For these denizens of Seattle's Sprawl, the only thing funnier than an Elf up from the preserves of Tir Tairngire is an Elf from the wilds who attempts to disguise his origins. My precautions, my plans, had been worse than for naught, they had betrayed me.

If my face was red before, it burned now with shame.

One Elf, distinctive for the black flesh and pink scar slashed over a milky eye, approached and wiped his hands on my jacket. "Geez, chummer, real wiz rags, 'kay?" Like a court jester, the jackanapes turned to his compatriots and bellowed, "His Majesty has sent his Minister of Fashion to us, chummers. Show some respect."

As the clown bent to drop his pants in derision, I twisted my wrist and raced the Harley's engine. Its bass roar exploded like gunshots off interior walls of this warehouse where the Ancients had gathered. The cycle's thunder shocked the Elf into a twisting leap backward. His pants slipped down around his knees, entangling his flailing limbs and bringing him down unceremoniously on his buttocks.

My effort at bravado earned me a momentary respite as the Ancients turned their scorn against the fallen Elf, but it was more than transparent to several other Ancients. One of them, lean even for an Elf, sliced through the crowd. Though she was not as voluptuous as I tend to prefer, her aggressive bearing and spirit were seductive enough. Yellow light flashed like a beacon in her mechanical eyes, and highlights shot from her long, coppery hair. Her gaze raked over me once, then again, more slowly. "You jacked, chummer?"

I shook my head.

"Magicker?"

I shrugged carelessly, hoping to give the impression of possessing more abilities than I, in fact, did have.

She shrugged wearily, then smiled, flashing long canine implants. "So yer a fern-witch come to the Sprawl to run with the Ancients, eh? Why don't the High Lord just shoot you misfits instead of sending you to us to die?"

I sensed the probe in her question, but I killed the smile it almost brought to my lips. Could it be they had been told I was on my way to Seattle, but not why I had been exiled? Did the High Lord think me so useless that he would consign my fate to hands such as these? If so, that would not be the first gross blunder he had made.

Before I could answer, the roar of another bike approaching caught everyone's attention. The syncopating rhythm of the bike's engine must have been familiar, for it thundered new life into the lethargic gang. The jester scrambled to his feet, tugging his pants into place. Grins broke over the faces of the rest, and my last inquisitor bared her teeth.

Blond hair flowing back from his shoulders, the leader of the Ancients pulled his bike alongside, slightly ahead of mine. He gave me a quick look, his corpse-white face showing no emotion, then killed his engine and parked the bike. Leaving his mirrored sunglasses in place despite the dimness, he swung off the Harley and stood there, stretching the muscles of his slender form like a cat rising from a sun-warmed nap.

"In from the Tir, eh, chummer?" He planted his fists on his narrow hips. "By the gods, you're a sight. Got your lunch in that backpack?"

"I was told that being armed would be a good idea if I wanted to survive here in the Sprawl."

He pulled off his glasses and hung them from his handlebars by a cord. "I hope you're better acquainted with whatever you have in there than you are with your fancy clothes. " He looked at me again, his black eyes searching and evaluating. "I'm Wasp, and I run the Ancients. We usually enjoy welcoming the High Lord's special pals, but that'll have to wait until later. Pearl, did you reach everyone?"

The jester nodded solemnly. "Everyone's itching for a fight after sitting out the night of fire. Keno and Johnny Dark are pulling together the Eastsiders. They'll meet us at the border on Westlake."

"Good." Wasp wandered across the floor to a billiards table. Pearl swept the balls into the pockets as Wasp drew a map from inside his vest, unfolding it and laying it out on the green felt. I killed my Harley's engine and followed, taking up a position at the far end of the table. Pearl stood at Wasp's right hand, and the female leaned on the table directly opposite the Ancients' leader.

"Look, chummers, here's the score. we're going to consolidate our territory. We're going to take the streets from Dexter to Aurora, starting at Harrison and going on down to Denny."

The whipcord samurai narrowed her Fujikon eyes. "That's Meat Junkie turf. They ain't gonna like that."

"That. Sting, is their problem. We're looking at an all-out battle." Wasp looked up at his assembled soldiers. "Kid gloves are off, chummers."

Sting still looked uneasy, and I sensed a tension between her and Wasp that ran deeper than a just disagreement over this little outing. I could not help but wonder if these two apparent rivals had once been lovers. "The kid gloves might be off, Wasp, but the Meat Junkies are tight with the Emerald Dogs. They can easily bring in more firepower than we can. Keno and Dark might be bringing in the Eastsiders, but will that be enough? Besides, the area you want covers Bob's Cartage and Freight, and we know the yakuza have designs on them..."

Her voice trailed off as Wasp's nostrils flared. "The yaks ain't in on this play. The Dogs got tore up By Raven's people on the Night of Fire. Doing this is going to be good for us."

"What about Raven?"

"What about him?" Sting's eyes snapped open and shut like the shutter on a camera. "We offered to help him on the Night of Fire. Maybe he'd help us against the Meat Junkies."

"He didn't want our help, and we don't want his. Besides, this isn't a gig Raven would buy into. It's just us."

In Wasp's words and Sting's reaction to them, I sensed another point of contention between them. It looked as though Sting wanted to depose Wasp, and judging by Wasp's anger, the battle for succession would intensify relatively soon. More important, I also gained the impression that someone or some corp was yanking Wasp's chain and Sting did not like it.

"Just us, huh? Just our blood, you mean." Sting spat on the ground. "Are they paying us by the pint this time? When are you going to learn that those corporators see pitting one gang against another gang as a real economical means of metahuman birth control!"

The remark slashed him, but before Wasp could reply, I broke in. "I was never given to believe the Ancients danced to a corporator's tune."

Wasp wheeled on me, giving full vent to his fury. "Who the hell cares what you believe? You're not even part of this gang, so you don't stand for shit, got it?"

Sting stabbed a finger razor down through the map. "Well, I am a member of this gang, and I think this deal sucks. You better have a good plan for this 'consolidation,' Wasp, because I'm sick and tired of shedding blood so a new Stutter Shack can spring up on some new corner."

"I do have a plan, Sting, one that should make even you happy." He pointed at the intersection of Republican and Dexter. "We link up here with the Eastsiders and just sweep down through the neighborhood. We take out pockets of resistance and move on. We just roll them up."

Despite the nods of assent from the gathered Elves, Sting remained unconvinced. "And what happens after we clear one block and move on to the next? The Meat Junkies will pour back in and occupy our building from the rear. Stupid plan, Wasp."

"You have a better one?"

"Yeah. We start at the north end of Aurora and the Eastsiders start at Denny Way. We work toward the middle and squeeze the Meat Junkies out."

Wasp shook his head. "Now that we've heard from the Custer Military Academy... "

"Pig!" Sting's hand convulsed, shredding the map. "You know your plan leaves us open to an attack by the Emerald Dogs!"

"The Emerald Dogs are not a factor!" Wasp bared his teeth in a feral snarl. "With our firepower," he growled as magical energy arced from left hand to right, "the Meat Junkies will die quick. This is not a protracted war, it's a lightning assault. In quick and force them out. Bang, done!"

"That's what you said the last time we tangled with the Tigers, but your corporator's intelligence bit, and we got gnawed real good." She swept her hair back from the side of her face and I saw the ragged scar from her left eye to her pointed ear. "I remember that fuck-up every day. With this plan of yours, the only thing that's going to get done is the Ancients!"

"That was different and you know it, Sting!"

"Do I? Have the corpgeeks cut your puppet strings?"

As Sting drew in a breath to continue her tirade, I sampled the gang's mood and knew my time had come. I coughed lightly and placed both hands palm-down on the table. "If you will forgive an uninitiated outsider making a suggestion..."

Surprised by my action, Wasp and Sting both glared at me, then nodded their assent.

"I would point out that caution against dividing your strength is well grounded when considering a battle, quick or long. On the other hand, having mobile flanking elements able to react to threats is also indisputably wise."

"Thanks for the flash from the front," Wasp sneered, evoking new laughter from his compatriots. "Now that we've heard from the Moronic Majority..."

"Wait!" The edge in my voice calmed the laughter, but not the tension that spawned it. "I have an idea. As you will recall Virgil admonishing the Romans, all that is necessary to win this conflict is to 'subdue the arrogant.'" I started to explain that with the sniper rifle in my pack, I could easily eliminate the leader of the Meat Junkies with a single, through-and-through gunshot wound to the head. I knew that the Meat Junkies would be disorganized and powerless without a leader. They would be impotent until another strong leader arose among them, and that would be a painful process. Before I could unfold my plan, Wasp cut me off.

"Dandelion talk and chip-dreams!" Wasp's anger gathered like a thunderhead. "I don't know this Virgil fellow—didn't catch his simsense show—but he don't know squat about battles in the Sprawl.

Neither do you. We've got a battle to fight tonight, and we ain't got time to nursemaid some greenie from the forests. All I can do is give you your first lesson: *I* run the Ancients. *I* do the thinking! *I* do the planning!"

"And we do the bleeding." Sting's comment sank in to the hilt and brought Wasp up short. She glanced at me. "I don't know what this Sears biker has in mind, and I don't care, but I do want some flexibility in this plan of yours. We have to be able to cover our backs in case the Emerald Dogs or Meat Junkies show us more than you guesstimate they have."

Wasp stared from Sting to me and back. "Fine, you want a reactionary force? Great. You, Pearl, Tiny, and the greenie. Pick out another half-dozen people, and you're it. We hit a hard point, you take it out. You happy?"

Sting took the minor concession, and with a sly grin, turned it into a major victory. " I'll be happy if we don't have to save your ass too many times. Fresh perspectives and other plans will keep us alive, Wasp."

"Then let's hope that if you are needed, you do succeed." Wasp turned from the table and pointed back to where our bikes waited. "Mount up, my brothers. Tonight we remind the city we do not tolerate encroachment on our turf."

A general war-whoop filled the warehouse, but I did not allow it to distract me. I saw Wasp watching me out of the corner of his eye, and I knew he had quickly assessed my role in settling the dispute between him and Sting. Whether by accident or design, I had mediated between them for the briefest of moments, assuming a position of power. Draping an arm around Pearl's shoulder, he whispered into his ear.

I smiled slightly, but knew I'd have to be careful. Who would detect malice in an accidental shooting during a rumble? A quick push from cover and I would make a perfect target for some Meat Junkie. If that was the game and those were the rules, I was more than willing to play.

✪

Knowing my Ranger Arms sniper rifle would not be of much use in the close combat I anticipated, I drew an Ingram from the Ancients' armory as well as enough magazines to last me well into the next century. As the roar of countless motorcycles filled the warehouse, I joined up with Sting, Pearl, and the rest of our taskforce. Tiny, the other Elf designated to join us, looked large enough—and ugly enough-to have been the result of an unholy union between Elf and Troll.

As I rode up and swung in beside him, he folded his arms across his chest. "You gotta name, chummer?"

I shrugged in an easy, almost friendly manner. "In the Tir, I was known as Alejandro Kylisearn, but among you, having a colorful nom de guerre is the way things are done." I stopped there, my voice betraying a dilettante's enthusiasm for a sinfully sinister adventure.

Tiny's face screwed up in confusion. "You need a street name."

"My thought precisely. I was thinking I would call myself..."

My voice faded to nothing as Tiny vehemently shook his head. "You can't name yourself. Only the leader can give you a name."

Pearl pulled up on my right, sandwiching me between him and Tiny. "I think, for now, we'll call you Greenie."

I graced him with a plastic smile. "You have no idea how that makes me feel, Pearl."

Further discourse with him was cut off as the lead elements headed out of the warehouse. We brought up the rear and I let Pearl's bike slide in ahead of mine. Tiny, for reasons only he could fathom, had obviously decided he would be my "pal." He joined me at the back of the pack. As we rode from the warehouse, a huge door slowly descended, shutting up the building.

Seattle's streets, laid out in a motley confusion of grids blanketing countless hills, glowed pink-neon beneath sodium lights. The day's earlier misting of rain and wisps of fog drifting in from the Sound, gave the Sprawl a sweaty, steamy feel. The tall, dark buildings closed in tighter than the redwoods of the Tir and I felt much the alien in this stone landscape.

As we headed down a hill, I saw the whole leather and steel line of Ancients writhing through the streets like a snake. Pedestrians froze like frightened deer in the glare of our headlights, or scrambled off into the haven offered by dark alleys. Normal citizens looked out from upper-story windows, exposing only their eyes and the tops of their heads. They believed themselves safe this time, but I could taste the fear on the wind.

In Seattle, the Ancients are regarded not so much as a biker gang, but a force of nature.

Wasp swung us east to pick up the Eastsiders, then headed us off west down Republican. The addition of the Eastsiders increased our forces by roughly half. From the hardware bristling on the Ancients' bikes and bodies, I judged we were as well-equipped as most private armies, yet I doubted we had the discipline and tactical training to be quite as effective.

Yet, depending on Wasp's performance as a battle-leader, I might revise my assessment of the Ancients. Many a leader is not fully adept at politics but is more than capable in a firefight. Though Sting had raised objections to past plans and assaults, the very fact of Wasp's continued leadership of the group suggested abilities I had yet to see.

As we reached the northern perimeter of the area we were to conquer, Wasp issued orders in a commanding voice. He had half his people dismount to act as shock troops, while the rest split into two groups. One group shot over to Aurora, and the other set off down Dexter. The mobile pincers would isolate the first block, from Republican to Harrison, while the others would clean it out.

That may have been the plan, but the Meat Junkies quickly raised objections. Pouring into the disputed area on Thomas Street, they formed up on Dexter on the other side of the monorail line. Their foot soldiers were arrayed behind two heavily armored trucks and a phalanx of riders. From what I could see, they outnumbered us, but their weaponry could not match ours. This mixed group of Humans and Grunges was, nevertheless, not about to give up their turf without a nasty battle.

A loudspeaker mounted on one of the trucks spewed a guttural curse that could only have come from the throat of an Ork. "Dandelion wine gonna run in the streets if you Ancients ain't cleared out in a minute."

In response, we remounted our bikes. Wasp turned to shake his head at Sting. "No, you and your team stand down. It was your wish. You stay on your feet and watch our asses."

"But!"

"No buts, Sting. It was your call. Now live with it." Wasp dropped onto his Harley's seat and raised his right hand. He let it fall, and like an electrical switch, it jolted power through the Ancients. Motorcycles screaming like captive beasts, the Ancients surged into battle.

The Meat Junkies likewise charged forward. As the two lines closed, one Ancient sighted a LAAW rocket in on the lead truck. It burned a fiery course through the night, but missed its target.

The missile struck a bike and scattered it into flaming debris, but did nothing to slow the onrushing war wagon. Sparks glanced from the truck's armored front as Ancients sought to stop it with small arms fire. The truck merely shrugged off their bullets as if they were raindrops spattering off the back of a rhino.

The first truck blasted into and through the Ancient line, plastering one bike and rider like a bug on its front grill. Another bike exploded as a wheel rolled over its teardrop gas tank, and that set the truck's tires blazing. Ancients scattered from in front of the truck, then turned their weapons against it, stitching holes across the vehicle's poorly armored aft section.

The truck's mate never even made it to the Ancients' line. Wasp slung his bike around and laid it down as gently as he could. His hands upraised, golden energy surrounded them with a magical nimbus. A sorcerous bolt of energy shot from his hands to skewer the armor plate on the driver's side of the cab. A second later, as the truck began to drift, a LAAW rocket struck it in the off-side wheel-well, blowing flaming rubber chunks all over Dexter. The truck's fender dug into the street, then the whole war-wagon pitched up in a somersault with a half twist. It came down hard, flattening its back before the gas tank exploded and sent up a column of flame taller than the surrounding buildings.

Sting turned her attention to the first truck as the Meat Junkies in it boiled out, guns spitting bullets as fast as the shooters could feed them magazines. Many of the Junkies hit the ground and didn't get up, but enough had Kevlar-lined clothes to keep them in the fray beyond the first couple of exchanges.

Sting's HK227 submachine gun steadily lipped flame. Instead of burning bullets with careless abandon, Sting picked her shots with deadly accuracy. When the passenger door opened on the cab, an Ork started to swing down, but jerked to a stop as three red holes opened in his chest. He slumped to the ground.

Midway down Dexter, the Ancients scythed through the Meat Junkie line. Bikes tangled as the two forces met head-on. Men and metal careened madly through the air as more than one Meat Junkie slid his bike into the Ancients. Like Cossacks driving their warhorses through peasant hordes, Ancients vaulted their bikes up over their foes, crushing Meat Junkies beneath them. Some Ancients did not survive the Kamikaze tactics, but the gaps opened in the Meat Junkie lines grinned back at us like a jack-o' lantern's smile.

Wasp pumped magical assault after magical assault into the Meat Junkie forces. The fireballs lit grunges into votive candles, while more magic darts savaged junkie bikers. Two other magickers joined Wasp in using magic to augment our physical weapons, but his tactical and strategic strikes were the most telling. He alone kept the small groups of Meat Junkies scattered and unable to mount a counteroffensive.

A heavy hand at my back pushed me forward, stumbling. I ducked and rolled, coming up with my Ingram ready to shoot whoever had touched me, but I kept my finger off the trigger. Tiny reeled back, twin holes ripped through his right shoulder, then tipped back over his own bike.

Concrete chips and lead splatter stung my face and hands as I leaped back behind my own bike. The shots had come from an up-stairs window in the building across the way, and looking up, I caught a glimpse of a leather-faced grunge ducking back from the window. "Sting, up there! Ork sniper."

She gave me a wild smile.

"Waiting for a hunting license? Go get him."

I kicked Pearl. "Come with me."

"Me?" Pearl snorted. "In your dreams, Greenie."

Sting turned on him. "Go with him, Pearl. We'll cover you."

I snagged my pack from my bike and looped one strap over my left shoulder. "On three?"

Sting nodded. "One, two, three, go!"

I sprinted forward, then cut left as the sniper reappeared in the window. A fusillade chewed up the window casing and the bricks around it, forcing him back quickly. Though the sniper could not have gotten more than a brief look at the scene below, I had no doubt he knew we were coming after him. Pearl matched my speed as we hit the sidewalk, but I stopped and let him vault up the brownstone's stairs all by his lonesome. When no gunfire materialized to cut him down, I ran up and entered the foyer two steps behind him.

What might once have been a fine, single-family dwelling was now divided and subdivided into so many living units that it was more like a kennel than an apartment house. It reeked of urine, gun-powder, and decay; faded paint flaked off the walls like dead flesh. A fresh stream of blood running from the doorway to a body at the base of the stairs pointed out the final resting place of one of the Meat Junkies in the truck.

I ran to crouch by his body, then scanned up the stairs to the first landing. I gave Pearl an "all-clear" nod that sent him sprinting up to where the second flight began. He signaled me to come up, but I hesitated a second to be sure the grunge at my feet was truly dead. Pulling off his mask of rat-skin and chicken-flesh, I felt for a carotid pulse and found none.

Reaching Pearl's side, I motioned for him to head up to the next landing. He balked and insisted I go. I slipped my right arm through the pack's strap, firmly anchoring it to my back. Peering into the Ingram's open bolt, I saw bullets ready to be fired and cautiously mounted the stairs.

Sweat started at my temples and rolled relentlessly down my cheeks as, step by step, I headed up. Unlike the first flight, these stairs opened onto a corridor that led back the length of the building. Any of the ramshackle doors could pop open, disgorging a whole gang of Meat Junkies. Making it worse was the fact that I had to divide my concentration between what might lurk above and wondering whether Pearl was about to shoot me in the back. It did nothing to bolster my confidence.

I bobbed my head up above floor level, then ducked down again as quickly as I could. I had seen nothing to suggest a trap, but the gunfire and explosions from outside provided enough competition that it was hard to be certain I had not missed something. I took another quick look, then took two more steps.

Again I saw nothing.

I had just turned to wave Pearl forward when the bullet hit me in the backpack. The impact tossed me across the stairway and bounced me off the railing on the far side. I hit hard and rebounded out of control. I dropped my Ingram, which clattered its way back down the stairs, me tumbling after it.

Clomping steps rushed toward me and the salty taste of blood made me panic. Adrenaline coursed through my body like lightning through a computer. Though my last somersault landed me flat on my back on the landing, I knew immediately what I had to do to avoid death.

My fist closed on the Ingram as the grunge appeared at the top of the stairs. Shoving the gun in his direction, I tightened down on the trigger. I made no attempt to fight the recoil, but just let it drag the gun upward. The bullets first tore into the stairs less than two meters below him, then sliced him open from groin to forehead.

Pearl looked over at me. "Blood in your mouth, not good. He must have gotten you bad."

"Dolt!" I spat and rose to a kneeling position. "The case was designed to protect what it contains from bullets and bombs. Kissing the rail put blood in my mouth." I ejected the Ingram's empty magazine and slapped a new one home. "Go!"

Seeing that my slow movements had gotten me shot, Pearl apparently decided that speed was the only way to outwit the Orks in the building. This worked beautifully for traversing my stairs again and then the next flight. but on the landing between the second and third floors, Pearl found himself trapped by the Ork sniper.

Pearl yelled for me to help him, but I hesitated. I'd seen the happy look on his face when he thought the Ork downstairs had mortally wounded me. If I let the sniper kill him, what would I lose but a watch-dog? Then I thought a bit more. I would also lose my bait.

From my position on the lower stairwell, I determined that the Ork had to be just inside the doorway of the apartment to the left of the stairs. With Pearl's shrieks of terror echoing in my ears, I retreated and shot the lock from that apartment's mate on the floor below.

Darting inside, I saw a woman and her two, wide-eyed gutterkin children huddled on the floor. I motioned them to silence.

I answered the next burst of fire from above with one of my own.

The Ingram's bullets tunneled up through plasterboard and ply-wood, covering the ceiling with powder burns. I heard a thump from above, then ducked back out of the doorway before the blood raining down could touch me.

I sprinted up past a cringing Pearl and secured the third floor. I stepped over the Ork's body, then stooped to pick up his AK-97 as-sault rifle. Crossing to the window the sniper had used, I shrugged off my pack and studied the situation below. While doing so, I unbuckled the flap on my pack.

The fortunes of war had shifted more in the Ancients' favor. The Meat Junkies, reinforced by two more war wagons, had managed to pull two or three groups of their people together behind a makeshift barricade. The Ancients concentrated their fire and magic on that formation, confident that the Meat Junkies would pull out once they could regroup.

Pearl drifted toward the window but I pulled him back from it.

"Idiot, get down. Do you want to get shot?"

"No."

"Good. Now, go get me the sniper's body. Strip off his ammo har-ness and give me the AK mags."

"Why?"

I looked at him. "If you want us to win this little battle, do it."

He set about his grisly task as I popped open the case. Its stainless steel exterior showed a dented hole from where the bul-let had hit, but the kevlar lining had caught the slug before it could damage my rifle or me. I pulled the rifle body from the foam pocket securing it, checked it quickly for any problems, then reached for the barrel.

As I screwed the SM-3's barrel to the body of the rifle, I caught my first glimpse of a massive ork goading the Meat Junkies on to great acts of heroics. Seeing him brandishing twin Uzis, the plan Wasp had not allowed me to share again flashed to mind. The trucks were just over 300 meters away, an easy shot with this gun and scope.

Down below, Tiny was up and moving again. He lumbered forward, his AK-97 smoking as he stabbed it into the face of a Meat Junkie and pulled the trigger. Yet even as he voiced a cry of triumph, I saw another Meat Junkie let slip the leash of a Barghest. Its unnerving yelp made Tiny hesitate, and in that moment of weakness, the infernal canine leaped for him, fangs bared and eyes as red as the fires of hell.

My brain instantly calculated the odds that I could bring the beast down before it killed Tiny, and the calculation said he would die. If he did not it was because, moving from the shadows, Sting intercepted the Barghest. The curved blades protruding from the back of her right hand sliced clean through the nightmare-hound. It slewed around and tried to snap at her just as its two halves were flying a meter or more apart.

"I got the ork, Greenie." His ammo harness landed at my feet. "What do I do with him?"

I nodded to the wall on the other side of the window. "Just stand him up there."

"But he's dead. He'll fall down."

"So hold him up."

Snapping the rifle's bipod into place, I looked up at the dead grunge Pearl was supporting. "Too bad you did not choose a more secure position from which to snipe, my friend. Right idea, wrong address, I believe they say." I pulled the collapsible stock into position and locked it down, then mounted the scope.

The flanking attack, led by Sting and Tiny, nibbled away at a junkie position, centimeter by centimeter. A junkie stuck the muzzle of a gun out and tightened down on the trigger. As his random fire punched a line of holes across Sting's chest, the Elf went down. I feared the worst for Wasp's rival, then I saw her roll to her feet and dive back behind cover. A second or two later, she was moving forward, albeit slower than before. The kevlar lining of her leather jacket must have saved her life.

The battle was by no means over and I wanted to make my contribution to the war effort.

"What are you doing?"

I slapped a magazine of .655 caliber bullets into the sniper rifle and rested the bipod on the lip of the window. "That's the Meat Junkie leader down there. If I take him down, they are done."

"Wiz, Greenie." Pearl murmured reverently.

I smiled. One gunshot and the gang would be leaderless. One gunshot and my position within the Ancients would be assured.

"Subdue the arrogant," I recalled the High Lord quoting Virgil as he exiled me for attempting to overthrow him. I settled the cross hairs on my target. I took up the slack in the trigger. "Subdue the arrogant, I shall," I breathed, stroking the trigger.

Pearl's jaw dropped. "What you did do, you ... "

I swung the sniper rifle around and jerked the trigger. Pearl smashed flat back against the wall at the center of a gory sunburst, then flopped forward onto his slack-jawed face.

The ork started sliding toward me. I filled my left hand with the Ingram and triggered a full magazine, blasting him out through the window. His body slowly arced over and landed headfirst on the steps, then rolled to the sidewalk. Stunned, Ancients looked up to me and then off toward the center of the battlefield.

The first 900-grain bullet had taken Wasp in the bridge of the nose and blown what passed for his brains out through a gaping exit wound. The Ancients' magical assault stopped abruptly and the fighting slowed as if Wasp alone had powered it with his sorcery.

I appeared in the window and brandished the sniper rifle. "You want a sniper, Meat Junkies?" I screamed like a madman! "I give you a sniper!"

My first two shots reached the Meat Junkies' stunned leader before he could even think to find cover. The first clipped him in the left bicep, whipping him around, with only his jacket keeping the severed limb anywhere close to his body. The next bullet punched into his right hip, coring him from flank to flank. The force of the second shot tossed him like a doll and he rolled to a stop in the gutter.

The Meat Junkies, leaderless and confused, crumbled and retreated. Sting shouted sharp commands, directing Ancient outriders to chase the Junkies from our territory. From my position, I played guardian angel for her, picking off stragglers who wanted to make their mark by killing her. By battle's end, the Ancients knew who their new leader was and I approved of their selection.

For the time being, anyway.

Before the High Lord cast me out of Tir Tairngire for treason, he asked if I had anything to say in my defense. "Better to reign in hell, than to serve in heav'n," I quoted Milton. And reign I shall, one way or another, in this hell of the Sprawl. ✪

COMING IN 2011
A brand-new *Shadowrun* novel:

Dark Resonance

By Phaedra Weldon

After seeing a game simulation of the Technomancers' Resonance Realms, an A.I. declares these realms to be its final destination—where it will ascend to a higher plane. A group of dissonant Technomancers convinces the A.I. that in order to achieve this, it must first bypass the Event Horizon. To accomplish this, a stable Rift must be created—only no one knows how to create such a rift, much less a stable one. That is, until the theories of Dr. Noble Caliban attract the A.I.'s attention, and a gestalt of Technomancer minds is formed to bend, direct, and use dissonance to open up the gateway to heaven.

Opening such a dissonant hole in the Matrix could trigger a new crash, and it's up to a Shadowrun team and the ShadowTalkers to free the minds of those Technomancers trapped inside the gestalt, and stop the Dark Resonance from contaminating the Resonance Streams—before it destroys the entire Matrix...

Netcat came up behind Kazuma, her left hand against his back. He was sure she could feel his heart banging in his chest. This wasn't the first time he'd faced the end of a gun—the last instance had been inside a coffee shop at the hands of hackers. Then he'd only been worried about himself and Montgomery. Now—

There was Netcat. And he felt an even stronger need to protect her.

He raised both hands, showing the intruder he was unarmed. "Look, just put the gun down—"

"Shut up, leaf-eater," the hacker curled his upper lip. "You did a pretty good job—making this place look like your grandfather was missing—same as your sister's place. But you're hiding something."

Anger burned fear away as Kazuma lowered his hands. "You were in my sister's home?"

"No—but I know about it," he shifted his weight to the side, leaning his head over his left shoulder, his gaze shifting to Netcat. "Well, well, well—girlfriend?"

Kazuma leaned his head to the right, keeping his gaze focused on Blackwater as he directed his next question to the AR window ever present in his peripheral vision.

>'CATIE? I'M OPEN FOR OPTIONS.
>I'M THINKING. DISTRACT HIM.

The intruder grinned. "Maybe once I do some serious damage to your pretty face," he pressed the gun into Kazuma's neck, "Then I can get to working on that pretty piece of leaf-eater behind you."

Kazuma gritted his teeth, refraining from saying anything smart. *You must always practice patience*, his grandfather had always said. *You must watch, listen to, and learn about your opponent. Seek out the weakness.*

And this man's weakness?

Himself.

>KAZ?

>YEAH?

>I CAN DISARM HIM.

>YOU CAN? GOOD—BECAUSE I—

Netcat's texting stopped and he tensed, sensing something else had happened.

>KAZUMA–

>WHAT?

"We're not alone," she said. "I can sense others—outside."

"Eh?" the hacker narrowed his eyes. "I didn't bring nobody else here—not when I can settle my score personal like—so don't go pulling that magic shit on me. You think you can put a spell on me and make me think I'm paranoid? Ask your boyfriend about how I treat mages." He pushed his gun's muzzle deeper into Kazuma's neck, who stood absolutely still. If Blackwater decided to get trigger-happy at this range, there wouldn't be much of him left from the neck up. "You recognize this gun, leaf-eater? It's the one that killed that magic piece of ass—and capped you too if I recall."

Kazuma glared at him, his mind flashing back to the woman staring up at him and the bullet hole in her forehead, then the pain where Blackwater's bullet had found his side. "Look, if she says she senses someone else here—she's serious." He licked his lips and tried to swallow, but the pistol pressing against his neck made him cough.

>CAN YOU REALLY SENSE SOMEONE ELSE OUTSIDE? OR WAS THAT A DISTRACTION?

>IT'S THE DWARF! THAT DWARF FROM YOUR APARTMENT. HE'S ACROSS THE STREET. AND THERE'S–

Abruptly, Kazuma's backbone tingled, and he was overcome with the feeling of being watched. He felt the first brush against the house node's web across his skin. Just a whisper at first, but it quickly became a pounding against his senses.

>CATIE—THERE'S ANOTHER TECHNOMANCER ON THE HOUSE NODE—

>CAN YOU HANDLE HIM?

Kazuma glanced at the hacker, who was watching him very closely.

>I LEFT A SURPRISE IN THE NODE JUST IN CASE—SO IF HE GETS IN—

The hacker moved before Kazuma could react—pulling his gun back and slapping it into the side of the Technomancer's head. The quick, sharp impact made stars explode in his vision and turned his legs to rubber as he crumpled to his knees.

"Kazuma!" Netcat yelled and knelt beside him, putting both hands on his shoulders.

"Give me the data you stole!" the hacker thundered. "You do that real fast and I just might let the little lady live. After I give her a piece of me, of course."

Kazuma had been about eight when he'd been thrown into his first fight. Just relocated to Los Angeles from Japan. Those hadn't been easy days—but they'd educated him on what it was like to take and deflect a blow.

Grandfather had taught the techniques—from birth to High School. But it had been up to him to test himself, and find what worked. And right now—with the blinding pain in his head—echoed by the pounding of the other Technomancer at the threshold of the house's environment node—the simple act of breathing was what he used as a focus. With each breath, he took in the essence of the datasphere around him, felt the wisps of it curl inside as he stepped just inside his AR.

He felt Netcat beside him, pulling up on his arms. Lowering his head, he leaned against her to feign weakness, to make Blackwater the victor over the wounded. But his muscles were far from silent as adrenaline pumped into his system, the years of practice announcing the coming move and calculating each step precisely.

Breathe in. Breathe out. Breathe in.

"You bastard," Netcat said, her voice low. There was a click, a *shuft* noise, and then something heavy hit the ground beside Kazuma. He opened his eyes enough to see the Manhunter's magazine on the floor in front of his left knee.

Kazuma knew they weren't out of the woods yet—the gun still had a bullet chambered. That one bullet could still kill one of them, if not both. He needed to act fast—and make no mistakes.

>MOVE BACK!

Kazuma gave the silent command to Netcat as he crouched down and to the left, his right arm reaching over to balance himself as he pushed his shoulder into the floor.

The hacker was fast, following Kazuma's sudden drop with his weapon. Kazuma twisted away, pushing against the floor with his left foot as his right foot kicked straight up.

The hacker fired.

The bullet split the air an inch away from Kazuma's right ear—just as his boot connected squarely with the hacker's unprotected neck.

Kazuma's side burned at the sudden wrenching movement as his right foot remained straight up for a few seconds. The Hacker gurgled, fighting to pull air into his shattered larynx before falling backward onto the floor, his useless gun clattering on the kitchen floor tile.

The whole movement took less than a second, but for Kazuma it seemed to last for hours. Those years of training released, his energy spent, the pain in his side and head overpowered him, making him tumble forward onto his chest, arms tucking beneath his body.

"My god," Netcat said, her voice incredulous. "You really *do* know Kung Fu."

Kazuma couldn't stop yet—a part of him was still watching the environment node, and he realized the new Technomancer had spoofed an ID and gotten inside. And not just with any ID—they were using the admin password. How they'd gotten it didn't matter. What mattered was that they could use it to lock the house down—trapping Netcat and him inside.

"He's in—I can feel him there."

"You can feel him in the node itself?"

Kazuma coughed several times as he nodded and managed to get to his feet. Leaning on Netcat, they stumbled to the back door, where she paused. "You can sense them in the Matrix, and I can sense them out here. The dwarf is out there—we can't go that way."

"Where's—?" Kazuma's voice was tense with pain. It felt as if any mending the auto-doc had done to his side had been undone. Putting his left hand to his side, it came away wet with blood.

"You're bleeding from your head as well," Netcat said. "Looks like it's me saving our asses again."

"Thanks—" Kazuma coughed. "For disarming the gun."

Netcat frowned. "I didn't—I thought you called a sprite."

He shook his head. "No—I didn't, And you didn't? So   was it the same thing that turned on the lights?"

Netcat reached down with her free hand and moved it over her stomach. It was a habitual move—one she'd done several times since their first meeting. "The Technomancer is at the front door. The dwarf is at the back. Is there another way out?"

"Basement. But we have to hurry—it'll take him a little time to work through the surprise I left. If we're lucky, it'll have already chewed through the house network, disabling any security I installed."

Kazuma led her into the hall closet. Netcat stood back as he—still clutching his unbelievably painful side—raised his right hand, tapping the small independent node running the basement. The back of the closet popped and shifted to the side, towels, raincoats and all disappearing with it. He motioned for her to go down the steps. Once through, he paused and hit the spring mechanism on the other side, watching to make sure the closet reset itself.

The basement was dark—and Kazuma had to get to the door under the front porch from memory. He hoped he wouldn't knock any of Hitori's and his toys around, which would alert anyone that they were downstairs. Netcat helped guide him just as a dark, chest-thumping humming started from outside.

"What's that?"

Netcat moved the old hinge locks on the door. "Sounds like a helicopter."

"Here? In this neighborhood?"

The house schematics weren't on the environmental node, and the other basement node was a closed system. The Technomancer wouldn't see it on the fly—though Kazuma was sure the guy could probably find it in a matter of hours if he put all his attention toward it. If someone used a thermal camera they'd spot Netcat and him right away. He tried not to concentrate on the presence. Something was wrong with it.

Something dark.

Frightening.

But it had been fleeting, and there were plenty of other things to worry about now.

The path under the house forced Netcat and him to crawl over the sloping ground to the wooden lattice concealing the underside of the porch. He continued doing it one-handed. Between calling sprites earlier, the sudden expulsion of energy, the wound in his side, and the throbbing pain in his skull, Kazuma was dangerously close to fading.

Netcat unlatched the latticework door and peered out. Kazuma had been balancing all his weight on his legs—mostly his thighs as they crawled. Both gave out now, and he fell forward into the dirt.

"*Oh no you don't,*" said Netcat's voice in his head. "*You are not leaving me like this—not like last time.*"

>CAN'T....

>OH YES YOU CAN. NOW GET UP AND GET US OUT OF HERE—THEN YOU CAN NAP.

Nap? Kazuma thought. *She's kidding, right?*

Netcat kept yanking on his arm as the sound of the approaching helicopter grew louder. Kazuma struggled to pull himself out of the crawlspace. The pair crouched at the side of the house, just at the edge of the front porch, completely hidden by the overgrown shrubbery.

"The dwarf and the Technomancer are leaving," Netcat said. "And a Shinobi just landed on the road in front of your grandfather's house."

"Will wonders never cease," Kazuma muttered. "Is it clear?" He'd pulled himself up to a sitting position, leaning heavily on the house. He saw the blood he was leaving, but shook his head. *No one's gonna look here,* he thought.

"They're going into your house."

Kazuma glanced up. "Who?"

"I sense an orc and a troll."

"I have no idea who they are."

Taking several deep breaths, Kazuma stood with an effort. Netcat leaned into him and they made their way to the next house—which looked abandoned. From there, they slowly walked to the house beside that one, keeping in the shadows.

Just before they crossed the street, a huge, familiar-looking van pulled up and parked in front of the Tetsu house. The two crossed the street, but before they reached the other side, Netcat stopped and stared at the van.

"No...it *can't* be."

Kazuma pulled at her, intent on getting to her friend's car. "We have to go. All that—" he nodded to the van and helicopter, the wind from its blades stirring up debris, "—is gonna—draw attention."

She nodded, but her gaze stayed on the van. "A human...two humans..."

Then they were walking quickly—as quickly as Kazuma could walk, at least—to the car. He fell into the passenger's side as she slid into the driver's. Netcat sat there as he watched her. He slumped in the seat—his eyelids growing heavy as the strain of what they had done caught up with him. "What..."

"It can't be him—why would he be here? Did that bastard come here to track me down?"

Not sure who she was talking about—and not caring—Kazuma closed his eyes—losing his fight with unconsciousness just as he heard her ask, "Slamm-0!—what the hell are you doing here?"

Mack monitored his AR window as he trained his pistol on the dwarf in front of him. Slamm-0! came in on his left, his Colt America at the ready. Preacher and Shayla appeared a second later from the back of the house.

The dwarf and the Blackwater became the center of Mack's circle. Mack recognized him as the same one on the vids Shayla had hacked in Tetsu's apartment.

With a sigh, he looked down at the fallen man. The damn fool wasn't moving. Had the dwarf taken him out? Was Tetsu somewhere in the house? "Slamm-0!—clear the back rooms. See if you can find anyone else."

Nodding, the blond hacker cautiously moved to the hallway and disappeared.

"There is no one else here," the dwarf said in a deep voice. "The Technomancers have left safely."

Something sparkled ever so slightly around the dwarf's hands—and Mack realized from his own years of battle in the field of elven magic that the dwarf had summoned a spell, but had not dispersed it. "You were at Tetsu's apartment," Mack said. "And I'd think twice before I let that that little spell go."

The dwarf looked up from the fallen hacker and narrowed his eyes. "Ah—Mack Carlin. Club owner, entrepreneur, currently running a shadowrun team from his club, SHOUT, in Los Angeles. You were once the lapdog of Princes, Mr. Carlin. I am curious to know where you stand at the gate of this age."

Mack felt his cheeks grow hot as Shayla's and Preacher's gazes flicked to him. None of his employees had ever known the complete truth about him, about his past and about what he had done or been in his youth. But somehow this stranger—this fucking dwarf—did.

The sparkling vanished as the dwarf wrung his hands out. "That's going to cause a headache—though I'm sure that once you're properly educated, you'll wish I'd used it on my intended target."

Mack pursed his lips. "The Technomancer?"

"No," the dwarf nodded at Blackwater. "This piece of shit."

"That piece of shit happens to be part of my team."

"Then you aren't as smart as I thought," the dwarf said. He reached into his jacket pocket—and all three instantly re-sighted their weapons on him. "No need," he said as he pulled out a paper card and offered it to Mack.

Knowing Shayla and Preacher would watch his back, Mack lowered his pistol and stepped forward, taking the card. *Draco Powell, Occult Investigator, Private license.* He read it aloud to his comrades as Slamm-0! appeared at the end of the hall.

"No one's here," he said. "And the node to this place is trashed. I tried two defrag apps—" he shook his head. "Whatever got ahold of it annihilated the joint."

"That would be the male Technomancer," Powell said. "The *Chikara.*"

"That word means power," Slamm-0! said. "You trying to say Kazuma Tetsu equals power?"

"Precisely," the dwarf said. "And you would be—" he frowned. "Not a player I am familiar with."

Slamm-0! smirked. "Call me a wild card, shorty. Who're you?"

Mack stepped toward Slamm-0! and handed him the card. "I'd tone down the insults—this guy could pretty much turn you into a frog if he wished."

Glancing at the card, the blond nodded. "Yep. I'll say." He looked at the floor and his eyes widened. "Whoa—that's Cole Blackwater." His gaze rose to the dwarf again, a different expression crossing his angular features. "You take him out?"

"No," the dwarf said. "It was Tetsu."

"A Technomancer," Shayla said. "Can they do *this*? I guess I never considered them to get physical."

"With a well-placed kick, anyone can do this," the dwarf said in a bored voice. "Mr. Carlin—I was hired by parties interested in speaking with Mr. Kazuma Tetsu. Unfortunately I arrived here to find Mr. Blackwater trying to finish the job he'd started at the Annex the night before last."

Mack rubbed at his chin. "Maybe you'd better start over."

"Indeed." Powell shoved his hands in his pockets and took a deep breath.

"Shouldn't we make sure Cole's okay?" Shayla said. "Is he dead?"

"No," Powell said. "But he is having trouble breathing. I'm afraid Mr. Tetsu broke his larnyx."

"Oh no—" Shayla started to go to Blackwater.

Powell held up his right hand and a transparent blue-white wall appeared between Mack's people and Blackwater. A mana shield. "Maybe you should listen to what I have to say before you decide to help this scum."

"Make it quick." Mack looked at Slamm-0! "I need you to check if Kenichi Tetsu kept anything in his house we can use to our advantage." He shrugged. "Impress me."

Slamm-0!'s eyes twinkled. "You got it." He vanished down the hall again.

"I have natural talents at my disposal—and there are some who would argue that my means of extracting information are at times—unethical." The dwarf smiled.

"You use bloodmagic," Mack said, remembering Powell's actions from the video. "Go on."

"Yes, I do. I work for parties—*interested*—in Mr. Tetsu and his abilities. When I heard he was involved in the break-in at the annex, I acquired permission to investigate. I discovered there was more than one blood pool present. Initial reports were correct that a shadowrun team had broken into the building and was gathering information when someone—perhaps one of the security guards—shot the girl. And one of her teammates had in turn shot the security guards.

"But I found another trace of blood not belonging to either of the involved parties. And this blood—" he frowned. "—I found interesting."

"You found Kazuma Tetsu's blood," Shayla said. "Blackwater said he'd shot him."

"Oh yes he did. Just after *he* shot the girl. The Technomancer did not."

Mack felt his chest tighten. "I already know what Cole Blackwater did. But my question is why? Why shoot your own teammate who's trying to help you?"

"Why did he shoot her? Because she saw something? Knew something? Got in his way? Only Blackwater could know that." He looked down at the hacker. "But I'm afraid he won't be speaking with his own voice ever again."

Preacher shook his head. "I knew I hated that bastard for a reason. Blaming Maria's death on some skinny leaf-eater."

"Did you do a thorough investigation into Mr. Tetsu's background? He's not a murderer. In fact, though he has had several courses in weapons manipulation due to his work in Knight Errant—his psych profile indicated he was not a killer. He doesn't have the mindset for it. To think he would kill that girl and two guards all at once?"

Mack ran his fingers through his hair as he signaled for his teammates to lower their weapons. "You seem to have all the answers. Care to tell us more?"

Powell held up his hand. "As far as you were told, the data wasn't important. Just a retrieval of information." He shook his head. "What you didn't know was that not only were you hired to retrieve it, but so was Blackwater. By the same Johnson—who knew what was in that packet."

"What?" Preacher barked.

Mack cocked his head to the side. "You're saying the same Johnson that contacted us to steal the information also hired Blackwater to steal it from his own team? Because the data itself is incredibly valuable?"

"Not valuable in terms of nuyen," Powell said. "But in terms of information. The packet you stole—and had stolen from you—was a list of Technomancers currently employed by Singularity. Names, addresses, profiles, bank accounts, residences."

Mack's eyes widened. "What?" He recalled his recent scans of the news. "Singularity's chairperson was talking about that—there was a information leak—" he cursed under his breath. "Wagner."

"Do you realize, Mr. Carlin—you and your group—that if that information is sold to the highest bidding corporation—the rights and lives of individuals on that list, and on the lists sold before it—would be forfeit? Their names, addresses, personal profiles—would be available for the most unscrupulous individuals to exploit?"

"That's—" Shayla swallowed. "That's almost like a slave market."

"Technomancers keep to themselves," Powell continued. "They live their lives very privately. They see what happens to those around them who go public and it frightens them. Technomancer disappearances and death rates have grown staggeringly since 2071, and even though there is a mandatory registration in effect for them, more than half will never step forward.

"Therefore it's been harder for those interested in their powers to find them. Your Johnson found a way—to sell them to the highest bidder. And he's made a small fortune doing it, and didn't care what happened to them. Unfortunately, Horizon decided to terminate the node he'd been using—and on that node rested one of the more important packets—a list of names of Singularity applicants who have some of the highest ratings in hacking, submersion, and information retrieval. These are the best of the best."

Mack's stomach turned. He'd always thought he could read a Johnson—know what their base ugliness was. But this—taking into consideration his past—this was an abomination. He cleared his throat. "How does Kazuma Tetsu figure into all this? Did he discover what this Johnson had been doing?"

Powell shook his head. "I don't think he realized to what extent the problem was. My assumption—without speaking with him—was that he was looking for his sister and had been secretly using his job and talents to find out what had happened to her."

"Hitori Tetsu," Mack said. "We saw her apartment. It was a lot like this house—everything as it was—but with the tenant missing."

"And Hitori's records at Horizon had been emptied," Powell said. "I found that interesting."

"Did you know he was a Technomancer?"

"No I didn't, even after reading his files. It was the search for his sister that made me consider his motives for being at the annex that night. It is my conclusion that Kazuma Tetsu knew nothing about what the Johnson was doing, but stumbled onto the information by accident. It was just chance that everyone decided to go after the packet of data on the same night."

"He probably bumped into Blackwater after they fought on the node," Mack said. "Blackwater said some hacker was there, and he was strong, stronger than he was used to. Moved like lightning."

"He moved much slower in the real world," Powell said. "And he was shot. It happened a month ago, by another gang of hackers at a coffee house. He and a detective from Seattle were in the same place when they struck. Coincidence? Maybe on the hacker's part. But the two of them—I think he asked this private investigator to help him find his sister."

"So what was it in that information that caught his attention?" Shayla asked. "And where is he now? His apartment was ransacked."

"No, it was only made to look as if it'd been tossed," Powell said. "Kazuma Tetsu and his girlfriend are still alive. There was fresh blood inside his auto-doc. They were there together, and they escaped."

"Wounded?" Mack narrowed his eyes. "They won't get far."

"Most Technomancers—like most addicts of the Matrix—are known for physical weaknesses—Tetsu is far from weak in body. Apparently he is also skilled in weapons and martial arts. I'm sure that although he's in pain, he's still very much a viable individual."

"But he's no Adept," Mack said. "Which could get him killed. Unless we find him first."

"Why?" Powell said. "Mr. Carlin—why are you here? I understand you originally believed the Technomancer killed your team member—but do you have any other contracts pending?"

Shayla, Mack, and Preacher glanced at one another. Mack hadn't told them about his conversation with Hestaby. Not because he was being deceitful, but because he'd kept his past private. None of his employees knew about his links to the dragon—or his former life working for him.

But this dwarf was sharp. And he was looking at Mack with piercing eyes. Mack didn't like him. And it wasn't his business why he was still looking for the Technomancer—that Hestaby had requested him to do so in order to find the dark resonance.

But all of them were expecting an answer. "We have a contract to find the Technomancer—because a Johnson wishes to find the information he stole."

"Then let me warn you that this Johnson may well be one of the buyers of this illegal information. I have information on one of them—an elf Poser. Her registered name is Charis Lorngeld. Human by birth. Have you met this Johnson in person?"

"No," Mack said, and was glad to see no reaction from Preacher or Shayla.

"He burned her, Boss," Preacher said, staring down at his former friend and comrade. "Can I have him?"

Whether or not the question was perfectly timed, its asking redirected the conversation. Mack nodded. "He's all yours, Preacher. I don't want to know how you do it, just get the information we need. Find out if Wagner hired him."

Preacher holstered his gun and bent down to hoist the unconscious hacker over his shoulder. He headed for the front door. "I'm taking the GMC."

After he'd gone, Mack looked back at Powell. "Where do you fit into all this?"

The dwarf smiled. "I'm an investigator. It's my job to know."

Mack glanced at the hallway where Slamm-O! appeared. The young man's face was flushed, his eyes wide. "What? You find something?"

"She's here!" he said, almost shouting. "Why the fuck is she here and who is this bastard?"

Mack felt a slight tap on his PAN and logged in. Two windows showed up on his AR desktop and he hit the *Okay* button to receive an incoming file. Raising his hands, he grabbed the corners of the small window and pulled in opposite directions, resizing it to see the grainy images better.

"I got this off a security camera a street over. Pretty primitive surveillance here—hacking wasn't a problem. But they caught this," Slamm-O! said breathlessly.

Mack started the jerky, poor-quality video. It showed the street in front of the store. A beat-up Honda was parked on the other side of the store's driveway, and two people were crossing the street to it. Squinting, Mack reached out and pulled at the image again to make it even larger. His commlink's processor strained at the speed it needed to re-pixel the vid and fill in the blanks. The image was even grainier, but he could make out a tall, dark-haired man leaning on the shoulder of a smaller, dark-haired female.

The two reached the car and she helped the man to the passenger's side. It looked as if he was clutching his side as he fell in and she shut the door. She paused when she moved around the back of the car, looking directly into the camera as if she knew it was there.

Mack froze the image and pulled up one of his profiler apps—one he'd used a while back to identify a kidnap suspect from a film even grainier than this one. The images sharpened slightly—

revealing a small, feminine face, short hair, and long, pointed ears. He captured the image and saved it. He looked at Slamm-O! and was shocked at the mixture of anger and worry on the other man's face. "You know her?"

"Yeah—she shouldn't be here. She's with this Tetsu, isn't she? That's him, isn't it? And he's leaning on her."

"May I see?" Powell asked.

Mack sent the image to him and Shayla as well.

"This your girlfriend?" Mack said.

"Yes," Slamm-O! barked, then, "No. I don't know. She and I hooked up—she's special. We had a slight falling out—"

"She ran here to Los Angeles?" Powell asked. "Did she know Tetsu?"

"I don't know," Slamm-O! said as Mack watched him fidget. "She might. She's got a lot of Tech-nomancer friends. Maybe he called her to help him. I just—" he put his hands on his hips and looked at Mack. "Why is he all over her?"

"Well," Shayla said. "Looks to me like if he wasn't all over her, he'd fall down. I think he's in pain."

"I'll show him some pain." Slamm-O! said. "If he gets her hurt, I swear I'll kill him."

Mack dismissed his desktop and frowned. "Look, I didn't hire you for your girl troubles. The fact you're after a Technomancer is a bit complicated, and I think you're crazy. And if you were smart you'd get out of that relationship real fast to save your—"

"It's more complicated than that," Slamm-O! said and he looked from Mack to Powell to Shayla. "She's carrying my child."

continued in *Dark Resonance*
COMING IN 2011
FROM CATALYST GAME LABS